To Lynnette
Dreams can co...
A
Dawn Kinzer

HOPE'S DESIGN

THE DAUGHTERS OF RIVERTON, BOOK 2

DAWN KINZER

To my daughters, Brooke and Ana
And my stepdaughter, Katrina,
May you always follow your dreams . . .

And unto one he gave five talents,
to another two, and to another one;
to every man according to his several ability;
and straightaway took his journey.
~ Matthew 25:15

One

Riverton, Wisconsin
June 1904

"Next stop, Martindale."

The end of her long journey—*almost*. The railroad didn't reach her final destination—the small country town of Riverton, Wisconsin. From what she remembered, with a population of over two thousand, Martindale was four times the size of Riverton.

Hope Andrews peered out the window at people on the platform saying farewell to passengers boarding the train. An elderly couple wiped tears from their eyes after giving a young man one last hug. He stiffened, as though embarrassed by their outward signs of affection, then softened and embraced the gray-haired lady before planting a kiss on her cheek.

One woman, wearing a faded dress and holding the hand of a little boy dressed in stained trousers, seemed to search the car's windows for a passenger. Her face lit up in recognition, and she waved frantically. Was she saying good-bye to a husband leaving home in search of work?

That man—talking to a porter. Despite the thick, hot air in the train car, Hope shivered. Similar build, hair color, and taste in clothes, but it *couldn't* be Henry. No one would divulge she'd traveled to the Midwest.

The stranger turned his face, giving Hope full view. Her shoulders relaxed, and she sighed in relief. Shame on her for letting even an imaginary Henry Shelton affect her—their relationship had been over for months.

A whistle blew, and the train inched forward. Cornfields and grazing cows would fill a portion of her scenery for the next year, maybe two. Quite a change from New York City, but for now, what alternative did she have? Because of Henry, she'd given up her home, her friends, and possibly any chance of becoming a real fashion designer.

Hope fingered the sketch pad in her lap. Discouraged by the rejections she'd received after submitting several dress designs, her parents had tried to convince her that God had given her creative abilities for a purpose beyond what she could even imagine. Hope desperately wanted to believe that possibility, but sometimes her faith waned. Her parents' enthusiasm came from experience. God always used them in big ways, no matter where they ventured. Somehow they knew the right things to say and do—as though the Almighty whispered instructions whenever they needed a little help. As much as she wanted to be like them, Hope didn't even come close.

A woman looking not much older than Hope and carrying a crying baby dropped onto the bench seat facing her. An off-key duet ensued with the wailing child as a little girl about four years old with brunette curls and soft brown eyes settled next to the lady, chattering nonsense and spitting one question after another.

"Hush, Marcie." The mother patted her daughter's thigh. With weary eyes and hair escaping pins, the poor woman appeared frazzled. She threw an apologetic glance in Hope's direction. "I'm sorry the baby's making a fuss. The train's movement should lull him to sleep."

It couldn't be easy traveling alone with two little ones. Hope offered an understanding smile. "Are you traveling to visit someone?"

"No, we're on our way home. We'll be getting off in Martindale." The baby gave a few last whimpers, then quieted. "We take the train every two weeks to visit my mother, clean her house, make sure she's eating properly. My husband and I keep trying to convince her to live with us, but she refuses to leave her home. It's difficult taking the children, but she looks forward to seeing them, so I do the best I can."

"You're a kind daughter to be so thoughtful." Hope, wanting to be like her own mother, strived to help others, but too often she acted on impulse and the results were less than positive.

At twenty-six, Hope's friends were already married and mothers themselves. They found it difficult to understand Hope wanting anything more than a family and Henry. She couldn't blame them—they didn't know the real man beneath the handsome, charming exterior.

Henry managed his temper in social settings where lack of control could damage his career as a lawyer. But away from observing eyes, he found various ways to punish her for displeasing him. Even now, thousands of miles away from him, her stomach churned at the memories. Hope refused to stay associated with a man who lacked genuine kindness, let alone become married to him. She'd broken their engagement, knowing she risked facing not only his rage, but public judgment.

If just seeing Henry's likeness set her heart pounding like a horse racing down the track at the Kentucky Derby, maybe she hadn't left the painful situation behind after all.

Though he claimed to love her, Henry had been unsupportive of her aspirations. He thought it foolish for her to think she could ever see her designs on the front cover of *The Delineator* or women using Butterick patterns to make the clothes at home for themselves.

Out of concern for her well-being, her wise and intuitive parents had pressed Hope to tell them what had gone wrong in the relationship. When she admitted she'd begun to witness mean and controlling behaviors, they believed her—a relief since Henry seemed a continual presence wherever she traveled in the city.

He never did anything to cause trouble—he was too smart for that. But because of his unwillingness to leave her alone, Hope's parents insisted she leave New York while they were out of the country. Although Hope refused to believe Henry would physically harm her again, they feared for her safety, and Hope knew her father wouldn't focus on his job at the Panama Canal if consumed with worry.

Ashamed she'd fallen in love with someone cruel and untrustworthy, Hope would have kept Henry's true nature to herself. But her closest friend, Charlotte, confused over the broken engagement, had insisted that Hope spend a night with her so they could talk into the early morning, just like when they were young girls.

Hope tried to discreetly keep the bruises on her arms covered, but while dressing for bed that evening, Charlotte had spotted darkened areas. Mortified, Hope had crumpled into a teary mess. Then, stumbling over her words, she'd explained the ugly marks Henry had inflicted when she returned his emerald ring, and she begged Charlotte to keep her secret. She'd agreed, and Hope had gained another ally.

There had only been one other physical encounter with Henry. He'd arrived at her home unexpectedly one evening while her parents were out, acting despondent over losing in court earlier that day. After reminding him that she wasn't alone—house staff still milled about—she'd allowed him inside. Hope carried an emotional interest in the eight-month-old case involving a child's death, and she believed Henry just needed a chance to talk about the disappointing verdict.

But the conversation quickly turned, and he begged her to accept his ring and renew their engagement. When she continued to refuse, he grew frustrated and slapped her. The horrified look on his face before he ran out the door had convinced Hope that Henry had never intended to harm her, but she couldn't trust it wouldn't happen again.

When Hope's father accepted the position in Panama, Charlotte tried to persuade Hope to stay with her family. She and her parents had considered the option. But, following much discussion and prayer, Hope agreed to put some distance between her and Henry, and Charlotte promised to keep Hope's whereabouts a secret.

⌘

Benjamin Greene stood in line for the train leaving Vilene. After getting up with the sun to pray with his father, he'd downed the scrambled eggs, ham, fried potatoes, and toast with blackberry jam his mother had insisted he consume before leaving. The hearty breakfast still satisfied his belly.

Ben appreciated Samuel giving him a ride to the train that morning. Although he'd spent almost a week at the family farm, there'd been little time to talk brother-to-brother without someone interrupting.

Older brothers, Samuel and David, had built homes on the property for their growing families, and younger sister Ruth still lived in the main house with their parents. On the family farm people were constantly in and out, sharing meals, chores, and conversation.

As soon as he stepped off the train in Martindale, Jake would bombard him with questions about the family, but like any older brother, Ben would first taunt Jake about missing out on their mother's Swedish pancakes and the maple syrup tapped from trees on the farm. He'd wait until later to pull out the two jars tucked in his bag.

If Ben and Jake had stayed on their family's land, it would have been difficult to support everyone relying on the farm's success without purchasing additional acreage. No one imagined the youngest in the family would inherit their great-uncle's farm outside of Riverton. But the uncle had never married, and he'd taken a liking to Jake early on. After Ben saw the overwhelming amount of work needing to be done, he offered to help Jake rebuild his dilapidated farm until Ben could figure out what he wanted to do with his own life.

What *should* he do? Devote years to milking cows and raising crops with Jake? It was a good, honest living, but Ben didn't feel passionate about that life—not like Jake. Ben had been reckless with the artistic abilities God had given him, and now he was paying the cost. He accepted that. Guilt challenged any joy he felt while painting, so until he found peace for what he'd done, he'd stick to his vow and keep his work a secret.

The train was ready for boarding, and Ben followed the gentleman ahead of him. Although a small breeze blew in through slightly opened windows, the warm car smelled of sweat and stale smoke, something he'd have to put up with during the two-hour trip to Martindale.

He scanned the car for an empty seat. There. Next to a gentleman dressed in a business suit. Across from him sat another man with his head leaning against the window and his hat covering part of his face. Ben took a step, then a middle-aged-looking woman coming toward him squeezed down the aisle and dropped her generously proportioned body next to the sleeping passenger. Ben would stay put and give the lady a moment to settle in.

"I see Charles and I have a new traveling companion," she said, then grinned at the man in the business suit, displaying a large gap between her two front teeth. Her hair mixed with brown, gray, and white strands reminded Ben of the coat on his brother's aging collie. "You get on at the last stop? What's your name? Where you headed?" Same kind of personality as old Shep too.

The man introduced himself as Jonathan Landers and explained he was getting off at Martindale, then opened his newspaper.

"Ahhhh . . . next stop then." She settled back, laid her hands over her handbag, and nodded to the gentleman sleeping next to her. "My husband, Charles Davidson." She patted his leg. "Say hi to this nice man, Charles."

He growled, shoved her hand away, and went back to sleep.

"I'm Mrs. Davidson. We're on our honeymoon. Both wi-dowed, we found love again."

Honeymoon? Didn't newlyweds show a little more inter-est in each other? Ben always imagined that if he ever got married—and that was a big *if*—it would be to someone he couldn't live without. Charles didn't seem to have the sligh-test interest in his beloved.

"I was having a nice visit with a woman in another car be-fore we stopped to let on more passengers, but she dozed off, just like my Charles. How nice that I have you to talk to. That other woman didn't have much to say, and I think it's such a bore just to sit here and stare out the window, don't you?" Her eyebrows lifted as a grin spread across her face.

Better to move on. Ben searched for another open spot. Only one left—across from a mother with a baby and little girl. He didn't mind children, and anything was better than being interrogated by a lonely woman on her honeymoon. Poor Mr. Landers.

℺

"May I sit here?"

Hope's focus moved up from her sketch pad, and her breath caught. The man with the nice voice not only had a kind and handsome face, but his cerulean-colored eyes mir-rored a deep blue sky, and his thick, light brown hair was the same soft shade as Charlotte's kitten. "Yes, you're welcome to." She glanced behind her. "The train has been moving for several miles. There was a problem with your seat?"

He slid in next to her, and looking sheepish, gave a nod. "You could say that. So, thank you." He lifted both hands in a defensive gesture. "I promise I won't bother you."

"See that you don't," Hope said, her tone light and teasing. The corners of his lips turned up slightly. Oh my, that smile, and those gorgeous eyes that hinted a sense of humor behind them.

"Ben."

"Pardon?" She needed to stop staring.

"Benjamin Greene. But friends just call me Ben." He held out his hand.

She took it. "Hope Andrews."

He reached across the space between the bench seats and held out his hand toward the little girl. "And your name?"

"Marcie." She giggled, then took his hand and pumped it.

Her mother nodded. "Helen Jones, and this is Luke."

"Nice to make your acquaintance." He opened a book and began to read, thereby ending conversation.

Did Hope say something wrong? Mr. Greene acted so cordial one minute, and the next, he ignored her—*them*. Of course, he did mention not wanting to bother them. But rudeness and consideration weren't synonymous.

Hope glanced sideways at him. Good-looking *and* literate. *The Call of the Wild*, a story about a sled dog and his adventures, had been published earlier that year. She'd seen copies displayed in a New York bookstore window. Mr. Greene wasn't wearing a suit, so probably not a businessman. Hope tried not to judge people by their clothes, but his could certainly be improved upon. With his lean but strong build, he'd appear commanding in a tailored suit.

Since her bench partner seemed absorbed in his novel, and Marcie was chattering to her mother without seeming to take a breath, Hope could get back to sketching. She opened the pad and continued drawing a bodice she felt would complement the skirt's lines.

Mr. Greene gave a low, almost inaudible, groan.

Something terrible must be happening in the story. "Did the dog get into trouble?" she whispered, without moving her eyes from her own paper.

"Sorry. Didn't mean for you to hear that," he whispered back.

Hope looked up and became transfixed by the depth in his eyes. Could it be possible to feel something for a man without knowing anything about him? She swallowed and forced her gaze away from his. "Well, I did. So, now you must tell me what caused you such distress."

Mr. Greene shook his head slightly, as though trying to decide if he should speak or not. He rubbed his face and groaned again, then nodded toward her sketch. "It's not quite right."

Heat shot up Hope's neck and into her face like a lit match set to dry kindling. She stared at her work. "Of course not—the drawing isn't finished."

"The woman's proportions aren't accurate." He squirmed in his seat, then pointed to the bodice. "Does any woman's chest stick out like that? Have you actually seen any with waists that tiny? No. And, despite her size, I don't think I've ever watched a women walk down the street with her . . . backside trailing way behind."

"It's—it's fashion." She tried to keep her voice down, but how dare he criticize what he didn't understand.

"It may be, but the proportions are still wrong." His whisper had grown in intensity too. "Art is often, and at its best, expressive. It doesn't always resemble a photograph.

But this doesn't make sense to me, fashion or not. The human body is beautiful in its natural form, why distort it? Why not draw clothes on people to show how they'll really look?"

"Obviously, you don't understand." How quickly his ill manners had turned her infatuation to repulsion. "What do you do for a living anyway, Mr. Greene?"

"I'm . . . I'm a farmer, Miss Andrews."

"Of course you are."

He narrowed his eyes. "You're insinuating that a farmer couldn't possibly be knowledgeable about art?"

Hope took a deep breath, but still forced her voice to stay low. "I'm not saying that all farmers lack culture—it's just obvious that *you* do."

"Are you fighting?" Marcie sat on the edge of her seat, her eyes wide.

"Honey, of course they aren't." Mrs. Jones raised her eyebrows at Hope and Ben, as though reprimanding two children. "They're just having a discussion."

Marcie squinted up at her mother. "They sure sound like they're fighting."

Luke awoke and let out a loud wail.

"Oh, no . . . here we go again." Marcie thrust her fingers into her ears. Then she looked up and wrinkled her nose. "Ooooh, what is that smell?"

Mrs. Jones blushed. "I need to find a place to change him. Marcie, stay here and don't bother these nice people." She picked up a bag sitting next to her and walked toward the back of the car with the baby.

Mr. Greene shrugged. "Truce." Then he returned to his book without another word.

Truce? Didn't she even get to vote? Hope sighed. Was Benjamin Greene any indication of the type of men she'd come across in this part of the country? At least he was kind to children, and she couldn't imagine him being malicious, unlike her former fiancé. Not that she was looking for a husband, or even a suitor. Her focus needed to stay on her future and making a place for herself as a designer. Nothing more.

Marcie set her doll aside and fidgeted in her seat. Her head bobbed this way and that as her eyes seemed to search the railroad car for something new to explore. It wouldn't do to have her mother return and find the little girl gone.

Hope moved next to the child and turned to a clean page in her sketch book. "Do you like to draw, Marcie?"

The little girl's face lit up. "Will you make some pictures for me?"

"I'll draw anything you like. But every time I do, you need to make something for me too. Agreed?" From Marcie's grin, this was certainly making better use of Hope's time than stewing about a man she'd never see again.

॰৪

Ben pretended to read, but in truth, he kept going over the same paragraph without retaining a thing. He stole a glance here and there when he sensed Miss Andrews was too absorbed in her drawings with Marcie to notice.

Without intending to, he'd offended the lady. His blunt nature had gotten in the way of having a nice conversation with a beautiful, intelligent woman. Why couldn't he just let it go? Why did he have to give his opinion—even if it was the truth?

But she was just as stubborn, and any real artist wouldn't waste time on something as trivial as fashion. Art was supposed to move people—make them feel something about life and themselves.

He didn't know why, but he enjoyed watching her with Marcie. Miss Andrews was good with children—it was obvious that both she and the little girl were enjoying creating their imaginary world on paper.

Rays of sunlight coming through the window rested on the woman's golden hair, making it shine like a wheat field waving in a summer breeze. Her lips were the same shade of pink as the bleeding hearts his mother had planted next to their house. Ben had also been struck by the color of her eyes. They were the same blue as forget-me-nots, and forget her, he would not.

Two

As the train pulled up to the Martindale station, Hope peered out the window for any sign of her cousin. *There!* That flaming red hair was hard to miss. Annie stood on the platform, shielding her eyes with her hands, her neck strained as though searching the windows of the train.

A wave of homesickness crashed against Hope's protective wall. Regardless of her independent nature, a sad reality had sunk in. Thousands of miles separated her from her parents, and their return date to this country remained uncertain. Even then, they'd return to New York, and whether or not Hope joined them depended on Henry's ability to let her move on with her life. Was it selfish to pray he'd find someone else to marry? Hope would never want anyone else to be harmed, but another love interest might make it easier to let go of his anger toward her.

Despite her eagerness to hug Annie, Hope couldn't miss how her traveling companion was struggling with gathering her things, carrying the baby, and keeping an anxious Marcie in tow.

"Would you like some help, Mrs. Jones? It may take a little while for my trunks to be unloaded, and you have your hands full."

She sighed and gave a tired smile. "Thank you. You'd think God would have created mothers with four hands instead of two. If I could just have your assistance in getting off the train, I'd be most grateful. My husband is waiting for us outside."

Hope carried an extra bag besides her own, took hold of Marcie's hand, and followed Mrs. Jones down the aisle to the door. She glanced out the window as Mr. Greene sprinted past with his bag tossed over his shoulder.

He apparently couldn't wait to put distance between them. Hope shook her head. "Rude *and* insensitive," she muttered under her breath. A gentleman would have offered to help a mother with two children disembark.

While drawing with Marcie, Hope had been able to set his insults about her sketches aside, but the little girl tired after a while and wanted to stretch out next to her mother for a nap. Hope had returned to her place next to the farmer and focused her attention outside the window. Absorbed in his book, he seemed to have forgotten their conversation, but his hurtful words still nagged at her. *It's not quite right. The woman's proportions aren't accurate. This doesn't make sense to me, fashion or not.*

She and Marcie made their way down the passenger-car steps, and the little girl broke free from Hope.

"Daddy!" She ran toward a man who lifted her into his arms and gave her a hug before putting her back on the ground.

"There's my husband." Mrs. Jones relieved Hope of her bag. "Thank you for your help with Marcie during the trip. You were a godsend."

"My pleasure." Hope waved good-bye to Marcie, happy to see the family reunited. But a hint of sadness slipped into her heart at seeing the husband embrace his wife and baby.

Maybe her friends were right. Maybe she'd made a mistake breaking off her engagement. She lifted her chin. No, she'd done the right thing—the *only* thing she could do in her situation.

"Hope!" a voice called from behind her.

She spun around, right into her cousin's embrace. "Annie."

After they hugged, Annie stepped back and locked arms with Hope. "You're finally here. It's been too long."

"Three years."

"And back then, I wasn't exactly my cheerful, fun self."

"I understood." During Hope's last visit, Annie had been a little withdrawn, even weepy at times, but Annie adored her father and his unexpected death had bruised her heart.

"I still miss my father, but they say time heals. I'm counting on that to be true. It also helps to imagine him up in heaven telling his silly jokes."

"He could make even the orneriest person laugh. I loved that about him."

"Me too." Annie's green eyes sparkled. "From your last letter, we have a lot to catch up on. But, we'll get you home and settled first."

"I need to claim my luggage. I brought several trunks and two large crates."

"I expected such. This way." Annie turned and pointed in the direction she'd come. "A friend who regularly collects shipments here for the Home Store needed to pick up his brother from the train, and he offered to help us. He's waiting in the area where your things will be unloaded from the baggage car."

"So, there *are* gentlemen to be found in the country." The

words slipped out before Hope gave them a thought.

Annie's eyebrows raised. "Pardon?"

"I'm sorry. I didn't mean—I promise to explain later." Hope gestured forward. "Come on. We shouldn't keep the man waiting."

They weaved through the throng of passengers disembarking and greeting loved ones until they reached the baggage car.

"Over there! One of my trunks is being unloaded now."

"You sign for your luggage, and I'll get our helping hands." Annie squeezed Hope around the shoulders. "I'm so glad you're here."

In no time, Annie returned. "Hope, this is my friend, Jake." Annie beamed at the attractive young man with mischievous blue eyes and light brown hair.

He flashed a charming smile. "Nice to meet you, Hope. Annie hasn't stopped talking about you. I don't think she took a breath all the way here from Riverton."

Annie's cheeks flushed. "Jake's only saying that because his quick tongue never met a match until I came along."

Jake threw back his head and let out a belly laugh. "Hope, your cousin tells it like it is—that's why I like her."

The pale rose color in Annie's face ripened to a cherry red.

She likes him! But did he feel the same way about her sweet cousin? When Annie said they had a lot to catch up on, she hadn't exaggerated.

Jake stood next to Hope's trunks and crates. "So, I'm guessing these are all yours." He waved a porter over. "I'll help you ladies into the wagon, and this gentleman will help me load the baggage."

Annie glanced around the area. "Where's your brother? Wasn't he supposed to meet us here?"

"He—uh—had to pick up a few things at a local store. It shouldn't take long."

With Jake's assistance, the women climbed into the wagon and onto a second seat behind the first. The back end of the wagon contained just enough room for Hope's belongings.

Jake finished loading, then got situated on the bench ahead of them.

He seemed familiar, but Hope couldn't place him. Maybe she'd met his family while visiting years back. "Jake, I'm sorry. I should have asked your last name. Did we meet when we were younger?"

"Couldn't have. My brother and I moved to Riverton only two years ago. Speaking of—there he is." Jake whistled and waved. "It's about time. There's room in back for those things."

Hope felt the blood drain from her face as Jake's brother stored several large tubes and a small box next to her luggage. The three-hour trip to Riverton would feel longer than her entire journey from New York to Wisconsin—*much* longer.

"I promised I wouldn't hold you up, and I always keep my promises," the newcomer said as he swung up onto the front of the wagon. "Hope Andrews." He looked as surprised as she felt uncomfortable. "You're Annie's cousin?"

"I am," she croaked out. Hope crossed her arms, then cleared her throat. "And apparently, Benjamin Greene, you're Jake's brother."

CR

Although still early June, the afternoon sun made riding in an open wagon uncomfortably warm. Several flies buzzed around Hope's head, and cows bellowed in the field next to the road. Her parched throat would welcome a cool drink, but if she accepted any more water from Annie's container, Hope would need to relieve herself in a wooded area at the side of the road. She'd rather die than make that request in Ben's presence.

"Oh, my goodness. What is that awful smell?" Hope covered her nose and tried not to breathe.

Ben turned around with a grin and a mischievous glint in his eyes. "Skunk. It must have sprayed something—or *someone*. Better not lean over the edge of the wagon. You never know what might happen."

"Very funny, Mr. Greene." She may have not been around skunks on a regular basis, but she wasn't ignorant of what animals could and couldn't do.

The wagon dropped, then bounced, throwing Hope into the air several inches. She gasped and grabbed on to the side railing with one hand and her hat with the other.

Annie clutched the edge of the bench as the wagon jostled back to level ground. "Goodness, Jake! We're not training to ride a bucking bronco in a rodeo."

"Sorry about that," Jake shouted over his shoulder. "A big storm came through two nights ago and the rain made a mess of the road. I'll keep a better eye out the rest of the way."

Hope winced as she settled back in place and readjusted her skirt. Still onboard, but bruises would soon follow.

"Take care that you do, brother." Ben gave Jake a light slap on his shoulder. "Miss Andrews is from New York City. She's probably accustomed to riding with cultured men in fancy automobiles, not simple farmers in wagons." By the sound of his voice, he thought the wild ride humorous.

Well, he wouldn't get the best of her. "You're absolutely right, Mr. Greene," Hope said in the sweetest voice she could muster.

"Have you ridden in an automobile?" An almost hopeful excitement seeped into Jake's tone.

She inched her sore bottom to the edge of her seat and held onto the backboard the men leaned against. No need to shout back and forth. "Many times. Someone I knew owned a Curved Dash Oldsmobile." Hope didn't plan to explain that the someone was her former fiancé.

"What's it like?"

"It's a little runabout that seats two people. The ride is smoother than a wagon's, especially this one," she teased. "But, it's not like gliding on ice, either."

"I'll have my own automobile someday." Jake gave one large nod. "You can be sure of it."

"Hold on, brother." Ben shifted in his seat to face Jake. "You don't know anything about those contraptions. I may not either, but trust me, they're not practical for our neck of the woods."

"Maybe it doesn't make sense to own one now. Not on our country roads. But they're the wave of the future." Jake grinned at his brother. "You can't stop a strong tidal wave, no matter how hard you try."

"I agree," Hope said, brushing a small spider from her skirt as though it were only a speck of dirt. "Intelligent and a farmer. What do you know? It *is* possible to be both."

Ben tossed a quick look at Hope. "If you think so little of farmers, why did you move from an exciting city and travel all this way to live in a small farming community?"

Jake shot Ben what looked like a warning. "Maybe she just wants to spend time with her cousin."

"I apologize if I've forgotten my manners, but you gotta admit, Jake, it's a little strange."

Annie opened her mouth, probably to defend her, but Hope raised her hand, signaling her cousin to remain quiet. More than once since she'd met him, Ben's actions and statements had felt impolite, but Hope wasn't without fault herself. Her mother had reprimanded her numerous times for asking inappropriate questions or making unsolicited gestures, assuming they'd be welcomed. "There's really not much to tell."

The wagon lurched, and Hope held on tight to the bench in front of her. "I don't plan on living here forever. Since my aunt is away and Annie is staying alone at their place, I decided to come for an extended visit. Annie and I haven't had an opportunity to spend much time together. That's all there is to it." At least, that's all they, or anyone else, needed to know.

"Hope, Riverton's just up ahead, and there's home!" Annie alluded to the white two-story house at the edge of town.

Nothing had changed in the years since Hope had last stayed in the welcoming and comfortable home. Peonies grew along the length of the front porch, their blooms various shades of dark and light pink. Carved loops adorned the corners of the entry to an expansive front porch. Several large maple trees grew to one side of the house, a white birch to the other. From their approach on the road, Hope also spotted the small barn where Annie kept her horse and small buggy, a fenced-in chicken coop, and a large vegetable garden.

Home for as long as she needed, but just how long would that be? How long before she could safely return to New York?

ɢʀ

Although Ben couldn't deny Hope Andrews was intriguing—and beautiful—and he admired her spunk, he was eager to put distance between the two of them. It had been a long time since he'd felt a strong attraction to anyone, but he couldn't risk losing his heart to another female again. The results had been too painful.

Those deeply-seated memories contributed to his less-than-chivalrous behavior toward her, even to the point of insulting her sketches, which actually held much promise. Another reason to guard his heart. She still had a chance to do something with her talent, while the door to that opportunity for him had closed long ago. But he would never explain, and Jake knew better than to try without experiencing Ben's wrath.

He envied Hope's freedom to express herself artistically without anything casting shadows on her creative light. Regardless, he'd try to curb his blunt words in the future and be more of a gentleman. He could at least help unload and carry in her bags and crates once they reached Annie's farmhouse.

What Ben most desired now was to put the past behind

and forgive himself for the wrong he'd done. Maybe by finding that kind of peace, he could once again embrace the joy he felt when using his God-given gift, instead of feeling guilty because of it.

Jake guided the horses to the front of the house, then pulled on the reins for them to stop. Both men hopped out of the wagon, and Jake helped Annie down from her perch, leaving Ben to assist Hope.

"We'll unload and carry everything in." Ben walked to the back of the wagon and released the drop-gate. He climbed up and shoved a large wooden crate toward the end, then hopped back out. He and Jake each grabbed hold and lifted the container from the wagon bed.

"Careful!" Hope rushed toward them and drew a clenched hand to her mouth. "Please be careful."

Ben groaned inside. Was she really afraid they'd drop the cargo? You'd think there was priceless crystal or an ancient artifact inside. *Doesn't matter. Whatever the crate contains, it's important to her.* He'd handle the load with care.

Her shoulders slumped. "I'm sorry. I didn't mean to sound ungrateful. I truly appreciate your help. Annie and I would have struggled for hours trying to move that piece ourselves."

"Right this way, gentlemen." Annie led the way up the steps to the porch. Hope held the screen door back while Annie kept the main door propped open and gave directions as Ben and Jake hauled in the precious crate and an additional box, then labored up the stairs with several heavy trunks.

"You should be able to get settled in now." Ben wiped his damp forehead with a handkerchief. "Annie, could I trouble you for a glass of water?"

"Of course. I should have thought to offer it myself. If you prefer, I have fresh lemonade chilling in the ice box."

"Thanks. That sounds even better." Ben tucked his handkerchief back into his back pocket.

Jake grinned at Annie. "I wouldn't mind some myself."

"I'll pour everyone a glass," Annie said as she headed toward the kitchen. "We're all parched from the dusty ride."

"I'll help." Hope started to follow, but Jake raced ahead and stopped her.

"Let me. You've been traveling for hours."

Her shoulders visibly relaxed. "Thank you, Jake."

Ben stifled a frustrated sigh. He would have shown he could be considerate and offered to help with the drinks if Jake hadn't beaten him to it. Ben had a feeling his brother's willingness had more to do with wanting a little time alone with Annie than it had to do with being polite to the redhead's cousin.

"I am a bit tired." Hope slipped into the rocking chair next to the fireplace after removing several books stacked on the seat. Annie had a habit of leaving novels in almost every room of the house.

After being cooped up on the train for thousands of miles, then thrown around in the wagon like a sack of potatoes, Hope must feel exhausted. "Did you travel the entire way by yourself?" Ben shoved several books aside, then dropped onto the settee across from her.

"Pardon?"

Was she so tired she'd forgotten he was even there? Or had she hoped he'd just disappear if she avoided him? "I asked if you'd made the trip from New York alone."

"Yes. I'm a grown woman, quite capable." A wave of sadness crossed her face. "I apologize for sounding a bit defensive. My parents are out of the country. I won't see them again for some time."

How long did it take to fill four glasses? A mix of deep and light laughter filtered into the room from the kitchen. Annie would be good for Jake, but he wasn't close to settling down, and Ben feared his brother would break the sweet girl's heart.

"Your parents are touring Europe?" Probably along with a group of other rich people. It turned Ben's stomach to see people abuse their wealth when they could use it for good. "What did you do that was so bad they didn't invite you?" Ben almost winced. He'd done it again. Why couldn't he think before blurting out his thoughts? Better yet, keep them to himself?

Color crept up her neck and filled her face as though she were about to bloom like the peonies outside. "Is that what you think? That I'm here only because they're off spending an extravagant holiday without me?" Her voice was tinged with anger.

"I assumed—"

"You assumed wrong." Hope took a deep breath, then seemed to give thought to her words before continuing. "Mr. Greene, I won't see my parents for two years, possibly longer. And that's only if they survive."

"I'm sorry. I don't understand."

"My father is working with the United States Army Corp of Engineers on the Panama Canal. My mother couldn't bear to be separated from him. Along with other engineers, they set sail from New York on the *Allianca*."

He couldn't go back and undo what he'd said, and by the disgust on her face he deduced she wouldn't accept his apology. But he could attempt more kindness. He purposely gentled his tone. "You said if they survive . . ."

Her expression softened after his words. "The work is dangerous—living conditions are horrendous. Families also risk exposure to diseases like yellow fever and malaria."

"Surely your parents won't be subjected to those same conditions."

"Their living quarters will be—more pleasant. But like anyone there, they risk serious illness."

How could Ben have been so wrong about her family? He'd always prided himself on being perceptive and having the ability to see things others missed. "Your mother willingly placed herself in such a position?"

"If you're judging her decision, you don't understand, Mr. Greene." Hope tilted her head and gazed deep into his eyes, as though she searched for an answer to a question she hadn't yet raised. "Though it hurt to say good-bye to them both, it gives me comfort to know they have each other to lean on. But my mother isn't traveling to Panama because she's afraid of being without my father. She's going with a loving heart and desire to serve God and the people there who are suffering." Hope's eyes glistened. "No matter how hard I strive, I will never be as good and courageous."

"Sorry it took so long." A blushing Annie strolled into the room with two glasses of lemonade, and Jake following closely behind with two more. "Jake told the funniest story about the trick he played on Ben when they were boys."

"I'm sure he did." Ben accepted a glass from his brother, took several sips, then emptied it. He hadn't realized how much he needed the refreshment. "Thanks, Annie." He clasped Jake's shoulder. "Little brother, you and I should head home. The cows need milking. Or did you forget you're still a farmer?"

"Right. Chores are waiting." Jake gave a slight bow in Hope's direction. "I'm glad you're here, Hope." He turned toward Annie. "And thanks for the invite for Sunday. That's nice of you to have us."

A look of horror flashed across Hope's face. Though it lasted only a second, Ben didn't miss it. He perched an arm on his brother's shoulder. "What's going on?"

Jake's grin swallowed his whole face. "To thank us, Annie invited us for dinner after church tomorrow."

Warmth flowed through Ben, and he struggled to hold back a smile. *Surprise.* He was actually looking forward to spending more time with the beautiful Hope Andrews.

Three

Ben opened the door to what looked like a regular tool shed from the outside and gave himself a moment to inhale the familiar smells of paint and turpentine—his haven.

The hideaway, private because he'd sworn his brother to secrecy as to its actual purpose, was built after they'd taken over the land. A pact between the two of them when Ben agreed to help Jake rebuild the hundred-acre rundown farm their uncle had left to him in his will.

Farming didn't stir Ben to get up in the morning. It didn't excite him or cause him to think about the future like it did his brother. Jake loved everything about growing crops and raising animals, and Ben loved his brother, so what else could Ben do but agree to help rebuild the inheritance? Jake couldn't manage the farm on his own, at least not yet. In return, his brother honored Ben's need to continue painting.

Benches lined two walls, a small table and a chair gave him a place to think and sketch, an easel stood nearby, and a small woodstove sat in one corner. Two smaller windows were added on the north and south to let in sunlight. He'd light a lantern before shadows cloaked the room, but right now the view from the large window facing west couldn't be missed.

As though brushed with watercolors, the evening sky was

washed with brilliant shades of pink, purple, and orange. A glimpse of heaven that reminded him God was a master artist in how he created the earth, seas, and sky. God understood Ben and the delight he felt with each brush stroke put to canvas. Because of that, Ben felt the closest to his heavenly Father while painting.

The Lord also knew why Ben could never share this part of himself outside of this room. Turmoil still lingered inside for the pain he'd caused another man. God had forgiven him, and even after all these years, his family continued to remind him of that truth. More than anything he wanted to find a way to forgive himself, but until then, keeping this place and his work unknown seemed like a necessary sacrifice.

He set the box containing the new oil paints he'd picked up in Martindale on a bench, then removed the cover from the tube he carried and pulled out several large pieces of canvas. The empty wooden frames waited to be covered. He stared at the larger one, mentally choosing a color palette that would capture Hope's striking blue eyes, honey-colored hair, and the blush that bloomed with her emotions.

Not that he intended to paint her—he just couldn't get her out of his mind. The conversation they'd had earlier that day replayed in his thoughts. It was clear she loved her parents, and they were good people. Hope didn't believe she could live up to the example her parents set, and that belief—however true or false—also seemed to burden her.

He respected the sacrifice Hope's mother was making to stay with her husband, regardless of the danger. What would it be like to have a woman love you so much she'd willingly risk her life for you?

Don't think about it, Benjamin. He'd never know that

kind of devotion. No woman would understand the difficult decisions he'd made or the life he led. His obsession with painting, the reason he kept his work hidden.

Without realizing it, Hattie had convinced him of that before he'd even come to Riverton. He'd been attracted to his sister's vivacious friend, but the night he planned to ask if he could court her, they'd gotten into a lively discussion about men and women's relationships with several other friends visiting his parents' home. Hattie hadn't grown up in the area, so she was unaware of what had happened between Ben and Percy years before—she had no knowledge that Ben was an artist. As far as she knew, like his brothers, farming claimed his heart.

That evening, Ben had thrown out hypothetical questions, and Hattie had made it clear she could never be interested in anyone who spent time on frivolous pursuits that didn't provide well. Her family had struggled financially her entire life, and she'd had enough of barely getting by. She needed financial security, and she saw herself married to a successful man who leaned toward serious work and leadership in the community.

If someone as sweet and gentle as Hattie felt that way about a husband's attributes, a simple painter who didn't even share his work, let alone sell anything, would never find someone who would accept a proposal.

Life sure would be easier if he could just be like his father and brothers, content taking care of animals and raising crops. Farming was an honorable way to make a living and a rewarding life for his family. But God hadn't made him that way, and he often questioned why.

The door to the shed creaked open, and Jake stepped inside. "The last of the chores are done. You coming up to the house soon?"

"Not yet. I want to get these canvases stretched and primed." Ben placed the largest frame on a bench and laid canvas over it.

"Sorry about tomorrow. I should've talked to you first." Jake stuck his hands in his front pockets. "But who turns down a decent home-cooked meal? Half the time I burn food, and you can't tell the difference between fully cooked and meat that's almost raw."

"It's fine, Jake." Ben flashed him a grin. "It was nice of her to ask. I appreciate the offer—I do. Annie's cooking beats mine any day." Besides, there was her interesting cousin to consider. "But from now on, try to answer for yourself. With all the work that needs to get done around here, Sunday is the best time for me to paint."

If his father knew, he'd encourage Ben to set creative projects aside on the Sabbath too. With the exception of necessary chores, like milking cows, Sundays were for worship and rest. But painting wasn't work, it was his life. Art connected Ben to God in the most intimate way.

"Come on, brother. When was the last time you spent an afternoon with friends? One Sunday out of a year isn't going to hurt you." Jake wiped his forehead. "Besides, no matter how many canvases you finish, no one will ever see them anyway."

"Jake, don't start on me again." Ben's fingers tunneled through his hair. "You know why."

"Just seems like a waste of talent, that's all."

Would his brother ever give up?

Jake stepped over to the larger window. "Sure is pretty,

isn't it?"

"The sunset or the cornfield?" Ben joined him and nudged his shoulder.

Jake shoved him back. "Both."

"You've done a good job at making this a working farm again."

"*We've* done a good job, the two of us. I couldn't have gotten this far without you, Ben. You know that." Jake laid his hand on Ben's back. "But we have a long way to go."

They stood gazing at what had become their livelihood after two years of backbreaking labor. To the left and farther down their stretch of land stood the barn and the milk shed. The wagon shed sat not far from the other side of the barn, which made hitching up the horses more convenient. But the ice house needed replacing before winter, and fences always seemed to require mending. The small amount of money that Uncle Marcus had left to help get them started on repairs depleted within those first few weeks. If all went well the coming year, maybe they could stop taking odd jobs to fund supplies for the farm and what Ben needed to paint.

The sun's few remaining rays shone through trees that edged the far side of the field up ahead. First one, then two more graceful animals stepped from the woods and onto the field where the cornstalks weren't yet high enough to hide them.

"Deer." As soon as Ben spoke, the whitetail took off, bounding over the rows of corn.

"Won't be long and they'll be dining every night on that corn, fattening up so we can enjoy venison this fall."

Ben sighed. "I don't know how you can kill those beautiful creatures."

"I hunt to eat." Jake turned from the window. "I'm going up to the house. Might read a bit before going to bed. I've almost finished *The Last of the Mohicans*."

Ben laughed. "Haven't you read that book three times already?"

"Five." He reached for the door handle.

"Wait." Ben leaned against the window frame. He'd just asked Jake to stop making decisions for him. It might seem unfair to bring up his concerns about Annie now, but it couldn't be avoided, especially since they'd be spending part of tomorrow together. "About Annie . . ."

Jake dropped his head back. "Ben, we're back to that again?"

"I think she may have some feelings for you, Jake."

"It's just one meal. There's nothing more to it."

"You could be right." Ben massaged the back of his neck. "I just don't want her to get hurt if she's hoping for something you're not ready to give. Ever since we moved to Riverton, Annie and her mother have been good to us, cooking some meals for us in exchange for fixing things around their house. Annie's been like a little sister, and we agreed to look after her while her mother's gone. Don't take advantage of her, or you'll have me to deal with, brother."

"Annie's a wonderful girl. She's pretty, smart, and fun to be around. But don't worry. I'm not going to do anything to give her the wrong impression. I've got a farm to run, and there's a lot more that needs to be done here before I can settle down with anyone." Jake opened the door. "But one day a woman is going to come along who will turn *your* world upside down, and I plan to be around to see it."

CR

Freshened up from her long journey and dressed in a clean nightgown, Hope cradled her teacup between her hands and climbed on top of the bed. She nestled back against the pillow and wooden headboard and gazed out the window at the setting sun, now almost hidden behind the trees. A light breeze fluffed the white curtains on either side of the open window to her right, and crickets in the yard and frogs in a nearby pond began tuning for their evening concert. The quiet was both comforting and disconcerting. In time, she'd get used to sounds so different from what she'd grown accustomed to in the city.

Annie dropped *Treasure Island* on a nightstand, then crawled next to Hope on the bed with her own cup of tea.

Hope moved over to make room. "Annie, my bedroom is lovely."

Delicate pink rosebuds with tiny green leaves adorned the wallpaper of the second-story bedroom. Her clothes filled the small closet and mirrored dresser opposite the bed. To the left, next to the door stood a washstand. A desk and chair placed beneath the window provided a perfect spot where she'd not only write her parents and keep them abreast of her life there, but also appreciate the view of the flower gardens and large apple tree below.

"Is there anything else you need to get settled in?"

"No, you've already done so much for me." Hope wrapped one of her nightgown's ribbons around her finger and smiled. "Thank you. For sharing your home, and for getting me a position at the store."

"You did that on your own." Annie stifled a yawn. "A local

girl applied, but your letter and experience at Macy's in New York convinced Mr. Carter you'd be an asset."

"I was honest and explained that I was only employed at the department store during one holiday season. But I learned a great deal while there, and I mentioned that after getting acquainted with *his* store, I might have ideas for drawing more customers in."

"People around here live simple lives, but I'm sure Mr. Carter would be willing to try anything not too extravagant. He would like your help with buying for the store, and he's also spread word that you'll be available to consult customers on the latest fashions." Annie set her cup on the nightstand next to her. "There won't be many hours to start—only two days a week—but you'll enjoy it. I promise."

"I'm sure I will, especially with you employed there too." Although she looked forward to the new adventure, Hope also felt a little nervous. "Regardless of how little I make, it's important that I contribute to the finances while here. I don't plan to take advantage of you or your mother's hospitality."

"Your offer is appreciated." The color in Annie's face deepened. "Selling the livery after Father died gave us enough savings to survive on as long as we're careful. We have chickens for eggs and a huge garden and raspberry patch in back. With my job at the store and Mother occasionally helping out at the hotel, we manage. But while she's gone, a little extra cash will come in handy."

Annie's honesty touched Hope. Money was a touchy subject with most people. When her father had shown her paperwork drawn up by his lawyer, Hope had gasped at the amount left in her hands—literally thousands—to be drawn

out as needed. But she had no intention of using any of it—
ever. Although they lived comfortable lives, her parents weren't wealthy. They'd depend on that nest egg as they grew
older.

Just as important was her determination to prove she
could make it on her own without her parents' financial support—or a husband's. The thought of depending on someone
her entire life scared Hope. She didn't want her parents taking care of her forever, and she certainly didn't want to marry a man in order to have food, clothing, and shelter
provided. She'd only marry someone she truly loved and
who viewed her as a partner—like how her father treated her
mother. Not someone to be bullied and controlled.

She couldn't fail at becoming a successful designer—she
just couldn't. Despite the obstacles, she had to make that
dream come true. Hope yearned to create beautiful things,
and designing could also bring financial independence.

Annie cleared her throat, drawing Hope's attention again.
"Along with a little housework, I could also use your help
weeding." She raised one eyebrow, and her eyes twinkled.
"It's a mighty big garden for one person to tend, and these
muscles can only take so much." She wore a pained expression as she rubbed her back.

Hope gave Annie a little shove. "I'll be glad to help, old
woman. And when I'm not at the store or helping around the
house, I can work on my designs."

"My cousin, a famous fashion designer." Annie made a
flourishing gesture in the air with her hand and winked at
Hope. "Who would have thought? Finally, I'll have something to brag about, even if it isn't about my own accom-
plishments."

"I wish I had your confidence in my future." Hope leaned back on the headboard and stared at the ceiling.

"Of course you'll be a great success. Why would you think otherwise?" Annie sounded like anything else would be preposterous.

How much should she confess? Perhaps all. "Sometimes I get frustrated." Hope lifted her head and caught the concern in Annie's eyes. "Ideas come to me all the time, but I have trouble transferring them to paper. And sometimes I struggle putting fabrics together to create what I envision in my head."

Annie's eyebrows lifted. "Then why try so hard?"

How could she explain? There was a lot more to it than desiring independence. Sure, she wanted to financially support herself, but she also yearned to be more like her parents. They made a difference in people's lives, and they enjoyed it, even when they faced what sometimes felt like insurmountable challenges. "Of course it would be nice to be famous, but when I help women feel pretty, it makes me . . . happy." Hope sipped her tea. "Do you remember me mentioning the neighbors in the blue house next to ours in New York?"

"The family with two daughters?"

"That's the one. Because Winnie is quite tall and thin, and Lula is short and thick around the waist, they were teased mercilessly by schoolmates with the 'Jack Sprat' nursery rhyme."

"'Jack Sprat could eat no fat, his wife could eat no lean.'"

"Exactly, only their names were substituted for Jack Sprat and wife. At sixteen and fourteen years, you can understand why they feared ridicule and refused to attend social functions. So one day, with their mother's permission and a seamstress's help, I convinced them to let me make some changes to their clothing."

"And?" Annie's voice relayed sincere interest.

"Fuller sleeves and skirts gave Winnie a more filled-out appearance, and several adjustments, like a different bodice with trim directing the eye away from the waist, made Lula look a little slimmer. Their delight warmed my heart. I knew then God had given me something to do." Not a purpose as grand or challenging as what others might be given, but one regardless.

"Annie, I have to learn how to express what's in my head or I'll go crazy. The only way I can explain it is to compare it to what Mozart might have experienced in my position—not that I'm that gifted by any means. But think about Mozart having symphonies or concertos ringing in his head without a way to play them or even write them down. God bestowed Mozart with talent, but he still had to learn how to write music so it could be shared with people through the centuries.

"It's the same for me. I have to do my part and take responsibility for developing my God-given gift. Otherwise, the creativity God has given me will go to waste, and I won't continue to embrace the joy I feel when a woman wears a garment I've imagined into reality. I want to create lovely clothes because I believe if a woman feels beautiful on the outside, she'll also feel good about herself inside. I know it sounds grandiose and conceited, but if Butterick accepts one of my designs, someday women across the country may sew and wear one of my dresses."

"It will happen." Annie sat back and hugged bent knees. "I know it will."

"I submitted several sketches before I left New York and asked that a response be sent to your post office box, but it may take some time before I receive a letter. When I dwell on it, I don't sleep or even think clearly."

"We'll just have to keep your mind occupied with other things." Annie sounded confident it would be an easy task, but then, she'd always been an optimistic soul.

"Oh, I haven't told you!" Hope, in her excitement to share the news, almost spilled her tea. "Before she left New York, my mother wrote to Eva Lancaster, an old friend of hers. She moved from Manhattan to Minneapolis after her father died. I was too young to remember her. The last several years, she's made quite a name for herself in fashion design. My mother asked if she might correspond and give me some advice."

"That sounds exciting."

"I want to learn everything I can from Miss Lancaster." Eva wasn't married, and she had a successful career doing what she loved. One woman who had proven it could be done.

Annie nudged her. "You'll let me see the drawings, won't you?"

"Of course. You always have good insight." Hope grimaced. "Unlike some people," she said under her breath, then sighed. She shouldn't allow Mr. Greene's opinion to bother her. He wasn't an artist.

Ben also couldn't have known how his disapproving words had stung and reminded her that even after working diligently, she still hadn't impressed any of her art teachers. They kept pushing her do to better, demanding that a true artist would never be satisfied, but would always strive for perfection. Her instructors wanted Hope to follow in their footsteps as real painters, but she had no aspirations of becoming a second Rembrandt or Michelangelo.

"How well do you know Benjamin Greene?"

Annie's eyes lit up with mischief. "Why do you ask?"

"Silly reason." Regardless, some insight might be helpful. "While on the train, he shared some critical remarks about my sketches—all unsolicited."

Annie scrunched her face. "It seems strange that Ben would have anything to say about some drawings, especially fashion designs." She shrugged. "Ben and Jake moved here two years ago after their great-uncle died and left Jake his farm. It was pretty rundown because the uncle was old and sick for some time. They've worked hard to bring the place back to life."

"So, it's just the two of them?"

"Their two older twin brothers, Samuel and David, and their sister, Ruth, all live on the family farm with their parents. Their father has been ill, so Ben went to see him and the rest of the family. That's why he was on the train."

"And Jake?"

"He stayed behind to take care of the farm." Annie blushed. "He takes his responsibilities to heart."

"Sweet cousin, you like Jake." Hope would get her to admit it.

"Of course I do. Everyone likes Jake. Ben may be quiet and serious, but Jake is . . . Jake is funny and charming. He's always willing to go out of his way for people—like today when he helped us home from the train station."

"And along with being very likeable, he's also quite good-looking, wouldn't you say?"

Annie gave an exaggerated sigh, then smiled. "Yes, I care about him. Jake has become a good friend. My mother occasionally hired both brothers to help around here, and Jake does errands and odd jobs for Mr. Carter at the store to help pay for improvements on the farm. So when he's around, we talk. Jake is nice to everyone. But, I'll keep my feelings to myself. It's safer that way. I don't want to get hurt, and I won't risk losing his friendship."

Hope understood guarding one's heart. However, despite Annie's denial, there was something special happening between her and Jake. "Maybe someday . . ."

"Maybe . . ." Annie winked. "And maybe I'll become Queen of England."

Hope sipped her cooled tea. "Well, here we are like two school girls sharing gossip. If only our mothers could see us."

Annie's lips turned up at the corners, and her eyes sparkled. "How many times while growing up do you suppose they sat like this at the end of the day?"

"They probably planned more adventures than what they'll ever tell." Hope traced the edge of her cup with her thumb. "They certainly maneuvered this one well."

"Hope, you're not sorry you came, are you?" Annie eyebrows furrowed above eyes that filled with worry. "I never wanted you to feel like this was your only choice."

"No! I'm glad I'm here." That was the truth. Hope felt more at peace than she had in a long time. "Please don't think otherwise. What I just said—it came out all wrong."

"Our mothers are both protective. Mine didn't want me to feel abandoned while she's in Michigan, and she'll be there indefinitely. Marie wasn't comfortable with any of the nannies she interviewed. But she can't take care of newborn twins herself when the older twins are only two years old." Annie raised her hand with palm up. "Who has two sets of twins only two years apart?"

A laugh burst from Hope's lips. "Marie has always had a tendency to do everything in a big way."

"You're right!" Annie held up her cup in agreement. "I may not be married with a lawyer husband, but I'm still a grown woman, and I can take care of myself."

"Of course you can." Hope had tried to convey the same about herself to her parents, and they'd agreed she was capable—under normal circumstances.

"And you can too." Annie wiggled into a different position on the bed so they faced each other. "Hope, I'm beyond elated that you're here, but I know for you to leave New York . . ." Annie eyes swam with sympathy. "That horrible man."

Without thinking about it, Hope's fingers found the area where bruises once marked her arm. "I wanted to stay in the city because my friends and the Butterick company are there, but my parents said they couldn't leave the country until I promised to put some distance between myself and Henry. They have enough concerns in Panama. I couldn't give them something else to worry about." Hope's lips teased into a smile. "Besides, how could I refuse to spend time with my favorite cousin?"

"I won't tell Marie you said that." Annie snuggled up beside Hope and put her arm around her. "You're a brave woman."

Hope leaned her head on Annie's shoulder. "Brave or not, I could never marry anyone who didn't support my dreams. And any man not courageous enough to go after his own would never understand what it takes."

Four

"Annie, why didn't you make me change into something more suitable?" Hope's pale blue silk shirtwaist and matching skirt felt ostentatious as she surveyed the families pulling up to the church in dusty buggies or farm wagons. "I want people to like me—not think I'm trying to impress them.

"You're lovely, and no one could ever think anything unkind of you." Annie's smile lit up her face. "So, quit dawdling."

Annie led Hope up the steps to the front doors of the church and down the aisle. As a newcomer, she expected some curiosity, but heat rushed into her face at the number of heads turning to catch a glimpse. Annie, however, either didn't notice or didn't care that they were being viewed like attractions in a circus sideshow. They settled into a pew on the left side and picked up a hymnal as Rebecca Hoyt began playing an introduction to the first song.

While attending her uncle's funeral, Hope had met the pretty blonde at the piano. Since then, Annie had shared through letters the scandal involving one of Annie's friends, Sarah, and the current reverend. Sarah and other customers had overheard Rebecca in the Home Store gossiping about an inappropriate relationship she believed was taking place between the reverend and Sarah.

After all the hurtful rumors she'd spread about the couple, Rebecca had attended the Methodist church for a while. But witnessing that she again attended the same church as Reverend Caswell and Sarah—now Mrs. Caswell—was surely a miracle and a testament to the power of forgiveness and the kind of people who lived in Riverton. Maybe Hope had been too quick to judge those gawking at her.

"Good morning, ladies," a male voice whispered from behind them. "Glad to see you made it on time."

Annie turned around with a soft giggle. "Good morning, Jake." She gave a slight nod. "Ben." Then she faced the front again with a smile that looked like it would never fade.

The congregation stood and began singing "What a Friend We Have in Jesus" before Hope could react and acknowledge the two men behind them.

Precious Jesus, help me. Hope sighed inside. Not only would she have to spend the afternoon with Ben, but she'd have to sit through an entire church service, knowing he could watch her every move.

Her cousin's beautiful alto notes harmonized with the melody, adding a rich layer to the music, but Ben's smooth tenor relayed emotion that spoke to Hope's spirit. The earnestness surprised her. She could almost feel the Lord standing next to her and taking her hand.

Remembering how Henry had mocked her propensity to sing off-key, Hope sang with a mere whisper, almost mouthing the words, so as not to offend anyone or intrude upon their worship with her lack of musicality.

"'What a friend we have in Jesus, all our sins and griefs to bear!'"

Her parents' favorite hymn—one they often sang or hummed around the house as they went about their day. One they might be singing this very moment.

"'What a privilege to carry everything to God in prayer!'"

It was the right thing for her parents to follow their calling, and she was proud of them. But Panama was so far away. Hope already missed them, and she also worried about them. They could contract a disease and even die before she'd have a chance to see them again.

"'Oh, what peace we often forfeit; oh, what needless pain we bear.'"

If she'd had her wish, the three of them would still be in New York, together and safe. Nothing felt sure right now. Not her parents' return, and certainly not Hope's future in fashion design.

"'All because we do not carry everything to God in prayer!'"

Though she knew the song by heart, Hope tried to focus on the words printed in the hymnal, but they blurred before her like a distorted watercolor. This would never do—crying in church, before the service had barely started. She tried to discreetly brush moisture from her eyes. If she ever needed Jesus as a friend, it was now.

CR

Ben leaned back in his seat and tried to focus on Reverend Caswell's sermon, which normally was easy to do. The messages were always challenging and inspiring, and Ben looked forward to them every Sunday. But today was different, and it had nothing to do with the reverend's words or his delivery. Ben just couldn't keep his mind off the woman sitting directly in front of him.

Hope hadn't turned around and acknowledged them like Annie. Why? Women. Hard to understand. Maybe she was trying to send a message. He'd been looking forward to spending the afternoon with her and another chance to—to what? Become friends? After his ill-mannered behavior the day before, he wouldn't blame her if she didn't feel the same.

If he had a sketch pad and pencil, he'd draw the feminine lines of her profile—the way she tilted her head when she turned to whisper to Annie. He'd include the silky, curling tendrils of golden hair that escaped from beneath her hat and rested on the upright collar wrapped around her neck. Ben had memorized her eye color, and without doubt, it matched the blue shade in her dress.

His gaze took in redheaded Annie sitting next to Hope. Being around Annie could feel like a Fourth of July with fireworks. She embraced life—and people—with excitement. Hope seemed guarded, but underneath her cool exterior she obviously loved and respected her family. She was passionate about art, but did those strong feelings include anything or anyone else? Two cousins so different. Like fire and ice.

Most people gravitated toward flames that offered warmth and comfort from the cold. Why was he so drawn toward the ice princess?

CR

The church service finished, and attendees stepped outside to visit under the June morning's clear and cheerful sky. Hope remembered some people from previous visits, like the sweet elderly widow Mrs. Jorgenson with silver hair and crystal-blue eyes who had been a school teacher during her younger years. Annie helped Hope with forgotten names and introduced her for the first time to others.

"I've been eager for you meet Mrs. Boyle," Annie said, almost pulling Hope toward a woman with four children of various ages—two brunettes and two redheads. "Her husband died a few years ago. Since then, she's become a popular seamstress in town. Her handiwork surpasses anything I've seen before." Annie poured out praise only when deserved. She slowed down and linked arms with Hope. "Mrs. Boyle, I'd like for you to meet my cousin, Hope Andrews."

Mrs. Boyle extended her hand. "Just call me Clara."

The woman's warm smile was all the embrace Hope needed. Despite the difference in their ages, they would become fast friends, Hope was sure of it. "I'm so glad to meet you, Clara."

They discussed clothes and preferred fabrics for several minutes before Clara's children pulled her away. Like Annie had mentioned, Clara did seem to know a lot about sewing. Hope's own skills were embarrassingly weak, especially considering her aspirations. An idea began to germinate. Would Clara consider working together? Hope would give it some thought and prayer before asking. With needing to care and provide for four children, Clara might not have any time to offer, and Hope certainly didn't want to take advantage of anyone.

Out of the corner of her eye, Hope caught Annie glancing to the left and right, as though searching for something—or someone. Her head stopped turning, and Hope followed her gaze to where Jake stood with a pretty brunette. He made a few gestures, as though telling a story. The young woman giggled, then smoothed the hair piled on her head.

Color matching Annie's hair rose from beneath her collar and flooded her face.

"Annie, I'm sorry." Hope wrapped her arm around her cousin.

"It's all right. I should be used to it by now." She reached up and squeezed Hope's hand resting on her shoulder. Annie grimaced. "I need to be careful, don't I?"

"You can try to fight it, or you can deny it, but you're in love, Annie." Hope almost envied her cousin. There was a time when she thought she felt that way about Henry, but she'd been more consumed with the idea of him than the man himself.

"If you need to talk to Ben before we leave, he seems to be in a heavy discussion with one of the other farmers over there." Hope pointed to the left.

"No need. I told Jake while we were in line to shake hands with Reverend Caswell to take their time and come to the house after they finished their business. But, I did almost forget that Sarah wants to see you." Annie shielded her eyes as she searched. "There she is." Annie strolled beside Hope in the direction of the pastor's wife.

"Annie! Hope!" The pastor's stunning wife with dark hair, deep blue eyes, and a rounded midsection waved. She stepped toward them, and a little blonde girl skipped beside her.

Design ideas burst into Hope's imagination like colorful paint thrown against a gray building. She couldn't help re-working Sarah's dress in her mind. If she took it in here, let it out there, added pleats and embroidery in that area . . .

Sarah embraced Hope, warming her heart with a welcoming smile. "I'm so glad you're here, safe and sound. Annie and I could hardly wait for you to arrive."

"Thank you. Everyone has been so kind." That certainly was true, regardless of some earlier stares in church. She'd only been there for two days, and she felt like she'd been greeted by half the town.

"It must have been difficult for you to move here from a city like New York, but give it a chance. I was very close to leaving when my circumstances changed, and I'm so glad I chose to stay. It changed my life—in all the right ways." Her fingertips lightly brushed the child standing next to her. "Hope, I'd like to introduce you to my daughter, Mary."

Hope smiled down at the little girl who looked to be about six years old. "Hello, Mary. My name is Miss Andrews."

"Hello." Mary gave a quick curtsey. "I'm pleased to meet you."

Sarah gave her daughter an approving smile, then winked at Hope. "Our family is growing, as you can see. Mary will have a brother or sister by the end of August." Sarah's countenance glowed as she moved her hand over her extended belly.

"Congratulations, Sarah. I'm so happy for you."

"Thank you." Sarah folded her hands in front of her. "There's been something I've been wanting to ask you. Annie told me she explained my interest in going to the mission field at one time before God made it clear my place is here."

Sarah combed through her daughter's hair with her fingers. "I'm aware your parents aren't traveling to Panama as missionaries, but from what Annie tells me, your mother will serve in any way she can, and I'd like to write her. My intention is to encourage and pray for her, your father, and people working on the canal. If there's anything else our church and community can do to help, we want to at least try."

The backs of Hope's eyes burned. "That would be wonderful and very much welcomed."

She'd been in Riverton less than twenty-four hours, and she'd already been moved to tears—twice. If this was a sign of things to come, she'd be an emotional mess before the end of the summer, but hopefully all for good reasons. The Lord had brought her here. What more did he have in store?

Five

Everything appeared in order, but Hope still adjusted a spoon here, a fork there on the dining room table. Then she rearranged the bouquet of daisies at the center. Why bother with such details? As soon as Ben and Jake walked through the door, they'd only focus on the heavenly smell of fried chicken, now keeping warm in the oven.

The two men had lingered after the church service to speak to Thomas Pederson about dealing with a coyote they'd seen roaming the area. Thomas, his wife Ellie, and their three children lived on a neighboring farm. Wild animals were never a concern in New York, but Riverton was far from any large city.

Lost in her own thoughts, Hope jumped at the sound of the doorbell.

"Can you answer that, please?" Annie poked her head out of the kitchen. "I'm finishing the gravy."

"Of course." She brushed her skirt and smoothed her hair. It meant so much to Annie to have the guests for dinner, Hope could make it through one afternoon with Ben. Besides, she needed to show her gratitude for his and Jake's helpfulness in getting her things from the train to Riverton.

She swung the door wide open and stepped aside to allow room for them to enter. "Please come in."

"My, oh my, just smell that!" Jake's grin almost reached from ear to ear.

"It looks like Annie can cook just like her ma." Ben swung an arm around his brother's shoulder and smiled. "I'm glad you talked me into coming."

Ben had a lot of nerve. First to assume that Annie had done all the cooking. And how impolite to admit that he didn't want to come in the first place. No one had forced him.

"Hi, Jake." She turned to his rude brother. "How nice of you to come willingly, Mr. Greene." Hope plastered a smile on her face. Then she addressed both of them. "Let me take your hats."

Ben held out his fedora, but didn't let go, forcing her to look up at him. "This town isn't much on formalities. So, considering that Jake, Annie, and I are on a first-name basis, don't you think it would feel a bit friendlier for you to call me Ben instead of 'Mr. Greene?'"

"I suppose I could manage that." Hope swallowed. "And with that, it would probably feel awkward for you to continue calling me Miss Andrews."

"I agree." Ben released his grip, an amused smile replacing his stare.

Hope felt a twinge. Did he think he'd won some kind of game between them? Maybe she just didn't have the stomach for putting on social airs. She accepted Jake's Stetson and placed both on a small table near the door.

"I'm glad you're here," Annie said, bounding from the kitchen, her face flushed. "Dinner will be ready in a few minutes. I hope you'll enjoy it."

"No worries there." Jake whistled an approval. "By the way that chicken smells, I'd wager the farm that dinner will be mighty tasty."

The blush in Annie's cheeks deepened. "Thanks, Jake." She gave a nod toward Hope. "I didn't do it alone. Hope stayed up late last night and made a luscious lemon pound cake, and she picked strawberries early this morning to layer on top—the first of the season."

Ben's eyebrows raised. "After your long journey, you still had energy to bake?"

Satisfaction at surprising him teased Hope's lips into a smile. "I wanted to offer something in appreciation for the help yesterday, and I enjoy baking. It gives me time to think."

"You men may wait in the parlor while we bring the food to the table." Annie pointed to the left.

"Oh, no. We'd never hear the end of your mother's scolding if we didn't help." Jake headed toward the kitchen, with Annie close behind.

"Annie, anything around the place you want me to take care of while I'm here?" Ben called after her.

She swung around before reaching the kitchen door, put a finger to her chin and gazed into the air, as though contemplating his question. "No, I don't think so. The back step you fixed is holding up fine. I appreciate your asking, though." She slipped into the kitchen.

Hope glanced at the dining table. It was foolish to place flowers in the center. They'd only be in the way of the platters and bowls of food. She moved into the room and picked up the vase.

"Can I help?" Ben's eyes fixed on her. He towered over Hope, and dressed in a dark suit instead of comfortable farm clothes, he appeared commanding. Not in a frightening way like Henry, who insisted he control situations—control her—but rather as a man who harbored great inner strength.

The same attraction she'd felt on the train pierced her resistance. She tried to free her gaze from his, but failed. "These will only be in the way."

"No, they won't. Leave them. They're nice." Ben nodded toward the bouquet. "You picked them for a reason, right?"

An unexpected shyness overcame Hope. "Daisies are my favorite flower. They always cheer me up because they remind me of the sun and happy times."

"You need cheering up?" He acted sincere—like he genuinely cared.

"No." She was going to sound like a child. "I have a small garden of daisies in New York. Seeing them in the backyard reminded me of home."

Ben nodded, apparently not judging her childish thoughts, then took the vase from her and returned it to the table. "Come on," he said softly. "Let's help get the food on the table before Jake finishes it off."

What a complicated man. He spouted arrogance, then turned around and acted kindly. Just as confusing were her feelings about him. One minute she felt repulsed by his behavior, but soon after, she wanted to get close and learn everything she could about him. Who was Benjamin Greene beneath his mysterious exterior?

CR

Ben placed several plates in the kitchen sink and followed his three dining companions into the parlor. Jake and Annie had carried the conversation during the meal, both sharing humorous anecdotes. They'd be good together—if his brother would admit it and make a commitment.

The two headed for the piano, where Jake slipped onto the bench and began pounding out a lively tune. What he couldn't do with his voice, he made up for with enthusiasm.

"Hope. Ben. Come join us." Annie stood to the side and blended lovely vocal notes with Jake's.

Ben caught Hope's eye and gave a nod toward the piano. "What do you think?"

"Trust me, you don't want to hear me sing. My attempts have been compared to a crow cawing as opposed to a nightingale's melodic voice. I have no talent whatsoever when it comes to music." Pink, the shade of apple blossoms, crept up Hope's neck and into her face, making her eyes appear even bluer. "But, please, you go on. I heard you in church this morning." She looked away and cleared her throat. "You have a wonderful voice."

"I—thank you." He'd offended her only the day before, but now she generously offered a compliment after confessing to lacking in the same area.

Ben thought someone like Hope, a city girl passionate about clothes, would have preferred roses or expensive orchids over simple daisies. Exhausted after the tiring trip to Riverton, she still went without sleep to make dessert for them. A cake so delicious, he wanted to ask for a second piece. This woman continued to surprise him.

An object to his left caught his eye. "That wasn't here before." Ben stepped over to the phonograph sitting on a small table in the corner. He'd only seen phonographs in catalogs and had considered purchasing his own, but what little he managed to save each month replenished his depleting art supplies. "Is this yours?"

"Yes." She moved next to him and ran her fingers over the edge of the polished oak cabinet supporting a turntable and large metal horn. "It was packed in the crate. That's why I was so zealous about you being careful with it. I couldn't leave it behind, and I'd have been devastated if it arrived damaged."

"If I'd known that box contained something so special, I would've been even more careful—not that I was reckless." Ben studied the machine, then faced Hope. "So, even though you don't sing, music is still important to you."

Hope bristled. "I may not have a talent for it, but that doesn't mean I don't know or appreciate good music—or need it in my life."

"No, that's not what I meant. You assumed . . ." But wasn't he guilty of the same more than once on matters concerning her?

Her eyes locked onto his. "I suppose I should have told you, but I believe one should respect another person's property, regardless of the monetary value."

Soft and meek as a kitten one minute, then strong and confident as a tiger the next. Hope was someone to contend with, someone who would challenge him on any matter, and not let him get away with excuses.

"You're right." Ben hiked his palms to his hips. "You're absolutely right. I apologize."

Hope's shoulders visibly relaxed as Jake and Annie switched to singing a ballad. "And I apologize. My father has told me that I jump to conclusions before obtaining all the facts, and I'm afraid he may be right."

"I've been guilty myself." Ben had never met a more complex woman. Hope wasn't afraid to be honest. A certain strength flowed through her, yet she admitted to weaknesses. He liked talking to this softer version of Hope—this vulnerable side—and he wanted to learn more. "What kind of music do you enjoy?"

She tilted her head. "Caruso is my favorite. Are you familiar with opera?"

"My mother was a professional singer before she married my father. When they married, she left that life behind to raise a family."

"How sad." Hope's eyes grew even more serious.

"You might think so, but she's very happy."

"But she gave up something she loved. Do you think that's fair?" Hope's tone dared him to convince her of his mother's contentment.

"I never thought about it being fair or unfair. She raised five children, and she's always said that teaching us to love and serve God was the most important thing she's ever done. Along with that, instilling the love of music in each of us became a new vocation for her."

"So, your mother made the right decision, even though it came at a cost."

"I'd say it's similar to your mother traveling to Panama to be with your father." A sudden realization. "When you truly love someone, you're willing to make sacrifices."

Hope held his gaze. "I couldn't agree with you more."

At that moment, it felt like something within them melded into a mutual understanding that couldn't be put into words.

Jake and Annie had stopped singing and seemed to have tuned in to the discussion. Silence filled the room, except for the light flapping sound the curtains made as a soft breeze blew through an open window.

Annie made the first move and stepped away from the piano. "I'll get us something to drink. Hope, will you help?"

Hope blinked and collapsed the invisible bridge between her and Ben." Yes, of course."

As she turned away from him, air rushed from Ben's lungs, as though he'd been released from a strong bond. What just happened?

CR

Hope picked up two glasses filled with lemonade and turned to leave the kitchen.

"Wait." Annie touched Hope's arm, keeping her voice quiet. "Are you all right? It felt like things were getting a little . . . *tense* between the two of you out there."

"I'm fine." Hope sighed. "I'm not sure what was going on, but it was like . . . we were the only two people in the room. I completely forgot you and Jake were there. Ben told me his mother chose to get married and have a family. It meant leaving her singing career. He said she was happy, and it brought back some of the same things Henry and I fought over, only this felt different. It made me wonder how different he is from Henry . . ."

Annie smiled. "Hope, Ben is nothing like Henry. Give him a chance, and you'll see."

"Why do you like him so much?"

Annie leaned against the counter. "At first, Mother and I got along fine after Father died. But after the first year, there were small repairs needed on the house and other places on the property. Jake and Ben had just moved here, and they were taking jobs wherever they could to help ends meet. Mother hired them to fix several things around here, but instead of taking money, they offered to do the work for some of her home cooking. It got to be a regular thing—us helping each other out that way. My heart fell for Jake, but Ben . . . he's like a big brother to me. And he looks at me like a little sister. I think he misses his own, and I may be the next best thing to having her here."

The way Ben teased, complimented, and protected Annie made more sense now. Hope was beginning to understand why her cousin admired the man.

Hope followed Annie into the parlor and handed Ben a glass of lemonade.

"Thanks."

"You're welcome." She smiled and sat next to Annie on the settee. "I'm sorry if I got a little out of sorts when you were talking about your mother." Hope chewed on her lower lip. How much could Hope tell them? Would these two men take her seriously? Or would they think her silly?

Ben opened his mouth, but Hope raised her hand to shush him. Annie trusted them . . . Hope would too. "I . . ." She took a deep breath. "I struggle with people telling me to give up my ambitions. So, when I hear that another woman has chosen to do just that, it's a bit discouraging."

Ben didn't laugh. He didn't snicker. He didn't even look amused. "Of course. Anyone in a similar situation would feel the same way."

"Really?" He understood? If it were possible for a human to float in the air, her body would have risen like a feather carried by the wind.

"I believe that God has a plan for each of us, Hope, and I also think he cares about what we want. But too often we're tempted to follow what someone else thinks we should do. Or we don't try because we're afraid of failure. Other times, what we imagine may be a little different than what God has in mind. It's not easy—it's actually impossible some days—but maybe we need to trust that God will work it all out."

"I couldn't agree more." The conversation had gone in an unexpected direction, but a positive one. Hope missed having similar conversations with her parents. "It's just difficult sometimes to hand over my heart's desires to God. I want to know what the future holds, but I also realize that his design for my life will be so much better than what I could create on my own. I also have to believe that God doesn't give us a talent, or at least a passion for something, unless he wants us to use it."

"Touché!" Jake raised his glass as though to toast. "Ben, do you hear this wise and brilliant woman? We are to use our God-given gifts. Not hide them under a bushel."

"I hear." Ben eyes shot flames at his brother, as though trying to stop Jake from saying anything further.

Hope didn't mean to raise any conflict. Better to move the conversation along. "Sometimes we start down one path, only to realize that direction was meant to be temporary." She sipped her lemonade. "For instance, Sarah Caswell prepared to be a missionary in Africa, but God's plan was for her to remain here and marry Reverend Caswell."

"Sarah and Peter grew up together and were very close, but he left for college and married someone else," Annie chimed in. "After his wife died, he moved back with his daughter, but Sarah had made plans by then to leave Riverton for the mission field."

"What stopped her?" Jake asked.

"Her feelings for Reverend Caswell and the fact that the missionary board changed their mind and decided to send a couple with medical experience instead."

Jake whistled and shook his head.

"But in the end, regardless of whether she went to Africa or not, Sarah is still serving God in ministry. It's what she was meant to do." Hope rubbed the moisture on her glass with her thumb. "I want to design clothes that make women feel beautiful when they wear them." She inched up to the edge of the settee and faced Jake. "If you could do anything at all, what would you choose?"

"That's easy." His face brightened like the sun rising over the horizon on a clear morning. "I'm already doing it. All I've wanted to do since I could remember is farm. Watch things grow. Tend to living creatures. Know that I could survive by my own two hands."

"You're one of the lucky ones, Jake. To have already found your way." Hope turned to her cousin. "Annie, what about you?"

Annie shrugged, then some twitches played at her mouth before her lips moved into a tentative smile. "I haven't told anyone this before, but I'd like to open a town library. Nothing big, of course. Just a small, quaint place."

Hope almost bolted from her seat. "Annie, that's a wonderful idea!"

"You really think so?" Annie's eyes shone.

Jake's forehead creased. "Why haven't you said anything before?"

"I was afraid people would think it ridiculous—or impossible for someone like me." Annie clasped her glass between her hands. "I'm just a store clerk."

"Annie, you're good with people," Ben said. "You're also smart and great at organizing, and you read more books than anyone I know—even Jake—and he reads a lot."

"Oh, my . . ." Annie's eyes grew as large as the cover to her hat box. "You really think I could do it?"

Hope leaned over and gave Annie a hug around the shoulders. "We'll help in any way we can." She looked at the two men, and they nodded in agreement. "That just leaves you, Ben. It's your turn to answer the question." Hope held her breath. She was about to learn something that would tell her more about Ben than she'd learned since arriving in Riverton.

Maybe he wasn't anything like Henry, and maybe she and Ben could be friends. Since he and Jake were so important to Annie, getting along with Ben would certainly make living in Riverton easier. Then there was that earlier moment. No denying the attraction—even if she didn't want to admit feeling drawn to him.

"Like Jake. I'm doing it." Ben stared down at his glass of lemonade. "All I want is to make a good living at farming." He spoke the words, but they lacked Jake's conviction.

Air escaped from Hope's lungs through a quiet sigh. There was some truth to what he said, but Hope wanted to find out what Ben *wasn't* telling.

Six

"Miss? Miss?"

"One moment, please." Hope turned toward the wall and returned a small lamp to a shelf as an excuse to close her eyes and take a deep breath, then she faced the woman bouncing a toddler on her hip. "How may I help you?"

A gruff-sounding man with bushy eyebrows and a thick mustache stepped in front of the lady, almost shoving her aside. "Excuse me! I was here first, and I've already waited ten minutes for you to pull down a lantern for me. If it takes any longer, I'll get it myself."

Hope met his glare. "Yes, sir," she said as calmly as possible. "You're right. You've been very patient, and I'll take care of you right away. I just wanted to acknowledge that she also requires some assistance." She peered around the man's wide shoulders and nodded at the mother. "I'll be with you as soon as possible."

The lantern he requested sat on a shelf too high for Hope to reach, so she pulled a ladder on wheels to that section. She retrieved the lantern and placed it on the counter in front of the impatient customer.

He grabbed the lantern, turned it left and right, then set it back down. "I don't want it." Without saying another word, he stalked toward the back of the store.

"Miss? Where can I find men's work gloves?" Bouncing no longer effective, the woman's son started to fuss.

"I'm—" Hope scanned the store and searched as far as she could see. "I'm sorry. I'm not sure."

"Can you please help me find them? My son is hungry and tired, but I can't go home without those gloves. Our puppy chewed my husband's last pair." Although the woman's tone remained civil, her moist eyes betrayed desperation. "My husband didn't want to take time away from the farm. He has so much to do. I thought my coming into town would help, but our boy is missing his nap."

Hope understood her eagerness to find what she needed and leave. The child was wailing, and people were starting to stare and whisper.

"Yes, of course." Hope wouldn't mind escaping herself right now. "Please wait right here." No sense in leading a customer with a crying baby up and down aisles. She scurried around the store until she found men's work gloves.

After grabbing an assortment, she returned to where she'd left the customer and laid the gloves on the counter. "Choose whatever pair suits you, and for the inconvenience you've experienced this morning, I'll give you 50 percent off."

The woman's face brightened. "Thank you!" She chose a leather pair and handed them to the little boy. Now that he had something new to occupy his attention, he calmed down. "These will fit perfectly."

"The cost is thirty-three cents, so I'll charge you sixteen." Hope would make up the difference with her own money. It was worth it to help the lady return home satisfied and as soon as possible.

"Would you please hold Jeremy?" She thrust her son into Hope's arms before she had a chance to object. It didn't matter—Hope would never refuse to hold a child. The young mother opened a small bag and counted sixteen pennies, which she laid one by one on the counter.

The little boy reached for his mother, and Hope returned him to her arms, but not soon enough to avoid the trail of snot from his dripping nose as he wiped it on her shoulder. Hope swallowed. "I'll write a receipt."

With gloves and baby in hand, the woman left with a smile on her face, and Hope remained with a wet yellow streak across her white shirtwaist. She grabbed an old rag and rubbed the marks until they were faint.

Courage isn't always about dealing with life-threatening situations, Hope. Sometimes bravery involves facing the unknown, taking on new roles, or embracing new adventures. Her father's last words as they parted ways in New York still played in her thoughts. She'd need to rehearse them often, especially after the morning she'd just experienced.

Hope blew a wisp of loose hair away from her face and shifted her weight from one foot to the other. She yearned to remove her boots and massage her aching feet. There was more to being a store clerk—or at least a good one—than most people realized. The weeks she'd spent as a clerk at Macy's in New York last Christmas season had somewhat prepared her, but she'd only had one department to cover, not an entire store's inventory.

Annie had explained that Mondays were one of their busiest days, but Hope hadn't anticipated feeling so overwhelmed. Several people expected her to know where obscure items were located in the store, even though she'd only been employed there less than a day. Dealing with impatient customers made her stomach queasy.

"How are you fairing, Miss Andrews?" Mr. Carter, the owner of the Home Store, placed two small boxes on the counter in front of her.

"There's a lot to learn, but I'm trying my best, Mr. Carter." Hope relaxed at seeing the warm smile beneath his mustache. "I'm thankful for the opportunity to work here." Her employer was known for his honesty and kindness. Along with that, nothing compared to this store for many miles.

"I apologize for not giving you more time to get acclimated, but one of the clerks was unable to come in today, so I'm afraid we're a little short-handed." He opened one box and pulled out a white cotton handkerchief with scalloped edges and a printed floral border. "An assortment of men's and women's handkerchiefs arrived this morning. I'd like you to arrange them in the glass case below this counter. Please make a note that cotton items will be sold for four cents each, and the linen, twenty-three cents."

"I'll be glad to, Mr. Carter." She enjoyed creating displays intended to capture a buyer's interest—one of her favorite responsibilities at Macy's. She'd taken the part-time job to earn money for Christmas gifts, but to also live in the midst of fashion—pieces sold by the store as well as shoppers wearing their finest.

"If you need any help—and I don't mean just with this task I've given you—please don't hesitate to ask. Any of the employees, including myself, will be happy to assist you."

"Thank you." Hope smiled and set to work.

Annie had insisted Hope would enjoy working for the store's owner, and she was right. From his interactions with customers, it was obvious he enjoyed serving them. Just now, he marched over with a chair for a frail-looking elderly woman who waited in line to pay for a soup kettle.

The Home Store, designed like a Spanish mission, was built in the center of town. With beautiful wood floors, large arched windows, and mirror-covered pillars, it could have fit in well with other city stores. The second story even included a separate room for women filled with couches, rocking chairs, and tables, as well as swings and cribs for their little ones. But along with serving Riverton, it accommodated the needs of farmers for many miles. A stable out back allowed them to shelter their horses while taking care of business at the store.

Hope fingered the cotton handkerchief. Although pretty and practical, silk would be nice for special occasions. Would Mr. Carter consider it? The store provided everything a person might need concerning household items or farm equipment, but the selection of clothes seemed mundane, and they were either hanging on racks or folded and stacked on shelves.

She already missed the department stores in New York and the many times she'd tingled with excitement while walking into a room lined with dresses made from beautiful fabrics. It would probably be the same for Annie if she'd ever have the opportunity to step inside a library with wall-to-wall books. Knowing where she'd moved from, Mr. Carter had expressed interest in Hope's opinion on what should be purchased for the store. Although folks here might admire the expensive clothing, she doubted Mr. Carter would sell very much. She guessed occasions for such attire didn't often rise in farming communities.

However, she could suggest making adjustments to the displays. Several dressed mannequins, with various accessories added, might stir a customer's imagination. A spark of excitement ignited. Yes, she'd mention it to Mr. Carter soon.

"Hello?" Someone rapped sharply on the counter.

Her daydreaming disrupted, Hope jerked to attention. "How may I help you?" Her face burned, and she tried to swallow.

The middle-aged woman with piercing eyes surveyed Hope. "You're new here."

"Yes, this is my first day."

"I'm Katherine Hoyt, and this is my daughter, Rebecca."

Hope's stomach clenched. She'd recognized Rebecca from seeing her at church the previous day. The mother with the pinched lips Hope knew by reputation. It would serve well to play to her vanity. Hope didn't need a customer complaining that she'd been lost in thought and inattentive. "Mrs. Hoyt, it's nice to meet someone so well respected in the community. Your husband is the local veterinarian, right?"

"He is . . ." Katherine Hoyt smiled, then narrowed her eyes. "And you are?"

"You're Hope Andrews, Annie's cousin." Rebecca offered Hope a smile. "We met three years ago when I played the piano at her father's funeral. But we only spoke for a minute then. I saw you at church on Sunday and recognized you right away."

"I see," Mrs. Hoyt said. "I didn't attend because I wasn't feeling well that day. If I'd been there, I would have made a point of introducing myself."

Hope tried not to squirm under the older woman's scrutiny and turned her attention to Rebecca. "Your playing was lovely, just as it was for my uncle's service."

"Thank you," Rebecca said, sounding genuinely pleased. "You came all the way from New York to stay with Annie for a while, correct?" She laid her purse on the counter that served as a barrier between them.

"Yes, I arrived last Saturday." Thank goodness Rebecca seemed less formidable than her mother—and how Annie had described her. If she couldn't answer Mrs. Hoyt's questions or find a needed item, she'd do what Mr. Carter had encouraged her to do—set pride aside and ask for help.

"New York!" Mrs. Hoyt sounded impressed. "Why would someone come from such a metropolitan area to a small town like this? What could possibly be here for you?"

"It's none of our business, Mother." Rebecca gave a short, forced laugh. "Whatever her reasons, they're hers."

"It seemed like a good time and opportunity for me to have an extended visit with my cousin." Hope didn't feel the need or desire to share anything more than that with either of them.

From what little she knew, Mrs. Hoyt was a snob who was mean to anyone she believed inferior. But Rebecca had shown unexpected kindness today. Maybe she'd changed from the meddling, arrogant person Annie had described in past letters.

Annie strolled over with an armload of dish towels, and caught Hope's eye. "Is there anything I can help with here?"

"Thank you, but no, we have no need for assistance. We're on our way out." Mrs. Hoyt gave a stiff, polite smile.

"We merely stopped for a moment to introduce ourselves to the new member of the Home Store staff."

"I appreciate your welcome." Hope meant her statement to include both women, but she kept her eyes on Rebecca.

"Yes, well, we'll be on our way." Mrs. Hoyt moved toward the front door. "Come along, Rebecca."

"It was nice to see you, Hope." Rebecca smiled at her, but only gave Annie a brief nod before following her mother down the store aisle.

Annie laid the towels on the counter and gave a low whistle. "I'm sorry. Only your first day on the floor and you had to deal with those two."

"Mrs. Hoyt makes me feel like I'm six years old and being reprimanded by my crotchety first-grade teacher." Hope leaned across the counter and looked up at Annie. "But Rebecca seemed—nice."

Annie's eyebrows shot up. "Nice? Have you forgotten what I've told you? How she spread those awful rumors about Sarah and Reverend Caswell having an affair? It almost destroyed their relationship, not to mention almost ruining their reputations. The reverend could have lost his job."

"That was years ago, and from what I've observed, she's been forgiven. Otherwise, she wouldn't be attending the same church as the Caswells, let alone serving as the pianist."

Annie scowled. "Still, that doesn't mean I trust her—or want to be her friend."

"I understand." Hope didn't blame Annie for her feelings, but something about Rebecca intrigued her. Hope reached across the counter and nudged her cousin's shoulder and grinned. "But, I know you'll also understand if I need to follow my own heart on this matter."

"Don't say I didn't warn you when she stabs you in the back." Annie picked up the towels from the counter. "You didn't have anything planned after supper, did you?"

Hope tilted her head. "Now, what type of arrangement do you think I could possibly have made in the last few hours?"

"I don't know. You could have decided to spend the evening with your new *friend*." Annie winked.

"You're incorrigible!" A soft laugh escaped Hope's lips. "What did you have in mind?"

"I'll explain later." A light ruby shade colored Annie's face. "Just be ready to go for a short ride."

Seven

Hope stepped down from the buggy and surveyed the two-story white farmhouse with the wide porch. The architecture included simple lines, but the home looked fresh and clean, as though recently painted. A lilac bush as large as a tree grew in front, as well as several rose bushes that needed pruning.

"Annie, are you finally going to tell me where we are?"

"Ben and Jake's farm."

Attracted to Ben, yet not completely trusting the mysterious man who seemed to be keeping secrets, she'd hoped to avoid him longer than one day. What was Annie up to? "Why would you bring me here without telling me?"

"I was afraid you'd try to talk me out of it." Annie tied the horse to a small railing next to the house so he wouldn't wander off with the buggy. "I'll explain once we find them." She perched one hand on her hip, and shielded her eyes with the other. The sun was just at the right height in the sky to blind her at this angle.

"Jake!" Annie waved wildly at him hiking up a slight hill with a collie at this side. He must have come from the barn below where several cows were mooing. She strolled toward him.

Hope remained behind. A meadowlark landed on a near-by fence and offered her a song before taking flight. The sun still shared some warmth, and Hope drank in the quiet and beauty surrounding her.

The couple drew near. "Hope, what is your cousin scheming now?" Jake, dressed in overalls, laughed and wiped his hands on a red handkerchief. Surrounded by the peaceful setting, no wonder he was so enthusiastic about farming and living in the country.

"I don't have a clue." Hope shot a questioning look at Annie. "Are you ever going to tell us?"

"Not until we're all together," Annie said smugly.

"I'll look for Ben after I wash up a bit." Jake shoved the handkerchief back into his overall pocket. "Please help yourselves to milk or lemonade in the icebox. I'd get it for you, but I don't think you'd want to be served with these dirty hands."

"Thanks. I'll pour four lemonades." Annie followed Jake and the dog up the porch steps, then turned. "Hope, are you coming?"

"You go on. I'd like to enjoy the view for a moment."

"I'll get the drinks and be right out."

Hope had never thought farms scenic, but the fields before her, basking in the fading sunlight, were breathtaking.

Where is Ben? The mere thought of him made her feel like she'd swallowed the Monarch butterflies dancing in the air next to her. Since Jake had just come from the barn, Ben obviously wasn't there. A small building that looked fairly new sat at a distance to the right. Odd place for a shed. Maybe Ben was inside putting tools away, or doing whatever else farmers did in sheds. Might as well explore. The sooner he was found, the sooner they'd all learn Annie's secret.

Hope reached for the door handle, but it swung open, and in her haste to move out of the way, she tripped and fell back on her bottom. She closed her eyes as a sharp pain shot through her hip. "Ow!"

The door to the shed slammed shut. "What are you doing here?"

Hope opened her eyes and looked up. Ben, a deep frown on his face, leaned over her. So he wasn't happy to see her. He didn't need to knock her down. "I was looking for you."

His brows knit together and confusion filled his eyes. "Why?"

She sighed. "If you help me up, I might be willing to tell you."

"Sorry. You surprised me." He reached down, and grasping her hand, pulled her up with such force she collided with his firm chest. His other arm wrapped around her waist and steadied her.

It lasted only a second, but it was enough. Hope's breath caught, and her heart felt like it was tumbling down a never-ending staircase.

Ben stepped back. "So, um, what are you doing here?" He glanced at the shed behind him, then up at the house.

"I'm actually not sure." Hope brushed what dirt she could feel from her skirt.

"But you just said . . ."

While in his embrace, she'd inhaled a familiar pine scent. She sniffed the air between them. "Were you painting in there?"

His face paled. "Why would you ask that?"

"You smell like turpentine." Her curiosity had been piqued, and she wanted to see inside. "Are you refinishing furniture?"

"Furniture?"

"What else would you be painting in a shed?"

His shoulders visibly relaxed, and the corners of his mouth twitched into a small smile as he pocketed his hands. "Right, what else would I possibly be doing?"

Why wasn't he giving her any direct answers? "Would you show me?"

"I don't think you'd find it all that interesting."

"You could be wrong. I might think it fascinating." Hope inwardly sighed. If she wanted answers, she needed to be willing to give them. "I have my reasons. While rummaging through our attic back home, I found the rocking chair my grandfather used as a boy. I thought it would be special to give it to my own child someday." Was that too personal? Letting him know that, despite their previous conversation about his mother giving up singing for her family, Hope wanted children? "But, I'm afraid I made a mess of it. You might be able to give me some ideas of how I might fix my mistakes when I return to New York."

Annie yelled and waved to them from the porch, gesturing for them to join her and Jake.

"Forget the shed." Ben gestured for her to follow. "There's something behind you riding all the way out here, and I'm curious to see what your cousin is up to."

They hiked back to the house and up the steps. Hope sat in a rocking chair next to Annie's, but the men both leaned against the porch railing and faced them.

Hope glanced at Ben and caught him staring at her. He turned away, and her cheeks warmed. "Annie, what's going on? The way you're acting, it must be something important." Hope needed to concentrate on what her cousin had to say, not think about that too short, wonderful moment in Ben's arms.

"I was talking to Mrs. Jorgenson earlier today about my idea for a town library."

Forget about Ben. Annie had Hope's attention now. "Aren't you rushing things? You never mentioned anything about a library until yesterday."

"True, but it's something I've dreamed of for a long time, and after your encouragement . . . well, I couldn't sleep last night. I began to wonder if I could really do it."

"Of course you can." Hope sat at the edge of her seat. "But first you need to have a building, and after that, there's so much more to consider. Like where you'll get enough books."

"I already have most of that figured out." Annie's eyes glowed. "And I've never seen Mrs. Jorgenson so excited! As a former teacher and always a book-lover, she has vast knowledge of what we might want available, and she has plenty of time to help get everything set up and established."

"That's wonderful, but—" Hope stopped herself. What was she doing? She had no right or desire to squelch anyone's dreams. "Tell us more."

"There may be a building in town that will work perfectly. Mrs. Jorgenson heard the other day that the town has claimed an abandoned house down by the river. The owner died two years ago, and they've never been able to find any living relatives. So, the property will be sold, with the proceeds going into the town treasury."

Jake hopped up and sat on the railing. "Where's the money going to come from to purchase it?"

"I don't plan to buy it—I want the town to donate the building. If we're going to have a public library, we need the community's support."

"I know the house you're talking about. It's pretty run-down, Annie." Ben rubbed his jaw. "It'll take a lot of work to get it in shape."

"That's where you and Jake come in. You're both handy with repairs and carpentry." Annie wet her lips. "And yesterday, you both said you were willing to help. Does that offer still stand?"

The two brothers eyed each other, and a big smile grew on Jake's face. He nodded. "It does, but we'll probably need more hands than just ours."

"There is one problem." Lines formed in Annie's forehead. "Someone else is interested in purchasing the property. If we can't convince the town council that we need a library more than we need money in the treasury, we won't stand a chance of getting the building and land donated."

Jake shrugged as though another buyer wasn't a problem. "Then, you'll just have to figure out a way to make them believe."

Only three days prior, Hope had arrived in Riverton not knowing how she was ever going to realize her goals while living in the small town. And now . . . she was seeing Annie's aspirations fall into place. It didn't seem quite fair.

Lord, please remove this seed of jealousy before it can take root in my heart.

Maybe it was only her own fault that she hadn't experienced any success with her designs. Maybe Hope needed to be more courageous and willing to take action like Annie. She'd spend every spare minute sketching from now on, and she'd set aside her pride and speak to Clara about her skills as a seamstress.

"Hope? What do you think?" Annie whispered in her direction.

"I'll do anything I can. I promise." Hope meant it. How could she not help? Annie had welcomed Hope to Riverton with open arms and done everything possible to make her feel at home.

Annie leaned back in her chair. "I'm so relieved. You don't know how worried I've been that you'd all think I was crazy."

"You, a crazy redhead?" Jake chuckled.

Annie made a silly face at him.

Their relationship seemed so easy, except that Jake didn't seem to have a clue as to how much Annie really cared for him.

⁊

No point in tossing and turning all night. Ben crawled out of bed, slipped his trousers and shirt on, and tiptoed down the stairs. Not that he needed to be quiet. Jake's snoring coming from the other room would drown out any creaks Ben made stepping on the old wooden boards.

He lit a lantern on the kitchen table, then stepped outside, closing both the front and screen doors behind him. The moon's glow gave off enough light, he could have made it to the shed without the lantern's help. An owl hooted in the distance.

Inside the shed, he lit a second lantern and set one on either side of a standing easel located behind him. He grabbed the canvas he'd stretched over a wooden frame earlier and prepped with white paint. A blank, fresh surface had the potential of becoming a vision that was both exiting and beautiful—like Hope. The more he spent time with her, the more he wanted to know and understand the woman within. She was like a lovely painting, with colorful tones and depth.

Ben picked up a piece of charcoal and began sketching a woman's profile—the very one he'd memorized during the church service the day before.

Hope had made it clear that she wanted her fashion designs to be accepted—loved by women. But she had yet to achieve her goal. Ben hadn't missed the brief disappointment in her face when Annie shared her excitement about the library and how opportunities had suddenly presented themselves. He understood the difficulty in celebrating someone else's success when your own felt elusive. Yet, with genuine enthusiasm, she agreed to help Annie.

Good thing he'd decided to check on Jake earlier that evening and stepped outside the shed just in time to stop Hope from entering. Ben had gotten after Jake for not keeping both women from wandering around the property, but his brother was right. It wasn't his fault that Hope surprised Ben. Keeping his artwork from the world was his choice—and his problem. That burden shouldn't be placed on Jake's shoulders.

She hadn't discovered his secret, but what would Hope have thought if she'd gotten inside and seen his work?

Despite the close call, for a brief but wonderful moment, he'd held her. Even if purely by accident. It would never happen again—it couldn't. He'd never toy with a woman's affections.

Until Ben could figure out his own life, his place was here, helping Jake. But Hope wasn't the type of woman who could be satisfied living on a farm, milking cows, and raising crops. She needed the excitement, lifestyle, and opportunities a big city offered. He could never offer her or anyone else that existence.

Besides, Hattie, the woman he once thought he might marry, had made it quite clear that women want and need financial stability. Even then, Ben had chosen to continue painting instead of pursuing a more lucrative profession.

He brushed the charcoal lines until no trace of them remained, stared at the empty canvas, then flung the charcoal against the wall. Why did he keep trying to fool himself? He didn't want to continue living this way—lonely, hiding behind a closed door.

But what do you do when you feel powerless to change anything?

Eight

Why couldn't she get the color right? Either the shade was too blue or overly green. Even holding the sketch in the direct sunlight beaming through the dining room window didn't help. Hope tossed the paper onto the pile of discarded failures accumulating on the table.

Her stomach growled. She hadn't eaten a thing since breakfast, and that was hours ago. Leftover ham from last night's supper, cheese, and fresh bread would serve her well. Maybe she'd find more success mixing paint colors after satisfying her gnawing hunger.

The doorbell rang. She wasn't expecting anyone, and Annie had left for her shift at the store without mentioning any visitors. Since Hope wasn't scheduled to work that day, she'd planned to spend time alone.

She peeked through the curtains covering the window to the left of the door. What could he possibly want? She opened the door with a casual air. "Hello, Ben." She smiled at the handsome, mysterious man with a twinkle in his eyes. "How may I help you?"

A wide grin grew on his face.

"Why are you looking at me that way?"

"What way?"

"Like the Cheshire Cat in *Alice's Adventures in Wonderland.*"

"If you invite me in, I'll show you."

"Please." Hope stepped back and made a waving gesture. "Come in."

"This way." He removed his straw hat and placed it on the small table next to the door with the ease of someone familiar with the house. Then he pointed to the oval mirror hanging between the coat rack and the staircase leading up to the second floor. "Take a look."

Oh, dear! How embarrassing. A pale green streak ran across her forehead, and a small blob covered the tip of her nose. Heat shot through her face. Why didn't she check the mirror before opening the door? "Please excuse me."

In the kitchen, it took only a minute to scrub the water-based paint from her face. She checked her reflection on the side of a shiny pot. Not a speck of green remained. Hope took a deep breath and strolled out of the room, expecting to find Ben waiting for her in the parlor.

Instead, he stood next to the dining room table, shuffling through the drawings lying there—*her* drawings. Hope could only imagine what he thought, and she prepared for an onslaught of degrading remarks.

"I don't recall you asking permission to look at my work," Hope said in a polite, but firm tone. "Besides, after expressing your strong opinions on the train, I wouldn't think you'd find anything on the table interesting."

"You'd be wrong." Ben held up her last attempt. "This one is actually—nice."

Nice. Hope groaned inside. She didn't want nice. She wanted stunning. Striking. Exquisite. "Thank you." She slid the dress design from his grasp. "But the color isn't quite right."

He glanced at it again and shrugged. "Looks fine to me."

Of course it does. She held up a peacock feather and pointed. "I'd like to show it in this rich, blue-green color, but I can't seem to get the right mix."

Ben studied the design, then her box of watercolors. "Add a small amount of that yellow in with what you already have mixed."

"I've already tried several other yellow tones. They only worsened the hue."

"But not that one."

Hope sighed. If she disregarded his suggestion, she might reap consequences later. "To appease you and avoid any further discussion . . ." Hope dabbed a clean brush in the yellow and mixed it in with the other paint. "I—I didn't think—this is it! The color is perfect."

"And it took a farmer to figure it out." His eyes and tone of voice let her know he was teasing her.

"I should be humiliated, but I'm actually grateful. Thank you." Hope offered a generous smile. No longer hungry and finally concocting the right shade of paint, she was eager to get back to her design. But, it would be rude to shoo him out the door. "Now what can I do for you? You must have had a reason for showing up at our door."

"I'm here at Annie's request."

"You saw her at the store?"

He nodded. "Jake and I came into town to get a few supplies. Annie got word that she could take a look at the house she wants to convert into a library, so she took her lunch break and headed over there with Jake. She'd like us to meet them there."

"My cousin isn't one to dawdle, is she?" Hope closed her paint box and dropped her paintbrush into a small can of water. "In less than seven days she's managed to set an idea into motion."

"Annie has never lacked enthusiasm." Ben grabbed his hat from the table and plopped it on his head as he opened the front door for Hope.

"I just hope it doesn't lead her down a long path of disappointment."

❧

Ben surveyed the front of the small run-down house and gave a low whistle. "It's worse than I expected." White paint—or what used to be white—peeled from the weathered exterior. Cracked windows bordered the warped door, and two of the four porch steps were broken through.

"Maybe the inside looks more promising." Hope climbed the steps, avoiding holes created by rotted wood giving way.

Poor Annie. Her excitement had blinded her to the difficult, if not impossible, task ahead of her. Ben took a deep breath and followed Hope into the house.

"I'm so glad you came. Isn't it wonderful?" Annie flung her hands into the air and twirled around. "Mrs. Jorgenson agrees."

The sweet older woman stood with her hands clasped and a grin on her soft, wrinkled face, as though thoroughly delighted. "It is something, isn't it? Riverton having its own public library."

Annie nodded heartily. "We still have to convince the town council, but I don't see how they could turn us down once they hear our plan."

Ben groaned inside. What was it about women and their fantasies? Didn't they see the wreckage in front of them? Filth covered the walls, animal droppings were scattered across the floor, and the place smelled like . . . The building should be torn down.

Jake was nowhere to be seen, so Ben would let Hope be the voice of reason. She may be the only person who could get Annie to open her eyes to the undertaking ahead. Only, Hope didn't refute her cousin's statements. Instead, she wandered from one room, seeming to hang on every word coming from her cousin's lips.

Annie pointed. "Books would be checked out at a desk here. We can fit in two small tables and chairs there."

"The light from this window is quite nice." Hope's eyes shone. "What do you think about having several reading chairs here?" Her imagination must have caught up to Annie's.

"Oh, that would be lovely!" Mrs. Jorgenson beamed at the other two women. "I was also thinking how nice it would be to plant flowers in the front yard. They'd make the library even more welcoming."

Next they'd be talking about hanging frilly curtains in the windows and serving tea and cookies to reading groups. Ben sighed. Were they trying to create a library or a ladies' club?

A door slammed from the rear of the house, and Jake sauntered in from another room.

Finally, another male influence. "Where have you been?"

"I was just out back checking on some things." Jake wiped his hands on his overalls and meandered over to the women. "The outhouse will have to be rebuilt. As far as the house itself, the foundation seems solid, so that's a relief. But this place won't be ready to open any time soon."

Annie hugged herself. "I'm in no hurry."

Yeah, right. Ben wiped his forehead. He was already sweating, and work on the place hadn't even started. Annie may claim not being in a rush, but if her current speed was any indication, *no hurry* could mean she wanted the library doors open as soon as next week.

"You mentioned a plan." Hope spoke softly. "How are you going to convince the town council to let you have the building without cost? And if they do, then what?"

"We've put together some ideas, haven't we, Mrs. Jorgenson?"

The older woman nodded and smiled.

Annie held up her hand and pointed to her pointer finger. "One. It will be important to get the townspeople and farmers involved. Ben and Jake are going to need help with carpentry and other repairs. For instance, we'll need bookshelves." She pointed to her middle finger. "Two. We've already spoken to several ladies who are willing to help clean and paint."

"Sorry to interrupt," Jake said, "but where is all the money going to come from to do these projects?"

"I was getting to that." Annie held up her ring finger. "Three. We plan to hold several fundraisers, yet to be determined, but we have a few ideas. Those events will also involve volunteers from the community, which will help more people feel like they're contributing to the library."

"It will be costly to fill this room alone with books." Concern flooded Hope's voice. "Most people living around here don't make large wages. There's nothing wrong with simple living, but you have to consider that even though people may be willing to give all they can, the contributions might still not be enough. What if it takes all the money you raise just to make the place habitable?"

"I've thought about that." The light in Annie's eyes dimmed. "I'm not ignorant of the challenges."

"I sure hope that's true." Not intending to reveal his doubt, the tone in Ben's voice did the job anyway.

Hope's eyes flashed. "Ben!"

Her reprimand in front of the others pricked his ego, but even worse was the hurt expression on Annie's face. That weighed heavily on Ben's heart. "I'm sorry, Annie, I didn't mean . . ." He didn't want to hurt her feelings. But if he tried to explain that he wanted to help and protect her, it might make matters worse. He'd just keep quiet, and then somehow find a way to make it up to her.

⚬⚬

With their visit to the intended library completed, Hope grew anxious to return to her sketching.

"Hope, would you mind riding with Ben and Jake?" Annie chewed the lower corner of her lip. "I need to take Mrs. Jorgenson home before returning to the store, and I've already been gone longer than I should have been."

"Of course, Annie." Hope glanced at the two men waiting. "Mr. Carter is an understanding employer, but we don't want to take advantage of his easy-going nature. We can talk more over supper."

"Thank you for coming, everyone." Annie helped Mrs. Jorgenson into her buggy.

Hope walked over to the wagon and Jake helped her up, then slid next to her so she was sandwiched between the two men. Jake seemed perfectly comfortable, but Ben squirmed slightly and inched away from her. Should she be offended? Did he find her unattractive or had he moved out of respect? He hadn't shoved her away the other night at the farm when she'd tripped outside his shed—he'd held on and seemed hesitant to let go. Hope folded her hands in her lap and tried to stay put as the wagon jolted and moved down the road.

Jake leaned forward and faced Ben. "Remember, we need to stop at the blacksmith shop. The new harnesses should be ready." He slid back and smiled at Hope. "It won't take up much time. Promise."

"I don't mind." Even if she did, it would be unreasonable to object. The blacksmith was just up ahead. Annie's house was on their way out of town, so it didn't make sense for them to take Hope there and then return. It would also take longer for her to walk the rest of the way home than it would for her to wait for Jake to take care of his business.

"Whoa." Ben guided the horses to a stop near the black-smith's building.

Jake jumped to the ground. "I'll take care of it." He strode through open doors leading inside where sounds of hammers striking metal rang from within.

She should be home, filling in the lines of the dress with that beautiful shade of blue. If she finished before noon the next day and was pleased with the results, she could still mail the design to Butterick and meet this month's deadline for submissions.

Instead, she sat next to a man who in every way seemed complicated. He could irritate her one minute and make her heart race the next. No man had ever confused Hope more.

The silence between them made it difficult to sit still, and she slid over a bit toward Jake's empty spot on the bench. She should say something—anything. Find out why Ben seemed so unsupportive of Annie's ideas for the library. The other day he expressed willingness to help, but his attitude today annoyed Hope. Even more importantly, his lack of enthusiasm had clearly hurt Annie's feelings.

"You're not going to get away with this, Jamie McFarland!" A tall, muscular man wearing a leather apron and covered with black soot rounded the corner of the building, chasing a scrawny male. He grabbed the man he called Jamie, spun him around, lifted him, and dangled him in the air like a puppet.

Jamie tried to break free. "I didn't mean to, Charlie! Honest!"

"You thieving scoundrel! I oughta hang you!" Charlie dropped him so his feet touched the ground, then with his right fist, made a swift upper cut to Jamie's chin.

Hope sat at the edge of her seat. "Ben! Please do something!"

"It's none of our business." Ben's jaw hardened. "It's better to leave it alone."

Charlie hit Jamie in the face, then the ribs, and the leaner man doubled over before he dropped to his knees.

Hope tasted bile. How could Ben not help the poor man? "I can't just sit here and watch!" She moved to the side of the wagon and prepared to step down.

Ben grabbed her arm and pulled her back onto the seat. "Don't be a fool. You can't get in the middle of that."

He called her foolish for wanting to stop a fight? Her throat burned.

Blood flowed from the corner of Jamie's mouth. "Please, Charlie . . . stop."

Jake strolled out through the doors of the blacksmith shop.

Hope stood. "Jake, help him!" She pointed to the scuffling.

Jake dropped his package on the ground and ran over to the two fighting men. "What's going on here?" He tried to pull the blacksmith away, got hit in the nose with Charlie's elbow, and staggered back. "Come on, Charlie. You don't want to do this."

"Ah—he's no good!" Charlie pushed Jamie away, and breathing heavily, wiped his brow. "I gave this lowlife a job at my shop—a chance to make things better for himself, and he stole from me."

Jamie sat on his ankles. "I'm sorry, Charlie. I won't ever do it again. I promise."

"You better believe you won't." Charlie spat on the ground. "I'm done with ya. I got my money back, but if I ever see you near my door again, I'll press charges and you'll end up in prison." Charlie stalked back into the building.

Hope took advantage of Ben's distraction and escaped the wagon. She scurried over to the two beaten men. "Are you all right?"

"You should get the doc to look at you." Jake put an arm around Jamie and helped him stand. "Want us to take you over there?"

"Thanks, but I'll be fine." Jamie rubbed his jaw.

"Stay away from Charlie." Jake picked up the package he'd dropped. "You don't need any more trouble."

"No worry there. I aim to keep my distance." Jamie brushed himself off. "Thanks for your help. I thought he was going to knock my head off. But I had it coming. It wasn't right what I did. I—I don't know what got into me." He shook hands with Jake, then trudged down the street with his chin down.

Hope wanted to hug Jake. "That was valiant, jumping in and stopping that bully from beating on this poor man."

"Valiant? Me?" A triumphant grin slid onto his face.

"He could have killed Jamie." Her stomach still churned from what she'd just witnessed. Her mind conjured Henry's face—those angry eyes. The pain from his words even worse than his digging grip that left marks on her arm for days.

"Charlie can get mighty angry when provoked, but he'd never take it that far." Jake took a handkerchief from his pocket and wiped the blood dripping from his nose.

"It was still a brave thing to do. Not everyone has that kind of courage. Even when I begged your brother to step in, he refused to leave the wagon." Her gut on fire, Hope couldn't even look in Ben's direction.

A look mixed with concern, horror, and apology flashed in Jake's eyes. He helped her into the wagon, got settled in himself, then nodded at his brother. "Let's head home."

Not saying a word, Ben lifted the reins and started the horses moving.

They rode in silence, each of them staring straight ahead, until they reached Annie's house. Hope's clenched hands remained on her lap. Ben hadn't even tried to protect Jamie from Charlie's blows. *Why?*

Jake helped her down from the wagon and walked her to the door. Hope turned to say good-bye to Ben, but he stared straight ahead, his face hardened.

She reached for the doorknob, then withdrew her hand. "Jake—"

"I know the fight upset you." He spoke softly, then sighed. "But don't judge someone you barely know. My brother . . ."

"Why didn't Ben try to stop him? Explain it to me."

"Hope, I can't." Jake shoved fingers through his messy hair. "It's his story to share. If and when he decides he can trust you."

Nine

Hope fingered the rejection letter from the Butterick Publishing Company concerning several drawings she'd submitted a month ago, two weeks prior to arriving in Riverton. What chance did she have to get her ideas noticed? Most of the designs chosen for patterns, as well as placement in *The Delineator*, were submitted by merchandisers who brought them back from European showings.

She sighed and stuffed the letter temporarily in a drawer behind the store counter. This would never do—this wallowing in self-pity. What would her mother think?

No need to wonder. In her gentle way, she'd tell Hope that thankfulness for the position at the Home Store and time spent with Annie would soften disappointment. She would also, in so many words, remind Hope that trusting God to show her the path he'd designed for her would provide strength to keep trying.

According to the large clock on the wall, she'd used her entire break going through mail Annie had picked up at the post office earlier that morning. With a raised chin and shoulders pulled back, Hope studied the customers milling in the aisles and around the displays. Though not the sixteen-story Butterick building in Manhattan, the Home Store was a lovely and friendly place. For now, it was also where she was employed, and she needed to focus on the tasks in front of her.

Clara Boyle, the widow with four children Hope had met at church, rushed to the counter. "Good afternoon."

"How nice to see you, Clara." Hope offered a generous smile to the seamstress. "How may I help you?"

"I'd like your opinion. I'm trying to choose between two fabrics, and I can't make up my mind which would be better suited for this particular dress. The pattern suggests several." Clara blushed. "It's a gift for Rose's fourteenth birthday. Somethin' to wear to church and for special occasions. There's never been much money to spend on fancy duds, and Rose never complains about her plain clothes, but she's at that age where most young women want to feel pretty."

"You're sweet to be so considerate of your daughter." Hope eyed the woman's bundles. "Let's take a look at your choices."

Clara laid two bolts of cloth across the counter—one pale blue silk and one lighter weight lavender with a tiny floral print.

"If I remember correctly, Rose is the oldest with brown curls and beautiful chestnut-colored eyes." Hope caressed the material lightly with her fingers, then picked up the Butterick pattern Clara had laid next to them. It showed a stand-up collar, three rows of pleats extending from the shoulder to the waist, and a wide lawn ruffle around the bottom. "I'd choose the lavender with satin ribbon for trim. It will complement her coloring and look feminine without appearing too sophisticated for her age."

"Oh, thank you. That's what I was leanin' toward, but I want her to be happy, and you being a fashion designer and all . . ."

"I'm more of an aspiring designer." She placed the packaged dress pattern back in Clara's hands. "Maybe someday you'll see Butterick patterns for my creations."

"Wouldn't that be something!" Clara grinned. "Are you workin' on ideas now?"

Not everyone understood Hope's passion. As a seamstress, Clara probably shared excitement over seeing beautiful fabric put together in a way that enhanced a woman's appearance. It was an art form of its own.

"I'm always sketching." Hope swallowed. "Between you and me, I submitted some of my best drawings to Butterick before leaving New York. But I received a letter this morning saying that although they display potential, my designs aren't quite up to their standard."

Clara's eyes widened. "That's wonderful news!"

"It is?" How could not being up to their standard be good?

"You have promise." Clara nodded as if to punctuate her statement. "Don't be discouraged. You just have to keep tryin'." She leaned forward, as though eager to hear more. "How does it work? Designs and patterns and all?"

"Hmmm . . . well, I only know some of what takes place." Hope smoothed the rejected blue silk and laid the bolt aside. She quickly glanced about to make sure no one else seemed in need of her. Giddiness tickled inside with the calm surrounding them. She'd have a chance to discuss her vision with a fellow enthusiast. "First, ideas are presented, and many of them represent what's new in Europe. Then, whatever is being considered is made up in muslins and modeled for designers and management. Each style is scrutinized for line, silhouette, and fashion. They probably have to consider practicality and suitability to the Butterick customer."

Clara held up the pattern envelope. "And these?"

"They're graded into sizes so a pattern can work for more than one body. Each woman is unique, which is wonderful, but it does make fitting clothes a challenge at times." Hope slipped the envelope from Clara's hand, then trailed her finger down the dress depicted on the front. "Then the patterns are printed on tissue paper. They're cut, folded, and inserted into envelopes complete with instruction sheets, so anyone in America can have a dress made that's also worn in Chicago, New York, or France. Once patterns are completed, garments are constructed, sketched with pen and ink, and engraved for colored fashion plates used in print."

"And that's what we see in *The Delineator*." Clara chewed on her lower lip. "But, even though the company is usin' European designs, they'll still consider yours. You should be so proud, Hope."

Oh, how she wanted to let those words reach deep inside. The rejection still smarted too much for that. "I am grateful there's still a chance for me. I think it's to my advantage that the Butterick family started out as simple tailors. They wanted fashion to be available for everyone. They also wanted to make dressmaking easier. So that's why even people living in small farming communities like Riverton have access to their patterns."

Hope unrolled the lavender material along the counter to keep things moving with her customer. "The company welcomes suggestions and ideas from the public. So, even though I'm currently living here, I have an avenue to submit my designs." She read the pattern instructions before measuring and cutting the fabric, then fidgeted with the material. Should she bring up the subject she'd been wanting to discuss with Clara for several days? "I know this seems a bit presumptuous, but I was wondering if we might help each other."

"How?" Clara seemed interested, which gave Hope courage.

"You're good with a sewing machine and needle and thread, but I'm embarrassed to say I'm not." She'd shown vulnerability and admitted her weakness, but what would Clara think of her now? "At least, I'm not as skilled as I want to be when it comes to making fine clothing."

Clara's eyebrows lifted. "Are you askin' me to teach you?"

"Yes, but more than that. What would you think about us working together?"

Clara's face lit up. "I could help put your designs together, and you could show me how to make things more fashionable." A smile spread across her face—a possible hint she felt inspired by the possibilities. "I do find it challenging to update one style to another. So many women ask for alterations on what they already own. You might also have a little more time to work on your sketches if you don't have to put the garments together yourself. But are you sure I can do your designs justice?" A frown creased her brow and her enthusiasm faded. "I wouldn't want to let you down."

Let *her* down? Hope couldn't be more grateful that Clara would entertain her idea. "I've been told you're the best seamstress in the area, and I really do need your help. So, are you willing to try it and see what happens?"

"Yes, indeed."

"Wonderful." Her lungs felt like they'd taken in fresh air. She'd acquired help, maybe even a partner. "Now, let's find the perfect buttons for your daughter's birthday dress." Hope folded, then carried the cut material to another counter nearby where Annie was shelving three bolts of gingham on the wall. Hope pulled out several small drawers that held pearl-like buttons.

Annie finished and turned around. "Another busy Friday. Only a few more hours before closing." Her face lit up with a grin. "Hi, Clara. Purchasing items for a new sewing project?"

Clara nodded. "A dress for Rose—for her birthday."

"Oh, my . . . the lavender will look lovely." Annie fingered the material. "You can trust me to keep it a secret."

"These are perfect." Clara held up a set of dainty buttons.

"You're absolutely right." Hope had spotted another set of buttons she was just about to recommend, but seeing the others next to the fabric, she had to admit that Clara had made a better choice.

Annie's eyes shifted from the cloth to somewhere behind Clara, and she groaned. "Trouble brewing. Rebecca Hoyt and Mrs. Jorgenson are heading right for us."

"I have delightful news!" Mrs. Jorgenson beamed. "I was just telling Rebecca about the library, and she wants to help."

Annie's mouth opened large enough a dragonfly could have swooped in. "I—I . . ." Her gaze moved from Mrs. Jorgenson to Rebecca, who stood prim and proper with hands folded in front of her.

"Trust me. You need what I can offer." Rebecca stared at Annie as though defying her to disagree.

"Trust *you*?" Annie shook her head as though the idea of Rebecca getting involved with the library was unthinkable. "Thank you, but we don't need your kind of help."

"Annie, what's gotten into you?" Mrs. Jorgenson's eyes saddened. "We should be grateful for anyone who is willing to join this huge undertaking, but especially someone who may have a voice with the town council."

"May I speak with you in private?" Annie gestured to the older woman to follow her, and the two of them stepped to the end of the counter and began whispering.

Clara fidgeted with her handbag. Rebecca stared at the floor. The tension hanging in the air was so thick, Hope feared choking on it.

Rebecca cleared her throat and smiled. "Clara, my mother means to tell you herself, but I'd also like to mention that she was delighted with the tea gown you delivered the other day."

"Thank you." Clara's shoulders relaxed, and she stopped fumbling with her bag. "I'm glad to hear it."

"Yes, well, you know how difficult it is to please her with anything. But you've mastered the art." Rebecca turned to Hope. "Clara's expertise with needle and thread is exceptional. No other handiwork compares."

Clara's eyes shone. "Thank you, Rebecca."

Hope should be tending to other customers wandering around the store, but she hadn't finished Clara's purchase. Hope prayed silently and tried to appear relaxed. This latest development could play out several ways, and she wanted to offer Annie support, if needed.

The whispering at the other end of the counter stopped, and the two women returned.

Annie faced Rebecca. "I'm willing to listen." Not even a hint of a smile—still, she sounded earnest.

"Good." Rebecca laid her handbag on the counter. "To begin, the town's approval is imperative. The council's next meeting is set for July fifth, which is just a little over two weeks away. So, you have that much time to come up with a detailed plan." She moistened her lips. "I can help write and present the proposal. As a teacher in Riverton, I can offer insight as to the benefits of having a library accessible to adults and students. I'd have no trouble expounding on what this could do for our community. Once approved, I'm willing to do whatever you ask."

"Hmmm . . . whatever I ask . . ." Annie drummed her fingertips on the counter. "It sounds like you're as passionate about this project as we are," she said with a hint of surprise in her voice.

"I know you have reason to distrust me." Rebecca's eyes focused on Annie. "I did things in the past that hurt your friends. But, please believe me. I would never do anything to jeopardize your plans. My students need this. The school's books and resources are so limited our children can't compete academically with those attending in larger towns. A library would open up other worlds to everyone in the community—worlds we don't have access to in a place the size of Riverton."

"All right." Annie sighed. "I'll gladly accept anything you can offer."

"Thank you, Annie. You won't regret it."

"When can we start working on a proposal?"

Rebecca picked up her bag. "We have a lot of work and not much time. Why not get some preliminary ideas down this evening?"

"The sooner the better. If we don't go to the meeting prepared, the council may decide to sell it to the other prospective buyer, and that would be heartbreaking." Annie glanced at Hope, who nodded. "Mrs. Jorgenson, are you able to join us at our house after supper?"

A warm smile spread across the older woman's face, and she winked at Annie. "I'll bring dessert."

Rebecca laid her hand on Mrs. Jorgenson's arm. "And I'll pick you up in my buggy around, say six thirty?"

"That would be lovely, dear." Mrs. Jorgenson turned. "I'll see you ladies this evening." She and Rebecca left the store together.

"I still need to get a few other items before heading home myself." Clara picked up the material and buttons. "I'll be back in just a moment to pay for these."

"No hurry, Clara, and if there's anything else I can help you with, please don't hesitate to ask." Hope slipped the button drawers back into place.

"Thanks, Hope." Clara marched down an aisle as though on a mission.

"So, cousin." Hope leaned against the counter and blew out a gust of air. "How in the world did Mrs. Jorgenson ever convince you to let Rebecca Hoyt, the woman you've detested for the past several years, join your crusade?"

"Frightening, right?" Annie gave Hope a weak smile. "She reminded me of some things. The first being that Rebecca has been forgiven by those she offended, so I have no cause to hold those past offenses against her. And . . ."

"And?"

"God gave everyone certain gifts. It would be wrong for me to stand in the way of Rebecca offering hers." Annie grinned. "Besides, she's right. We can use all the help we can get."

Ten

ere she stood in the Pedersons' backyard, surrounded by people who had welcomed her with open arms and included her in their Fourth of July festivities, and her mother and father were doing all they could to alleviate hardships for people struggling thousands of mile away. As proud as Hope was of them, their sacrifices made her feel small and insignificant in comparison. All she could do was honor them the best she could by becoming the woman they believed her to be.

She set drinking glasses at the end of a long table behind the large farm house. Carefree children's laughter carried toward her. Smiling, she took in all the activity and chatter around the yard. It would have been nice to have had a brother or sister.

Ellie and Thomas Pederson had invited Annie and Hope to join their family gathering, and warm-hearted Ellie made Hope feel right at home. Ellie was Reverend Caswell's sister, so other guests included the reverend, Sarah, and their daughter Mary, as well as Sarah's grandmother, Abigail Hansen. Hope had learned that Mrs. Hansen, who was now resting in a chair beneath a shade tree, could be a bit crotchety at times, but she also had a tender spot when it came to Sarah.

Ellie's two sons, John and Isaac, played with a ball and bat, while her daughter, Grace, pushed Mary on a swing hung from a large oak tree.

"I hope the boys show up soon." Ellie placed a large pitcher of lemonade on the table next to the glasses, then covered the top with a small towel to keep the flies away. "It's such a warm day, I don't want to bring out the milk or potato salad until they're here."

"Boys?" As far as Hope knew, Ellie's family was all present.

"Ben and Jake Greene."

Hope's heart thumped double-time. Ben would be spending the day here? She'd avoided him since the fighting incident and had barely spoken to him even at church services except for forced, polite conversation. She still wondered what Jake meant when he alluded to Ben having reasons for not stepping in to stop the beating. How could anyone stand by while one person hurt another?

Ellie shooed a honey bee away from the table. "I suppose I shouldn't call them boys, but I've grown to think of them almost as younger brothers. They've been a great help to Thomas, and the children adore them." She pointed to the left. "Their farm is just through the woods on the other side of the cornfield over there."

Hope's shirtwaist felt damp beneath her arms, and she wiped moisture from her brow. The noonday sun was beating down, but it wasn't so hot beneath the maple tree's canopy that she should be melting like a burning candle. Was this God's providence? She and Ben thrown together at a small, friendly gathering when she still hadn't made peace with him?

Her mother's letter explaining her efforts to share God's love with the people in Panama had jolted Hope into realizing that whether she agreed with Ben's actions or not, being rude or withholding kindness didn't make her more noble than him—maybe less.

"Just in time!" Annie placed a large roaster of steaming baked beans on the table and ran to greet the wagon pulling up to the side of the barn.

Hope smoothed her skirt and loose strands of hair, then put a genuine—and slightly nervous—smile on her face. She looked up and moved forward to greet the newcomers, and her smile faltered. Only one Greene brother had arrived. Jake.

"Where's Ben?" Ellie stood alongside Annie as Jake disembarked from the wagon. "Is he following behind?"

Jake tied the horse to a post, then reached into the wagon and pulled out a basket filled with ripe, lush strawberries. "He, uh, sends his regrets."

Ellie sighed. "Oh, no. I hope he's not ill."

"Nothing to worry about." He cast a glance in Hope's direction, but it lingered only a second before he gave Ellie a grin. "Where are those baked beans you promised? I could smell them cooking all the way over at our farm. I'm not fooling, either."

"Sure you could." Annie's eyes shone as she laughed along with him. Could it be more obvious how she felt about Jake? "Right this way, and bring the berries with you."

"The children will miss having Ben here. We all will," Ellie said as she followed them back to the tables now laden with food.

Yes, we all will. That realization struck a chord in her heart. Hope felt a surprising loss at his absence as she helped bring the last few dishes from the kitchen.

What had she glimpsed in Jake's eyes? A hint that Ben's refusal had something to do with her? Had she offended him so much by her frustration over his lack of defending a man that he would actually stay away from the celebration? He deserved to be there more than she did. Maybe her accusations had bothered him more than she thought.

Hope should be relieved Ben wasn't coming today. It wasn't in her to pretend that everything was fine when, in reality, tension between them had remained as thick as paint exposed to the sun's heat. Left too long, it could possibly harden.

It wasn't in her to live with the ache of unfinished business. Words spoken by her mother echoed in Hope's mind, reminding her that she couldn't just look at the fruit a person produced in his life—she also needed to dig down to the roots to truly understand someone.

She jolted to a stop between the kitchen and a picnic table, and a platter of golden ears of corn almost slipped from her hands. She wanted to know Ben. Not just the man he willingly exposed, but also the deeper part of him that might make it possible to become real friends. Somehow she had to make things right between them.

The platter made it safely to the table, much to Hope's relief. Before leaving for Panama, her father had promised that God would open doors for her. But she also held some responsibility to do her part. *Lord, if you provide an opportunity to make peace with Ben, I'll try to be brave enough to take it.*

"Gather around everyone." Reverend Caswell grabbed Sarah's hand. The handsome pastor and his beautiful wife, both with dark hair and deep blue eyes, made a striking couple.

"Hush, children!" Sarah's grandmother, Mrs. Hansen, tapped her cane on the ground. "Listen to the reverend."

The boys and girls giggled, then quieted, as though they knew the elderly woman meant business, but was still soft under the crusty exterior.

"Before we fill our bellies with the wonderful food prepared for us, let's pray." Reverend Caswell bowed his head, and everyone followed suit. "Thank you, Lord, for the country we live in and the blessings we receive here. Help us to never take for granted the freedom we have or the sacrifices it has taken to attain and keep that freedom. Thank you for this food that we're about to enjoy. We also ask, Lord, that you bless and protect Hope's parents with comfort, friendship, good health, and your divine guidance. Amen."

"Amen!" they all added in unison.

Hope glanced at each individual, wishing she could put into words how much it meant to her—to hear a prayer for her parents while being surrounded by people who had become like family.

The adults found places at one table, while the children sat together at another. Once the youngsters' plates had been filled, dishes were passed around to the others.

"Hope, how do you spend the Fourth of July in New York?" Thomas, who reminded her of a Norwegian Viking, slathered butter onto a biscuit. "Must be pretty exciting in a big city."

All eyes focused on her, displaying an eagerness to hear the answer. Hope dabbed her mouth with a napkin and took a drink of lemonade. "Well, like here, it's hot in the summer. So, my parents and I have always spent the holiday at Coney Island. We picnic at the beach."

Jake stopped chomping on a chicken wing. "Do any swimming in the ocean?"

"Sometimes." She smiled. "My favorite thing is to spend time in the amusement parks. Luna Park is filled with thousands of outside electric lamps. It's beautiful when they're all lit up. One of the popular rides in that park is called 'Trip to the Moon.' Steeplechase Park has wonderful roller coasters and a Ferris wheel. I also love the scale models of the Eiffel Tower and the Palace of Westminster's clock tower."

"We must go back someday so you can show me everything." Annie popped a strawberry into her mouth.

"Of course." Hope returned her cousin's smile. It would be great fun to show Annie the sights, but when would it be possible to return to New York? For now, she needed to make sure enough time and distance kept her safe from Henry. "Thomas, would you please pass the biscuits and blackberry jam?" That little diversion did the trick, and conversation went in other directions.

Hope had left out the part that included Henry joining them the previous Fourth of July after he'd begun to court her. She should have listened to her inner voice then. When he'd expressed excitement over a new park opening that would primarily contain freak shows, her stomach had roiled at his comments. He'd expressed no compassion, but only enthusiasm over the plight of people who would most likely be employed because of their disfigurements and trials.

But she'd been taken in by Henry's good looks, charm, and popularity, and she'd refused to accept what her gut knew about his true character. She should have stopped seeing him after their visit to the park that Fourth of July. If she had, she wouldn't have accepted his proposal some months later and avoided painful consequences.

Four months had passed since she'd broken their engagement, but the horrible memory of that night still lingered, threatening to steal any contentment she might find in Riverton.

Hope savored the soft biscuit and sweet, fruity jam as her gaze traveled around the table. Everyone was enjoying the meal, conversation, and companionship. Everyone except Ben, because he wasn't there.

She laughed at jokes, joined in conversations, and even played several games of badminton because she didn't want to ruin anyone else's fun, but her heart wasn't in it.

The reverend and Sarah finished a game of croquet with the children and found chairs in the shade. There wouldn't be a better time. Hope slipped into a vacant chair next to them.

"The children beat us, Hope. Can you believe it?" Sarah's laugh was filled with lighthearted joy, and her eyes twinkled. Her hand caressed her expanding middle. "Oh, my, this child is active. Only three months to go. Ellie better be prepared. She may have her hands full when the time comes."

Hope gasped. "You're giving the baby to her?"

"No, no, no!" Sarah laughed. "She's going to be my midwife." Sarah rubbed her tummy again. "It will be a special delivery with Auntie Ellie helping to bring him or her into the world. Ellie's one of my closest friends, and she was like a sister to me even before Peter and I married."

"Oh." Hope relaxed.

"Glad we got that cleared up." Reverend Caswell cocked his head. "Something else on your mind besides babies?"

"Yes, there is." Hope slid to the edge of her chair, then folded her hands in her lap. "Reverend—"

"Friends and family call me Peter." The warmth in his eyes said he considered her one or possibly both.

"Peter, thank you for including my parents in your prayer." Hope's throat thickened. "It meant a lot to me."

He nodded. "Sarah and I have been praying for them, and we'll continue until they return."

"I know, and that's why I wanted to have a few minutes alone with you. I received a letter from my mother yesterday." Hope had savored every word—several times. "She's in good spirits, and so is Father, but the conditions for most workers are deplorable. Accommodations for canal employees provide little protection against wet weather or jungle life. Some are using old boxcars or tents for housing. Anything with four walls, a roof, and a floor is considered living quarters. There's no cold storage, no fresh milk, and little meat. Distilled water is delivered to each house daily. When it it's not available, they have to boil any water they can find."

Sarah frowned. "It's worse than I thought."

"I knew various diseases would be a threat, but I can no longer close my eyes to the extent of sickness and death. Malaria and yellow fever are only two possibilities. There are many others. My mother writes as though she's not vulnerable, and I know she believes God will protect both her and my father. I wish I had her faith, but I'm scared." Hope's eyes burned as her vision blurred, and she caught Sarah's eyes filling with moisture along with her own.

Peter grimaced. "Regardless of faith in God's provision, the government has a responsibility there."

"My mother sounds optimistic that help has arrived. Mary Hubbard, the newly appointed Superintendent of Nurses has come with the Chief Sanitary Officer, Dr. Gorgas. They also brought two other nurses with them."

"Daddy!" Mary came skipping toward them and leaped into her father's lap. "Come push me on the swing!"

Sarah leaned over and tickled the little girl's side.

Mary giggled. "Push me on the swing, Daddy! Please."

"Anything for my girl." Peter jumped up from his chair, threw her over his shoulders, and ran toward the swing with the little girl bouncing against him, laughing all the way.

"God has led your parents to Panama for a reason, Hope." Sarah leaned forward and squeezed Hope's hand.

"Thank you for listening. It means a great deal to me that you care so much about their welfare." She'd left friends behind in New York, but God had certainly surrounded Hope with wonderful people here in Riverton.

"We'll continue to pray for them and their safe return. In the meantime, seek what the Lord wants of you."

What *did* he want from her? Her parents were ambassadors of his love and peace, and if she were to be like them— like Christ—Hope needed to become a peacemaker.

"Please excuse me, Sarah. There's something I need to do." Hope headed for the house and entered the kitchen through the back door.

Ellie folded a dish towel and laid it on the counter. "Is there anything I can get for you, Hope?"

"Yes, there is something." She had to risk his rejection. "Would you mind if I took supper over to Ben?"

CR

Hope rapped on the front screen door to Ben's farmhouse, then waited. The only sound she heard was the blood whooshing through her ears as her heart pumped faster. This was a mistake. She should have waited until Jake left the party and come with him, but she'd slipped away quietly, afraid he'd try to dissuade her.

She took a deep breath, opened the door, and stepped inside. "Ben, are you in here?"

No response. Hope tiptoed through the rooms to the kitchen. Used dishes were piled in the sink, but the counters were clean. She set her picnic basket on the small table, bare except for a light blue tablecloth with several red stains— possibly berry juice. The window over the sink faced west, so the sun's last rays brightened the kitchen with a warm glow.

She peered through the dust-covered glass at the barn and fields below. A cow mooed. Maybe Ben decided to start the evening chores without Jake. Hope opened the back screen door, skipped down the steps, and began hiking toward the barn.

A crow cawed from the top of the small building to her right—the very shed that Ben had almost stood guard over the day she and Annie had visited. What was so secret about an old shed that probably only held farming or gardening tools?

She shouldn't investigate, but this might be the only time to find out what was so important in there. Hope would just peek through a window. That would be it. She wouldn't enter, no matter how tempted to go inside and poke around.

No sign of Ben anywhere. If she was going to do this, now was the time. Hope glanced back at the house and around the yard, then strode up to a window on the side of the shed. Although the sun shone through large windows facing the west, several lanterns were also lit inside, giving Hope a clear view through the window on the south side.

Ben's back was to her, but he stepped to the right, and Hope gasped. Stunned, she couldn't move.

He tossed a paint brush into a jar filled with liquid, wiped his hands on a towel, and then turned off the lanterns. Hope ducked beneath the window and then around the corner to hide until he left the shed and headed toward the house. Her horse and buggy were tied to a post in the front of the house, and the picnic basket was sitting on the kitchen table, so escape seemed impossible.

She might only have a short moment, but her resolve to stay out of the shed dissipated like steam rising from a boiling kettle. The door to the kitchen slammed, and Hope grabbed her chance. She slipped inside the warm shed, which would have been stifling had he not left several windows open, then stood in the middle of the room, not knowing where to let her eyes feast first.

Paintings, mostly nature scenes, stood propped against two walls, three or four deep. Though alone, she stepped with caution, as though fearful of waking someone. Awe filled her as she perused the stacks of artwork and drank in the display of talent on the canvases. In one piece, water cascading over rocks evoked a feeling so strong, she could almost hear the rushing water.

Hope turned toward the spot where Ben had been working, and the wooded scene on the easel drew her. So vivid were the details and colors, she almost believed she could step into the painting if she got close enough. The way he painted beautiful, feathery moss growing on trees . . . Hope reached, her fingertips almost brushing—

"Don't!"

She whipped her hand back and swung around, her face burning.

Ben stood there, his jaw clenched. "The paint is still wet."

"I—I'm so sorry!" She tried to swallow, but her throat felt as dry and scratchy as dead pine needles.

"What are you doing here?" Angry eyes bore into hers, and his chilled tone confirmed his displeasure.

A slight shiver raced down Hope's spine. She'd overstepped boundaries by investigating the shed's contents. "I thought you might have stayed away from the party because of me. So, I brought you some supper as a peace offering." She bit her lip, hoping it would stop her chin from quivering and her eyes from watering. "I didn't expect to find this . . ." She waved her hand, pointing to the painting on the easel. Hope blinked, but the effort was lost—a hot tear slid down her cheek.

"Why are you crying?" Ben's face scrunched, but his voice had lost its fire. "I know it still needs some work, but is it that bad?"

"Bad?" Hope threw her head back, then faced him, wiping the remaining tears from her eyes. "No—it's that good! Why didn't you tell me you could paint like this? That you could paint at all?" Her gaze returned to the detailed canvas. Ben was an artist like her—no, he was far better. But now they shared common ground, and perhaps it was a place where they could meet and become good friends. "I should have known from things you said, the suggestions you made about my own work. I don't understand why you've kept your talent a secret."

Ben led her to a wooden chair in one corner of the room. "Please sit down," he whispered and offered a small smile. She complied, and he pulled a stool next to her.

"I'm listening." Hope folded her hands in her lap.

His eyes softened. "First of all, I didn't stay home from the picnic because I was worried about myself. Things have been awkward between the two of us, and I didn't want my presence spoiling the day for you."

"I'm sorry you missed the fun." Did he hear her sincerity? He would have enjoyed the games, the food, the camaraderie the men had shared. "And I missed having you there."

$$\infty$$

Ben couldn't control his pleasure at seeing her cheeks darken. His lips slid into a smile at hearing her admission—and one she didn't intend by the look in her beautiful blue eyes.

She fidgeted for a moment. "So, you're a painter, and a remarkably good one."

"I appreciate your assessment, but I'm mediocre at best." Ben sighed. It hadn't been easy keeping his work a secret all these years. Maybe this was God's way of giving him someone to talk to who could understand. It wasn't that Jake didn't try, but he couldn't grasp the passion Ben felt about art.

"You must know that your work is far from average." Hope lifted her chin and quirked an eyebrow. "How have other artists, gallery owners, or collectors responded to your work?"

"My brother is the only person who knows I paint."

Hope's forehead furrowed. "Don't you want your work to be seen and enjoyed?"

"No." Ben squirmed. "My paintings aren't for public viewing. They're private."

"But . . ." Hope looked away, as if mulling the concept over in her mind, then turned back to him. "But shouldn't a God-given talent like yours be shared?"

"That may depend on someone's view. Is it wrong to offer up one's creativity for God's pleasure? To paint for him alone?"

"No . . . if that's what God wants." Hope reached out and grasped his hand between hers. "But your paintings could help bring peace to a troubled person or help soothe an aching soul. They're a little bit of heaven on earth."

"I can't, Hope."

"Then, please tell me why."

Jake knew, and he'd never told anyone. Could Ben trust Hope as well? If he were to ever have any chance at an honest friendship with her, he'd need to know one way or another. Maybe it was better to find out now than to wonder.

"Can you keep a secret?"

"Of course."

"I mean it, Hope." He wiped the sweat trickling past his temple and down the side of his face.

She sat at the edge of her seat. "I promise!"

Ben glanced toward the ceiling and heaved a sigh. "You look at my paintings and see something good in them."

"They're not just good—they're brilliant."

The corners of his mouth twitched. "All right. Through your eyes, you're able to see something that's worthy. But all I see is failure at accomplishing my vision—what's in my head. An inability to transfer what I either view around me or what I envision from my imagination. Whatever I paint always falls short. They'll never be good enough to hang on any wall."

"That's not true." Hope scowled. "Give me the opportunity to prove it to you."

"That's not possible."

"You're insufferable, Benjamin Greene."

"And you don't know the whole story."

She stood and lifted her clenched fist. "Then you'd better share it before I bop you on the nose."

"It's my penance, Hope." This was it, the time to cleanse his soul. Keep nothing back.

She slunk back down into the chair. "Your penance? You can't keep talking in riddles, Ben," she whispered.

"Here's the entire truth." Time to risk looking like a weak fool. But if she didn't see him that way when he finished, he might possibly gain an ally. "I was fifteen and in love with Mary Sue Higgins. A bully who also liked her kept stealing my art supplies. He'd make fun of me, claiming I'd never be a real man. He ripped up a drawing I'd worked on for hours, a birthday gift for Mary Sue. I was so angry, I wanted to hurt him badly, but I just stood there with the shredded pieces balled up in my hands."

Ben was right back there at school. The sounds of students happy to be out of classes for the day, the smell of summer heat and sweat, and Percy Sanders' black eyes filled with hate.

"You know the Bible says to turn the other cheek, so I walked away. Only, Percy didn't stop. He came at me until I fell, then he shoved my face into the dirt and called me a coward, along with several other ugly names. Schoolmates closed in around us, and Percy urged them to taunt me. Jake tried to pull him off, but he was much smaller than Percy. I managed to get free, but I was in such a rage, I rammed my body into him as hard as I could."

Ben closed his eyes, his breathing ragged. He had to finish the story. "Percy fell backwards, hit his head on the school's concrete steps, and blacked out. Our teacher heard shouting through an open school window, but by the time he got to us, the whole thing was over. Percy was rushed to our local doctor's office."

Hope had paled, but she hadn't left the shed. "Then what happened? Was Percy all right?"

"No." Ben cleared his throat, then took a deep breath. "The impact to his head did something. He lost sight in both eyes."

Hope gasped and put her hands to her mouth.

Ben couldn't blame her. It still horrified him after all these years. "Everyone who saw what happened all testified that Percy had started the fight and I had tried to walk away. They swore I was acting in self-defense.

"Mary Sue's parents claimed I lacked self-control and refused to let her have anything more to do with me. But even if they had, I think Mary Sue was a little afraid of me after what she'd witnessed. I didn't sleep for two nights, trying to re-sketch her gift in time for her birthday. I got it done and took it to her house. But she refused it and said it had come at too great a cost—to Percy."

Hope gazed to the right and seemed to escape into her own world for a moment, then she turned to him with glassy eyes. "Even at that young age, it must have hurt a great deal to lose the girl you cared about in connection to your art— the other love in your life."

Hope understood. A little bit of the pain that Ben carried melted away. Yes, maybe they could be friends, the kind who confided in each other. "It's made it difficult to trust people, women, or my work."

"So, you don't share your paintings or even the fact that you're an artist with anyone because you believe it's your punishment for your part in Percy going blind." Hope jumped up from her chair. "You were defending yourself. Yet, you're going to let an accident that happened years ago keep the rest of the world from seeing beauty and hope— God's creation—through your work."

He'd been wrong! She didn't understand at all. "How could I possibly receive praise or money for something that was part of another man's loss? My eyes still work. I can paint and tell the difference between red and blue! I still have that much, but Percy will never see the shade of his wife's hair or the color of his baby's eyes. I'm to blame, and I need to pay for it."

CR

The truth hit her like a steam engine going full speed. "That's what Jake meant when you wouldn't get involved in Charlie and Jamie's fight. Jake said there was more to it, but he couldn't explain—it was your story to tell." It made so much more sense now. Jake had said Ben wouldn't tell her his reasons until he trusted her. Did he trust her now? Or would he have kept his secret if she hadn't found his paintings and demanded an explanation?

Ben raised his palms, displaying streaks of dried blue and green paint. "I'll never use my hands to hurt another person again."

She'd called him a coward that day for not stepping in to stop the fight—the same thing Percy had called him on the school grounds. No wonder he'd become so irritable with her.

Her heart ached for the fifteen-year-old artist who was not a boy, yet not a man when he experienced such trauma. There still had to be a way for him to share his gift. His talent shouldn't be hidden forever.

"I'm so sorry, Ben, for what you've carried all these years." Hope reached toward him, and not waiting for him to respond, laid her hand on his. "But I . . ." She closed her eyes. *Lord, help me. Give me the right words.* She raised her eyelids. Ben was staring at her.

"But what, Hope?" He squeezed her hand.

His warm touch made her heart sprint like a thoroughbred racing down a track. "Do you remember that Sunday afternoon after I first arrived in Riverton? You and Jake came for lunch after church."

"I remember."

"You said then that you believed God has a specific plan for each person. That no one should worry about people's opinions, only what God thinks. Did you mean it? Do you really believe that?"

"I do . . ." Ben's voice had taken a defensive tone, and his body stiffened just enough for her to notice.

Hope's breathing became shallow, and it felt like her lungs were starving for air. "That afternoon we shared our desires for the future, or at least Jake, Annie, and I did. We talked about how, even though we see our lives going one way, we can head in that direction, and then suddenly our paths can go in a different direction. I may have a plan for my future, but God's design is always better than whatever we can imagine."

"God knows best."

"He does." She wrapped her hands around his. "Do you have any dreams, Ben? Did you ever?"

"Of course. There was a time when I wanted to have my paintings shown in a gallery or hanging in homes. Not so I'd be known or to make a lot of money. To have them inspire or bring some kind of pleasure would be enough for me. Those aspirations had to die." He slipped away from her and stood. "Hope, you have to accept that I can't bring myself . . ." Ben squeezed his eyes shut tight as though in pain, then opened them, exposing his sorrow. "My paintings are and will remain between God and me. They'll never leave this room."

"Ben . . ."

"I don't want to talk about it anymore." He returned the stool to the corner. "I think we should go up to the house. We can share the supper you brought."

They left the shed and walked side by side, but Hope carried a heavy heart. She wanted so much for him, and she believed God did, too, if only Ben would accept it.

In her sadness, she grieved his unwillingness to even explore the possibility, but there was something else at stake. Hope was drawn to him, but she could never consider having a close relationship if he didn't understand how important it was to not give up on a dream.

Hope was convinced his talent should be shared, but Ben wouldn't back down.

Well, neither would she.

Eleven

Hope glanced at the store's wall clock. How could it be almost four? A sale had prompted greater numbers to walk through the doors that day. Hope had little time to breathe between tending to customers, but her spirits were so light she barely noticed her throbbing feet.

"Annie, when are you taking a break?" Hope tried to temper her excitement.

"I'm taking a few minutes for a glass of cold water now. This July heat is unbearable." Annie wiped her glistening forehead with a white embroidered handkerchief, then rearranged several items on the china display in front of them. "Did you need help with anything? It's been like a beehive in here all day with people buzzing in and out."

"I missed my scheduled break because of taking care of a customer who couldn't make up her mind between a bolt of green cotton fabric and a bolt of green cotton fabric."

Annie raised her eyebrows.

"I'm serious. Same material, but the shades of green were light and lighter. I could barely tell the difference."

Annie chuckled.

"I mustered all the patience I could, and then I prayed for more." Hope gave a small laugh. She didn't see the humor in it then, but could now. "The important thing is that she left the store happy, and Mr. Carter told me to take some time for myself as soon as business slowed down. So, I'm taking a break with you." Hope would have leaped into the air if it had only been the two of them in the room. "I couldn't wait until tonight to tell you."

"Come on. That glass of water is beckoning me, and I need to find out what's got you all lit up like a firefly on a summer's night." She led the way to the back room, opened the ice box, and poured two glasses of chilled water. Annie took a quick drink and sighed, a mixture of relief and pleasure on her face. "Out with it."

"Annie, I finally heard from her. Eva Lancaster!" Hope pulled an envelope from her skirt pocket and grinned. "This letter came today."

"Well, what did she say?" Annie plopped down in a chair at a small table and gestured for Hope to do the same.

She slid onto a seat, withdrew the letter from the envelope, and unfolded the paper so it lay flat on the table. "Let me read it to you." Hope cleared her throat and took a deep breath.

> Dear Hope,
>
> Please forgive me for not responding sooner, but I just received your mother's letter. I've been in Paris for several months and have just returned to Minneapolis.
>
> Although we haven't corresponded frequently over the years, I always think of your mother fondly and how kind she was to me while I lived in New York.
>
> If you ever make a trip to Minneapolis, I'd love to have you join me for supper. It would

give me great pleasure to share anything that might help you in the world of fashion. If you bring some of your sketches, I'll give you an honest opinion of your designs. In this business, you'll need to accept criticism along with any praise or you'll not survive. It takes a great deal of courage to put our creative work—our hearts—out there for the world to judge. It can help to hear the truth from a friend before doing so.

I've been thinking of your parents in Panama and the work they're trying to accomplish there. I'll pray for them every day. I'll pray for you, too, that you would seek God's guidance in all you do and that God's plan is made known to you, whether it be in the fashion world or elsewhere. Peace be with you.

Warmly,
Eva Lancaster

Annie propped her elbow on the table and dropped her chin into her hand. "My goodness. She sounds like a wonderful lady. Sophisticated, smart, and nice."

"Doesn't she? And can you imagine staying in Paris for several months? I don't think I'd sleep a wink the entire time. I'd be too afraid of missing something." Hope smoothed the letter, then folded it and returned it to the envelope. "I need to go to Minneapolis as soon as possible, Annie."

A knock sounded on the door, it opened slightly, and Rebecca poked her head around the side. "May I come in?"

"What is it, Rebecca?" Annie sat up and her expression grew serious. "Not bad news, is it?"

"No! Not at all." Rebecca stepped inside and joined them at the table. "I just talked to the mayor. The council is calling a special meeting tonight, and they want Mrs. Jorgenson, you, and me to be there. This is it. They must have made their decision. They're either going to sell the house to the interested buyer or let us have our library."

◌੨

Hope had tried to work on a design for a jacket and skirt while Annie attended the town council meeting, but she couldn't concentrate, so she'd read again the letter sent by her closest friend, Charlotte, savoring the news from New York. She enjoyed hearing about the parties, the couples courting, and who was now in the family way. Relief always accompanied each message confirming Charlotte thwarting Henry's latest attempt at enticing her to disclose Hope's location.

Although grateful for Charlotte's loyalty, Hope also ached at putting her friend in a precarious position. But Charlotte believed Henry wouldn't risk bruising his reputation by harming her. She'd warned him that she wouldn't keep her tongue still if he did, and he'd already experienced embarrassment over the broken engagement to Hope. He wouldn't want his friends and associates aware of his darker side—or thinking him weak. With his usual flair, Henry had presented Hope's disappearance as a reaction to *his* decision to call off the wedding. She didn't care what people thought, as long as he left her alone.

The clock on the mantel chimed nine times. For the last hour, she'd prayed that God's will would be done and that Annie would have peace about the council's decision, whether they accepted or denied the proposal for a library.

Restless, Hope pulled back the lacy curtain from the parlor window and peered outside. The sun's last rays were peeking through the trees on the horizon, but Annie was nowhere in sight.

It must be a good sign that she'd been gone for several hours. Annie would have returned earlier if the library proposal had been turned down. Or, she could have been upset and gone somewhere to be alone.

If only Hope had been permitted to be there. Even the possibility of her cousin's disappointment made Hope nervous. Annie had put so much of her heart into planning all the details, even to the point of listing hundreds of books that would cover all the genres she wanted to see on the shelves. Hope paced for several minutes, then put a kettle of water on the stove.

A horse neighed. Hope strained her ears, then rushed to the door and swung it open. Annie waved, and a large grin spread across her face. She drove around to the side of the house toward the stable and carriage house where she'd unhitch the horse and settle him for the night. Rebecca followed Annie in another buggy, but she disembarked in front of the house and tied her horse to a post.

Hope stepped out onto the porch. "Rebecca, I've been as anxious to hear about the meeting as a father waiting for his first babe to be born." She held the door open and stood aside. "Please. Come in and make yourself at home. I'll make some tea."

"Thank you." There was a gleam in Rebecca's eyes, but she didn't share any news, which Hope appreciated. Whatever the verdict, it was Annie's moment, and it shouldn't be taken away from her.

Hope brought a tray with three cups of steaming tea, dessert plates, and a larger plate piled with sugar cookies into the parlor at the same moment Annie stepped inside. Hope set the tray down. "Oh, Annie, I can't stand the suspense any longer."

Annie grabbed Hope by the waist and twirled her around, laughing. "It's ours! The members unanimously agreed to let us turn the old house into a town library."

Hope hugged her cousin. "That's wonderful, Annie. I'm so happy for you."

"I couldn't have done it without Rebecca and Mrs. Jorgenson. Their interest helped convince the council that a library was important in a small town, and that we could make it work."

Rebecca's eyes glistened.

"Are you all right, Rebecca?" Hope offered her a cup of tea and sat on the settee next to her.

"I'm fine." Rebecca turned away for a brief moment, then cleared her throat. "I know the library is important to you, Annie. But, you don't know . . ." She took a deep breath. "It means a great deal to be a part of it. I know you're not fond of me, and the only reason you agreed to let me help is because the council might respect my position as a teacher."

"You're right." Annie stared into her cup. "I didn't like you because you were mean and arrogant. And I didn't trust you after what you did to Reverend Caswell and Sarah. You almost tore them apart."

"Annie . . ." Hope needed to stop this before a night of celebration turned into something entirely different.

"But, I've seen you work hard to change." Annie paused, seeming to choose her next words carefully. "These past weeks, I've actually grown to trust you." Her eyes warmed, and she offered a half smile. "I'm grateful you're devoted to building the library. I was telling the truth when I said I couldn't do it without you."

Hope breathed a sigh of relief. *Thank you, God.*

"I'm glad, Annie." Rebecca sniffed. "Really glad."

Annie took a gulp of tea, then reached for a cookie. "We have a lot of work ahead of us, but I think it's possible to have the library in full operation before September."

"That gives us only six weeks. Are you sure that's feasible?" Hope's head began to swim with all that had to be accomplished within that timeframe.

"It's been all laid out, and since the town council agreed to the schedule we proposed, we have to stand by our word and at least open the doors by the first Saturday in September. Otherwise, we lose our credibility with them and the town."

Hope rubbed the side of her teacup with her thumb. "I think you're asking too much of yourself. Maybe you should trust the townspeople for a little understanding and grace if things don't go as planned."

"I understand why Annie is so adamant that we open by then." Rebecca spoke as though she'd already given the timing some thought. "If we ever need to go back to the town council for anything pertaining to the library, we'll have al-

ready proven that we can follow through on our commitments."

Annie nodded. "We have access to some books through
the library in Martindale. The town and librarians have
agreed to share some of their books on a rotation basis. As
soon as we build up a strong offering, we'll lend them a
number of books for a set amount of time as well. Both
towns benefit."

"Of course, first things first." Rebecca seemed to bring
some necessary logic to the mix, balancing out Annie's enthusiastic energy. "We have a list of volunteers who are willing to do manual labor on the old house. Bookshelves also
need to be built. But before any of that can be done, we need
to raise money for supplies—and for enough books to get us
started."

"That's where the fundraising event comes in, but when
and where?" Hope took a large bite of her sugar cookie.
Good thing it almost melted in her mouth. She could have
easily choked on it as distracted as she was by the conversation.

"A Saturday would be best, when there are more people
in town doing their shopping. Let's plan for August thir-
teenth. That only gives us three weeks, but we can't hold it
any later than that." Annie put her teacup on the tray, then
almost jumped from her seat and began to pace. "I believe
the best place is on the library's front lawn. You know, draw
attention to the location. Let people get a feel for what we're
trying to accomplish. Help others experience a sense of our
vision."

"It's perfect." Rebecca caught Hope's eye. "We need to
make some notes. Is there paper . . ."

"I'll get it." Hope was on her feet before Rebecca had finished the question. She found paper and a fountain pen in a desk drawer. "I'll try to write as fast as you two come up with suggestions."

"We need to solicit donations for the auction, but I think there might be people who would be willing to set up booths of baked and canned goods for sale and then donate the proceeds to the library." Annie's tone became more excited the longer she talked. "What if we included games for the children?"

"Make it a community event, almost like a fair." Rebecca's eyes brightened.

"Those are wonderful ideas, but we have to advertise if we're going to entice anyone to come." Hope scrawled as fast as she could. "I'll be happy to make colorful signs to post in the businesses around town." It would be fun, and it would also give her some satisfaction to use her artistic talents for some good. "We can get flyers printed in Martindale and distribute them and flyers there too."

Rebecca brushed cookie crumbs from her fingers onto her dessert plate. "I'll submit an article to the newspapers in the surrounding towns—at least those large enough to have papers. They may not print it, but I can at least try."

"I've already promised the town council that I'll keep detailed, accurate records of any donations and raised funds and how the money is spent." Annie went to the desk, withdrew a ledger, and held it in the air. "I purchased this the other day on faith." She grinned, then sat next to Hope. "Jake and Ben will help us find people who are willing to offer their time or goods for sale the day of the event. Mrs. Jorgenson has a way with many of the women in town—they love and respect her. Mr. Carter may give us permission to put up a sign at the store, and I mean a *large* sign, explaining the need for donations."

Hope laid the pen down and reached over and squeezed her cousin's hand. "You're making your wish come true, Annie."

"Riverton is going to have its own library. Imagine that." Annie beamed. "A place here in our own community where children and adults can explore and go on so many adventures just by opening the pages of our books."

Hope smiled with confidence that the library would come to fruition and provide a blessing to the community.

Annie looked at Rebecca and then Hope. "I've prayed for something like this, and now that it's really happening, it's all a little overwhelming. Not that I don't believe we can follow through or that the work will be too much. But just in seeing that God is good and faithful, just like you said, Hope."

"I understand." It was a bit thrilling to be a part of Annie's journey and watch her grow into a closer relationship with God through this experience. She'd prayed along with Annie for the library to become a reality. Yet a hint of envy nagged Hope. When would God give her the desires of her heart? When would her own dreams come true?

Truth whispered a needed reminder within. The first night Hope arrived in Riverton, she'd told Annie that God would do his part, but she also needed to do hers. Eva Lancaster had not only invited Hope to join her for supper if she ever visited Minneapolis, but she'd offered to give her opinion on Hope's sketches. That would never happen unless she made the journey.

She'd make arrangements in the morning.

Twelve

The dark sky showed some paling at the horizon. The sun's first rays would lighten the morning from grays to various shades of blue until the sphere rose in full glory to greet the world and announce the beginning of a new day.

Ben sat hunched in his wagon, clutching a package wrapped in brown paper. Despite the early August morning's chill, sweat dripped down his sides, and he wiped moisture from his forehead.

What was he doing here? Maybe he shouldn't have come, but he'd promised himself he'd make it up to Annie after making hurtful comments doubting her ability to create a library. Sure, this was one way, but there were others, and he'd done all he could to help make the fundraiser a success, hadn't he?

Then why had he wrestled most of the night with this decision—prayed for guidance and felt certain this was what God wanted?

Lord, why have you asked this of me?

Maybe he'd heard wrong. Or while sprawled across the bed unable to sleep, imagined God whispering his desire. He also couldn't shut out Hope's challenging words to use his God-given talent. Her phrases kept haunting his thoughts. Maybe she was right, but he wasn't ready to step out into the world as a painter. Maybe someday, but not today. He didn't want to disappoint her, like he did that day in the shed. If only she could understand it just wasn't that easy for him to put the past behind him. There were days when he felt guilty for even enjoying a beautiful sunrise or sunset.

Ben groaned. Now that he was here, he needed to finish the task, then escape before anyone spotted him. He jumped down from the wagon, then reached for the package. People would soon rouse from sleep and begin their daily routines, if they hadn't already.

Like a nervous animal fearing predators, he scanned the surrounding area as he snuck down the road and then crept up the porch steps. He propped the parcel against the inside railing where someone would find it. The note attached explained its presence. Ben sprinted down the steps and behind the hedges lining the yard.

Halfway back to the wagon, he halted. His heart beat as fast as a pheasant's wings during mating season. What was he thinking? For years, he'd known his own mind. Now a few questions from Hope made him doubt. Foolishness. He'd just made a huge mistake.

There had to be time to retrieve the package before anyone discovered it. It would only take a few minutes to return, grab it, and slip back to the wagon. Ben turned around and raced back, careful to remain hidden by vegetation. He leaned against a tree and poked his head around to view the house.

Too late. Rebecca's father stood on the porch, clutching the brown-paper-wrapped offering.

CR

Hope glanced at her watch. Ten minutes late. Where was Annie? They'd barely had time to speak during the busy morning with both of them giving directions to participants in the fundraiser. But they'd promised to meet at that location so they could visit the booths together, greet each person who had contributed, and inquire if anything else was needed as the event got underway. She and Clara had agreed to donate an item to the auction—a garment designed specifically for the winner by Hope and sewn by Clara.

The soon-to-be library's yard almost looked like a small county fair that bright, warm August afternoon. Booths had sprung up around the perimeter, and they were also lined up in a row down the center. Mrs. Carter had offered to lend the red, white, and blue ribbons and banners they displayed outside their home during their Fourth of July celebrations. Mr. Carter had also donated matching balloons, which were tied to each booth. Some of the men in town who played in a small band gathered in a corner of the yard with a violin, banjo, trumpet, and drums. Their lively music added a sense of gaiety and celebration to the air.

"Isn't this exciting?" Mrs. Jorgenson's cheeks were flushed, and her eyes sparkled. "It looks like we're having a party."

Hope nodded. "It's remarkable how many people are donating to the cause, and the best thing about it is that they're not only feeling like they're a part of making the library happen, but they're having fun doing it too."

"It's truly become a community effort, hasn't it?" Mrs. Jorgenson smiled. "My goodness, I made several apple pies and a pound cake, but the other pies, cookies, and cakes here were donated by the ladies from our church."

Hope surveyed the long table filled with desserts. "Annie must be beside herself to see so much support. It's confirmation that she's doing the right thing for the town."

"Have you poked around at the other displays?"

"Not yet. Annie and I were supposed to do that together, so I've only seen several after they were all set up. Sarah's grandmother and several of her friends are selling preserves and honey. She showed me jars of her rhubarb preserves and strawberry jam, and they all looked so tempting, sparkling like jewels in the sunlight."

"Her preserves would win a prize if they were entered in any contests. I'm sure of it."

"So many people have been generous. Mr. Carter offered a mantel clock for the auction, and he's also contributing a woodstove to keep the library warm in winter. Rebecca's mother donated that lovely pale blue and peach quilt for the auction. Can you believe she made it herself?"

Mrs. Jorgenson screwed up her face. "Oh, believe me. Katherine Holt has been letting everyone know within earshot that the quilt was made with her own hands, and I think she'd describe every stitch in painstaking detail if anyone would let her." She made a gesture, as if brushing her comments away. "Forgive me for being so . . ."

"Honest?" So, even gracious Mrs. Jorgenson was human. In a funny way, it was a relief.

"It is stunning, and I should be more grateful for Katherine's willingness to part with it." Her lips turned up into a mischievous smile.

Hope winked at her, then shielded her eyes and searched the crowd for Annie. Still no sign. "Rebecca is helping with the children's games. They're a lively group. I'm glad she enlisted the help of some of the older youth from our church."

"Looks like my ladies need a little help themselves. Several people are waiting in line."

"Yes, please, take care of them, Mrs. Jorgenson." Hope had been so focused on their conversation, she hadn't paid attention to the growing number of people milling around the booth. She overheard several mention they'd come from Martindale.

"Hope! There you are." Annie rushed to her, sounding almost breathless.

"Right where I said I'd be."

"I'm sorry I'm late, but . . ." Annie pulled on Hope's arm. "You've just got to see for yourself!"

"See what?" Hope could barely keep up with her cousin.

Annie dragged Hope toward the area sectioned off for the auction. Folks crowded there seemed to focused on one object. Annie asked several people to step aside, and then she pulled Hope in closer to where a long rope extended between two poles to keep admirers several feet away from the auction items.

Hope's breath caught. No wonder this contribution had caused such a commotion.

Rebecca slipped in next to them at the rope. "I had to take another look, but don't worry. I left the games in good hands."

"Still no idea of where it came from?" Annie peeked around Hope to see Rebecca. "Seems strange that no one has claimed it."

"All I know is that my father found the donation on our porch this morning, wrapped in brown paper with a note attached saying that it was to be placed in the auction to help raise funds for the town library. So, I went to the school on my way here and borrowed an easel so we could display the gift properly."

Perched in front of them was a framed painting about eighteen inches by twenty-four inches of a little boy in overalls running through a grassy field with a collie close at his side. The boy's face expressed pure delight. Not only beautiful, the painting felt joyful. You could almost hear the little boy's laughter. The painting was unsigned, and people around them speculated not only about the artist, but who could have parted with such a precious piece.

Hope spotted Jake staring at the painting. He turned and the stunned expression on his face confirmed what she already knew. Ben's artwork. No one else could paint like that. No one else she knew would anonymously give away something so personal. *Why?* Why would he take such a public risk if he wanted to hide his talent?

Something had softened his resolve to never display his work. Somehow, Ben had overcome his pain and made this lovely offering, even if only she and Jake would recognize the painter. Her heart melted with gratitude at the sacrifice.

The auction was only two hours away, but it now felt more like two days. An idea mushroomed, then exploded, sending adrenaline rushing through Hope's body.

God, are these thoughts from you? Or had she devised the plan out of her own agenda?

CR

The loud, fast-talking auctioneer's voice started to fade, and Hope heard a hum in her ears. She blinked her eyes and inhaled. So nervous about losing the painting, she'd forgotten to breathe. That wouldn't do, fainting in the middle of bidding, especially since it had come down to her and an unfamiliar, well-dressed lady. She must have come from one of the surrounding towns, most likely Martindale, as it was the largest in the area.

Mr. Carter stepped up and leaned close to her ear. "Don't let her see you hesitate, Hope," he whispered. "If she witnesses any doubt, she'll know she can outlast you."

"Thank you, Mr. Carter," Hope whispered back. Then she lifted her hand to raise her bid again.

"I would have bid more myself, but I could see in your face how much you want this painting."

"I do, Mr. Carter, for reasons I can't explain."

"Art can have a deep effect on people, and this one seems to have made quite an impression on you. Good luck, Hope." He turned and headed toward a group of several men observing the action.

You can do this. She raised her hand again.

Annie tugged at Hope's sleeve. "Are you sure you can afford to go higher? Don't misunderstand. I'm thrilled about all the money we're raising, but don't get carried away and do something you'll regret later."

"Don't worry, Annie. I know what I'm doing."

Dear God, please make that lady stop. Hope's heart was pounding so hard it would break through her rib cage if she didn't win soon. She was just as concerned at the rising bid as Annie. Hope couldn't go much further. She received a monthly allowance from her parents' accountant that she shared with Annie. The two of them didn't eat much, and they used what they could from the garden, but she insisted on giving Annie a sum every month to help with expenses that came with a home and animals.

Her wages from working at the store two days a week didn't amount to a great deal, but she used them for personal things. Hope had been saving to purchase a new paint box—the latch on hers was broken and not repairable. She was beginning to run out of art supplies, and there was that lovely peach silk fabric she had her eye on. But she'd sacrifice those things for as long as needed. She had plans for the painting—more than just hanging it on her bedroom wall.

There was the additional money her parents had given her access to, but that was for emergencies, and purchasing artwork certainly didn't fall under that category. Besides, she didn't want to take advantage of their generosity. Hope could use a portion of what she'd set aside for her trip to see Miss Lancaster in Minneapolis. No time to question that decision. Somehow, she'd find a way to make up the shortage.

Hope raised her hand one last time. That was it. She couldn't go any higher. *Please, God.*

"Going once, going twice . . ." the auctioneer yelled.

All eyes were on the other bidder. She shook her head no, then looking at Hope, gave a slight nod.

"Sold to the young lady over there!" The auctioneer pointed his gavel at Hope.

"Ahhh . . ." Hope gasped in relief as Annie hugged her. Over her cousin's shoulder, Hope saw Ben standing like a pillar not far behind them as the crowd separated to move around him.

He cocked his head and his eyes narrowed, as though he were studying her. Then he turned and stalked away.

⟡

Ben sat on the back step of the library, away from the masses and noise. The band's latest tune floated through the air, but the waltz helped calm his nerves.

From the moment his painting was displayed, people had speculated about the donor. They wanted to know the artist's name. Someone stubborn enough might pursue that knowledge until they discovered Ben. Secrets were hard to keep forever, but he wasn't ready for his to become public. Whether he'd paid the price or not for blinding Percy remained debatable. But once he exposed himself as a painter, Ben would face criticism about his work. Could he deal with impartial judgment? Possibly be viewed as a fake? A fraud?

Sure, people here seemed to be moved by the painting, and he'd overheard comments filled with praise, but it was only one canvas. Other pieces might not live up to this one. Besides, what did farmers and small-town folk know? They couldn't tell the difference between a masterpiece and a complete fiasco.

His stomach muscles clenched. When they first met, Ben had criticized and misjudged Hope for expressing the same sentiments—that farmers couldn't possibly know or understand art. How arrogant of him. *Forgive me, Lord.*

A burly man stepped from the outhouse, checked his suspenders, and slammed the door behind him. He nodded acknowledgement to Ben, then sauntered toward the front of the building.

Jake and Hope came around the other side.

"We were wondering where we'd find you." Jake propped one foot beside Ben and rested an arm on his thigh. "Why didn't you tell me?" He kept his voice low. "Good grief, Ben. You hide your paintings from even your friends and family, then you put a picture out there for the whole town to see."

"I know." Ben tunneled his fingers through his hair. "It was a mistake."

"A mistake? To not tell me, or to do it at all?"

"Both. I struggled with the decision all week. Didn't sleep at all last night. I wanted to help . . ."

Hope sat on the other side of Ben. He met her eyes. *You did it.*

I shouldn't have. Silence circled the three of them like the breezes fluttering the trees.

"Why do you regret it?" She knew his story, and her concerned tone confirmed she cared. "Are you sure there wasn't something more to it?"

He didn't see any judgment in her expression. "What do you mean?"

"Maybe there's a part of you that wants to be free of secrets." Hope's voice was gentle and soothing. "Do you think that could be true? That you're ready to share your work?"

"I had a lapse in judgment, that's all." Ben squeezed his eyes shut for a moment and shook his head. "So many people were giving whatever they could to the cause. My paintings are all I have, and I thought God was nudging me to give one away. Maybe it was his voice in my head, or maybe it was my own ego. Maybe deep down, I wanted to see people's reaction. But I still didn't want anyone to know it was mine. So I left the painting unsigned, wrapped it up, and left it at Rebecca's early this morning. Then I came to my senses, but it was too late. Dr. Hoyt had already found it."

Jake draped an arm around Ben's shoulder and gave him a sly smile. "It's me and Shep in that painting, isn't it? In our fields back at the home farm."

"Yeah." Ben rubbed his eyes, then turned to Hope. "I knew you'd figure it out as soon as you laid eyes on the painting, but I took a risk that you'd keep silent. I never imagined you'd bid on it." He'd lost control of his art with one impulsive decision, and he needed to feel in control again. Ben peered into understanding eyes. "Sell the painting back to me. I'll pay the full amount."

"It's not for sale." Hope's voice was soft, but firm.

"Why?" Ben couldn't pull himself away from her gaze. She'd already done so much to support Annie and the library. Why sacrifice more than needed? "The whole point of the auction was to raise money. Nothing will be lost."

Jake nudged Ben's shoulder. "Hey, do I get a say in this? The painting is of me and my dog. Don't I get a chance at it?"

"I repeat. The painting isn't for sale." Hope clasped her hands in her lap. "But if you're afraid that someone will ask questions, I'll hang it in my bedroom for as long as I live in Riverton. Eventually, it will be forgotten. In the meantime, I won't disclose to anyone in town that you're the artist without your permission. Not even Annie."

Hope liked the painting that much? Enough to pay an extravagant amount—and then keep it hidden—because it would make him more comfortable? She'd even keep his secret from her cousin. Gratitude flowed through Ben's veins and merged with humility. He didn't deserve such a friend.

Hope stood and towered over Ben, the sun providing a golden halo around her head. "But I highly suggest that you let Annie into the inner circle of Benjamin Greene's secret society soon. She's as loyal as they come, but she's also a smart redhead with a fiery temper beneath that sweet disposition. Trust me, you don't want her figuring it out on her own."

Thirteen

"Excuse me, young lady, are you employed here?"

Hope jolted from her daydream and returned to her place behind the counter in the Home Store. She was no longer in Minneapolis dining with Eva Lancaster, reveling in the praise flowing from the designer's lips after seeing Hope's sketches. She focused on the middle-aged woman with raised eyebrows standing before her. "Yes, how may I help you?"

"I'm looking for a lightweight yarn in pale yellow. I'm crocheting a baby blanket for my new granddaughter. I also need white cotton thread for tatting, and I'd like to look at the shuttles. My daughter-in-law is interested in learning how to tat."

"How nice of you to teach her. I'd like to learn myself. The lace makes lovely dress collars and cuffs." Hope gestured to the left. "Right this way." She led the customer to another section in the store and laid out several skeins of yarn in light yellow shades. "Do any of these suit you?"

The woman chose one and felt the wool's texture. "This will do nicely. I'll take several."

Hope searched for another skein to match while her customer picked out thread and a new shuttle. With purchases in hand, the woman thanked Hope and left the store with a smile on her face. If only customers' requests were always that easy. Earlier that morning, a cantankerous older gentleman insisted she find a man to help him when she could have just as well assisted him herself.

Her cousin was better suited for this job. Somehow Annie found patience for customers who couldn't make up their minds, and her vivacious personality and sense of humor put a smile on the most dissatisfied-looking faces.

She may not be as natural at the job as Annie, but Hope did her best, and she appreciated the income, now even more important after the sum spent on Ben's painting. Replenishing funds necessary for her trip to see Miss Lancaster in Minneapolis, as well as her dwindling art supplies, would require being extra careful with earnings. Regardless, it was worth every penny to have the painting in hand.

The framed canvas hung in her bedroom on the wall opposite the bed. There she could gaze at it in the evening before turning off the lamp and view it first thing in the morning. The warm colors, the boy playing with his dog, the way the wind seemed to blow through the tall grass—in some way they soothed her soul.

As she studied the painting, Hope had discovered little things missed at first glance—the sheen on the collie's coat, the delicate butterfly on a wild flower, a deer observing from the edge of the woods surrounding the field. Those details made the picture come alive, and in some surreal fashion Hope felt like she was experiencing the world through Ben's eyes.

She had plans for the painting, and before long Ben might be thanking her for being so persistent in obtaining the piece.

Annie strolled up and dropped several small boxes on the counter. "Do you think you can stand to work with us lowly clerks for the next four weeks?" She grinned and winked. "Until the famous Miss Lancaster declares you a prodigy and takes you under her wing?"

Hope returned the grin. "Dear cousin, I appreciate you having such faith in me, but that reality is pretty far-fetched." Twenty-eight days left to build up her courage. Even the remote possibility of Miss Lancaster offering to advise her beyond that meeting kept Hope's mind reeling. "Just knowing that I'm getting an opportunity to show her my drawings gives me the chills. I'm excited, but at the same time, I'm terribly frightened that she's going to declare my designs are a travesty and an abomination."

"That's not going to happen, and I'm going to be there right beside you to witness every moment so I can relive the evening with you for days after."

"Oh, Annie, I'm so glad you're going to Minneapolis with me. I know it's for only one night, but we'll have such a good time in the city. I've read the West Hotel is quite grand."

"You're used to the fancy hotels in New York, but I've only seen them in magazines." Annie eyes sparkled. "Can you believe it? Good things are happening for both of us. We raised the money needed for the library, and if all continues to go well, it will be open in two weeks. And only two weeks later, we'll be on a train heading for the city where you'll meet someone who could change your life."

"Hope, you're just the person we need." Sarah waddled toward them, glowing and looking strong and beautiful, even in the last days of her pregnancy.

Rachel Kahl followed close behind, carrying a bundle wrapped in brown paper. Hope had met the young woman with dark hair and hazel eyes at church, and she was immediately attracted to the nineteen-year-old's sweet nature.

"What can I do to help?" Hope focused on her two friends. Whatever they required would be far more fun than waiting on the challenging customers she'd served earlier.

"First things first. We have an announcement to share." Sarah wrapped an arm around Rachel's shoulders and gave her a slight squeeze. "Or, at least Rachel does."

The pretty girl blushed as she smiled. "I'm getting married!"

"Rachel, that's wonderful!" Annie hugged her. "Congratulations. When is the happy day?"

"Saturday."

"As in tomorrow?" Annie squealed. "That doesn't give you much time to plan a wedding."

"I know. My parents are as nervous as cornered rabbits." Rachel wrung her hands. "Not because they don't want me to marry Caleb. They think he's wonderful, and they've given us their blessing. But they didn't expect to marry me off quite this soon."

"Then what's the rush?" Hope couldn't imagine anything improper.

"Caleb was just offered a teaching job in Madison. It's a wonderful opportunity because of the available college courses nearby that will help him become a professor someday. The only problem is that he needs to move there right away. He doesn't want to go without me, and I don't want to be separated from him either."

Annie sighed. "How romantic."

"And exciting. You'll be off on your own adventure." Hope swallowed the bitter taste of envy. Her time would come according to God's design, not hers. This was Rachel and Caleb's opportunity to create and share the life intended for them. "So, why do you need my help?"

"We're just going to have a small wedding at two o'clock in the afternoon with family and a few friends at the church. Reverend Caswell is officiating. Then a simple reception at the house. But, I . . ." Rachel glanced at Sarah.

"Rachel won't have a wedding gown." Sarah smiled at Hope. "So, we'd like to add something to her Sunday dress to make it feel special."

Rachel perked up. "Not that there's anything wrong with the dress. It's like new, and Mrs. Boyle did a wonderful job fitting and sewing the garment." She laid down the package she carried and opened it, revealing a lovely blue dress. "I just never expected to get married in it. I always thought I'd wear my mother's dress, but it doesn't fit, and there's not enough time to alter it."

"We're just country folk, but you have a wonderful sense of fashion, Hope." Sarah helped spread the dress out on the counter. "We thought you might suggest a piece of jewelry, a sophisticated hat, or something that might serve as a lovely veil."

Hope trailed her fingers over the fabric. Nice, practical, and Clara's perfect stitching was some of the best Hope had seen—even in New York. Still, the dress wasn't what a bride envisioned wearing on her wedding day.

An idea germinated and within seconds grew into something that excited and frightened Hope. Could she do it? It was worth trying, and she'd create a backup plan just in case she failed. "Rachel, would you be willing to leave the dress with me until morning so I can give it some thought?"

"I—I don't know . . ." Rachel bit her lower lip and turned to Sarah.

"I think it would be all right, Rachel." Sarah gave her a confident smile. "Hope will take good care of the dress and be prompt in returning it."

"I promise to bring it to your home in plenty of time before the ceremony." Even if Rachel insisted on taking the dress with her, Hope could still carry out her plan if Clara agreed to help. Without her, Hope would still look for a way to make the existing dress more elegant.

"All right." Rachel smiled. "I trust you."

"Good. I'll get to work on your wedding attire this evening." Hope grinned and re-wrapped the dress in the brown paper.

Rachel and Sarah left the store, not realizing the literal meaning behind Hope's words.

❧

Hope rubbed her eyes, then poured strong coffee for them both. "Clara, I can't thank you enough, or Rose for taking care of her siblings all night. It would be impossible to do this without you."

"No need for thanks." Clara accepted one of the steaming cups. "I'll admit that I had some reservations. I thought we should have asked Rachel first, but now, seein' this dress, I don't know how she couldn't help but love it. Besides, Rachel has always been kind to me and my children, especially after my Frank passed. I'll do anything I can to make her wedding day special." Clara took a sip, then set down her cup, away from the garment in front of her. "I'm so happy she's found love again."

"Again? She had another beau?"

"Oh, you didn't know?" With nimble fingers, Clara moved a threaded needle through a small section of the gown's left sleeve. "Caleb's younger brother, Martin. He and Rachel were very close, but Martin drowned several years ago. Early in November when the water was frigid, and the river hadn't completely frozen over. He'd gone out lookin' for a missing heifer. He was only seventeen."

"So young. His death must have been heartbreaking."

"Rachel was devastated. When Caleb came home from college for the funeral, the two of them spent some time together, then started writing after he went back. Now, two years later, they're getting married. God is sure full of surprises with how he takes care of things."

"Yes, I guess he is."

"Now take the two of us. Did you ever think we'd be sitting here together in the wee hours of the morning, puttin' together a wedding dress?"

"No, can't say I ever imagined it." Tired as she was, Hope still laughed. "I've been working on this design for a while, and I plan to submit it to Butterick, but I needed your skilled fingers to bring it to life."

A light shade of pink filled Clara's cheeks. "Good thing I've sewed for Rachel before. If the dress fits that mannequin, it should fit the bride." Clara snipped the thread. "Finished."

Hope set her coffee aside, her fingers slightly shaking. "Time to see if we've mastered the task or not." She took a deep breath and gestured toward the mannequin.

Clara draped the light blue satin gown over the form. Hope had been saving the fabric for herself, but knowing how perfect the color would look on Rachel, and now seeing how gracefully the material fell to the floor made the sacrifice worth it. The silhouette was soft and feminine, and the fabric would flow as Rachel walked. The top piece of the dress was created with sleeves fitted at the shoulder down to the elbow, an open square neckline, and a gathered bodice. The trumpet-shaped skirt flowed softly over the hips, flaring at the hem. A short train trailed in the back.

Clara's fingers traced the left sleeve. "It's beautiful."

Hope stood back and crossed her arms over her chest, a wave of disappointment flowing through her tired body. "Something isn't right."

"Not right?" Clara's eyes widened. "Did I do something wrong?"

"No, not at all. Your work is impeccable." Hope sighed. "It's my fault. The gown just doesn't look like a wedding dress."

"But with so little time, I think we've accomplished a miracle." Clara, now looking even more weary, dropped into her chair. "Without your satin, what would we have to work with?"

Hope sat in the chair across the table from Clara. "It's just that I wanted it to be so much more . . ."

"Are you two still working? It must be almost four in the morning." Annie appeared, from what felt like nowhere, tying her robe.

"We thought we'd finished, but now I'm not so sure." Hope yawned, then rubbed her burning eyes. They'd been up all night. Lack of sleep was one thing, but feeling disappointed with their efforts was another. "What are you doing up at this hour?"

"I came down to use the outhouse and get a drink of water." Annie shuffled toward the kitchen in the back of the house.

Clara and Hope sat quietly, staring at the dressed mannequin.

Hope's focus strayed from the gown to the curtains hanging on the window behind it. "How could I have been so . . ." Hope leaped up from her chair, now feeling quite awake. "Of course it's wrong. My design wasn't originally meant to be a wedding dress." She faced Clara. "It's so clear. What's missing?"

Clara's eyebrows furrowed. "It's missing lace, but we talked about that. Neither of us have any tucked away that would be suitable, and there's not enough time to ask one of the lady's in town for tatting."

"We don't need to. It's been right here in front of us the whole night."

Annie lumbered into the room and yawned. "I'm going back to bed." She headed toward the stairs leading to the second floor.

"Wait." Hope chewed her lower lip. This could go either way. "Annie, we need your help. Actually, we need your lace curtains."

"My new curtains?" Annie swung back around, her mouth wide open. "The curtains I saved for and waited three months to buy?"

"I promise I'll replace them—as soon as I can." Hope rushed to the mannequin to state her purpose. "I know it would be a sacrifice, even for someone as generous as you. But, these lacy curtains could turn this dress into an elegant wedding gown—one that would be special, like Rachel."

Annie thought for a moment, then she re-tied her robe and pulled a chair close to one of the windows. "Why can't I ever say no to you?" She climbed up and slid one of the curtain panels from the rod. "Hope, I know you mean well, but you have a tendency to act in haste. You don't even know if Rachel will be interested in wearing anything different than what she's already chosen."

"She's going to love it. Trust me." Hope stepped onto a chair next to a second window. Oh, my. Eager to get started, Hope had proven Annie's statement to be true. She'd moved forward again with an idea without consulting an important party. "Clara, I'm sorry. I haven't even asked if you're willing and able to work longer."

"Of course I am. I wouldn't think of leavin' now." Clara perked up as though she'd had a full night's rest. "We have plenty of work ahead of us, so we'd best get started."

"Thank you." Hope smiled, then stepped down with her arms full. She draped one of the panels decorated with white lace over the dress on the mannequin, and a delicate shade of blue showed through the transparent overlay. "We'll make a second dress from the curtains and the blue one will serve as an undergarment. Sheer sleeves edged with lace will replace the satin sleeves. We should also have enough lacy material for a veil." Hope hadn't experienced this kind of excitement in a long time. She pointed to the end of the table. "That blue satin ribbon over there will go around the waist."

It would be perfect—just perfect.

ॐ

"I—I can't believe you made something so beautiful—for me!" Rachel's eyes lit up as Hope held the wedding dress for her to see. "I want to hug you both, but I'm afraid I'll crush my new dress."

"We made a veil to match." Hope, trying not to squeal in her own excitement, nodded at Clara to show Rachel the veil, and Clara draped the lace over her own arm to display the delicate piece.

"Oh, my . . . it's just lovely. We must show Mother." Rachel, beaming, took the dress in her arms and held it with care. "She went upstairs right before you arrived, but said she'd be down shortly. She has a surprise for me too."

"Rachel, what's going on down here?" Millie Kahl moved down the stairs, carrying a cream-colored satin garment. She stopped several steps from the floor.

"Mother, Hope and Clara have done the most generous thing." Rachel held the dress against her front. "Isn't it the most gorgeous wedding dress you've ever seen? They worked all night. It's a wedding gift, but I don't know how I'll ever repay them for their kindness."

Hope's heart would surely burst any minute. Rachel loved the dress, and if it would make this sweet girl feel even more beautiful as she said her vows and pledged herself to the man she loved, it was well worth losing a night's sleep.

"That's wonderful, dear." No one could have missed the crack in Millie's voice. "The dress is beyond exquisite." She looked at Hope, her eyes filled with disappointment. "How thoughtful of you both to have worked so hard for my daughter."

"Mother, what's wrong?" Rachel clutched the wedding dress to her chest. "What are you holding?"

Millie's weak smile lacked cheer. "It's nothing, dear. I'll just go put it away, and then we can have a quick cup of coffee with Hope and Clara before we need to finish preparations. We still have much to do."

Hope had to speak up. "Mrs. Banks—Millie—you also have a dress for Rachel, don't you?"

"It's nothing." Millie looked from Hope to Rachel. "Really."

"Mother, is that your wedding dress?" Rachel's tone was warm and loving.

Millie nodded. "I wanted you to have something nice to wear, so I altered it the best I could. I wanted it to be a surprise."

"You must have been up all night working, too, only without any help." Hope reached over and touched the smooth fabric. "You poured your love into this dress."

Millie's chin quivered, and pools of liquid emotion welled in her eyes. "She's my daughter."

"Oh, Mother . . ." Rachel leaned over and kissed her mother's cheek.

Hope's eyes stung, and by the looks of it Clara was fighting her own tears.

"You should wear your mother's dress." It didn't matter that Hope had good intentions. She'd rushed ahead and neglected to think of the possible cost to others. She should never have given Rachel a dress without consulting her mother. Hope touched Rachel's arm. "Clara and I will understand."

Clara dabbed at her eyes and nodded. "Of course we will."

"Well, I won't!" Millie sniffed. She fingered the lace on the gown in Rachel's arms, then gave her a warm smile as she cupped the bride's chin in her hand. "My sweet daughter, I've always wanted the best for you, and that means you're going to wear this lovely dress and be the most beautiful bride Riverton has ever seen."

"You mean it?" Rachel's eyes lit up.

"More than that, I insist." Millie smiled. "Now, Clara and Hope, would you like that cup of coffee? I'm sure the dress will fit perfectly, but would you like to see Rachel in it before you leave?"

"We would love that." Clara glanced at Hope, as though offering assurance that it would be the right thing to do.

"Thank you. Of course we'll stay." Hope had no misgivings. Millie's peaceful countenance and the warmth in her voice assured Hope that her blunder was forgiven.

Clara moved Rachel and her mother toward the stairs. "We can help ourselves to the coffee, Millie. You help Rachel into the dress."

Mother and daughter headed up the staircase to the second floor, and Clara led Hope to the kitchen where they found a hot pot of coffee sitting on the stove. Clara poured each of them a steaming cup.

Hope took one, then followed her friend back into the parlor. "Clara, you were right to have reservations about making Rachel's wedding dress. I should have asked her and Millie's permission before we even started."

"I got caught up in the excitement too. I guess we both learned something." Clara sat on settee and motioned for Hope to sit next to her.

"Ladies, here comes the bride." Millie's grin almost stretched to both ears. She reached the bottom of the stairs, then turned her attention to the top.

Clara and Hope joined her. Rachel stepped into view, and Hope gasped, then caught Clara's eye. The bride was breathtaking as she descended. The dress flowed with light, airy movements, and the lace added elegance. Rachel's dark hair was swept up beneath the veil, her face glowed, and her hazel eyes sparkled with the joy of young love. She reached the bottom step with a big smile spread across her face and led them back into the parlor.

Millie sighed. "Honey, you look like a princess."

"I *feel* like a princess!" Rachel turned around for them to view all sides of the dress. "Hope—Clara—I can never thank you enough. Caleb is going to think he's stepped into a fairy-tale."

Hope clasped her hands to her chest. "I couldn't be more honored. You make the dress look like it came from one of the finest stores in New York. Maybe even Paris."

As they stood admiring Clara's stitching and sharing the humor in Annie's new curtains being utilized, Hope couldn't rid herself of the nagging thought that something was still lacking.

"Ladies, you'll have to excuse us." Millie turned to her daughter. "We should get you out of the dress until it's time to prepare for the ceremony. We still have some other things to get accomplished and there isn't much time."

An idea came to mind, and Hope needed to speak up now or she'd lose the chance. "Clara, would you help Rachel change and hang up the gown? I'd like to speak with Millie."

Clara gave her a questioning look, but didn't refuse. She grinned at Rachel. "Back up the stairs, Princess."

Millie motioned for Hope to sit. "What is it?"

Hope needed to be tactful, especially after her initial blunder. "Although Rachel is a stunning bride, it suddenly occurred to me that something is missing."

"Missing?"

"She came into the Home Store yesterday with Sarah to find an adornment for her blue dress."

"Yes, but now she's not wearing that garment." The light dimmed in Millie's eyes. "And I was so busy trying to finish altering my dress, I didn't even think about what she might wear with it."

"Do you have any jewelry that I might see?" Hope's idea could be brilliant, or it could be disastrous.

"Just a few pieces, nothing fancy or worth much."

"Even so, we might find something that Rachel would like."

Millie shrugged her shoulders. "You're welcome to look. I'll get the box from my bedroom." She left the parlor, but returned in less than a minute and laid the wooden box with swirls carved on the top next to Hope.

She opened the box and searched the contents. Millie was right. Aside from several lovely brooches, the rest of the items were inexpensive trinkets, a pearl necklace with a broken clasp, and a man's watch. Nothing that would do.

Her fingers grasped a velvet bag at the bottom of the box, and she held it up for Millie to see. "May I?" At Millie's nod,

Hope pulled the drawstrings and opened the bag, then removed a delicate gold chain and a locket with a pearl in the center. Old, but exquisite.

"Oh, my . . . I'd almost forgotten about that." Millie took it from Hope, and with the chain draped over her fingers, she let the locket dangle in front of them. "It initially belonged to my grandmother. She gave it to me on my sixteenth birthday. I wore it every day until Rachel was born, then put it away for safekeeping. You know how children are—grabbing at everything. Rachel was fascinated and wouldn't leave it alone. She was a strong little one, and all it would take would be one little tug and the chain would have broken."

"This is it. This is what's missing." Hope could have hugged Millie. "The locket will compliment Rachel's wedding dress."

"Are you sure?" Millie squinted. "It's been around for years."

"But that's what makes it so special. It's an heirloom, something passed down through generations. It's been a part of your life and memories, and something she can wear long after the wedding dress is no longer suitable." Hope grinned. "It's perfect."

"If you're sure." Millie's eyes lit up, and excitement filled her voice.

Clara strolled into the parlor. "The bride will be down soon."

"Millie, please show Rachel the locket and see how she feels." Hope stood. "Clara and I will be on our way."

Millie turned nervous eyes on Hope. "Don't you want to wait—hear what she decides?"

Hope put her hand on Millie's shoulder. "You can let me know later. I think this moment should be between mother and daughter."

"What if she doesn't like it? We'll have to find something else."

"Trust me. She's going to love it."

"Thank you. For everything." Millie looked at Hope, then Clara. "This is going to be one of the best days of her life." With the necklace in hand, she almost skipped up the stairs.

Clara perched her hands on her hips and gave Hope an amused smile. "What was that all about?"

"I found a lovely heirloom necklace in the bottom of Millie's jewelry box and suggested that she offer it to Rachel as something special to wear on her wedding day."

"Nice thought."

"It's still a shame that all the work Millie put into her wedding dress is wasted." Inspiration rushed in like a locomotive without brakes. Hope stared at the empty stairs Millie had just ascended. "Clara, would you say that Rachel and her mother are now about the same size?"

Clara wrinkled her forehead. "Yes, I think they're close."

Hope raised an eyebrow at her friend.

"Are you suggesting?"

"We have four hours." Hope bit her lip in excitement.

"Are you sure?"

"We could manage, but it would take both of us." Hope took a few steps, then wiped her damp forehead. "Maybe it's a crazy idea. We've already worked through the night, and there's your family to consider."

"I could go home long enough to check on the children and help Rose with breakfast." Clara brushed lose tendrils of hair from her cheek. "We've come this far with the wedding, I'd like to at least try. What's a few more hours out of our lives?"

"All right. But this time, we'll talk to Millie before rushing head-on." Hope raced up the stairs with Clara close behind, then knocked on Rachel's bedroom door. "Millie, are you in there?"

Millie poked her head out. "Did you come to see Rachel?"

"Could we look at the wedding dress you altered?"

"Of course. I'll get it." In less than a minute, Millie stepped out of the room with the dress in her arms, her questioning gaze moving from Hope to Clara, then back again.

Hope held the gown in front of Millie, studying several areas. She grinned at Clara. "Millie, do you have anything special to wear to the wedding?"

"No, there hasn't been time to—are you suggesting?" Millie gasped. "I can't wear a wedding dress to my daughter's wedding. It wouldn't be appropriate."

"Of course you can't. But it looks like the gown will fit you, and if we made some changes . . ." Hope picked up the train and handed it to Clara.

"If it's all right with you, Millie, I can cut the train and hem the bottom so the skirt falls at the same length all the way around." Clara had caught the vision. Even after working all night, she seemed energized by their mission. "It would take me hours to sew by hand, but I could finish it in time for the wedding if I used my machine."

"And I have lovely wide black ribbon that will work well as a sash, as well as delicate ribbon for a little trim." Hope had a completed picture in her mind. "We can change the Vneck by adding a panel of black satin. I think I have enough in a box at home."

Millie covered her mouth with her hand. "I'm overwhelmed."

"Just say yes, Mother." Rachel swung the bedroom door wide open. "There's no one else to pass down the dress to, and you deserve to have something pretty to wear."

"One more thing." Hope was itching to get started. "A matching hat would be a finishing touch. I visited the millinery the other day, and the elderly owner is closing the shop soon, for good. Her inventory is quite small, but she has one plain white hat on her shelf, as well as a large black plume in stock. She lives not far from her shop. If closed, I might get her to open for this special occasion, and I'm sure she'd give me a good price on the hat and plume. And if you agree to all of this, Millie, it would be my gift."

"This is all very exciting, but it's too generous. I couldn't possibly . . ." From Millie's expression, she was struggling with wanting to accept, but not knowing if she should.

"It would be an honor to do this for you." Hope glanced at Clara for help.

"Hope's right. If your guests like what we've done for you and Rachel, they might spread the word. You'd be doing us a favor."

Millie's chin quivered. "All right. Thank you." She hugged Hope, then Clara. "Thank you."

"We'd better get to work if we're going to have everything back to you in time for the wedding." Exhilarated, Hope would do everything she could to help the mother of the bride feel as beautiful as her daughter.

Hope led the way back down the steps and outside into the sunshine where she took a deep breath of fresh air. "Oh my, Clara. I was feeling terrible because I'd neglected to think about Millie's feelings concerning Rachel's dress. But I think I just redeemed myself."

"Your heart was in the right place, and it's all worked out."

Yes, everything had been resolved despite Hope's impulsive actions, and much of it due to Clara's help. Hope glanced at her friend as they strode down the street. They'd worked well as a team. How many more opportunities would there be to see what they could accomplish together?

Fourteen

After taking a swig of water, Ben dropped to the thick grass under a maple tree on the library's front lawn. Hunger gnawed his empty stomach, and he eagerly opened the basket Annie had delivered containing chicken sandwiches, egg salad sandwiches, apples, and oatmeal cookies.

The sound of a hammer pounding came from inside the soon-to-be library, and laughter burst from a group of youth volunteering their time to paint the outside of the building. Despite spending time teasing and chasing each other, they'd accomplished a great deal.

He should probably wait for the others to come, but he hadn't eaten for hours, and the smell of food wafting from the basket stimulated his insides again.

"May I join you?" Hope stepped into the shade offered by the large tree's canopy, escaping the sun's hot rays.

"Didn't you and Annie put this meal together?"

"True." Hope gracefully lowered herself to the ground.

He opened the basket, grabbed an apple, and rubbed it against his sleeve. But instead of taking a bite, he stared at the fruit clutched in his hand. "Hope, I've wanted to ask—I mean—we haven't talked." Ben lifted his gaze to see her sitting prim, with her hands in her lap.

"Go ahead."

"The truth?"

"Always."

"I wouldn't want anyone else but you to have my painting, so I'm not only humbled, I'm also honored you bid at the auction." Knowing that something personal to him remained close to Hope made him feel connected to her in a strange way, even when they were apart.

"Ben, you can't possibly know how happy that makes me." Hope's gentle voice was like a pink watercolor, soft and feminine. "I hung your painting in my bedroom, out of sight, like I promised. It's a treasure. When I open my eyes in the morning, I experience joy through that little boy, and before I close my eyes at night all I see is hope."

"Thanks for keeping your promise. And thank you . . ." Words felt inadequate. "To know that it brings out those emotions means a lot to me." All he'd ever wanted was to help people feel something through his paintings.

"I understand. Perhaps more than you realize." Of course she understood. In a different, but somewhat similar way, Hope desired people to react to her work.

So, the question of where the artwork hung was answered, but curiosity about whether people had continued to speculate on who painted the picture of the boy with his dog had plagued him since the day of the auction. Ben tossed the apple from one hand to the other. "I need to ask. Are people still wondering?"

"About the painter?"

He nodded. Then, trying to act nonchalant, shrugged. To make a big deal out of it now that several weeks had gone by would seem egotistical. Ben couldn't deny pride played a part, but his reasons for asking were also laced with fear. He wasn't ready to expose himself as an artist.

"I told anyone who asked that the painting was given anonymously. That's the truth. Some people have speculated that the artist was a friend or customer of Mr. Carter's, since his reputation and influence is widespread. It's also been suggested that someone wanting to do a good deed from Martindale sent it." She shooed several flies buzzing around the food basket. "But the person who can't stand not knowing where the painting came from is Annie. Even more than knowing the artist, she desperately wants to meet the generous donor."

Ben focused on the fruit in his hand. "I've been thinking about what you said after the auction, and you're right." He raised his gaze to meet Hope's. "Annie deserves to know, and she needs to hear it from me. If she ever found out another way, it would hurt her."

"Yes, it would. She'd be devastated." The serious tone in her voice convinced him that he needed to be upfront with Annie as soon as possible. "That would be followed by anger and a desire to inflict great bodily harm to you." The corners of Hope's full lips lifted into a hint of a smile. The imp was teasing.

Her eyes twinkled, challenging him, but he resisted an urge to tickle her until she gave in and apologized for having a little fun at his expense. Then he'd surely be tempted to kiss those lips that piqued a desire to taste their sweetness. How would she respond if he did? Would she welcome the playfulness? Or would she reprimand him for not treating her like a proper lady?

Maybe another time—another place. Ben pulled himself back to reality. The hunger he'd begun to feel for her couldn't be fed.

"We're here, and I'm starved." Annie marched up to them with Jake in tow.

It was disappointing to have his time with Hope interrupted, yet a relief. She enticed him, intrigued him, and also confused him. Ben thought he'd understood and accepted the past and the future. Then she entered his world, and now he questioned if he'd been wrong to shut out the possibility of having someone to love and share his art—his life. More than anything, Hattie had desired financial security in marriage—something he couldn't promise. But if he was right, Hope wanted a partner who understood her creative passion, and wasn't that what he yearned for too?

"Sorry to make you wait—unless you didn't—but I had to insist that Jake get cleaned up." Annie wrinkled her nose. "Trust me. You would not have wanted to come within a few feet of him."

"Someone had to take down the old outhouse so we could put up the new one." Jake ruffled Ben's hair, then plopped down next to him. "I always manage to get the dirty jobs, while pretty boy here gets the easy ones." He reached for the basket of food, put his hand in to grab an item, but stopped and handed the basket to Annie. "Ladies first."

They passed the basket around, then sat quietly for a moment, filling their stomachs. Ben enjoyed the cool reprieve the tree offered from the hot August sun.

Annie glanced from Ben to Jake. "You know how much we appreciate your help, don't you? Especially since this is harvest season. For you to take time on a Saturday to come here . . . well, I owe you."

"Hey, Annie . . ." Jake nudged her shoulder with his. "You know we wouldn't be here if we didn't want to be."

"Time and weather have been on our side. We'll start working in the hay field on Monday." Ben grabbed a cookie and passed the container to his brother.

"We can stay a few more hours, then we'll have to head home to milk cows and get some other chores done. Now that we've decided to try dairy farming like some of the other farmers in the area, we've been adding to the herd." Jake bit into the cookie, then closed his eyes and made sounds of pleasure.

"I understand you needing to get back to the farm. We've come so far already, I'm sure we'll be ready to open as planned." Annie brushed crumbs from her skirt. "Rebecca and I have already begun categorizing and shelving books."

Hope glanced behind her, then turned back. "Am I imagining it, or is Rebecca happier than I've ever seen her?"

"I've noticed changes in her too." Annie grinned. "You know . . . I think I almost like her."

"That would be a switch!" Jake chuckled and stretched out on the grass.

Annie gave him a little shove in the side. "I think Rebecca has been trying to find ways to prove to people she's not as mean and conniving as she used to be."

"Whatever is causing the transformation, I hope it continues to work."

"Hope and pray, Jake." Annie laughed. "I'll admit that Rebecca has been a great help. She's devoted many hours to getting the library ready. The inside looks welcoming, don't you think, Hope?" Annie looked to her cousin, who nodded. "Not all of the shelves are filled with books, but we have a good start."

Hope passed the container filled with cookies to Ben. "There's a good mix of nonfiction and fiction for adults, and one corner of the back room has been designated for children's books."

"I want to make it inviting and magical." Annie wore a faraway expression. "Mrs. Jorgenson has this wonderful idea of offering a story time for the younger ones on Saturday mornings. People who come into town to do their shopping can leave their children with us while they shop or while they look for books themselves."

"Have you figured out how you're going to run a library and still work at the Home Store?" Ben admired Annie's passion and willingness to throw herself into providing the town with a library, but at this point it was all on a volunteer basis.

"Rebecca, Mrs. Jorgenson, and I will work out a schedule for us to work in the library, and eventually we'll train other volunteers." Annie gave Jake a smile. "And your brother agreed to make a trip with me to Martindale once a month to rotate inventory with the library there."

So Annie had found another way to spend time with Jake. If his brother was as smart as Ben thought, he'd finally realize that Annie was in love with him, and he'd admit to himself how much he cared for her too.

Jake threw a handful of grass at Annie.

She blew it out of her face, and swept it from her shoulders. "I guess you're ready to go back to work." She gave him another shove, then stood.

Ben glanced at Hope and felt a pang. Could they ever be that free with each other? He wanted to be more at ease with her—he wanted to share himself without holding back. But until he could trust her completely, he couldn't allow himself.

"What's all the shouting?" Hope stood, and facing the library, shielded her eyes.

"Oh, no!" Annie grimaced. "It's that grouchy Mr. Stone from next door. He complained the day of the fundraiser that we were making too much commotion. Can you believe it? He lives alone and rarely leaves his shack. You'd think the old codger would like a little company and entertainment to liven up his day."

"Have you sat and talked with him?" It was strange that Ben had never met the man. The town was small enough that he knew most of the residents, at least by name.

"I tried the day of the fundraiser, but he was too riled, and I was probably too defensive." Annie sighed. "But something has to be done. We can't have him causing disruptions every time people want to visit the library. He'll scare them off."

"Don't worry." Ben laid his hand on her shoulder. "I'll see what I can do." There had to be something more to Mr. Stone's complaints than a little noise.

"Wait. I'll come with you." Hope packed and closed the picnic basket. "There's still food left. Maybe Mr. Stone would like something to eat while we talk."

Ben couldn't keep back a proud grin. *That's my girl. My girl.* When had he started thinking of her that way? "Good idea. A full mouth may stop him from yelling at us."

Mr. Stone stood shouting at a young man who looked fifteen and who held a brush in one hand and a small bucket of paint in the other. "You people think you own the world!"

The older man shook a crooked finger at the boy. "Well, you don't!"

The youth looked at Ben and Hope with wide eyes that asked for help.

Mrs. Jorgenson had been working in the flower gardens in front of the library with a young woman, but now she walked over and stood next to Hope.

"You can go back to work," Ben said to the painter with a nod of assurance. Ben relaxed his stance and offered a genuine smile as he sent up a silent prayer. "Mr. Stone, you hungry?"

☙

Hope held her breath. The man certainly wasn't the friendly type, but Ben seemed to be ignoring that fact.

"What if I am? You think you can bribe me to be quiet?" Mr. Stone's angry tone sounded closer to growling than speaking.

"I have no intention to bribe you for anything. I'd like to have a word with you, but out of consideration I also don't want to waste your time. Figured if you hadn't eaten, we might as well kill two birds."

Mr. Stone shuffled his feet. "Well, I guess I could eat. If you're offering."

"I'm offering." Ben pointed to a small group of empty chairs on the lawn that would be placed back inside the library at the end of the day. "We can sit over there."

How cleverly Ben had taken command of the situation while keeping the older man's self-respect intact. Hope slid onto the chair opposite Mr. Stone, and Mrs. Jorgenson sat next to her.

"I hope you don't mind that I've poked my way in." Mrs. Jorgenson whispered to Hope. "I've known Warren Stone for years, and I might be able to help."

Ben held up two sandwiches. "Chicken or egg salad?"

The thin, elderly man held out a wrinkled hand littered with dark spots and crooked fingers with knuckles twice the normal size. "Chicken. Egg salad gives me stomachaches." He unwrapped the sandwich and took a large bite. After swallowing, he wiped his mouth on his sleeve. "Not bad."

"Glad to hear it." Ben cleared his throat. "Mr. Stone, no one wants to bother you or disrupt your life by putting a library here. It's meant for the good of the town, and you're a part of the community too."

Mr. Stone grunted and slapped his thigh. "I don't understand why you all think there's a need for a library anyway. It's just going to cause trouble. Look at all those young people carrying on. The library will become a place for them to meet and cause all kinds of nuisance. Mark my words." He bit off another bite of sandwich and talked around it, his right cheek puffed out. "A man can't even think! I built my house on the river so I could have peace and quiet, and now it's been stolen from me."

Hope's stomach was growing uneasy, but it wasn't the lunch she'd eaten. Mr. Stone was like a boulder that wasn't going to budge. How could Ben still smile and remain so calm? He'd revealed an endearing inner strength, and she inwardly cheered him on.

"Is there something else that's bothering you that you're not telling us?" Ben leaned forward, but he kept his voice calm and caring. "I'm having a hard time believing that a little noise from people having a good time is what's really upsetting you."

Mrs. Jorgenson cleared her throat. "Warren, I know the house belonged to Jonas. Is that what's really bothering you?"

"It was his home." Mr. Stone's eyes filled with anguish. "He was my best friend, but he was more like a brother. After our wives died, we still lived next to each other for years. I didn't have anyone else and neither did he. After he passed, I could at least walk through the rooms of that house and remember all the good times we had together." His voice cracked. "But now everything is changed, and I won't even have that anymore. Everything is being taken away from me."

His irritability made sense now. Hope glanced at Mrs. Jorgenson and saw the empathy in her eyes. The elderly man was still grieving the loss of his closest friend. Every stroke of the hammer on the library's walls was like pounding a nail into his heart. How was Ben going to handle this new development?

"I'm so sorry. There was never any intention to disrespect Jonah's memory." By the pained expression on his face, Ben also hurt for the man. "Can you look at the situation another way?"

"There is no other way!"

"There may be." Ben shifted in his chair, as though preparing to say something important. "Instead of looking at the library as a horrible thing that has destroyed your friend's home, maybe you could think of it as a monument to your friend and his legacy left to the town. A place where everyone will remember him."

Mr. Stone perked up. "You mean like name it after him?"

Ben eyed Mrs. Jorgenson. "What do you think?"

She thought for a moment. "Hope, would Annie agree to it?"

"I can't speak for her, but it wouldn't hurt to ask." Hope couldn't imagine that Annie would care about the name being changed from the Riverton Library to something else. It was most important that the doors opened and the community used and enjoyed the library. And that the closest neighbor didn't harass patrons.

"The Jonas Hall Library has a nice ring to it." Mrs. Jorgenson tapped her chin with her finger. "The town council would have to approve, but I think at least a plaque with his name would be in order. After all, Jonas did donate the land and building to the town."

"That would be wonderful. Really wonderful." Mr. Stone's body relaxed, and a slight smile grew on his face. He almost looked huggable.

Mrs. Jorgenson leaned forward. "Warren, what are your favorite books? I want to be sure to have them available for you when we open."

His face darkened to red. "I—I don't read. Never learned how."

"Didn't you go to school?" Mrs. Jorgenson sounded alarmed.

"Did, but had to quit to help on the farm. My wife did all the reading we needed."

"Well, if you could read, what would you choose?" Mrs. Jorgenson spoke with kindness and without judgment.

"What are you interested in? Is there any place you'd like to visit?"

Mr. Stone seemed to hesitate, then he licked his lips. "Always wondered what it would have been like to live in the Wild West. Be a real cowboy."

"Then that's where we'll start." Mrs. Jorgenson smiled. "I'll teach you how to read."

"I'm a old man! My chance to learn is long past gone."

"Warren Stone," Mrs. Jorgenson said with authority, "are you doubting my ability as a teacher? I've taught numerous children how to read over the years, and I can certainly teach you."

Pure joy spread across the elderly man's face. "All right, I'll take you up on your offer." His grin quickly faded. "I don't have any money to pay you."

"I don't require payment. But you can help us put the tulip and daffodil bulbs in the flower gardens in front of the library. And I'll expect you to assist with weeding come spring." Mrs. Jorgenson stood. "Come along, Mr. Stone. There are several bags of bulbs left to stick in the ground."

Fifteen

"Did I witness a miracle or did I imagine what just happened?" Hope turned to Ben, who seemed slightly stunned himself. "One moment Mr. Stone is angry and can't understand the need for a library, and the next, he's agreeing to help Mrs. Jorgenson plant tulip bulbs in the yard."

Ben chuckled and shook his head. "God is faithful."

"He certainly is." Hope released a large sigh. "Something good actually came out of what could have been a disastrous situation. Mr. Stone will learn to read, and a whole new world will open up to him. And I like the idea of naming the library after his friend."

"Let's pray the council agrees."

"Everything is coming together for Annie. I'm so happy for her."

"Are you?"

"What kind of question is that? Of course I am." Hope focused on her hands in her lap. "But, I'll admit, I'm a little envious too. Aren't you?" She looked at him. "You once had visions of being a well-known painter. I can't believe that you don't still wonder what it would be like to see your work hanging in a gallery."

"Doesn't matter. That path is no longer an option for me." He stretched out his legs in front of him. "I'll try to get a moment with Annie today to tell her about my art. Can't put it off any longer. Wanted you to know that she may . . ."

"Have a lot to talk about when we get home."

"She'll either be thrilled, or she'll want to hang me for keeping it a secret from her for two years."

"Knowing Annie, probably both." It was a good thing he'd warned her. Hope would be prepared for both ranting and a lot of questions. It would be a late night for sure, but it would be worth it. She couldn't abide keeping Ben's secret from Annie much longer, especially when one of his paintings hung in Hope's bedroom.

"How are your sketches coming?"

That was unexpected—him asking or caring. "I think they're improving, and now if I ever have trouble mixing colors I know who to go to for help."

Ben laughed. "Yes, you do."

"Do you really want to know how I'm doing? With my designs, I mean?"

His laughter-filled eyes grew serious. "I really want to know."

"I received another rejection from Butterick, along with a request to keep submitting. They see potential in my work, but the designs aren't what they're looking for at the moment. I'm trying to be encouraged by the fact that they don't want me to give up."

"I agree. That's great news."

"There's more." Butterflies stirred inside Hope.

"Oh?"

"I'm taking a trip to Minneapolis the second weekend in September to see a friend of my mother's."

"Minneapolis?" His forehead furrowed. "What does that have to do with Butterick?"

"Eva Lancaster is a fashion designer who has done quite well for herself. She and my mother met while Miss Lancaster lived in New York, and she's willing to look at my sketches." Surely he could see the significance. "I'm sure I'll learn a great deal from even a few moments with her."

"How long will you be gone?"

"One night. Annie is traveling with me. We'll spend Saturday afternoon in the city and the night at the West Hotel, which will be a costly, but I want our first trip to Minneapolis to be a real treat. Annie has never stayed in a luxury hotel, and I need a taste of what I miss from New York. We often don't appreciate something until it's no longer within reach."

He gave a low, quiet grunt. "And Miss Lancaster?"

"We're invited to dine with her that evening." She didn't expect him to shout with excitement over her opportunity, but he could have shown even a little enthusiasm. Minneapolis wasn't New York or Paris, but it was the closest thing she had right now.

"I'm sure you'll have a good time." He stretched his arms in front of him and then behind his back. "I gotta get back to work."

"All right . . . I should check in with Annie and see where she needs help." *Men!* And they claimed women were hard to understand. He almost sounded disappointed that she was looking forward to spending a little time away from Riverton.

He headed in one direction, and Hope went the other, searching for Annie. There she stood, next to one of the flowerbeds, speaking to Mrs. Jorgenson and Mr. Stone and nodding her head. Mr. Stone shook Annie's hand, then followed his soon-to-be teacher to a patch of dirt where tulip and daffodil bulbs were laid out.

Annie grinned at Hope. "The Jonas Hall Library."

"So I hear." Hope embraced her cousin, then drew back. "I think it's perfect."

"Yes, perfect." Annie's smile drooped, and a shimmer of moisture covered the beautiful green eyes that now focused somewhere behind Hope's back. Annie swiped beneath her right eye. "Men. I don't understand them."

"Funny. That's just what I was thinking." Hope turned. So that's what had caused Annie's sudden change of emotions.

Jake seemed to be joking with a young woman who had recently moved to Riverton with her parents and younger brother to re-open a bank that had closed after the owner decided to move to a larger town. The pretty brunette, around twenty years old, had volunteered to help Rebecca catalog the books, and in the process had apparently caught Jake's eye.

"You have to come with me." Annie clutched Hope's hand, and her nails dug into Hope's palm as she pulled her toward the bench where Jake and the temptress sat side by side.

"What are you doing?" Hope was mortified. "You can't go over there and reprimand him for paying attention to some-one else."

Annie stopped short. "Thomas left instructions for me before he headed back to his farm, and I'm going to make sure they're carried out. That's all." Her lower lip quivered. "But I'm not going over there alone. Not with him hanging on her words like they're dripping honey."

Hope's heart ached for her sweet cousin. Why couldn't Jake see how much Annie loved him? How devoted she was to him? "I'll go with you."

Their shadows almost covered Jake and the seductress before he noticed they were standing right in front of him.

The young woman was probably very nice and shouldn't be thought of in derogatory terms. Like most people in Riverton, she was most likely taken in by Jake's charming ways, and Hope didn't have any reason to think such ill thoughts, despite how protective she felt toward Annie.

"Annie, you need something?" Jake looked at her with an innocence that relayed the fact that he didn't have any idea of how much his flirting with this girl hurt her.

"I wouldn't have interrupted, but could you please look at the roof before you leave for the day?" Annie's voice was smooth and controlled. She was hiding her emotions well. Not easy for her, Hope knew.

"Annie and Hope, have you met Miss Oakland?" Jake's eyes twinkled as he gestured toward the newcomer. "You probably already know that her father is the new banker in town."

"Nice to meet you, Miss Oakland," Annie said with a slight tip of her head. "We appreciate you helping Rebecca catalog the books for the library, especially being so new to our community."

Good girl, Annie! "Hello, Miss Oakland. And yes, thank you for your help." Hope extended a smile, praying it looked relaxed and genuine.

"Please call me Laura." The slight bloom in her cheeks made her unusual blue-violet eyes even more striking. They reminded Hope of the pansies that grew in Annie's backyard.

"It seems friends use less formality here, and if Jake is yours, I'd like to be too."

"Of course." Hope glanced at Annie and glimpsed her clenched hands behind her back.

"Jake, I really do need you to check the roof before you leave to milk cows." Annie's calm voice lacked its usual warmth.

"All right, I heard you." Jake sat up from his relaxed position on the bench.

"Thomas has replaced most of the roof, but he couldn't get to the front part where most of the books are already shelved." Annie's voice hitched. "He started on that area this morning, but he was up all night with a sick cow and had to head back to the farm to tend to the animal."

Jake scratched the back of his neck. "If I'd known, I would have fixed it earlier today."

"I know. It's not your fault. Thomas didn't realize the roof was in such bad shape until he climbed up there this morning. He'll replace that part of the roof on Monday, but dark clouds are forming in the west, and he's afraid rain is coming our way."

"Those clouds over there? That's nothing, Annie." Jake leaned against the bench. "We got blue skies and sunshine. Those clouds will blow over. Even if there's a slight shower, it won't last long."

"If you don't have the time, I can ask someone else." By the tone of Annie's voice, she was working hard to keep calm. "Nice to meet you, Laura. You're welcome at the library any time." Annie swung around and took several steps.

Hope put her hand on Jake's arm, tilted her head Annie's direction, and gave him a weak smile.

"Wait!" Jake jumped up from the bench. "Annie, wait."

She faced him, the crestfallen look on her face showing her disappointment.

"I'll climb up there and take a look."

"You promise?" Doubt saturated her tone.

"I promise."

༄

The second-story bedroom felt hot enough to roast a small chicken. Now that the August sun had turned in for the night and black clouds moved across a darkening sky, a cool breeze teased the curtains to perform a delicate dance.

Hope turned the knob on the bedside kerosene lamp. Annie and her mother hadn't switched to using carbide lamps like several people in town, but Hope didn't mind. From what she'd learned, carbide lighting was inexpensive but prone to gas leaks and explosions, and although electric lights were becoming popular in New York, it would most likely be some time before smaller communities like Riverton embraced them.

A mosquito buzzed around her head, and she batted it away. Pesky thing! Hope tucked her knees in close to her chest and wrapped her arms around them to keep her thin nightgown from billowing as the wind cooled her warm body. A storm was brewing. She'd need to lower the window, but not yet.

Her cousin, dressed in a white summer nightgown, leaned against the bedroom door frame. "May I come in?"

"Of course." Hope waved her in. "I didn't realize you'd come home. I'm sorry I needed to leave before you finished at the library. It must have been working under that hot sun all afternoon that caused my headache, because I felt much better after I got back here and cooled off."

"The heat was bothering other people too. It was best for you to come home and rest." Annie sat on the edge of the bed. "It's been quite a day."

"A long and productive day. Quite a few townspeople pitched in—you should be proud."

"I am. Proud and happy." Sadness in Annie's voice relayed something different.

It broke Hope's heart, especially at a time when Annie would otherwise be spinning around the room with her face lit up like a beacon. "I'm sorry Jake hurt you today by spending time with Miss Oakland."

"I should know better than to let it bother me. Jake sees me as a little sister—nothing more."

"I'm not so sure, Annie. I've seen the way he looks at you." Since she'd arrived in Riverton, Hope had caught Jake watching Annie more than once while she was unaware, his eyes filled with affection. He adored her.

"You're sweet to try to make me feel better, but I need to accept reality." Annie's shoulders heaved a large sigh. "Then there's his brother. After you left, Ben pulled me aside to tell me that not only is he an artist, but he donated the painting hanging on your wall." She sounded—stunned. "No wonder he's felt compelled to offer his opinions on your work."

"It was probably a lot to take in, but I'm glad Ben finally told you."

Annie sprawled across the bed, then propped her head on one hand. "It was about time." Her finger traced a pattern on the quilt covering the top of the bed. "I'm just a little hurt and disappointed that it took this long for Ben to be honest with me. I thought we were better friends." Her accusing eyes met Hope's. "He said you've known for a while."

"Remember when I took supper to him on the Fourth of July? I surprised him while he was painting in the shed. I wasn't exactly invited into that private world—it was more like an invasion into hostile territory until a peace treaty was agreed on."

"But that was almost two months ago, and you didn't breathe a word of it to me." Annie sounded bruised by Hope withholding information.

Opposite of her usual cheery voice, the accusing tone felt like a knife making a slow cut into Hope's heart. Of course Annie felt betrayed. Wouldn't Hope have struggled with similar feelings in her cousin's position?

"I wanted to tell you. I did, Annie, but I couldn't." Every part of Hope yearned to reach out to her cousin. "You don't know how difficult it was to keep that secret from you."

Annie bolted up and sat across from Hope. "We rode out to the farm, so he could show me himself."

"Ben wanted to share that part of his life with you, Annie, because he cares about your friendship." Hope reached over and grasped Annie's hand. "Even though he may not admit it, I think it's torn him up inside to keep that part of himself locked up from you."

"He did seem a bit relieved—but I didn't know if that was from finally coming clean or the fact that I didn't punch him." A twinkle returned to Annie's eyes. "He's talented, isn't he?" she asked, her voice filled with recognition and awe.

Hope nodded. "His work is breathtaking."

"One day we might be able to say that we know a famous painter," Annie whispered with enthusiasm.

"In order to become famous, you first have to be willing to let people see your art." Hope's focus shifted, and she gestured toward the picture hanging on her wall. "Now you have your answer as to who painted that beautiful piece, but unfortunately Ben doesn't want anyone else to know about his remarkable ability."

Annie twirled one of her red curls around her finger. "That is a bit of a problem." She looked at Hope and raised an eyebrow. "So what are we going to do about it?"

"I'm working on an idea . . ."

Lightning exploded across the sky, its bright flash obliterating any shadows in the room for a moment. A loud boom of thunder followed, echoing through the night. Raindrops began to fall, first slowly, but only for seconds before the heavens opened, releasing a torrent.

As Hope rushed to close the window, a gust heavy with water sprayed her with cool droplets. Outside, trees bowed to the wind as if worshiping its strength. She slammed the window shut and rearranged the disheveled curtains. "I didn't expect the storm to come in so—" Hope turned around to face Annie right behind her. "What's wrong?"

"He wouldn't, would he?" Annie's eyes were as large as the asters she grew in the backyard, and her chest rose as she gasped for air.

"Come on." Hope wrapped her arm around Annie's shoulder, led her back to the edge of the bed, and coaxed her to sit. "What's got you all worked up?"

"I have this terrible feeling in my stomach." Annie squeezed her eyes shut. "He promised me."

"Who promised you what? You're not making any sense."

"Remember, Thomas was concerned about a section of roof on the library, but he had to get back to his farm before he had a chance to take another look. Jake promised me he would take care of it."

Hope squeezed Annie's shoulder. "Then why are you so worried?"

"He could easily say one thing while distracted by another."

"He wouldn't do that to you."

"I've seen it before. If something piques Jake's interest, he can change direction as fast as a hummingbird can switch course in flight. I didn't get a chance to talk to him again before he left the library today, and I didn't see him at the farm either. I'll give you one guess as to what—or who—grabbed his attention." Annie rubbed her temples. "One thing is for sure . . . I won't get any sleep tonight."

Hope took Annie's hand in her own. "There are other certainties. We can pray, and God will hear. Another is that I'm going with you first thing in the morning to see if there's any damage."

There wouldn't be any rest for either of them until they knew the building was safe from devastation. Annie had worked hard to make the library a reality, and she didn't deserve to have her dreams dashed now.

Sixteen

Hope couldn't bear to look at Annie. Not yet.

A portion of the library's roof had caved in over the front room where books had already been shelved. Wind strong enough to topple several trees and break large branches from others nearby had ripped through the space, scattering papers and catalog files from the desk top in all directions, donating them to the muddy mix.

Not saying a word, Annie stepped to one shelf and trailed her fingers down the spine of one book after another, as though saying good-bye. Then she moved to the table standing beneath the gaping hole in the ceiling that exposed a gray, drizzling sky. She opened the cover to *Little Women*, her shaking fingers attempting to separate the soaked pages. Tears streamed down her cheeks.

It was painful to watch, and Hope covered her mouth to stifle a sob.

"*David Copperfield.*" Annie began to whisper book titles as if honoring soldiers fallen to their death. "*Heidi.*" She held the book to her chest before laying it down again. "So much ruin. How could we ever ask townspeople to donate their hard-earned money again?"

A floorboard creaked, and Annie and Hope turned in unison toward the door.

"Annie . . ." Jake, gripping his hat in his hands, stayed

close to the door. Ben stood not far behind him.

"Go away, Jake!" Annie's eyes filled with tears as she half-cried at him. "I don't want you here!"

"I'm so sorry, Annie." Desperation rang in his voice. "I'm here to help—both me and Ben. We'll do whatever you say."

"I don't need your help, Jacob," Annie sputtered. "I was stupid to ask for it yesterday. I should have known I couldn't count on you."

"I know I let you down." Jake took several steps closer.

"Me and everyone else in Riverton." Annie wiped tears from her eyes, then her cheeks, as though defying any attempt to soften her heart toward him. "What happened anyway, Jake? Laura Oakland?"

Color flushed Jake's face, and he turned to Ben.

"Tell her the truth." Ben nodded toward Annie. "She deserves at least that much."

"Rebecca Hoyt invited Laura—Miss Oakland—and me to supper at her home. They insisted, and I thought it might be a good opportunity to get to know Dr. Hoyt better." Jake glanced back at his brother. "Ben said he'd take care of the milking, so I accepted the invite."

"Don't bring me into this mess." Ben sounded frustrated. "If I'd known you'd made a promise to Annie, I never would have agreed."

Jake squirmed. "I should have just told them I had things to take care of, but I forgot about the roof. I'm so sorry!"

Hope caught Ben's eyes, and from what she could read in them, he was almost as angry with the situation as Annie.

"Jake, I don't believe you accepted an invitation so you could talk to a vet. There was more to it." Annie's chin quivered. "I don't want your help—and I don't want to be your friend anymore."

"Awww, come on, Annie." Jake reached for her.

Annie drew back as though his touch would scorch her. "You just don't get it. I've loved you since the day you sat at our table and downed two pieces of my blackberry pie, even though it might have been the worst tasting concoction made this side of the Mississippi."

Jake's eyes filled with pain. "Annie, we've been good friends, but I never believed you could love me, well, not in the way . . ."

"I did—love you." Annie's face flamed as red as her hair. "I'm not so sure anymore. But even if I still did, it doesn't matter because it's obvious you don't feel the same way. If you cared at all about me, even as a friend, you wouldn't have betrayed me."

"Betrayed you?"

"You know how much this library means to me. Yet, having supper with the new girl in town was more important than your promise to take a little time to check the roof." Annie picked up the damp copy of *Little Women* and cradled it against her chest. "That's just the way you are, Jake. You're charming and fun-loving, but you're incapable of making any commitments—even to me."

"You got it wrong, Annie."

"I don't think so." Annie turned away from him. "Please go, Jake. I don't want you here."

Jake looked at Ben, who kept a stern face and shook his head, then he glanced at Hope.

"You'd better go, Jake," Hope said softly. Annie had every right to be upset about the mess, and now she was probably also embarrassed about blurting out her feelings. She never

would have confessed to loving Jake under normal circumstances, but this wasn't an everyday situation, and her emotions had to be struggling to stay beneath the surface.

"No." Jake stiffened his back, hitched his thumbs on his
belt, and faced Annie. "I'm not leaving—not yet."

Hope felt Ben's warm and gentle grasp on her shoulders.
He attempted to direct her toward the door, but she
shrugged him off. "What are you doing?"

Instead of answering, he grabbed her elbow and led her
outside. There he released her.

"Benjamin, what on earth?"

"We have no business in there right now."

"Are you crazy? Can't you see that she's devastated?"
Hope felt confident her cousin was desperate for someone to
rescue her from being in the same room as Jake.

"I'm not blind, Hope. Of course she's upset. She has plenty of reasons to be angry and hurt." He stared at the building
as the inhabitants' escalating voices spilled from the open
door, tripping over each. Then silence blasted through the
opening. "Think she killed him?"

"That isn't funny." Hope took several steps toward the library. "Annie needs me."

Ben jumped in front of her. "What they *need* is to be
alone." His warm eyes peered into hers. "You want to fix everyone's problems, but this time you have to let things take
their course."

"First jokes, then insults." Hope blinked to soothe the
prickles assaulting her eyes. What was wrong with trying to
be helpful? It wasn't like she was planning on galloping into
the building on a white horse, brandishing a sword. But he
was right. Fixing problems made her feel good, like when

she took it upon herself to make a wedding dress for Rachel.

The corners of his lips curved into a small smile. "Look—I think Annie is perfect for Jake, and he'll figure that out, but without our interference."

"But the mess . . . I don't want Annie to think I've abandoned her." Based on the look on her face earlier, Annie felt overwhelmed by the work it would take to put everything back in order.

"There'll be time to clean up later." He tilted his head toward town. "We still have time to get to the church service if we hurry. The best thing we can do now is pray for Annie and Jake, and we can rustle up some help while we're there."

"I suppose you're right." Now they had less than a week to make repairs and still open the library by the first Saturday in September, but Hope had already seen the way townspeople had pitched in with enthusiasm to get the building ready. "At least Annie and Jake have stopped yelling, so that's a good sign things might be on the mend. I don't want this mistake to come between them."

"Just because people fight or have their differences doesn't mean they don't care about each other." Ben winked at her. "Sometimes it's proof that they do."

Was he talking about Jake and Annie, or the two of them?

Seventeen

Ten minutes after leaving Jake and Annie alone at the library, Ben trailed Hope down the aisle as the congregation stood and began singing the first verse of "Holy, Holy, Holy! Lord God Almighty." He slipped in next to her where she found an opening in a pew three rows from the front. He didn't need to witness the stares—he felt them. Hope seemed oblivious to the tilting heads from the row directly across and those in front of them, worshipers trying to get a glimpse of the couple. Were they a couple? Warmth flowed through his veins at the possibility.

This was nice—sharing a hymnal with her—singing and praising God's mercy and might. Although Hope's beautiful lips barely whispered the lyrics, her countenance glowed. He'd pray that she'd someday be liberated from worrying about what people thought of her voice and feel free to sing from the heart just for God.

The song ended and heads bowed in prayer. As they did, Ben's arm brushed against Hope's. He reached for her hand, and his fingertips grazed hers before she clasped her hands in front of her. Did she notice his move was intentional? Or did she think it was only coincidence?

Ben tried to concentrate on the message, and although he was usually immersed in the reverend's sermons his mind wandered. Hope might be struggling with similar questions.

Had Jake and Annie made peace? Or had he crushed her heart? Ben had suspected months ago that his younger brother wasn't being totally honest with himself or Annie about his strong feelings for her. It was about time the truth came out, for both their sakes.

Then there was the mess at the library. How were they going to get all the water soaked up and the roof fixed, and how many books could be salvaged? Where would they find help? This was a busy time for farmers. Most were in the fields from sunup until sundown. Jake and Ben had already set aside some of their own chores to make time to work on the library. Now there was so much more to do, and with the library set to open in six days the pressure seemed greater than before.

They stood to sing the last hymn, and even though he knew the song by heart, Ben took advantage of sharing the hymnal with Hope so he'd have an excuse to stand close to her. He caught another whiff of her perfume. It smelled like spring. Light, not heavy like that stuff Mrs. Hoyt doused herself with. You could smell that woman coming twenty feet away.

"Please be seated." Instead of making his way down the aisle to greet people as they exited the church, Reverend Caswell motioned for his wife to join him from her seat in the first row. "You come, too, Mary."

Sarah rocked a small bundle in her arms while Mary moved up and down on her tiptoes with a grin as wide as a quarter moon and as bright as a full one on a cloudless night.

Reverend Caswell couldn't have beamed more himself. "As most of you know, ten days ago we welcomed into our family a little boy, Joseph Martin Caswell. We want to thank you all for the kindness and generosity extended to our family—and your patience at having to wait to meet him. We haven't gotten much sleep, as you can imagine." Chuckles rippled through the church. "But as tired as we are, we feel honored and blessed to have him. Children are a gift." Heads nodded, and some murmured agreement. "You're welcome to take a look at the handsome little prince, but I have to warn you that he's probably getting hungry, so just a quick peek."

As if in agreement, the infant let out a short cry, and the congregation burst into laughter. The reverend led his family to the front door of the church where he could personally welcome those in attendance.

Hope seemed deep in thought, so Ben remained seated beside her until most of the crowd had spilled into the warm sunshine outside.

"Ready?" Ben stepped aside to let Hope go ahead of him down the aisle. "But if you'd like more time to sit and think—or pray—we can stay."

"No, we should find Thomas and ask him about fixing the roof." She perked up, and she grew a sweet smile. "Besides, I've waited long enough to catch a glimpse of the new little prince. That's what the reverend called him, right?" They sauntered down the aisle, side by side. "With those two parents, he's bound to have all the traits you'd think should come with royalty. He'll be charming, kind, wise, generous, and handsome."

Ben raised an eyebrow. "You've read too many fairytales. He'll most likely tease, play in dirt, climb trees, and challenge any limits his parents give him."

"Is that what you did as a boy?" She stopped and faced

him, a hint of smile on her face. "Rebel against your parents?"

"No." Painful memories of the boyhood fight that changed everything assailed him. "I just managed to hurt them in other ways."

The smile fled, and her eyes filled with recognition, then regret. "Ben, I'm sorry . . ."

"We'd better see the newcomer before we lose our chance," Ben said with a lighter tone than he felt.

"Yes. The baby." Hope turned on her heels and made straight for the child, with Ben close behind.

They said their congratulations, and then he stepped back. Ben liked babies as much as anyone, but hovering like a mother hen over one? Leave the cooing to the women. Still, if he ever had a son, he'd be itching for the day when he could take him fishing or riding, and every boy needed a dog to play with and explore.

"Would you like to hold him?" Sarah, her eyes shining with pride, swayed back and forth in lullaby rhythm. Did all mothers perform that dance? His sister, Ruth, did the same thing when his nephew was born.

Hope cradled Joseph in her arms as she moved left, then right.

Hmmm . . . not just mothers.

"You have a sweet baby brother, Mary." Hope smiled at the six-year-old sticking close to her sibling.

The little girl grinned, showing a gap where a front tooth was missing. "I love him even when he cries at night."

Ben crossed his arms and leaned his backside against the rear pew and grinned. *Just wait until he threatens to put worms down your back.*

The sun's rays filtering through the stained glass windows behind Hope surrounded her with light, making her glow like a blond Madonna with child. His heart and hands ached to paint Hope just like that, but even the most masterful artist couldn't capture the essence of what he was seeing and feeling at that moment.

Thomas and Ellie sent their three children outside, then Thomas sauntered over to the pew and mirrored Ben's position.

Ellie peeked at the baby. "You precious little boy." She gave Sarah a hug. "Have you heard from your parents?"

"We received a telegram from my mother. She sent their love, and said the news raised my father's spirits. They both wish they could be here." Sarah smiled, but her eyes betrayed sadness. "My father's health is failing, and I don't know how much longer he'll be able to hold on. After all this time separated from them, I can't bear the thought of losing him just when we've made plans to move them here to be with us."

"We'll keep them in our prayers," Ellie said.

Ben nudged Thomas. "Where are Sarah's parents?" he whispered. "I assumed they were both deceased. I've never heard her mention them."

"They're in San Francisco." Thomas lowered his voice. "Sarah was raised by her grandmother here in Riverton. Her parents headed out to California without her after her father got into some trouble with gambling. Sarah didn't even know they were alive until two years ago."

A low whistle slipped through Ben's lips. "I can't imagine what it would be like to grow up without my folks."

"Family is everything." Thomas shifted his body, and after uncrossing his arms he gripped the pew railing behind him with both hands. "We can laugh about the women cooing over the baby, but man-to-man, becoming a father was one of the best days of my life."

"Same here." Reverend Caswell stepped next to Thomas.

"Peter, good sermon this morning." Ben reached out to shake the reverend's hand.

He accepted with a grin, then scratched the area at the top of at his clerical collar. "Can't wait to get out of this thing. Every time I move, the edge rubs on a mosquito bite, and the itching is driving me crazy."

Thomas chuckled. "Your wife went through hours of labor to give you a son, and you're complaining about a little bug bite?"

"I'm rightfully humbled. Thanks, friend." Peter grinned, then glanced at the women still fussing with the newborn. "He is a miracle." He gripped Thomas's shoulder. "I can't tell you how grateful I was to have Ellie there during the birth."

"You've already thanked me—several times."

"Remember when Ellie first mentioned she wanted to become a midwife? How you balked at the idea?"

Thomas nodded. "I had good reason. I thought she had enough to do with taking care of four children and helping on the farm."

"What changed your mind?" Ben was sincerely interested. From everything he'd witnessed, these two men seemed to have happy, strong marriages. Could he ever have the same?

"Peter and I had several long conversations, and he convinced me that I needed to figure out God's will and not trust my own understanding of how my relationship with Ellie should work." Thomas looked in his wife's direction, his countenance filled with love and admiration. "One night while I was alone in the barn milking, I decided to pray, and right then and there, God opened my eyes. Helping bring babies into the world was something that was in her, and I had no right to stop Ellie from using the gifts he'd given her. I had to forget my stubborn pride, but trust me, it's been worth it just to see the joy it gives her. She also helps the doc once a week, and she always comes home excited about what she's learned. Seems she's got even more energy that she pours into our young'uns."

Ben glanced in Hope's direction. She'd need that type of husband—one who would encourage her. He could be that man.

Hope was starting to fidget. She turned her head, and her worry-filled eyes met his. Now that the service was over, and there was no sign of either Jake or Annie, Hope must have started to feel anxious.

"Where's Annie? Didn't she come to church this morning?" Sarah took the infant from Hope. "She's been so eager to meet Joseph."

"I wanted to have a few minutes with the baby and share your joy before relaying some bad news." Hope clasped her hands in front of her chest. "Annie and Jake are both at the library. Unfortunately, the storm last night did quite a bit of damage. There's a huge mess to clean up, and repairs need to be made to the roof as soon as possible. Annie is so heartbroken, she had to get right to work. But they—we— need as much help as we can get. Annie can't do this on her own."

Thomas groaned. "I knew I shouldn't have left yesterday before making sure the roof was solid."

"Please don't blame yourself," Hope said. "It wasn't your fault. Besides, the important thing now is that we give Annie our love and support, because she could use a large dose of both."

"I'll take my family home, then come back into town and get that roof in shape. If I have to leave to do the milking, I will, but I won't rest tonight until that part of the building is fixed.

"Our children can help too," Ellie said. "They need to change out of their Sunday clothes, but we'll all pitch in."

"Sarah will need to rest at home this afternoon, but I don't think God would mind me working on the Sabbath for a good cause." Peter scratched the side of his neck. "I'm actually pretty handy with a hammer and nails."

"Thank you." Hope hugged Ellie. "This is wonderful."

Ben's heart swelled in admiration and appreciation. Hope had explained what happened to the library without blaming Jake and his negligence. She could have crucified him, but she didn't even mention he'd been asked to check the roof. Ben was becoming more aware every day that Hope Andrews was one special woman.

◯ଷ

"That's all we can do for now, Annie. Besides, you're exhausted, and you haven't eaten a thing all day." Hope tugged Annie, her clothes now damp and dirty, through the entrance before closing the library door behind them. "We need to get you home."

Annie lumbered down the steps and onto the lawn. There, volunteers were gathering their cleaning supplies.

"Thank you, everyone. We couldn't have managed without your help." Despite the appreciative words, her familiar smile had gone into hiding, and her weary voice relayed some sadness.

"The roof is as good as new, Annie." Thomas threw his tools into the back of his wagon. "Shouldn't have any more trouble."

"Thanks for taking care of it, especially on a Sunday."

Hope didn't miss the tear balancing on the edge of her cousin's eyelashes. Even after all the help and encouragement, Annie looked like she was still struggling with her emotions and the huge setback because of water damage.

"No problem." Thomas jumped up into the wagon seat. "You need anything else, you let me know."

"You don't have a treasure chest filled with gold buried anywhere on the farm, do you? We could sure use it to replace lost books." Annie's attempt at humor brought a slight smile to Thomas's face.

"It'll all work out, Annie. You'll see." He waved as the wagon began moving down the road in the direction of his farm.

"Thomas is right." Rebecca set down the pail and rags she'd used to clean. "Mrs. Jorgenson and I will come over tomorrow, and the three of us will come up with a plan to get more books. Maybe the library in Martindale will be able to spare additional copies—just until we're able to purchase more." Rebecca put her arm around Annie. "I'm so sorry, Annie. Jake mentioned wanting to talk to my father about a problem he was having with a cow, so I invited him to supper. But I would have insisted that he fix the roof first had I known."

Jake had told the truth about why he'd gone to supper at the Hoyts'.

Hope glanced in Ben's direction, then back. "Rebecca, could you please keep Annie company for a moment? I need to speak with someone. It won't take long."

"Come on, Annie. My feet are tired, and they hurt. Let's sit in your buggy and rest a bit." With her arm still around Annie's shoulder, Rebecca nudged her away from the building.

Volunteers had taken their tools and cleaning supplies and dispersed, but Ben and Jake remained, now deep in conversation next to their wagon. Hope hesitated. Maybe she should leave.

No, with Annie clamming up, there was no other way to find out what had transpired between her and Jake while alone at the library that morning. Annie had barely said a word all afternoon, which felt disconcerting, considering friends looked to her to keep things lively and cheerful. Instead, she just kept cleaning, her thoughts locked within. Jake had remained at her side, unusually quiet, seeming to sense that starting a conversation was not only futile but possibly dangerous.

"You men heading home?" Hope kept a slight distance, ready to escape if not a welcomed intrusion.

"Hope, you gotta help me." Desperation etched Jake's features. "I'll do anything to make things right with Annie. Whatever it takes to fix things."

"I believe you, Jake, but the only time I've seen Annie more wounded was when her father died." Hope stepped closer. "She loves you, and that's what makes her disappointment even worse."

"I know . . ."

"Jake, have you told Annie how you feel about her?"

He nodded. "I tried, but I don't think she believed me."

"How *do* you feel?"

"Go on, Jake. Tell Hope." As Ben leaned against the wagon, his eyes remained focused on his brother.

"I've had strong feelings. For a long time." Jake bent over and leaned on his knees as he exhaled a deep breath. Then he stood and shoved his hands through his hair. "Ben warned me that if I wasn't careful, I could hurt her. But I kept burying my feelings. Her admitting that she loved me about made me drop to the ground."

"How could you not have known? It was so obvious."

"She's always teased and joked around with me like my sister, Ruth, so I thought I was just a brother to her."

"She loves you, but you'll have to win her trust again." Hope offered a smile. "Don't give up, but don't rush her."

"Nice and slow. I get it." Jake sighed. "I left a hammer and a box of nails out back. I better fetch them." He marched off with his head hanging low.

Ben straightened and shoved his hands in his front pants pockets. "Rough day. For both of them. But I'm glad they finally got some things out in the open."

"Yes, but unfortunately it took a disaster, and now it appears that Annie's not speaking to him." Hope glanced back at the buggy where Annie and Rebecca rested. She couldn't leave them waiting much longer.

"How today went—it makes me appreciate even more that I'm able to trust you."

"Trust me?"

"You know, to keep certain things to yourself even when

it may be difficult." His gaze fell to her lips and warmed them without even the slightest touch, quickening her heart. "Without trust, there is no relationship."

Hope wet her lips to cool them. "We have a relationship?"

He bent closer. "I think it's promising," he whispered in her ear, sending a shiver down her neck and spine. "And you?"

"I think there's hope," she whispered back, and he laughed at her teasing play on words.

Though she tried to offer a charming smile, a sharp pain stabbed her neck as muscles there tightened. What would he think—what would he feel— if he knew she'd arranged a meeting with a gallery owner while visiting Eva Lancaster in Minneapolis the following week?

Ben lacked faith in his work, but once a respected person in the art world saw Ben's painting and confirmed his exceptional talent, maybe he could believe it too. Hope had been willing to lose his friendship and anything else they might have together in the future because she believed making that appointment was the right thing to do.

But what if she was wrong?

Eighteen

I'm not going." Hope closed her dresser drawer. "I can't leave you behind or Mr. Carter in a mess."

"Hope, no! You can't be serious." Annie slumped on her bed next to the bag Hope was packing for the journey to Minneapolis in the morning. "You've planned and looked forward to this trip for weeks. You'll miss staying at the West Hotel. And dining with Miss Lancaster."

"What else am I supposed to do? Since that salesman from Milwaukee visited, half of the store employees have come down with the flu, and even Mr. Carter has been in bed since yesterday. I can't let him down. He's been too good to me."

"With my help, the store will be fine. There's no need for you to stay behind." A tear escaped one of Annie's big green eyes. Her red, blotchy face betrayed that she'd had a good cry before even stepping inside Hope's bedroom. "Of course I'm disappointed I won't be going with you, but I can't let that get in the way of you making the trip. It's important that you don't miss this opportunity to spend time with Miss Lancaster."

"But, Annie . . ."

"Please, Hope. You've stood by me these past weeks and worked hard to help get the library ready for the opening. By the grace of God and good people who volunteered, we met our deadline. Although the shelves aren't filled, we have enough books to call it a library, and the children enjoyed Mrs. Jorgenson's story time so much on opening day, I'm sure even more will attend tomorrow morning. Everything isn't perfect, but it's a start." Annie stood and grasped Hope's shoulders, her serious gaze sending a message. "You're always looking out for others, but now it's time to do something for yourself. It's your turn, Hope."

"Sweet words, but—"

"You're not worried about traveling alone, are you?"

Hope raised an eyebrow and smiled. "How quickly you've forgotten that I not only came much of the way from New York unaccompanied, but aside from the last months in Riverton, I've lived in a large city my entire life."

"I haven't forgotten." Annie's lips slid into a teasing smile. "Just wanted to make sure you still remembered." She released her grip on Hope and curled up on the bed.

"You're right. I can't pass up this opportunity to have Miss Lancaster look at my work. I also promised my mother that I'd share every detail of my trip with her in my next letter, and I'd hate to disappoint her. She's feeling so far away from everything familiar."

"I understand." Annie squinted and pointed to a flat rectangular object wrapped in brown paper, propped against the wall. "What is that?"

"That?"

"What are you up to, Hope?"

"Can I trust you to keep a secret?"

"How can you even ask that? You know you can."

"Even from Jake? The two of you have spent a lot of time together these last two weeks. Since the calamity at the library, he's stuck to your side like lint to a wool skirt."

"Hope?"

"It's a painting."

Annie bolted upright. "You're not—"

"I am. I have an appointment with a gallery owner to show him the painting." Hope's confidence in her decision weakened at seeing the look of horror on Annie's face.

"Ben will be furious."

"Maybe. Maybe not. It will probably depend on the result. He could be grateful."

"Knowing Ben, I doubt it." Annie grimaced. "He'll just feel that you've stepped into sacred territory."

"He has a gift. It needs to be shared."

"Your opinion. On the shared part."

Hope cringed at hearing Annie's words. The truth sometimes hurt. "But don't you think others will agree once they see his artistry?"

"It doesn't matter how many people feel the same way as you if Ben wants to keep this part of his life to himself."

"But if I could help him move beyond his fear . . ." Wouldn't that be worth breaking a promise of silence about his artistic skills?

"You think he's a coward?"

"When it comes to his art, yes, I do. But most of us are afraid of some form of rejection, aren't we? Take you and Jake, for example."

"It's not the same thing."

"Close enough. You were afraid to tell Jake how you really felt about him. But if you'd never blurted out that you loved him, those feelings would still be hidden deep inside, and you'd be frustrated and miserable."

"True. It wasn't how I wanted it to happen, but it forced us to talk about our friendship. I had no idea that he'd been confused for a long time about his feelings for me. It's going to take some time for me to trust him, but now we can try to figure things out together."

"That's what I want for Ben. The opportunity for him to hear how talented he is so that he can make decisions based on that information instead of hiding his work in a shed out of guilt over something that happened years ago."

"I'll keep your secret, and I'll pray for you." Annie wrapped her arms around Hope's shoulders. "Because if this doesn't go well . . ."

◌

Hope surveyed the West Hotel's immense lobby, the largest in the country, as she waited to check in. The last time she was in a place this grand, she and Henry had met his cousin, a senator from Maine, and his wife for the evening. The lovely time over dinner had been marred by Henry making fun of Hope's aspirations as a designer, even though his cousin's wife seemed quite interested in what Hope had to say.

Like a blacksmith shaping iron on an anvil, it struck Hope that she'd changed since moving to Riverton. She still never wanted to see Henry again, but she no longer struggled with fear when he came to mind.

Forget him, Hope. Focus on the present, and leave the past behind.

She pushed thoughts of Henry aside and tried to memorize every detail around her so she could give accurate descriptions when she returned to Riverton. If only she could have seen Annie's reaction to the elaborate architecture— thick pillars, the gabled roofs, bay windows, towers, and dormer windows. It was all so beautiful, and a slight wave of disappointment fell over her at not being able to share it in person with her cousin.

Not only did the hotel have 407 rooms and 140 baths, but it had also been the temporary home of Mark Twain. Hope had saved that piece of information as a surprise for her cousin, and now she wouldn't have the heart to share it. Annie had copies of *The Adventures of Huckleberry Finn,* and *The Adventures of Tom Sawyer*, but her favorite book by the author was *A Connecticut Yankee in King Arthur's Court*.

Hope thanked and tipped the bellboy for carrying her small trunk to her lovely room, then she closed the door behind him and flung herself across the bed. Just to catch her breath. Too excited to sleep the night before, she'd dressed at sunup to get to Martindale in time to catch the early train. Somehow she'd managed to get the horse and buggy to the livery. They'd be waiting for her there when she returned.

Exhaustion was settling in after sitting near a family with three active little boys during the long train ride from Martindale to Minneapolis. Good thing she was able to force down a small meal on the train. Not having to seek out a place to dine in the middle of the day, she could spare the time to close her eyes for a moment, and the bed felt so comfortable . . .

ଓ

Hope woke with a jolt. How long had she slept? It couldn't have been more than a few minutes, could it? She opened the case to the watch dangling from the gold chain around her neck.

No! How could I?

More than an hour had passed. Nervous energy surged through her body. She didn't have much time to freshen up, change, and get to her appointment at the Woodlin Art Gallery. After sending numerous requests for a meeting, she'd received word that Mr. Woodlin might only have a few minutes to offer in the middle of his busy day, so she couldn't risk being late.

She flung open her trunk and pulled out a blue suit she'd been told complemented her eyes, but also gave a business-like air. As the person representing Ben's work to an influential man in the art world, Hope wanted to make a good impression—not too soft and feminine, but also not brash. Men seemed to have a difficult time accepting strong women in the business arena.

The gallery was only four blocks from the hotel. It should be an easy walk—one of the reasons she chose to stay at the expensive hotel, besides looking at it as a treat and a small taste of what she was used to in New York.

Hope stepped outside the hotel and into September sunshine. Size and weight made carrying the wrapped painting cumbersome enough, but protecting it from pedestrians jostling her wasn't going to be as easy as she imagined. She spotted a nearby streetcar headed in the right direction and raced to get on.

Four *city* blocks added to a fair amount of distance, but the ride went much faster than if she'd tried to maneuver her way on foot to her destination. The streetcar stopped at a corner and Hope spotted the gallery just ahead.

"Please excuse me." Hope squeezed between a robust man who smelled of cigars and a hefty gentleman with thick glasses as she struggled to disembark.

The toe of her boot caught in her skirt as she stepped from the car, throwing her off balance. She clutched the painting, and teetering for a second, twisted her ankle. Sharp pain shot through her foot. Her eyes watered, and she almost dropped to the ground.

Hope couldn't stop now. She hobbled the rest of the way to the gallery door. Thank goodness a doorman was present to help her in.

Breathless and fighting back tears, Hope limped toward the receptionist sitting behind a large mahogany desk.

"Good afternoon. I'm Mrs. Mayfield. How may I help you?" The pretty woman in a stylish dark plum suit offered a warm smile, which helped put Hope a little more at ease, though her ankle throbbed.

"I'm Hope Andrews. I have an appointment to see Mr. Woodlin at three o'clock."

Mrs. Mayfield checked an appointment book lying open in front of her. "You're a few minutes early. Mr. Woodlin is currently in a meeting. His schedule is very tight today, but I'm sure he'll see you as soon as possible. Please take a seat." She gestured toward several comfortable-looking chairs. "I noticed you struggling a bit with your foot when you walked in. Are you going to be all right? Is there anything I can do to help?"

"Thank you for being so considerate." Hope tried to speak with assurance. "I twisted my ankle on the way here, but I'm sure I'll be fine once I rest a moment." She sank into a large, soft chair and tried to ignore the pain by focusing on the artwork adorning the walls.

What had she done? By coming here, she'd not only broken her promise to Ben, but she now suffered with a sprained ankle. If the swelling and tenderness got any worse, she might not have the strength to find her way to Miss Lancaster's home. Maybe Hope deserved to lose her opportunity for trying to prove she was right about Ben's talent. He'd be furious once he knew she'd betrayed his trust, but she'd have to tell him at some point. Was coming here worth risking what they'd only begun to build?

A half hour passed as Hope watched people come and go, but still no Mr. Woodlin. She pushed herself up from the chair and tried to walk to the receptionist without putting much weight on her injured foot.

Hope attempted a smile. "Excuse me, but do you know if Mr. Woodlin will soon be free to see me?"

"He'll come down as soon as possible, but I'll go find out what I can. If anyone comes in, please tell them I'll be back shortly." Mrs. Mayfield put down her pen and climbed the stairs to the second story, then disappeared.

There was nothing more she could do but pray, so Hope moved back to the chair and began to do just that. She prayed Mr. Woodlin would soon meet with her, then love Ben's work just as much as she did.

Ten minutes or more later, Mrs. Mayfield returned with a beautiful blue and gold tea cup, the contents steaming. "I'm sorry. Mr. Woodlin is still in the same meeting, but I've brought you jasmine tea if you care to have some."

"Yes, thank you. That's very thoughtful." Hope accepted the cup and sipped the warm liquid. It did help calm her jittery stomach. This waiting was excruciating.

An hour later, Mrs. Mayfield gave Hope a sympathetic look. "Would you like more tea?"

"No, thank you." Close to five o'clock and closing time for the gallery, and Hope still needed to store the painting and freshen up at the hotel before her dinner with Miss Lancaster. Should she leave now? But she'd already waited for nearly two hours. After all she'd endured that afternoon, she couldn't accept giving up now, despite her physical agony.

Not only hungry, Hope desperately needed to use a powder room. Hope toddled over to the desk, leaned over, and whispered, "Is there a . . ."

Mrs. Mayfield nodded and pointed. "Take that hall, turn right, and you'll find one on the left at the end of the hall."

What if Mr. Woodlin came down to see her, and she was gone? She might not have another chance.

"Don't worry." Mrs. Mayfield must have seen Hope's hesitation. "I'll chain him to the desk and keep him here if I have to."

Hope nodded with gratitude, found her way, and returned as quickly as she could. Still no Mr. Woodlin. An ornate grandfather clock bonged five times, and her queasy stomach made her want to retch.

Fifteen more minutes crept by. Hope's throat started to close in. A drop of liquid plopped from her lower eyelash onto her right cheek. She whisked it away.

The grandfather clock ticked away six minutes. The passing of three hundred and sixty seconds no longer available to her. If she stayed any longer, she'd likely make a mess of her own opportunity by showing up late for her dinner engagement with Miss Lancaster. But if she left now, she'd fail at getting Ben's work seen and leave feeling defeated after wasted efforts at the gallery.

"Miss Andrews?" The distinguished-looking gentleman descending the staircase wore a tailored charcoal gray suit.

"Yes. I'm Miss Andrews." Hope clutched Ben's painting in front of her.

"I apologize for keeping you waiting." He reached the bottom of the stairs and extended his hand in greeting. "Arthur Woodlin."

Hope accepted the firm grip with one of her own and shook his hand. Mr. Woodlin's blue-gray eyes reminded Hope of the pigeons back in New York.

"I apologize, but I only have a moment to spare. I'm hosting an event for loyal gallery patrons, so I know you'll understand that I can't be late."

"Of course." Hope tried to clear her dry throat, but didn't have much success.

"I should have left the gallery fifteen minutes ago. However, I do admire your tenacity, so I'd like to see what you brought."

With trembling fingers, Hope unwrapped the painting— Ben's art—and her chance to prove that his work had value.

Mr. Woodlin surveyed the framed scene of the little boy playing in the field with his dog. "Miss Andrews, I'm curious. What makes you think this painting has any merit? Why do you have so much interest in promoting this artist?"

"I'm not a professional painter, Mr. Woodlin, but I've studied art history, I've sat in studios for months where skilled painters have shared their knowledge, and I've enjoyed many hours in New York's finest galleries. I'd like to think that I've gained some understanding of what makes art exceptional."

Now wasn't the time to hold back. *Be bold, Hope.* "But, there's more to art than what can be taught through books or in classrooms. For most people, it comes down to feelings. What does a particular piece evoke within? What does it say to the heart? I know what I feel when I look at this painting—and other paintings by this artist—and I believe they need to be shared."

"Well said." His warm smile helped calm Hope's breathing. "In order to make an appraisal of the work, I'd like to spend more time with the painting than what I have now. If you leave it with me, I'll commit to shipping it back to you unharmed and at my expense."

What should she do? Could she believe him? Because the painting was created for the auction to raise money for the library, Ben had never signed it. What if someone else claimed the work? Hope said a quick prayer for guidance. She'd trusted Mr. Woodlin to give an honest evaluation of Ben's talent, so she needed to trust him in this too.

"It's a deal, Mr. Woodlin."

"Very well." He shook her hand again. "Mrs. Mayfield will take care of you and set everything up."

"Thank you, Mr. Woodlin." She'd done it. Hope had presented Ben's work to one of the most prestigious galleries in the Midwest. She'd sing if she could carry a tune, and she'd perform a jig if the celebratory act wouldn't result in killing pain. She couldn't break out in song or dance, but she could send a prayer.

Thank you, Lord, for giving me the strength to wait for Mr. Woodlin, and thank you for the opportunity to leave Ben's work with him. Right or wrong, I've brought the painting this far. I can do no more. It's in your hands, and I know that I need to trust your plan for Ben, whatever that future holds.

Hope gave Mrs. Mayfield the painting and her address in Riverton just as the grandfather clock bonged five thirty. She would have brought her portfolio with her, but without Annie to help, there was no way she could carry both the painting and her designs. There was no other choice but to make her way back to the hotel to get them before finding her way to Miss Lancaster's. The lovely lavender gown she planned to wear that evening would remain in the hotel room, unworn. Hope wouldn't have a spare minute to change.

With her heart pumping and her ankle hurting, she hurried back to the hotel to get her designs before catching another streetcar going in the direction of Miss Lancaster's home. She got off at her stop and breathed relief at how much easier it had been to move without carrying the painting, only to realize she'd gotten off three blocks too soon.

The sky, now dark, sprinkled Hope's face with moisture. She'd have to hurry to make it before the clouds opened and blessed the ground with a deluge. Anxious to reach her destination, Hope pushed forward, despite the pain shooting from her ankle with each step.

There! The numbers on the house matched those on the slip of paper in her hand. Almost out of breath, and wincing in agony, Hope climbed the steps and reached the covered porch before the rain broke free and poured from the heavens. She clutched her safe and dry portfolio to her heaving chest with one hand and tucked several locks of loose hair behind her ear with the other before knocking on the door. This was it. After tonight, her whole world could change.

The door creaked open about six inches, and a short, elderly woman looking like Mrs. Claus with her light blue eyes and white hair smiled up at Hope. "May I help you?"

"Hello." Hope felt better already in the lady's calming presence. "I'm Hope Andrews. Miss Lancaster is expecting me."

The woman covered her mouth with her hand. "Oh, dear, oh dear . . ." She swung open the door. "Come in. Please. I'm Mrs. Newman, the housekeeper."

"Is something wrong?" Hope hadn't misunderstood the invitation or the date and time. "I know I'm a few minutes late, but I had a little trouble getting here." By the woman's distraught expression, tardiness wasn't the issue.

"You didn't get the message, did you?"

"What message?"

"Miss Lancaster sent a message to your hotel several hours ago."

"I never got it." Hope hadn't given any thought to checking for messages when she returned to the hotel for her portfolio. Her only concern was getting to Miss Lancaster's as quickly as possible.

"Here, sit down. Make yourself comfortable." Mrs. Newman led Hope into the parlor and guided her to a settee covered in deep red velvet. "I'm so sorry. She was looking forward to spending the evening with you, but she received word about her mother. She's been ill for several months, but this afternoon she took a turn for the worse and isn't expected to make it through the night."

Poor Miss Lancaster. She'd gone to be with her dying mother. Hope would have done the same thing. "I understand."

"Perhaps you can come another time. Once Miss Lancaster has been able to lay her mother to rest and grieve."

The sweet housekeeper meant well, and Hope tried to push her disappointment aside. "Yes, perhaps." She stood, still holding her beloved designs close to her heart. "I should leave."

"Would you like something to eat before you go? A cup of tea or coffee?"

"No. Thank you. I'm not hungry." Nausea had replaced the earlier cavernous feeling in her stomach. Hope reached the door and opened it to the sound of rain pounding on the porch roof. She'd fought for Ben. Why not fight for herself? "Could I—"

"Could you what dear?"

"Nothing, Mrs. Newman. Nothing at all." Hope could have left her portfolio, but Miss Lancaster hadn't requested it, so leaving the designs behind felt a bit presumptuous.

"Are you sure you want to go out in this weather? You're welcome to stay."

"You're very kind to offer, but I'll be on my way." Hope smiled at the housekeeper in an attempt to assure the nice lady she'd be fine.

The cool rain was almost refreshing as it beat against Hope's heated face, and the drops sliding down her cheeks blended in with her tears, hiding them from anyone wondering what a young woman was doing alone on the streets of Minneapolis that time of night.

❧

Hope's damp hair hung down her back over the comfortable nightgown. Her drenched suit lay across a chair in the room to dry, but she doubted it would reach that point by morning, when she needed to pack and leave for the train station.

From her bedroom window, she had a good view of the wet street below and the corner café where she'd forced down some chicken soup to help ward off her body's chill. It wasn't that September evenings were cold, but the mix of wind and cool rain had penetrated her clothes. Of course the sky had begun to clear as soon as she stepped into the hotel lobby. Her timing had been impeccable the entire day.

The trip felt like a complete failure. She'd hoped for so much more.

Lord, what are you trying to tell me? Am I wrong to share Ben's talent—a gift you've given him—with others? Am I wrong to have dreams of my own? Where are you?

What if she never got the painting back? What was she going to tell Ben? He trusted her to keep his secret. He may never forgive her for what she'd done.

It would be a long time before she could make the trip back to Minneapolis. She'd come all this way to have her own opportunity crushed. Hope couldn't blame Miss Lancaster, and she didn't want to blame God, so what was she supposed to do with her disappointment and anger?

Even Minneapolis wasn't as enjoyable as she'd anticipated. Without anyone there to share it, the fancy hotel had lost its luster. Hope missed Annie. She missed her parents. She even missed Riverton.

Hope had never felt so alone.

Nineteen

I shouldn't have come, Annie." Hope's insides were knot-ted up like a ball of yarn toyed with by a kitten. "How can I face Ben and pretend that I didn't leave his painting in Minneapolis?"

"Both Jake and Ben would have questions if I'd driven out here by myself." She pulled on the reins and guided the horse to the side of the house where they could tether her. "They're anxious to hear what happened with Miss Lancas-ter."

"You mean what didn't happen." Hope climbed down from the buggy and grabbed the basket with the molasses cookies they'd baked earlier.

"That wasn't your fault." Annie reached for the pile of clothes she'd mended for the "all-thumbs boys." She'd taken pity on their lack of ability with needle and thread. "Besides, I think they're just plain impressed that you made the jour-ney at all, especially alone."

"I'm glad Mr. Carter gave us both the day off from work-ing in the store. After the trip not going as planned and not getting home until almost supper yesterday, it's helped to have today together."

"Me too. You needed time to talk and sort through some things."

The front screen door slammed. "Good evening, ladies!"

Jake ran down the porch steps and grabbed the bundle from Annie's arms. "If we'd known you were coming, we would've waited supper."

"We've eaten." Annie beamed up at Jake.

"I cooked tonight, so trust me, you're better off missing it." Jake leaned toward Hope and inhaled. "Do I smell cookies?"

"Freshly baked this afternoon." Annie reached into the covered basket and pulled one out for him.

He took a bite and a grin spread across his face. "Heaven."

Annie put her arm through his. "We waited to drive out till now, figuring you'd be busy in the fields this afternoon."

"We were," he said between chews. "Corn for silage. But that's done for the day, and so is the feedin' and milkin', so we can enjoy the rest of the evening—and more cookies." He reached for another, then pointed to the shed. "Ben's in there. No surprise."

Hope gazed at the shed, then glanced back at Annie and Jake. They were heading toward the porch swing, and Annie had Jake engrossed in a story about a customer who had come into the store earlier that day looking for a gift for his wife's birthday. Her wild gestures and contorted facial expressions had Jake almost doubled over from the humorous situation.

No point in standing there like a crane pretending to hide. Hope couldn't remain invisible to the couple forever. Besides, it would be much better to speak to Ben privately and explain what she'd done—or left undone—in Minneapolis. No sense in dragging Annie and Jake into the mess if it could be avoided.

She squeezed her eyes shut and anticipated a loud and chilling creak that would grow more obnoxious as the door to the shed opened, but not so much as a squeak. Ben must have fixed the hinges. She sighed with relief, and slipped inside without her arrival being announced. Good. She hadn't wanted to disturb him if he was absorbed in his work. No—that wasn't entirely true. She wanted an excuse to prolong having to make any confessions.

His back toward her, he faced the large window and a canvas propped on an easel. With graceful strokes of muted pinks, yellows, and lavenders, he created a soft sunset. Not the brilliant display one sometimes viewed in awe, but calming and peaceful, like a blanket covering the sky as it bid God's creation good night.

The sun's rays streamed through the window in front of Ben, and as the sphere dropped lower its beam must have blinded him. He rubbed his eyes and turned toward her, his face lighting up as bright as the descending fireball in the sky.

"Hope, I didn't hear you come in."

"You must have oiled the door hinges."

Ben nodded and chuckled. "You noticed. Then it was worth the effort." He laid his paintbrush and palette on a bench, then leaned against it with a smile that matched the sparkle in his gorgeous blue eyes. She loved that he no longer minded having her in his sanctuary. That fact helped ease some of the tension in her shoulders. "So, tell me about the big city. Did you enjoy meeting Eva Lancaster?"

If she looked into those caring eyes any longer, she'd melt into a puddle at his feet. She needed to keep her wits about her—at least until she disclosed her other reason for making the trip. After that, the fire in his eyes might be enough to singe her, so best to keep her distance.

"Well . . ." Hope took several light steps to her right, trying not to put too much weight on the foot with the sore ankle. How long could she delay? A sheet was draped over a painting propped on another easel sitting to the side, but the cloth had slipped down, exposing a corner of the work. "What's this?" She pulled the covering away and gasped.

There, on canvas, Hope danced in a field of daisies. A light breeze teased the white summer tea dress and blew her freed blond hair back slightly. It was like staring into a mirror, the likeness so real. No, he'd made her better. Hope's eyes filled, and she tried to blink back the pools from spilling. He'd painted a glow into her cheeks, and pure joy shone from her eyes. Was that how he saw her? Beautiful and free? Innocent? At that moment she'd give almost anything to be the woman he'd created in his imagination.

"You're not saying anything. I can't tell if you—"

Hope wiped her tears, then faced him. "I've never sat for you, how did . . .?"

Ben stepped closer. Even without physically touching, the warmth radiating from his body reached her. "You still haven't told me if you like it or not," he said in a low and gentle voice.

"It's so beautiful I don't know what to say." Hope didn't deserve to be painted like a goddess—an angel. She was neither, and he'd feel the same as soon as she told him the truth about her venture to the art gallery.

The depth of caring in his eyes bathed her in desire as his fingers filled with so much talent brushed back escaped strands of hair fallen across her eyes. With tenderness he tucked them behind her ears, as though offering her a whispered caress. Her shallow breaths competed with her pounding heart—one tempted her to dissolve into his arms, while the other urged her to flee.

"You wonder how I could paint you without your presence here." He searched her eyes. "I can because you're always with me."

"Ben . . ."

"Please hear me out, Hope." He took her hand in both of his. "It means a lot to have someone to talk to—someone who understands my work."

"It means a lot to me too."

His gaze lowered and he leaned in, lightly brushing her quivering lips with his.

She didn't move or protest, but pressed in closer, giving permission. She wrapped her arms around his neck and he tightened his hold, one hand warming her back, the other cradling her head. The kiss deepened, sending heat through her body. Hope could have remained in his embrace until she lost all strength to stand, but Ben withdrew, his chest heaving, his breathing heavy.

He held her head between his gifted hands and leaned his forehead against hers. "I care for you, Hope. More than I can put into words right now. That's why I had to paint you—to show you. And it's why I need to stop kissing you, even though everything in me is yearning to continue."

Her head was swimming with his declaration, and her heartstrings sang for her to admit she'd fallen in love with him. "But would he believe her after what she'd done? Had she risked too much? Until Hope knew, she'd move with care. "I have feelings for you too."

"It feels like springtime in the dead of winter to hear you say those words." His lips caressed her temple. "Because I know I can trust you."

Hope's determination to explain her mission at the gallery weakened. He'd depended on her, and she'd gone against his wishes. Could she be sucked into the ground like dirty bath water tossed out on a hot day?

She drew back and pressed her hand against his chest, his beating heart thumping against her palm. No matter the outcome, he deserved the truth. Keeping it from him would only hurt him more.

"I have to tell you something." She slipped from his grasp, and wringing her hands, took several steps back. The confused look in his eyes made her throat feel like it was coated with honey. She tried to clear it, but with little success. "Seeing Miss Lancaster wasn't the only reason I went to Minneapolis."

Ꮖ

Ben braced himself against a bench. Hope's voice, normally strong and determined, sounded fearful. "Are you sick?" People sometimes traveled to the city to see doctors who specialized in illnesses a small-town doctor couldn't treat. He couldn't imagine his beautiful Hope lying in a hospital, but if it came to that, he'd never leave her side.

"Sick?" Her eyes widened. "No—no, it's nothing like that."

"Good." He sighed with relief, and his shoulders relaxed.

Hopes eyebrows drew together. "Do I seem like I have something wrong with me?"

"No. But what other reason could you have to go to Minneapolis?"

"I took your painting of the boy and dog to the Woodlin Art Gallery." She bit her lower lip. "I wanted to show it to Arthur Woodlin."

"Why?" Ben gripped the bench behind him. He needed to understand. Why would she go behind his back? Hope knew how important it was to him that she keep his secret.

"I thought he might want to see more of your work. Perhaps purchase some of your paintings or display them. At the very least, confirm what I know." She talked fast, not giving him a chance to interrupt. "That you're a talented painter. My intentions were good. *Please* believe that my intentions were good and honorable."

Ben felt like he'd been kicked in the stomach by an angry mule. He thought he knew Hope. Even after convincing himself that he would never find a woman who could accept his life as a painter, Ben had risked opening up his heart to her. And she'd responded by deceiving him. "Honorable? Hope, you had no right." His groan morphed into a growl. "I never gave permission—"

"Ben, I'm so sorry. I should have told you about the appointment before I left for Minneapolis." Hope closed her eyes, but a tear escaped and slid down her cheek. "I believe so much in you that I convinced myself I had every right to take the painting to the gallery because the artwork belonged to me." She straightened and opened her eyes, revealing pain. "I told myself that it was selfish for you to keep yours hidden."

"You've got it all wrong. After what I did to Percy, it's selfish to paint at all—putting sunsets, rivers, and fields on canvas and receiving praise for them when he'll never see any of those things again."

"It's not guilt you feel for Percy's blindness that's stopping you. It's fear. I think you're hiding behind that accident because you're afraid of not being good enough." A tear clung to her lower lashes. "But, you are good enough."

Maybe he should feel humbled—even grateful—for her strong belief in him, but how was he supposed to let go of the hurt and anger that rumbled in his gut? How could he trust her again?

◌ℛ

"Did you even see Eva Lancaster?"

"No." Hope swallowed the sob rising in her throat. The entire trip had been a disappointment. She'd failed to accomplish anything but hurt Ben.

"So, it was *all* a lie?" His tone no longer harsh, he only sounded—wounded.

"No. You—I—" Another tear trailed the first, but Hope didn't have the energy to wipe them away. "My purpose for going to the city was to see Miss Lancaster. We had plans to have supper at her home on Saturday evening, just like I'd told you." She glanced up at Ben, but his eyes were so intense, she couldn't bear the weight of his gaze and looked away. Unexpected exhaustion encouraged Hope to close her eyes, curl up somewhere and retreat, yet she forced her feet to remain in place.

"But the entire day was one disaster after another." No more tears. Hope took a deep breath. She needed to tell him the whole story. "I went to the gallery first to meet with Mr. Woodlin, but I was worried that I'd be late for our appointment and in my hurry, I twisted my ankle getting off the streetcar. I arrived on time, but he was in a meeting, so I sat there waiting for hours, afraid I'd be late to Miss Lancaster's, but wanting so much for him to see your work. Finally, Mr. Woodlin came down to the reception area, but he explained that he needed leave for an important event and wouldn't have time to meet with me."

"So, he never actually saw the painting."

By the tone of his voice, Hope couldn't tell if Ben was relieved or disappointed. "Only briefly, and as an apology for breaking our appointment, he said if I left it with him, he'd return it with his appraisal."

"You left the painting there?" Ben growled and shoved his hands through his hair. "Whatever possessed you to—?"

"I was trying to be helpful." Enough was enough. Good intentions were behind her decision. Ben didn't need to make her feel worse than she already did.

"And that's you, Hope. Little Miss Helpful." The sarcastic way he said it made it sound like she made a habit of messing things up for other people.

A spark ignited in her belly. "If it means anything to you, after wasting my afternoon trying to do something nice for you, I hurried to Miss Lancaster's home and arrived drenched, and then was told she wasn't there. She'd left just minutes before I arrived because her mother was close to death." Hope stared into Ben's eyes.

"So my trip was a total waste of time. And for what? To be bullied by an ungrateful, arrogant, rude—" Hope clenched her fists at her sides and closed her eyes to barricade the emotional river. She'd told herself she wouldn't cry. Nothing she could say would change how he felt about her decision to take the painting to the gallery, so she needed to stop trying. After a moment, she opened her eyes.

Ben reached for her, but Hope slipped from his grasp. "Hope . . ."

She limped out the door without giving him a chance to say another word.

A few steps later, Hope stopped. Even though she'd meant well, it was a mistake to take the painting to the gallery without Ben's knowledge. Annie had warned her, but Hope had been so confident she knew what was best for him, she'd refused to listen.

She needed to apologize—convince him she was sorry. Make things right. She walked back to the shed. Hope took a breath and turned the knob, moving the door enough to slip inside, but she didn't move beyond the door frame.

His back facing her, Ben threw a cloth over the lovely painting that only minutes ago had made her feel beautiful and loved. But she'd broken his trust, and he couldn't—or wouldn't—forgive her.

That was it then. Benjamin Greene was done with her.

CR

At the sound of the door clicking into place, Ben turned around, expecting to see Hope standing there, but the space was empty. Had he ever felt this lonely? So full of regret?

Hope hadn't done anything out of maliciousness. She didn't mean to hurt him, of that he was sure. But he'd been so quick to condemn what she'd done—actions she'd taken because she believed in him so much, she risked losing her own opportunity. He was a fool, and he'd behaved like the very men he despised for how they treated women.

What if Hope was right? What if hiding his work—his talent—was the opposite of what God wanted, and Ben had been deceiving himself out of fear? By not showing anyone his paintings, he was protected from rejection.

Lord, what am I to do? Have I been so wrong all this time?

He slipped the cover from the painting and gazed at the woman with eyes the color of a bright afternoon sky and hair that reminded him of sunshine.

Ben groaned. What was wrong with him? He'd spoken without thinking—*again*—and insulted her.

What was he doing hanging out in the shed? He needed to go after her. He swung open the door and raced toward the house, just in time to see the back end of the buggy moving as fast as the wheels could handle the road out of the farmyard.

Too late. Ben sank down on one knee. He could saddle a horse and follow her home. A weight settled on his shoulder, as though God had placed his hand there.

Wait.

Like most men, Ben didn't understand women. What if going to her was what she wanted—needed—from him?

Wait.

With his whole being, Ben wanted to chase after her, but if God was telling him to stay put . . . it was best to give her a little time. Maybe it wasn't for Hope's sake but his that God wanted him to hold back. His thoughts and feelings were all jumbled, and more damage could be done if he didn't untangle them before talking to her.

Was he ready to completely forgive her? He'd only

learned about her betrayal that night, and forgiveness wasn't something Ben gave without thought and a willingness to never bring up the uense again.

Of course he'd forgive. He loved her and had begun to believe it might be possible for them to have a life together.

But tonight had brought heavy doubt.

He was convinced that she cared deeply for him, but Hope's strong desire for his success in the art world had led her to betray him. She continued to push him toward public recognition. Was it because she believed that strongly in him? Or was it because she'd be ashamed to be with a man who wasn't as prominent as the men she'd been accustomed to spending time with in New York?

Ben wanted Hope in his life, and he thought she enjoyed living in Riverton, but she'd alluded to returning to New York in the future. If not there, she might have opportunities with Eva Lancaster in Minneapolis. If he failed as an artist, he couldn't ask her to stay in the small farming community and hold her back—he loved her too much.

Those weren't the only questions needing answers. Others swirled around in his head, almost making him dizzy. How did he really feel about his painting being left in the hands of a gallery owner? If he were honest with himself and Hope, he'd admit to having more than a flicker of interest in the man's evaluation.

The frightening part—what would it mean for Ben if his work didn't stand the test of careful scrutiny? If told he had no talent, could he continue painting? Or would his passion for art dwindle? Ben hoped he would carry on for the sheer joy of creating something out of nothing, but if that ability were lost . . .

On the other hand, his world could drastically change if the gallery owner liked Ben's work. That remote possibility both excited and scared Ben. Could he finally let go of the guilt he'd carried for years and finally accept the freedom to claim the title *artist*?

Twenty

Ben's kiss played in Hope's mind as she wrapped a bolt of navy-colored flannel discarded by a customer. Two days had passed since she'd last seen him and confessed to taking his painting—*her painting*, not that that mattered now—to Minneapolis. She hadn't made the decision on impulse, aware he might become angry with her. At the time, she was still willing to take the risk because she believed she knew best. But she hadn't prayed for direction. When was she going to learn? When was she going to seek God's divine wisdom instead of running ahead of him on her own?

She'd meant well, but that didn't excuse her blunder. Hope could pretend she'd shown the painting to Mr. Woodlin for Ben's own good, but that wasn't entirely accurate. Truth bathed her with shame—she'd also done it for herself. Love for him had taken root deep in her heart, but she wanted more from him than what he could presently give.

Prestige and money didn't matter to her. She didn't care if he was a poor farmer or a wealthy businessman. But she did yearn to have a husband who wasn't afraid to take risks, and, despite her encouragement, Ben still insisted on keeping his paintings locked away in his shed, safe from any critical eyes. Fear wasn't the only problem. Guilt over Percy's blindness still plagued Ben, but Hope didn't lack sympathy there. She'd prayed daily that Ben would forgive himself.

What if she someday became a successful designer? Would Ben ever leave the farm and his comfortable sanctuary to live in a large city? If not, could she give up her dream for him? The man she loved was kind to even the most disagreeable, joked around with the children in the community, watched over her cousin like a little sister, was loyal to his family, and loved God with a passion. The way his eyes lit up when he saw her made her feel . . . special.

Hope had left one relationship in New York, only to find herself in one almost as complicated.

"Only a week before we turn the calendar's page to October. Customers are starting to plan for colder months ahead." Annie laid a bolt of gray wool on the counter, then frowned. "Well, don't you look like cream that's been sitting out in the heat too long."

"Sour?"

"Curdled. Your face is all scrunched up, like you have a stomachache." Annie grasped Hope's hand. "Or is it your heart that's ailing?"

"Confusing emotions, Annie. They ebb and flow like the tide at Coney Island. First I'm angry, then hurt, and that turns into sadness until I'm angry all over again."

"Ben?"

"Ben, Eva Lancaster, my parents . . ." Hope perched her elbows on the counter and laid her head on her hands. "I'm such a mess."

"You'll hear something from Miss Lancaster soon. It's only been a few days since you returned from Minneapolis, barely time for her to send a note and for it to arrive. And the last letter you received from your parents said they were doing well and in good health. Right?" Annie lifted Hope's chin and looked directly into her eyes. "Right?" She drew the word out, then the corners of her mouth tipped up.

"Yes, you're right—*this* time." Hope couldn't stop a slight smile from twitching on her own face. "Don't let it go to your head."

"Oh, heavens, I'm reminded too often that I make a fool of myself." Annie winked. "Let me hang on to this one victory, cousin."

"You may cling to it with both hands." Hope tossed her a spool of ribbon. "Tie it up with a bow and display it for all the world to see."

Annie grinned as she grabbed the spool. The end of the ribbon wrapped around her right arm and trailed through her fingers. "I may do just that."

A small laugh escaped Hope's lips. "You always cheer me up."

"It's one of my gifts." Annie's eyes sparkled. "Glad to see it's doing some good."

"It is." Now, if Hope's talents could someday be put to use. "I'm trying not to be selfish or too disappointed about Miss Lancaster cancelling our dinner engagement. Last night, I painted a card and wrote a note expressing sympathy for her struggle, and I sent it off earlier today. I miss my own mother, but at least I have some assurance she'll return from Panama." In her correspondence, Hope had made no mention of her drawings or any expectations of the designer. Miss Lancaster had far more important things with which to concern herself.

"It was thoughtful of you to consider her feelings." Annie's leaned next to Hope on the counter. "I'm funny and cheerful, and you're generous and kind. If we could put ourselves together into one person, we'd really be a catch."

"Right now, I wouldn't be surprised if Benjamin Greene thought of me closer to a fish that has been lying in the sun too long and has started to stink." Hope pinched her nose shut and made an ugly face.

Annie pulled Hope's hand away from her nose. "Ben will come around. He cares too much to not fix things between you." She startled, as if stung by a bee. "Oh, my goodness."

"What is it?" Hope raced around the counter. "Are you all right?"

"I got so busy helping a customer, I completely forgot that Mr. Carter asked me to report on some inventory in the back room. I'd better take care of it right away." Annie scurried off toward the back of the store.

A familiar customer approached, holding two bolts of cloth. "Hope, dear, Clara is making a new dress for me, and I can't decide between these two." Mrs. Hawkins laid similar fabrics on the counter—one a midnight blue, the other forest green. "What do you think?"

"This shade of blue will look lovely with your coloring." As Hope smiled at the woman, a chill skittered down her spine. She shook off the strange feeling, wrapped the fabric in paper, and tied the package with a white ribbon.

Mrs. Hawkins fingered the ribbon. "How lovely. It makes me feel like I've just purchased material suited for a fancy gown."

Hope had suggested replacing twine with the prettier, more feminine trimming to make such purchases feel special for female customers, and Mr. Carter had agreed after the other clerks wholeheartedly supported the idea. The positive response from the clientele had put a smile on her face many times since.

"I'm indebted to you." Mrs. Hawkins tucked her change inside her purse. "My husband says I have a terrible time making decisions, and he's right. I'd probably still be standing there, not knowing if I should pick the blue or the green if you hadn't helped me choose."

"You're welcome, and any time you want a woman's opinion, please feel free to ask." Hope offered a generous smile. Something didn't feel right, though Mrs. Hawkins wasn't a threat. "I'll be glad to help."

"A gem." Mrs. Hawkins gave a quick nod. "That's what you are." She draped the strings to her handbag over her wrist and picked up the package from the counter.

"That's very kind of you to say, Mrs. Hawkins. Thank you for coming in."

As Hope bid the woman good-bye, she glanced to the left and almost lost her stomach. She could barely breathe. Wearing a satisfied grin, Henry stood a mere six feet away. It was pointless to leave. He'd follow. At least here, surrounded by other people, he'd never make a scene. Henry revealed his darker side only in private.

"Hello, Hope."

She grabbed onto the counter to steady herself. Strong, she had to be strong. Henry would use any signs of weakness against her. *Breathe, just breathe.* "What are you doing here?"

Hope had been in Riverton for over three months, and it had been longer since she'd last glimpsed Henry. Aside from being a bit thinner than she remembered, he looked the same. Tall, dark wavy hair, dimples, and eyes the color of German chocolate cake. If only his true demeanor were half as sweet.

With an arrogant air, he sauntered up to the counter. "I've missed you, Hope." His smile would have charmed any woman who didn't know him, but Hope knew him too well.

She glanced around for help. Mr. Carter was in the back room, as was Annie. Most customers milled farther from her counter than they usually did.

"I didn't like how we left things, and I wanted another chance to talk. You didn't make it easy to find you, but persistence paid off, and here I am." His self-satisfied smugness grated on her.

"How *did* you find me?" she whispered. "When I left New York, I didn't make my destination public knowledge." Charlotte would never have told him where Hope was living, and several other friends had agreed to keep it a secret as well, without knowing the truth about her relationship with Henry.

"After Charlotte slammed the door in my face several times, I called on your friend, Louise Jackson."

Hope caught Mr. Carter eyeing them, and for a moment she thought he might rescue her, but a clerk led him to another location. It would be a relief to have Henry shown the door, but the store was filled with customers. For Mr. Carter's sake she didn't want to make a scene, and she certainly didn't want to start any gossip. "What did you say to that poor girl? And please lower your voice."

"Louise has always had a soft spot for me, and tears on the third visit convinced her I was sincerely pining away for you," he said in a more subdued tone. "She decided you and I had a misunderstanding, and I deserved a second chance."

"Word can't express what you deserve."

"I'm going to take that as a compliment." His grin carried pure evil.

"It wasn't meant as one." How was she going to get rid of him? "Henry, I'm employed here. I don't have time to discuss what you want or don't want. You need to leave, and I don't mean only the store."

"I can't."

"Why not? There's nothing here for you."

"I'm not leaving Riverton until we talk." His eyes softened and his shoulders dropped. "I'm not here to make trouble," he said softly.

"Then why are you here?"

"To apologize for being a cad." Henry fingered the fedora in his hands as though nervous. "I'm staying at the Sherlock Hotel. Please have supper there with me tonight."

Hope wasn't going to be taken in by his sudden contrite demeanor. "No, Henry. I don't want anything more to do with you."

Even as the words passed her mouth, Hope knew it wouldn't matter what she said. Henry wasn't leaving Riverton.

"You'll change your mind." He tipped his hat to her, placed it on his head, and sauntered out the door.

❧

Ben wiped the remaining trails of shaving cream from his face with a towel and surveyed his reflection in the small mirror hanging above the sink. First the left side, the right, then the chin. Good. Clean without any nicks. He didn't want to meet Hope looking like he'd gotten caught in barbed wire.

His hands gripped the edges of the sink as he bowed his head. *Lord, help me find the right words.* How many times had he whispered that plea during the day? Once he'd decided to ride into town that evening to talk to her, he'd begged God that Hope would forgive him for being an ungrateful clod, but he'd also prayed for his own change of heart.

He'd wrestled with ongoing questions since the night she'd confessed to taking and leaving his painting at the gallery, and he'd forgiven her. But putting what she did behind him was a different matter, because he wasn't sure he could count on her to not do something similar again. He wanted—*he needed*—to forgive and forget this time.

After seeing his parents fight and make up for years, Ben knew from their example that love wasn't always easy, but challenges didn't make a commitment to another person any less real or powerful. He didn't know any married couples who cared and honored each other more than his parents.

It had taken a spunky, stubborn, independent woman coming into his life to realize how much he wanted that for himself. A gal who used her artistic talents to sketch dresses, of all things. And she *was* talented. He just hadn't humbled himself in front of her to admit it, but he would. He'd encourage her to draw whatever she wanted, as long as it made her happy.

"So, you're finally going to talk to Hope?"

Ben glanced at the mirror at Jake leaning against the doorframe. "I need to set things straight with her. Right now it feels like she's on one side of the Grand Canyon, and I'm on the other."

"And you're ready to build a bridge to the other side."

Jake rubbed his jaw. "It's about time." He leaned over and patted Ben's shoulder. "You better get a move on, brother. You don't want to arrive too late. I hope it goes well. I really do."

Twenty-one

Pleased with the lines of the skirt, which flared slightly at the bottom, Hope studied the design. Wool, with the exception of silk for the high collar and part of the bodice. Now color. She dipped her paint brush into pale sage watercolor paint and added a green wash to the sketch. At first, she'd envisioned swirls of beige embroidery on the bodice and down the skirt along both sides of the center panel, but the dress would look more elegant and finished if it included similar stitching along the hemline and bottom of the sleeves.

A rapping noise on the door jolted Hope, and she dropped her brush on the table. Her heart matched the rhythm of a sewing machine needle pulsing at full speed. Her intuition whispered the answer, and her breathing quickened.

A second knock sounded. A quick peek through the curtains hanging on the window to the side of the door confirmed her suspicion. *Henry.*

She'd tried to forget—even for a moment—the encounter with Henry earlier that day, but it had been foolish to think he'd disappear without seeking her out again.

Hiding wouldn't do any good. He must have asked around town where she lived after he left the store earlier that day, and now that he knew, he'd continue to show up until she finally convinced him she'd never change her mind. How she was going to do that, Hope didn't know. But her parents didn't raise a coward, and if her mother had the strength to risk dying from horrible diseases in Panama, her daughter could face one delusional man.

Annie, helping with inventory at the store, wouldn't be home for a little while. However, Hope needn't go into battle alone. *Lord, if not an army, could you please spare a few angels?*

Several more knocks followed. "Hope, please let me in. I know you're in there." Henry sounded calm, despite her not immediately responding.

"Go away, Henry." Hope leaned against the door, breathing heavily. "There's nothing you can say or do that will change my mind. What you're doing—showing up here—is a waste of time. Go back to New York."

"I can't. I care too much about you." He almost sounded sincere. "I just want to talk, and I'm going to stay right here until you give me a chance to say my piece."

"Then say it and leave," she said firmly.

"I'm not going to shout through a barrier." Henry's tone raised a notch, a sign he was beginning to get irritated.

She wouldn't let him inside, but she'd open the door and give him a chance to speak his mind in the chance it might appease him for now. Henry was stubborn enough to stand there all night, and Annie didn't deserve to come home and face a man whose agitation could morph into anger the longer he felt denied and out of control. Hope wanted no harm to come to her cousin, but she knew Annie well enough. As soon as she spotted Henry, she'd become protective and confront him.

One deep breath, then a moment to allow her heavenly reinforcements to arrive, and Hope swung open the door. Her suitor—her opponent—stood only several feet away with an enormous bouquet. The mixed shades of yellow, red, and orange dahlias were spectacular—like fireworks. The last of the season, they could have only come from one garden in town. He either sweet-talked the proud owner into parting with them with some lie, or offered her more money than she could refuse.

Hope didn't move beyond the threshold, but instead stood as tall as she could and crossed her arms. "Why are you here?"

"These are for you." He held the flowers toward her.

"I can't accept them."

His eyebrows knit together. "But, they're your favorite." Henry sounded like he couldn't believe she'd reject his gift.

Of course he would think she preferred them—his mother did. No matter how many times she told him, Henry never remembered that simple daisies were Hope's passion. And that wasn't the only thing he hadn't paid attention to when they were together.

"Henry, I don't want flowers from you. I don't want anything to do with you. Why can't you believe that?"

"I traveled all the way from New York to see you, and you won't even have supper with me. Don't I at least deserve a few minutes of your time?" His eyes implored her to agree.

"No, I can't say that you do." This nightmare had to end. "But I'll let you say what you need to, and then I'll expect you to walk away."

"Agreed."

Hope caught his smug expression before it slipped away.

Giving him this opportunity could be a mistake, but she'd try one more time to help him see reason. Weak in the knees, she stepped out onto the porch.

Henry laid the bouquet on the porch swing, then faced Hope, his expression softening, his eyes filling with emotion, almost as though he sincerely cared for her.

"What is there left to talk about, Henry?" Hope, standing straight with her hands clenched in front of her, didn't back down from his gaze—the one that used to make her melt like chocolate put to flame. "Let's get this over with."

Henry kept his eyes fixed on her. "I love and miss you, Hope, and I want you to come back to New York. That's all there is to it." His lips curved slightly upward into a weak smile. "I know I have a tendency to get a little intense."

"A *little*?" The man could exaggerate. If he'd been a fisherman, he would have fit right in with telling tall tales of catching fish ten times their actual size. "Henry, you couldn't discuss me working in fashion without you pacing and your jaw almost locking into place. You even said once that you wouldn't allow it. No wife of yours would ever do anything but manage your home and have your children."

Henry tried to shush her, but she wasn't going to stop now. Hope searched deep within for courage. "You bragged to your cronies and your business associates about your beautiful fiancée. But if another man even said hello or opened a door for me, you accused me of flirtations."

"You're beautiful. Can't a man be both proud and protective of his loved one?"

"But it was the way you did it. Like I was some kind of possession." A memory surfaced, so vivid it felt like she was reliving it. "I overheard you once. Making bets. You made disgusting wagers about our wedding night." It still made her nauseated to think someone she had loved could be so crude. "I can't live that way—I *won't* live that way. I'm not property to be bullied and bossed, or to be placed on a shelf as a pretty decoration or toy until you decide to take me down to play or show off."

"Hope, I'm truly sorry for my past insufferable behavior. But I'm here because I do love you—not because I want to own you and prop you up on display like a prize." His piercing stare never wavered, even when she attempted to peer into his soul. "I want to be the man you deserve, and I'll do whatever it takes."

A genuine tone filled his voice, and was that a hint of moisture in his eyes? He should have performed on stage. Henry was an incredible actor. It would have been easy to believe him if she hadn't seen the calm too many times before the storm hit again.

"I know you want me to return to New York with you. That much I *do* believe." Hope hugged herself. She'd be brave and finally say her piece, no matter the consequences. "But it's not out of love. You never loved me. You only wanted to control me, and I embarrassed you when I broke our engagement. After all, who wouldn't want to be your wife?" She scoffed, the idea ridiculous to her now. "The brilliant, dashing, and successful Henry Shelton?"

"I was good to you. I would have given you anything your heart desired," he almost growled, as if still in disbelief she'd left him—was still refusing him. That expression—the threat outlining his glare—that's what she knew lurked inside.

"You would have given me everything but my freedom, Henry." Hope closed her eyes and begged God for strength one more time. She swallowed and opened her eyes again before meeting his.

His eyes narrowed just enough for Hope to notice. "You talk like you were a prisoner."

"Not a prisoner yet, but I would have ended up feeling that way." She'd tried so hard to explain before, and she'd tried again, but he couldn't hear what she had to say—not really. Not if his following her to Riverton was indication.

He pushed his hand through his hair as though trying to keep his frustration under control. "That's absurd."

"We've been through it all before, Henry." Hope would never have been this bold in New York, but she'd grown stronger these past months in Riverton. "You wanted to bind me to you and your wishes. You wanted to make me into someone I could never be, someone who would be a wife and mother, but silent in the marriage. I have a voice, Henry, that needs to be heard. And I have a talent that I believe God wants me to use."

Henry shook his head. "Hope—"

"I can't live in your shadow, waiting for you to beckon me to your side. When I didn't behave as you wanted, you hurt me." Her fingers instinctively moved to her face. Physical bruises had faded, but emotional ones had not.

"I'll never hurt you again, Hope. I promise." He reached for her, but Hope stepped back. "You know I can afford to stay until I convince you that we should be together."

"You're crazy, Henry." She gathered her courage and stared into his stormy eyes. "What are you going to do? Follow me everywhere I go, like you did in New York? Threaten me until I marry you? Love doesn't work that way."

"I'm telling you, I won't leave town without you."

"Only a few minutes ago, you agreed to that very thing."

"You misunderstood. I never said I would leave River-ton."

"Get out of town, Henry. For your own sake. I have family and friends here who watch out for me. I'm not alone, and I'm not afraid of you," she said with conviction.

"Maybe you should be." His voice sounded threatening.

Hope took several steps back.

"Did you hear me, Hope?"

"Yes, Henry, but did you hear me?" She crossed the thre-shold and slammed the door.

○℞

Ben drove his wagon into the Annie's farmyard and spotted an unfamiliar man watching him from the front porch of her house. Had the stranger just arrived, or was he leaving? Dressed in an expensive suit, he obviously wasn't lacking financially, and he had looks that would make most women swoon.

"Evening." Ben gave the man a nod. "Nice night."

The stranger, without saying a word, gave Ben a searing look before descending the porch, climbing into his buggy, and taking up the reins.

After tethering his horses, Ben watched the visitor move down the road before running up the steps to the front door. Who was that man? Couldn't have been a salesman—he didn't have any samples with him that Ben could see. Be-sides, anyone trying to sell something wouldn't be that rude.

Ben held a bouquet of Black-eyed Susans, the closest thing he could find to daisies, in one hand while he tried to smooth his hair with the other. This was it. Hope was either going to let him in or not. Either way, he wasn't leaving until he had a chance to apologize for hurting her feelings after she returned from Minneapolis. Even if he had to sleep on her porch all night and Jake had to take care of the farm chores himself. His little brother owed him anyway.

A large bouquet of flowers lay on the swing. Shouldn't they be in water? He'd mention it to whoever answered the door. Ben rapped on the door. He didn't have to try twice. The door swung open.

"Henry, I told you—" Hope's mouth stayed open, but no other words came forth.

"Did I come at a bad time?"

"No—I—" Her cheeks blossomed with color.

Ben had never seen Hope so flustered.

"It's good that you're here." Her focus shifted to the flowers in his hand.

"For you. The closest I could come to daisies this time of year."

"They're lovely, Ben. Thank you." She accepted the bouquet. "I'll put them in water."

"You probably want to do the same for those." Ben pointed to the swing.

Hope grabbed the blooms that had been tossed there, but handled them as though they were undesirable weeds. "I'll get rid of these."

Why did she sound sad? Had the flowers been from that stranger? Henry?

She gestured to the swing. "Please make yourself comfortable while I put your bouquet in a vase."

His bouquet? But not the other? "Would you like my

help?"

"No, thank you. I'll be right out." She reached the door, then whirled around. "I'm sorry. I'm not being a good hostess. Would you like coffee? Tea? Lemonade?"

"I don't need anything, but thanks for asking." He had terrible timing. Hope was obviously distracted, and it probably had something to do with the gentleman who'd been there earlier.

Ben waited for Hope to return, then followed her to the swing and sat down beside her. What had he walked into? "Hope, who's Henry?"

She sat quietly, her right thumb massaging her left palm, as though struggling with how to answer. "He's the reason I'm here." Hope looked up at him with eyes that begged for understanding. "I haven't mentioned him before because I thought, while in Riverton, I could keep that part of my past private. I was wrong." She laughed softly. "I guess you and I are similar in that way. We've both had our secrets."

"Who is he to you?" Ben's breathing labored, but he had to know.

"We were going to be married, but I broke off the engagement before moving to Riverton." Her voice held so much sadness.

"And he's here to . . ."

"To convince me to go back to New York and marry him."

"Are you going?" Ben could barely force the question through his lips.

Her forehead furrowed. "No, I'm staying in Riverton."

Relief rippled through his body. "You still love him?"

No answer came. She just stared at the floor. Hope's thoughts must have drifted elsewhere.

"Hope?"

"I'd rather not talk about Henry," she said softly.

"All right." Ben swallowed his questions. As much as he wanted answers, he'd respect her wishes and stop pushing.

She tilted her head. "It was kind of you to bring the flowers."

He was glad to see a smile surface and the sadness flee her eyes. "I've been thinking and praying a lot these past few days about your trip to Minneapolis and what you tried to do for me. I know you meant well, and I want you to know that I've forgiven you for going against my wishes."

"Thank you." Her smile broadened.

"I've also been asking myself a lot of questions." Ben cleared his throat. This wasn't easy, but Hope deserved to hear his admission. "I have to confess there's a part of me that's grateful you did something I couldn't. I don't know what will come of you leaving my painting with Mr. Woodlin, but maybe it's time for me to find out if I have any real talent."

She reached over and grasped his hand. "Ben, you can't imagine how happy that makes me."

Ben yearned to pull her into his arms and feel her close, breathe her fragrance, kiss her soft lips, but he used all the strength in his body to refrain.

They'd admitted they cared for each other—they'd shared a passionate kiss—but now that her former fiancé was trying to win her back, how could Ben tell her he loved her? That he longed to know if she loved him? It would only make her decision more difficult if she were already conflicted about her feelings for the other man.

There must still be something between them for Hope to

feel she needed to leave New York to get over him, and for the man to come thousands of mile to see her.

Besides, what did Ben have to offer? A simple farmer, he had little to no money. By his attire, the man Hope had been engaged to obviously had wealth and could provide Hope the type of life in the city she was accustomed to and probably wanted, high fashion and all. Ben couldn't offer that. Even on the slight chance he'd hear anything from Mr. Woodlin, there was no guarantee it would be encouraging news.

Ben couldn't tell Hope how deep his feelings were rooted and risk being rejected again because of the path he'd chosen as a painter. As much as he loved Hope, this time he might not recover.

Twenty-two

Hope slowly shoved the plate of scrambled eggs and toast away from her. "Annie, it's considerate of you to make breakfast, but I'm not hungry." Last evening's events had played through her mind over and over all night. Dealing with Henry, standing up to him.

Then Ben showing up unexpectedly. Hope could have savored their peacemaking if Henry's presence earlier hadn't overshadowed Ben's visit and forced her to admit she'd been engaged. Hope hadn't imagined it—he'd acted differently after her confession. Regardless, she couldn't keep the information from him forever—not if they were to have the kind of relationship she desired.

"I wish you'd try to eat something." Annie placed a second plate on the table for herself. "You didn't have any supper last night."

"Seeing Henry made me lose all appetite, but I will take a cup of coffee. Please." An uncontrollable yawn forced Hope's mouth open, and she covered it with her fingers. "Excuse me."

Annie set a steaming cup next to Hope on the table, along with a small pitcher of fresh cream.

"Thank you." Hope poured a generous amount of cream into her coffee, then also indulged by adding a spoonful of sugar, then another. She inhaled the aroma before taking a sip.

Annie slipped into her chair on the other side of the small kitchen table. "I'm guessing that, along with no supper, you didn't get any sleep last night."

"I barely closed my eyes." Hope bit the bottom of her lip to stop the quivering that threatened to make way for tears. "When Ben told me last night he'd forgiven me for showing Mr. Woodlin his painting, I thought we might have a chance to be together. But after I told him about my engagement to Henry, Ben acted aloof the rest of the evening. He needed to know. I couldn't keep it from him forever, but it seems to have changed how he looks at me. I thought he cared for me, and I even hoped he might love me. But now what am I supposed to believe?" She fingered her coffee cup, then sipped the sweet mixture, now tepid. "And what am I supposed do about Henry?"

"Now that Henry's had a chance to talk to you, don't you think he'll leave town without causing any more problems?"

If only. "Henry is stubborn, and he likes getting his own way. He won't give up, because his ego can't accept that I won't change my mind."

"What are you going to do?"

"I don't know." Which is why she'd tossed all night. "Not yet."

Annie's expression grew even more serious. "You need to talk to the town marshal."

"What would I tell him? Henry hasn't done anything wrong. He made an appearance in a public place, and he showed up at our front door and asked to talk. That's all. He didn't actually threaten me or try to hurt me."

"But he's hurt you before."

"That was months ago, and it's his word against mine. I didn't contact the police, so there's no record. I didn't think anyone would believe me, other than my parents." Hope sighed. "I never thought he'd follow me." She'd hoped he wouldn't.

"For as long as he's here, you need to be careful." Annie tapped her fingers on the table. "You aren't on the schedule to work at the store tomorrow or Saturday. I'll tell Mr. Carter I'm taking your place today because you aren't feeling well. It won't be lying." She pushed her eggs around her plate with her fork. "You shouldn't risk going to the store. He could show up there again, and it would be almost impossible for you to avoid him."

A weight would lift from Hope if she didn't need to worry about assisting customers with Henry watching or trying to speak to her. "Oh, Annie, are you sure? You wanted to spend the day at the library. You have the load of books from the library in Martindale to catalog and shelve."

"I'm sure. Rebecca offered to help with the books, and now that we have a system in place, the two of us are having no trouble managing what needs to be done on a weekly basis."

"All right. I'll take you up on your offer. Thank you." Hope's stomach growled, a sign she was already feeling better. She slathered butter and blackberry jam on a piece of toast and bit into the sweet mix. "It would be nice to spend the day on a new design I started for Mrs. Graham."

"Didn't you and Clara already design and make the dress she won at the auction?"

"We did, and she liked it so much, she asked us for a two-piece suit." Hope had been ruminating over several ideas, and getting lost in her work would help keep her mind on something besides Henry and Ben.

"That sounds like a perfect way to spend your day." Annie's voice trailed off, and she held her coffee cup in front of her face, looking deep in thought.

Hope laid her half-eaten toast down on the plate. "Annie, what's going on in that head of yours?"

Twenty-three

Hope glanced back and scowled. Henry leaned against the tallest oak on the church lawn, watching her as she strolled toward the church.

"Are you sure you want to do this?" Annie sounded a bit apprehensive.

"I haven't stepped outside of the house for three days. I won't let Henry keep me hostage because I'm afraid of facing him. It's Sunday, and he's not stopping me from attending this morning's service. Plus, I desperately want to talk to Ben." She lifted her chin and linked her arm through Annie's. "Besides, Henry wouldn't have the nerve to cause any trouble with practically the entire town present."

"I wouldn't make any wagers on that." Annie kept pace with Hope. "He's shown up at our door every day, trying to talk to you, with no luck. Henry may be getting desperate enough to make an irrational move."

"I almost wish he would. Then maybe we could put an end to this nonsense." They picked up their skirts a few inches in order to walk up the steps into the church without tripping. "Something has to give, Annie. I keep waiting for him to get so frustrated that he busts a window or tries to break down a door."

Annie grabbed Hope's arm. "Hope, do you think he'd actually go that far?"

"You just said it yourself. Henry may do something stupid."

They reached the top of the church steps. "Wait. I need to tell you something before we go inside." Annie pulled Hope over to let others pass. "When Jake came over for supper last night, he had a lot of questions about your relationship with Henry. Ben had mentioned the engagement. So, I explained everything about Henry and his cruel tendencies. But I made Jake promise not to say anything to Ben or anyone else."

"Annie, I wanted to handle this myself."

"I know. But, I'm worried. And Jake thought I had every right to be. It's one thing to be brave and another to be unwise." Annie squeezed Hope's hand. "From what you've told me, Henry could be dangerous, and I don't want anything to happen to you."

"It won't. I promise." Hope tried to sound convincing, but Henry had been so relentless the past few days she couldn't predict how far he'd go to get her attention. Her nightmares had returned, and she'd gotten very little sleep since his arrival. Charlotte's letter warning Hope that Henry knew she was in Riverton hadn't arrived in time to prepare her, but it wouldn't have made any difference if it had arrived earlier. She'd have to face him, regardless. "Come on. Let's go in."

They stepped out of the sunshine into the dim building entrance before entering the familiar place of worship. Like a gentle breeze, a sense of peace touched Hope as they strolled down the aisle into the rainbow of light filtering through the colorful stained-glass windows lining both sides of the room. Soft organ music played as parishioners filed in. Rebecca practically glowed as her fingers caressed the beautiful instrument that had replaced the old, beaten up piano only a few days earlier.

It didn't take long for Annie to slide in next to Jake sitting on one of the polished wooden pews. Hope waved good morning to Sarah and responded to Mary's grin with one of her own before joining Annie in the pew.

Ben sat on the other side of his brother. He didn't greet her or even look her way. An invisible knife jabbed her heart, and her face warmed. Was he miffed because she hadn't told him about her broken engagement sooner? Without a declaration of his feelings and intent toward her, Hope hadn't felt obligated to tell him, and wouldn't have that night if Ben hadn't seen Henry and asked about him.

"Hope?" Jake whispered as he leaned over Annie toward Hope. "Can we talk after the service?"

"About what Annie told you last night?" Hope whispered back.

He nodded. "You need to see the marshal. If you don't tell him about Henry Shelton, I will. That man is dangerous. And there's something else you should know. Ben thinks there's a chance you're still in love with Shelton. I told him differently, but you need to clear that up as soon as possible."

Ben thought she had feelings for Henry? How could he have gotten that impression? At least his strange behavior made a little more sense now.

Despite the warm temperature in the room, an icy chill slid down Hope's back and she shuddered. She glanced behind them, knowing what she'd see before she even turned her head. Henry sat two rows back, staring at her. He tipped his head and smiled, as though nothing wrong had ever transpired between them. Her mouth went dry.

The congregation stood to sing the first hymn, and as Rebecca played the introduction on the organ Hope got Jake's attention. "I'll see the marshal tomorrow morning. First thing. Will you go with me?"

He nodded and gave her a wink. Annie sighed and gave Hope a quick hug around her shoulders. Ben, his head tilted to view the exchange, appeared confused, but as soon as Hope caught his eye his focus returned to the front.

Hope didn't need to read the lyrics to the first hymn. "Beautiful Savior" had been a comfort to her since she was a young child, and her mother sang it as a lullaby. She closed her eyes and asked the Holy Spirit to soothe her aching heart with the song's sweet words—if even for a moment.

Fair are the meadows,
Fair are the woodlands,
Robed in flowers of blooming spring;
Jesus is fairer,
Jesus is purer;
He makes our sorrowing spirit sing.

☙

As her gaze rested on the cross hanging at the front of the sanctuary, Hope mouthed the words to "Onward Christian Soldiers." More than ever, she needed God's help, protection, and guidance. How hard did she need to fight to accomplish her dreams and convince Ben to stop punishing himself for having his own? How many internal wounds did she need to suffer while trying to convince one man she wanted him—and another she did not?

The last stanza was sung, and Rebecca played an additional verse as people put hymnals away, picked up any personal belongings, and began to file out row by row to greet Reverend Caswell at the door. Hope followed suit with Annie and Jake close behind, but Ben was engaged in a discussion with a farmer sitting directly behind him. Was it so important that it couldn't wait until later, or was Ben finding a way to avoid her?

"Good morning, Reverend Caswell. Wonderful sermon." Hope extended her hand and attempted a convincing smile.

"Thank you, Hope." The corners of his mouth rose slightly, and his striking blue eyes lit up with humor. "But a pastor sees more of his congregation than they realize," he whispered. "I don't think you heard a word I said."

"I'm so sorry." Her cheeks burned. Hope thought she'd hidden her discomfort. "I'm afraid I was a bit distracted."

"Don't be embarrassed. I'm not offended. Please don't tell anyone, but my mind sometimes wanders during the service too. I only bring it up because a little bird told me you're having problems with a certain individual."

Hope's head turned to her cousin, and she raised her eyebrows.

"Tweet, tweet." Annie's face flushed.

"Annie . . ."

"Well . . . there are people who care about you."

"She's right, Hope, and if you need someone to talk to, or if Sarah and I can help in any way, please don't hesitate to come to us."

"Thanks, Reverend. I'll be speaking to the marshal tomorrow, first thing."

"Marshal Gates was in church this morning, and he's over

there talking to several of our members. I grew up with Chester, and believe me, he wouldn't mind hearing your story now."

"I don't want to bother him. Tomorrow is soon enough." Hope pulled Annie close to her. "We shouldn't hold up the line any longer. Thanks for your concern."

"I meant what I said, Hope. We don't want to intrude, but Sarah and I would like to help as much as we can." His eyes said he was serious. Hope could trust both of them.

"Come on, Annie." Hope tugged her cousin down the steps. Before she reached the bottom, she scanned the area. Even with all the people socializing and the children playing tag on the lawn, it only took a moment to spot Henry leaning against the same oak tree, watching her every movement.

"What's the rush?" At the bottom of the steps, Annie brushed loose, curly tendrils from her face.

"Annie, can I still visit this afternoon?" Jake stood a few feet away, twirling his wide brim hat in his hands.

"Yes, please. I'm looking forward to it." Annie flashed him a bright grin. "Fresh banana cake and hot coffee will be waiting."

"We could go for a walk down by the river. Give us a chance to talk about those new adventure novels you brought from Martindale."

Annie glanced at Hope. "I don't think we should venture too far from home today. We could play a game or two of Pinochle."

"Pinochle sounds good. I might even win for a change." He placed his hat on his head, took several steps back, then turned and headed for his wagon where Ben stood talking to several men.

Annie sighed as she watched him walk away. "He sure is handsome, isn't he?"

"He is." Hope blocked Annie's view and perched her hands on her hips. "But we have more important things to discuss at the moment. Before we went into church, you said you'd only told Jake about Henry. So what's the truth? How many more?"

"Besides Reverend Caswell, no one else." Annie peered over Hope's shoulder. "Sarah is waving to us."

Hope turned around to see Sarah gesturing for them to join her and Clara. "Looks like we're being summoned." As she headed toward the group with Annie at her side, Hope glanced back to see if Henry had left. No. He was still there, keeping an eye on her.

Maybe if she visited with the other women, he'd tire of this game and leave the churchyard.

"Hope, I'm glad we have a chance to talk." Sarah cradled five-week-old Joseph in her arms while Mary played Drop the Handkerchief nearby with a group of children.

"What's on your mind?" Hope couldn't resist touching the baby's dark, silky curls, so soft on her fingertips. The little boy already resembled his mother. A whisper of envy lingered for a moment in Hope's heart. Maybe she'd have a son or daughter of her own someday.

Sarah glanced at Clara, who nodded for her to go ahead. "First, we wanted to ask what you'd think about the Ladies Aid Society sending several boxes of gifts to your parents for Christmas. It's not that we think they require charity, but the ladies send needed items to missionaries in other countries. With what your mother has shared in her letters, it sounds like they're ministering in a variety of ways to the people there. We were wondering if they and the other workers might like to receive some hard-to-get items in that location. It would mean a lot to us to help make their Christmas special."

"I—I don't know what to say." Hope didn't try to stop the pools forming at the corners of her eyes. "I'm overwhelmed by your compassion. My parents have been donating supplies out of their own funds because they can't stand to see anyone lacking. I'm sure they'd welcome your support. Even notes of encouragement are greatly appreciated."

Clara grinned and clasped her hands together, obviously pleased with Hope's approval. "We still have three months before Christmas, but by deciding to proceed now we'll have time to talk over some ideas at the next monthly meeting, purchase or make the items, and get the boxes sent out in time to arrive for Christmas."

Annie wrapped her arm around Hope's shoulder and squeezed. "There you go. A rainbow moment in the midst of a storm."

"Storm?" Clara's eyebrows rose. "The sun is shining, and there's barely a cloud in the sky."

"It's nothing." Hope dabbed her eyes with her fingertips. "Annie was just referring to a little problem that has come along, but we're handling the situation."

Clara squinted her eyes, as though she didn't quite believe the explanation. "All right. If you say so." She gave a small shrug and smiled. "Hope, I was also wondering if I could ask for your help. One of the ladies in town asked me to make her a new dress from a pattern she saw in *The Delineator*. She hasn't seen her son in five years, and now he's bringing his wife home to meet her, along with their three-year-old daughter."

"Oh, my goodness. What a special occasion." Hope could only imagine the anticipation the woman must feel about meeting the new members of her family.

"You must be talking about Blanche Shepherd," Annie said. "I heard her mentioning it to several ladies in the store the other day."

Sarah shifted the baby from one arm to the other. "There's no sweeter woman in town, and she's missed her son, so I've been thanking God that Teddy is finally making this visit. His father was a difficult man, but now that Mr. Shepherd is deceased, it probably feels safe for the son to return."

Annie nudged Hope. "See?" she whispered. "Some people pay heed to dangerous situations."

"Quiet." Hope gave her a slight nudge back, and smiled at the other two women to defuse any questions that might be surfacing. "I'd love to help."

"I knew you would." Clara appeared satisfied. "What Miriam has chosen is lovely, and it would certainly be a nice dress. But, meeting her daughter-in-law and granddaughter for the first time deserves something special. Her form is also a little difficult to fit, and I've been struggling to get the fabric to lay the way it should on her body."

"Between the two of us, we'll come up with something flattering." Hope gave a quick thought to her plans for the coming week and what days she was expected at the store. "Can you start on Tuesday? I have the entire day to give." She refused to let Henry's presence control her actions any longer, and hopefully, once the marshal got involved, Henry Shelton would no longer be a concern.

"That sounds perfect. Come in the morning around nine o'clock." Clara let out a big sigh. "I can't tell you how much I appreciate your help."

"I'm looking forward to it." Hope meant it. A new project would help distract her from thinking about what had been happening, and not happening, with Henry and Ben.

Hope and Annie said their good-byes, then headed toward their buggy while Hope tried to keep a discreet watch on Henry. Though important she know his whereabouts, she didn't want him getting the impression she was interested in speaking to him. Better to ignore him as much as possible.

As Annie climbed into the buggy, Hope turned her head just enough to keep aware of what was happening around her and spotted Henry striding toward them. There was nowhere to run. She'd just have to stand her ground.

He arrived at her side with a huff. "Hope, we need to talk."

"There's nothing to talk about. It's over. There isn't anything you could do or say to change my mind." Hope heard Annie step down from the buggy as she quickly surveyed the churchyard. Several couples were still engaged in conversation while their children raced across the lawn, including the reverend, Sarah, and the marshal Reverend Caswell had pointed out. But all seemed oblivious to Henry's presence.

His hand locked around her arm, and his fingers dug in. She flinched. "When are you going to stop this foolishness?" he asked in a deep, growly tone.

"Let me go!" Hope struggled against his firm grip.

"Leave her alone!" Annie shoved him from the side.

A jolt freed Hope's arm. She spun to see Ben yank Henry away and swing him around. Ben held the top of Henry's shirt in his clenched fist, and he drove that hand into Henry's chest until he was up against the buggy.

"You heard them." Veins in Ben's neck pulsed, and the color in his face matched the shade of ripe tomatoes.

Jake, his lips pressed into a straight line, stood to the left with raised fists, appearing eager to jump into the mix if needed.

"No one treats a woman like that." Ben gave Henry a shove, then released his hold. "You need to get out of here."

℞

Ben couldn't stand the thought of another man touching Hope, for any reason or in any way. He'd raced over there as soon as he witnessed the distressed expression on Hope's face. As much as he wanted to clamp his fingers around the man's throat, Ben kept his hands close to his side. He couldn't lose control. Not now. Not ever again.

"You're telling *me* what I can and can't do? Who are you, Farmer?" Shelton sneered. "You think you have a chance with her? She'll never be happy in this backward town." He faced Hope. "You know I'm telling the truth, Hope."

"Please go back to New York, Henry." Hope was flushed, and she sounded humiliated.

Ben clenched his fists, but he didn't raise them. "Leave or the town marshal will have to get involved."

"I've had enough of your interference." As soon as the words came out of Shelton's mouth, he hit Ben with a left jab that caused his teeth to bite his tongue, and then with a quick torque at the waist, Shelton followed that strike with a strong right punch.

At impact, the air whooshed from Ben's lungs. He doubled over and stumbled back.

"No one tells me what to do." Shelton, sounding like an arrogant scoundrel, almost growled his words. What had Hope seen in him? "Certainly not some uneducated farmer who shovels manure for a living and smells like it too."

The anger simmering in Ben's gut boiled into rage. With his head still down, he rammed Shelton, surprising him and knocking him to the ground.

"You got him, Ben!" Jake shuffled sideways around the two brawlers.

"Keep Henry down." Annie yelled as she ran by them. "I'm getting the marshal."

"I can't just stand here! I need to do something." Hope sounded desperate.

"No, you don't," Jake said in a commanding voice. "Ben's gotta do this on his own."

Out of the corner of his eye, Ben glimpsed the bottom of Hope's skirt as Jake pulled her away from the scuffle. Didn't she think he could handle Shelton?

Several men gathered.

"Enough of this!" The reverend tried to grab hold of Shelton and drag him off Ben, but the two were entangled.

Shelton's knee digging into Ben's groin sent pain shooting through his body. With fury in his gut, he rolled Shelton onto his back. Ben moved to sit on him and gain control, but as he lifted his leg over the other man's chest, Shelton raised his left shoulder from the ground and swung. Pain exploded near Ben's right temple.

Ben's fist returned a blow to Shelton's left jaw—his other fist followed with a hit to the right jaw. Ben raised his arm to go at it again, but Shelton's eyes closed, and he let out a low groan. Ben froze.

"I'll take it from here." A burly man wearing a badge and a revolver stepped forward, and extending a hand, helped Ben up.

"You're welcome to him, Marshal." Ben swiped at the blood trickling from a cut on the side of his head.

The lawman grabbed Shelton and forced him to stand. "I should lock you both up. One in the cell, and one in the town's ice house. Give you time to cool down. But I'm going to let you go with a warning." He narrowed his eyes and pointed to Henry. "And you—Annie gave me a brief run-down. We don't take kindly to the likes of people like you, and we also protect our own. I'm strongly suggesting you leave town by tomorrow morning. If you're still here at noon, I'll ask Miss Andrews here to give me a full report and press charges for assaulting her."

"She'd never do that to me." Shelton tucked in his loose shirt. Somehow his smugness remained.

Hope stepped forward. "Yes, I would."

Shelton picked up his hat, then focused on Hope. "I'll be at the hotel if you change your mind and want to talk."

"Good-bye, Henry."

Shelton glanced around the remaining group, shoved his hat on his head, and stalked off.

The marshal waved back the men who had circled to observe the fight. The women had stayed near the church with the children. "Get on home, everyone. Nothing more to see."

Reverend Caswell also encouraged his parishioners to leave the area.

Hope turned to Ben with sad eyes. "You're bleeding."

"It's just a little cut."

"I'm not so sure." She lightly touched the wound. "You might want the doc to have a look."

"Well, you sure gave Mr. Henry Shelton a walloping." Jake patted Ben's back. "Good job, brother!"

"No help from you."

Jake grinned. "You didn't need any. You came to the rescue and taught that no-good—you taught him he couldn't come around here and make trouble." His smile faded. "What's the matter?"

"You need to ask?" Ben rubbed the battered knuckles on his right hand. He'd done it again—allowed rage to draw him into a physical battle.

Hope grasped his hand, her eyes locking onto his. "Ben, this wasn't the same situation as when you brawled with Percy. Henry threw the first punch, and you were just defending yourself—defending me. No one got badly hurt. You may believe fighting is always wrong, but sometimes it can't be helped when doing the right thing."

Words of wisdom, but would he ever be able to accept them?

Twenty-four

Ben sat still while Hope dabbed the damp cloth on his wound and wiped blood from his head. He was tempted to bat her hand away, but gritted his teeth and bore the pain like a big boy. He didn't say a word while she administered the bandage.

Should he be glad Annie and Jake were hiding out in the kitchen, making something for them to eat? Ben had a long list of questions for Hope, but what if he didn't like the answers?

He silently inhaled Hope's sweet, yet light and fresh scent. He liked it. Not like that horrible stuff some women wore—heavy and sickening—the kind that lingered like smelly cigar smoke in an enclosed room.

Why didn't she say something? She'd tended to his wounds, and now she stood there, silent, packing up the medical supplies. The quiet made him crazy. The only sounds were his breathing, Jake and Annie clanking in the other room, and the rustle of her putting things away.

Hope placed the extra bandages in the box and closed the lid. She took his hand. "Would you sit with me outside on the porch swing? I think the fresh air will help . . ."

"Help?"

"I have a lot to explain, Ben, and it's not going to be easy."

He nodded, then followed her outside. Ben sat on the far

side of the swing, not knowing what was acceptable at this point. Whether they had problems between them or not, he shouldn't be alone with her when all he wanted to do was take her in his arms.

They rocked slowly, the chain creaking. Embarrassed by Henry's behavior in the churchyard, the thought of being entirely truthful put her nerves on edge, but the encounter had forced her into this position. The time had come for Hope to share a painful part of her life with Ben.

As her feelings for Ben had grown, so had her desire for him to respect her. His opinion mattered. But what would he think of her now? Her lack of judgment and inability to see through Henry's facade? Hope still harbored shame for remaining in a relationship with the cruel and deceitful man and not putting an end to the relationship sooner. She'd kept holding on to the possibility that Henry would become the same man in private that he displayed in public, but after he physically lashed out in anger and hurt her, Hope realized that waiting for him to change could put her in danger.

Hope folded her hands, then unfolded them and smoothed her skirt. Where to start? Maybe if she began, words would flow like a river through an opened dam.

"I met Henry at a party given by a family friend. He wasn't like the man you witnessed today—angry, arrogant. Quite the opposite, he was charming and attentive. Henry is a lawyer, and although he works for one of the most prestigious firms in New York, he talked about using his position to help those in need. I believed he was sincere." Hope clasped her hands in her lap, and dug her fingernails into her palm. "I only tell you these things because I don't want you to think I'm a woman who falls for a man for shallow reasons."

Ben shifted his position, and laying his arm along the back of the swing, he faced her. "I would never believe that of you." His tone sounded convincing.

"Thank you." She tried to smile. Would he still feel that way after he heard the entire story? "Several months after we met, he asked if he could court me, and seven months later, we became engaged. My family and friends were ecstatic that I was going to marry someone who was educated, well-traveled, and moving up in the social world. I had a wonderful life." Or had she merely experienced an illusion of happiness because her friends were so envious of the attention Henry had showered on her? "But when we started talking about what our lives would be like once married, it was clear that Henry believed strongly in wives supporting their husband's goals while giving up their own."

"He wanted you to give up designing?"

Hope fingered the chain suspending her side of the swing. "He said I would have to stop all that 'nonsense.'" Hope could still hear his commanding voice—his hurtful words. "He would give me permission to paint pictures of fruit and flowers to pass my time, but he absolutely forbade me to pursue anything he considered a job. During one of his rages, he literally tore up a design I'd worked on for weeks, intending to submit it to Butterick."

"Don't most people believe that married women should give up any employment?" Ben's voice had dropped to a whisper.

Had she misjudged again? Was Ben just like Henry? "When *most* women get married, they do focus only on being wives and mothers. But it's not true that all give up their careers. I want to be a good wife, I do. And I'd love to have children someday, but I can't pretend that my passion for creating something beautiful out of nothing doesn't exist." Hope turned and gazed into Ben's eyes. "Nor can I believe that God would give me this desire in my heart if he didn't mean for me to do something with it."

Ben nodded. "I understand that struggle."

Of course he did. Her heart softened once more toward him. He was a gem. The contrast of Henry's selfishness and Ben's empathy had taught her that. "Fortunately, my parents did too. They'd never approve of me marrying a man who couldn't honor a God-given talent, and they gave their blessing to break the engagement, which I did three months before coming to Riverton."

"And Shelton was hurt."

"I think he was more angry and humiliated than hurt. Henry grabbed my arm so hard, his fingers left bruises."

"Any man who could do that to a woman, especially someone he claims to love, doesn't deserve a wife." Ben's voice held compassion, but his eyes conveyed anger.

"I thought the same." Hope took comfort in Ben's protective words, and a large sigh escaped her lips. "Henry continued to pursue me, but when gifts and flattery failed, more of his true character was revealed." Her pulse quickened at the memory. "One night he arrived at our home and asked to see me privately. My parents were out for the evening, but he was so upset about a court case he'd lost, I agreed to let him in. I prayed I could calm him down with a cup of tea and a listening ear, then send him on his way.

"I should never have allowed him to step foot inside. But I was still feeling guilty about breaking the engagement and not thinking clearly, and since I'd been following the case involving a child's death for months, I wanted to find out what happened.

"We went into the parlor, and I dismissed the servants so they wouldn't hear. But instead of talking about his disappointment over the case, he begged me to take back the engagement ring and marry him. When I refused, he struck me hard across the face. Ashamed by his behavior, he ran out the door.

"By the time my parents returned, my face was swollen and bruised. I never reported the incident to the police because Henry is a prominent lawyer, and there were no witnesses."

Ben's jaw stiffened.

"My parents were livid. Henry returned the next day, apologized profusely in their presence, and promised to never touch me again." Hope's face burned now as the memory of that horrible night played out in her mind. "My father threatened him and told him to stay away. But like a shadow I couldn't leave behind, he continued to follow me." Her palms were sweating. Hope had wanted to believe he'd never be violent again, but after what she'd experienced in the churchyard, she couldn't depend on any promises Henry made.

Ben fisted his hand in his lap, as if he could protect her from the past. "He was trying to intimidate you."

"Not knowing if I'd see him every time I turned a corner made it difficult to live a normal life. So, when my parents decided to travel to Panama, they insisted I move here to live with Annie for a while."

"What you've gone through . . ." Ben released a sigh, then rubbed his eyes. "The words I'd use to describe Henry Shelton shouldn't be said in front of a woman. I wouldn't blame you if you stopped trusting men altogether." His sympathetic gaze found hers. "You living in Riverton makes even more sense now."

"I gave up so much because of Henry. My friends, my home, and maybe even a real chance at becoming a designer. Last year, Butterick built their fifteen-story headquarters in New York. Did you know it's now one of the largest magazine publishing companies in the country? Can you imagine all the activities inside that building? Besides putting out *The Delineator*, everything from seamstresses making sample garments to workers printing and shipping sewing pattern envelopes.

"I walked by there every chance I got, stared up at that tall building, and thought about walking through its doors someday. That may never happen now." The reality of those losses broke her composure for a moment.

"I'm sorry, Hope." Ben handed her a large red handkerchief. Not very feminine, but clean.

"Thank you." She wiped her cheek and tried to smile. "The truth is that I've found many blessings in Riverton. Annie and I have grown closer, and I've made new friends here with Reverend Caswell and Sarah, Thomas and Ellie, Jake, you . . . And I've got the job at the store and time to sketch. There are many reasons to be thankful."

"Glad you can see it that way."

"I *choose* to see it that way. I can't wallow in regrets or what could have been. I have to move forward with my life and look for the good around me." She'd just poured out her heart to him, shared her darkest secret, and he seemed empathetic to the situation, but how did he feel about *her* now?

Hope closed her eyes to gather her courage. "Now that you know the truth—that I don't want anything to do with Henry—is there any chance for you and me?" She opened her eyes and peered into his, yearning to see warm acceptance, even love.

"I see . . ." Hope couldn't bear to look any longer. Eyes that were once filled with laughter, teasing, and friendship were now filled with nothing more than compassion for someone who had been wounded. She could have been a cow with a broken leg and received the same response.

A Monarch butterfly lit on a yellow mum growing in a container on the porch. Its wings fanned back and forth before it took flight again. Soon it would migrate to a warmer climate. Right now she wished she was small enough to climb onboard and escape Ben's pity.

He cleared his throat. "It's not that I don't care for you, Hope." He shifted on the swing. "Maybe because we hadn't made a commitment to each other, you felt you didn't owe me any explanations about Shelton and your past relationship. But finding out about him only because he showed up in town makes me wonder if you might be keeping other secrets."

"I've told you everything, Ben. There's nothing more to tell." Hope longed to search his eyes, yet feared what she'd discover.

"Maybe so, but after all that's happened since you're arrived in Riverton, I'm not sure I can rely on you to be honest with me." He took a deep breath. "I'm sorry, Hope. I won't be with anyone I can't completely trust."

❧

Ben's stomach growled. It was his own fault he was hungry, but he couldn't sit across from Hope and share a Sunday dinner after seeing the pain in her eyes. He'd hurt her deeply, that he was sure of, and there might not be a way to fix that . . . at least not any time soon.

How long had he been sitting there alone in the church? Ben laid his sketch pad on the bench. Painting always soothed his soul, and he could have sequestered himself in his shed for several hours, but he'd felt drawn back to the peaceful sanctuary. He pulled out his pocket watch and flipped the cover open. Three twenty. He told Jake he'd pick him up by four so they could get back to the farm for milking. The cows couldn't wait.

He was no softy, but wooden benches sure felt harder by the minute. Ben slid his body over and lay down with his hands behind his head. A perfect view of the stained-glass window depicting the crucifixion hung before him.

A door slammed in the back, and he raised his head to see who had come inside.

"Ben, what are you doing in here?" Reverend Caswell strode down the aisle toward him. "You all right?"

He bolted upright. "Yes, Reverend. I'm fine. Just came in to sit a spell. Think. Pray."

"Sounds like good reasons." The reverend leaned against the pew on the opposite side of the aisle. "Parishioners like to call me Reverend out of respect, but I prefer my friends just call me Peter when we're not in formal settings."

"I'll try. And thanks. For thinking of me as a friend."

"Sarah left one of the baby's things here this morning, so I told her I'd fetch it. Good excuse to get some fresh air." Peter relaxed his arms across his chest. "I've got some time to sit if there's anything you want to talk about. Anything you say will be kept between us, if that's the way you want it."

Maybe this is what Ben needed. He'd sat there praying for answers for several hours. Maybe God sent Peter there for this very purpose. "Actually, I could use someone to talk to. Jake is a pretty good listener when he tries hard enough, but as brothers go, he's biased when it comes to me."

Peter crossed the aisle and slipped next to Ben in the pew. "Let's hear it. What's eating at you?"

For the next twenty minutes, Ben poured out everything. First, that he was a painter—and that disclosure raised Peter's eyebrows, but he didn't stop Ben and ask questions. Peter let Ben continue to talk. How he felt about Hope and his struggle with trusting her after she took his painting to Minneapolis when he'd specifically told her to keep his work a secret. Then, just when he thought he'd gotten past that, Henry Shelton showed up. But the most difficult of all was telling Peter how he'd blinded a young boy because of fighting, and how that very morning he'd broken his vow to never to raise his fists again.

"I'm ashamed of myself." Ben tilted his head back and sighed. "God must be so disappointed."

"Shelton had it coming." The conviction in Peter's voice hinted that he approved of the fight. He chuckled. "Don't look so surprised. Christians are supposed to stand up for what's right, and unfortunately, talking doesn't always do the job."

"You don't understand. I was so angry, I could have lost control and really hurt that man."

"But you didn't." Peter laid his hand on Ben's shoulder. "The Bible says a lot of things about loving people, but it also mentions righteous anger. Jesus himself got angry when there was due cause. Today you only did what was necessary to protect someone you care about, and then you pulled back. Shelton walked away with only a few cuts and bruises—and without wounding Hope."

"So, you're saying brawling is justified?" A man of the cloth condoned beating another person?

"No. But I do believe that sometimes as Christians, we must fight both physical and spiritual battles in order to serve the kingdom of God. Earlier today, you physically fought someone who was on the path of possibly doing someone harm. Since then, you've been fighting with forces unseen."

"So, what am I supposed to do?"

"Pray for wisdom and strength. Truly forgive Hope for any wrongdoing—put it all behind you. And forgive *yourself*."

Twenty-five

The sun's rays falling on Hope's shoulders gently pushed the October morning chill from her body, and she finally began to relax in the company of good friends who had gathered outside of the church—Clara, Rebecca, Ellie, Sarah, and of course, Annie. Concentrating on the sermon had been impossible knowing Ben sat two rows behind. She'd repented several times during the service for her lack of attention, but she could almost feel his stare. Had Ben also struggled with how their last conversation had ended—his declaration that he couldn't be with her?

Clara touched Hope's arm, drawing her attention. "Blanche had tea with me yesterday after her son and his family left for their home in North Dakota. They had a wonderful visit while here, and I think it did her heart good. Anyway, she's intending to come by soon to thank you in person."

"I was certainly glad to do it." Designing something that was fashionable but also flattered the woman's curvaceous figure had been a joy.

"She lit up like a full moon when she slipped on the dress and looked in the mirror. I've ever seen her so happy and confident. You helped her welcome her family home with pride."

"Thank you, Clara." That was exactly what Hope had

wanted to accomplish—why she believed God had given her artistic talent. She was supposed to use it to make people happy, not keep it to herself.

"As a matter of fact"—Clara's eyes sparkled— "we've received so many compliments on garments we've worked on together, I was wondering if you'd consider a more serious business proposition. One that would require a bigger commitment to each other and the town."

"What are you proposing?" Hope braced herself. Clara was glowing with enthusiasm, but Hope feared her friend's plan might entail more than what they were prepared to undertake.

"What would you think about the two of us opening up our own dress shop here in Riverton? I'm sure we'd have plenty of business to make it worthwhile. Now that Rose is fourteen, she's a big help with the other three children, and I'd get a lot more sewing done in an actual shop without the young ones underfoot."

"I—that's not . . ." Hope wanted to help this dear friend who had come to her rescue several times, and she didn't want to disappoint Clara, but she'd never considered staying in Riverton long-term until her friendship with Ben had grown into deep feelings for him.

And now that he'd made it clear a future together was impossible, Hope had contemplated moving elsewhere before her parents returned from Panama. If not back to New York, perhaps Minneapolis or Chicago. In a town as small as Riverton, she'd continually see him at the Home Store, church, and social functions, and the invisible chasm between them created a heartache she bore in silence. Only Annie knew how Hope felt about Ben—she'd fallen in love with him.

Hope pushed thoughts of Ben aside. "Oh, Clara, that's a lovely idea, but I'm not sure how long I'll be living here. I never moved here with the intention of making Riverton my permanent home."

"I know." The twinkle in Clara's eyes dimmed, yet didn't completely extinguish. "But, please, think about it. There would be nothing to stop you from still submitting your ideas to Butterick, and they might take you more seriously if you ran a successful shop."

"I'll give it considerable thought. I can do that much. Don't give up just yet. Perhaps we can come up with a way for you to still open a shop of your own without my ongoing partnership." Hope would do whatever she could to help Clara, and she'd contemplate what she might contribute to the venture.

Annie, listening to their conversation, nudged Hope. "Tell Clara about the letter from Eva Lancaster that arrived yesterday."

"What did it say?"

Hope tingled all over again, just thinking about the words she'd read at least twenty times since. "She apologized for missing our supper engagement while I was in Minneapolis, and now that she's had time to grieve her mother's passing and put some things in order, she'd very much like to see some of my designs. She's asked me to send a portfolio."

"Hope, that's wonderful! If she likes them, it could be the start to something big for you." Bless Clara's heart for her enthusiasm and wanting the best for Hope.

"Regardless of whether she thinks the designs have merit or not, she's promised to offer some guidance. For that, I'll be eternally grateful."

"I'll be praying for a quick and positive response."

"Thank you, Clara."

The woman was a treasure. As Hope had gotten to know her, she'd discovered that Clara's oldest son had died after being kicked by a horse, and she'd also lost her husband only two years ago. A blacksmith, he'd tried to earn extra money for their large family and had fallen while fixing a barn roof. Now she had four children to support on her own. Clara was an inspiration of perseverance and faith. If Hope was ever going to open up a shop of her own, she would be honored to have a partner like Clara.

Hope peeked around Annie for just a moment to catch a glimpse of Ben. He'd said good morning and given her a smile when he greeted all the women in the group, but didn't say another word. Now he was talking with a group of men, mostly farmers who were probably discussing crops and the harvest. Hope moved her eyes back to the circle of women who were chattering around her. She would have been mortified if Ben had looked their way and caught her staring.

Two weeks had passed since his fight with Henry, who'd left town the next day. The marshal confirmed it. Two weeks since Hope had shared everything with Ben about her past relationship with the arrogant lawyer. Two weeks since she and Ben had spoken. Was it always going to be like this? The two of them avoiding each other? *Lord, please show me how to fix this.*

Sarah, Ellie, and Rebecca finished their own conversation a few feet away and joined the other three women, forming a circle.

"Ellie delivered another baby the other night." Sarah's

voice held pride for her sister-in-law. "That makes four now, doesn't it?"

"It does. Except I needed help with this one. The baby was breach. So in the calmest voice I could muster, I asked the father to get Doc Burnside." Ellie wiped her brow. "Thank the good Lord everything went well, and a healthy little girl was brought into the world."

Annie nudged Rebecca. "It looks like people in Riverton are doing their duty to supply you with children to teach." Her focus returned to Ellie. "Was it the family who took over the farm next to Ole and Martha's? They came into the store the other day with a little boy in tow, and the expectant mother looked so uncomfortable, I was a bit nervous she was going to have that baby right there in the store."

Ellie nodded and laughed. "Sweet woman, but very shy, so it may take her a while to feel at home here. We'll need to do everything we can to make her welcome."

"That's something we should talk about at the Ladies Aid Society meeting this week." Sarah's son began to fuss in her arms, and she jostled him to calm him. "Oh, and Hope, remember to bring the list your mother sent. We only have a month before we need to send supplies and gifts if we want to make sure they'll arrive by Christmas."

"I will." Never in her life had Hope imagined she'd be attending Ladies Aid Society meetings. She'd always thought of them as gatherings for older women who quilted as an excuse to sit around and gossip. But she'd been wrong. This group of ladies ranged from young women just starting families to great-grandmothers. They chatted and laughed as they unselfishly contributed to making life easier for those less fortunate by donating quilts, food, and clothing. Hope had also become aware that they delivered meals to new mothers and people who were housebound because they were ill.

"This is a busy week with the Ladies Aid Society meeting on Thursday, and then the church hayride on Saturday night." Ellie counted silently on fingers. "We'll have five wagons, including ours. That should be enough."

"The children have been looking forward to it all week." Rebecca draped a heavy black shawl on her shoulders. "It's been heartwarming to hear them invite friends from school to join us."

Annie grinned. "Hope has never been on a hayride."

"She's been reminding me all week that first-timers get buried in the hay as an initiation." That bit of news unnerved Hope, but it sounded like most of the congregation participated in the event, and she never wanted to be afraid of trying anything.

"Don't let her teasing get to you. Hayrides are fun. It's mostly singing and telling stories," Clara said.

"She's right," Sarah said. "My grandmother will stay with the baby, but our hayrides are tame enough for Mary to come along."

Sarah, Ellie, and Clara said their good-byes and left to join their families. Jake practically swooped Annie away to talk by themselves. That left Hope standing alone with Rebecca.

"Annie says everything at the library is going well."

"Yes, quite well. A number of people come in on Saturdays while in town getting supplies, and the children love to search for new books. It's like a treasure hunt for them. I don't know how Annie does it. Spending as much time as she does there while still working at the Home Store most days." The corners of Rebecca's mouth curved up. "Annie and I weren't always fond of each other, but we've become good friends. At least, I think we have."

Hope returned the smile. "I know she'd agree."

"It's interesting how perspectives can change." Rebecca waved at several children who called out their good-byes to her as they left a game of tag, then climbed into the back of a wagon.

Other parents were gathering their children as parishioners began dispersing, probably heading home for their Sunday dinner and afternoon of leisure.

"I was just thinking the same thing about the Ladies Aid Society." Hope lifted her face to the sun's warmth. "I've been surprised by how much I enjoy spending time with the women."

"See there? That's just what I mean. You probably never thought after living in New York that you'd feel at home in a small town like Riverton. Yet, you've been here less than six months, and already you're a large part of the community."

"That's kind of you to say." The reality that Riverton now felt like home warmed Hope's insides like a cup of hot chocolate on a bitter cold January night.

"I mean it. You've made a place for yourself. That's why people here were so willing to rally around you and make sure that that troublemaker Mr. Shelton left. You may not know this, but more than one person besides the marshal spoke to the man and warned him not to come back. Including Ben."

"No, I wasn't aware." Gratitude for their support cascaded over her like fresh water, cleansing her from some of the pain and embarrassment she'd been carrying.

Rebecca seemed hesitate to speak. "I know it's none of my business, but may I ask how you and Ben are getting along?"

Odd question, considering she and Rebecca weren't close. "Did Annie mention anything about us?"

"No, she hasn't told me anything. When we're together at the library, she mostly talks about Jake. But it was clear the way Ben handled Mr. Shelton that he cares for you, and no one has to be terribly observant on Sunday mornings to notice that you and Ben have been maneuvering to stay clear of each other."

Hope's shoulders dropped as air rushed from her lungs. "It's that noticeable?"

Rebecca raised her eyebrows. "Like a snowman at a summer picnic."

"I don't know what to do. He's just so stubborn—and proud."

"He's a man." Rebecca's eyes softened. "I've experienced heartache with more than one myself."

Remembering Rebecca's history in Riverton, Hope stole a glance at Sarah and Reverend Caswell, and Rebecca's gaze followed for a brief moment.

"It's all right. I know Annie told you how I became a crazy person because I believed Reverend Caswell was the man for me. But I was wrong, and I got over my feelings for him a long time ago. Sarah had a lot to do with that. It's a long story, but she forgave me for some horrible things I said and did, even when I didn't want forgiveness. That gesture rekindled our childhood friendship. It also helped me accept that she's the right match for him." Rebecca glanced in Ben's direction. "I'm not saying you should forget about him. I just want to remind you that if he's the one God has chosen for you, everything will somehow work out. And if he's not, then God will heal your heartache."

"You've really been able to move on? Even with seeing Sarah and the reverend together all the time?"

"I have, and I sincerely wish good things for them. But I won't deny that I'd still like to find real love someday. I'm a romantic. Annie can testify to all the romance novels I check out of the library." Rebecca gave a little laugh, but it was laced with some pain.

"And have a family?"

Rebecca tipped her head.

"I'm sorry. Did I say something wrong?"

"No, not at all," Rebecca sighed. "It's just . . . I can't have children of my own," she said softly.

"I'm so sorry, Rebecca."

"Thank you. I've accepted it, but reminders are still painful." Rebecca's expression became contemplative. "I was engaged once, but my fiancé broke things off when I told him there wouldn't be a family to go with the marriage. He didn't handle the news well. I couldn't blame him. When Peter—Reverend Caswell—moved back to Riverton a widower with a small child, I thought my prayers had been answered." She gave a slight shrug. "You know how that turned out. So, I have to keep believing that someday the right one will show up. Of course, I'd still love to have a family, but unless God provides a miracle, it won't happen for me."

"Psalm 37:4 says, 'Delight thyself also in the Lord: and he shall give thee the desires of thine heart.' We need to remember that."

She'd spoken Scripture to encourage Rebecca, but as soon

as the words left Hope's lips, a disturbing awareness assailed her. Had she been striving so hard on her own to create opportunities to use her talent that she'd risked missing any created by God?

Twenty-six

If it weren't for the occasional stalk that poked Hope and made her itch, the bed of hay felt almost cozy and warm once she nestled into it. Annie had made herself comfortable next to Hope at the head of the wagon, and Jake sprawled on the other side of Annie. Ben had helped riders board other wagons before jumping on the end of theirs as they left Thomas and Ellie's farm. Hope felt a twinge of sadness when he remained at the opposite end of where she sat. Why hadn't he volunteered to chaperone one of the other wagons?

Their wagon carried adults, families claimed a second wagon, a third had been filled by ages thirteen to nineteen, and the last held rambunctious children old enough to be on their own, but too young to be accepted on the same wagon as those older than twelve. Along with several other parents, Thomas and Ellie chaperoned that latter, probably because their own three, John, Grace, and Isaac were onboard with their friends. Clara had also volunteered to ride with them because of her three younger children, giving Rose a chance to have an evening free of responsibility on a separate wagon. From Hope's limited view, the big people seemed to be keeping the little people corralled. At least no one had fallen out—yet.

The wagon jostled left and right as it traveled down the

trail flanked by trees. This late in October, little foliage still clung to almost-naked branches, allowing the full moon's radiance to light their way.

"Was this road made just for hayrides?" It seemed like a huge task to Hope for an occasional outing.

Jake sat up, chewing on the end of a hay stalk. "Do you want to know about the farmer who originally owned Thomas's farm, fell in love with a girl at the neighboring farm, and how he cut a trail through the woods so he could visit her, even in the dead of winter and during horrible blizzards?"

"Of course. Sounds romantic." Hope could stand to hear a happily-ever-after ending.

"I could tell it, but it would be a fairytale."

"Jake!" Annie gave him a shove. "That's mean."

"Sorry, Hope. Didn't think you'd fall for it. But isn't a joke better than a ghost story while riding in the *deep, dark* woods?" He raised his hands like he was going to attack Annie and made an *ooh*ing sound.

"That's your defense?" Annie's reprimanding tone didn't fool Hope. Her cousin adored the man. "Hope, we're riding through a sugar bush."

"Pardon?"

"Maple trees—lots of them. Ole Larson owns the property, and he makes syrup. He sells some to stores in the area and gives the rest away."

"I know Mr. Larson. He's the older man I see every Sunday at church with his sweet wife, Martha." They'd smiled and greeted her every Sunday since her arrival in Riverton.

Jake grabbed a fresh piece of hay and stuck the end in his mouth. "In mid-February to mid-March, when the sap starts running, he'll come out here with a small crew to tap the trees. He can't do all the work on his own anymore. Thomas helps, and last year, Ben and I came over a couple of times to help take buckets off the trees. It's fun."

Annie turned to Jake. "You told me once, but I can't remember. How much sap can you get from one tree?"

"About twenty gallons, and that only amounts to about two quarts of syrup." Jake removed the hay from the corner of his mouth and flicked it over the side of the wagon. "Sap contains a lot of water, so it has to boil down over a hot fire for about five days to thicken up."

"I had no idea." The next time she ate pancakes, Hope would have a greater appreciation for the pools of maple syrup she poured.

The students in the wagon behind them began singing a lively tune, but the lyrics were carried away with the night's breeze.

"Listen to them." Annie, always drawn to music, pulled herself up and sat on her ankles. "Come on, everyone." She started waving at their companions. "We don't want them to have all the fun."

"You start us, Annie," someone shouted.

She played around with a few notes, then seemed to find the pitch she wanted, and her clear voice belted out the new song by George M. Cohen, "The Yankee Doodle Boy." She'd been singing it around the house for days, so she knew the verses well, but the rest joined in on the chorus. After once through the sad ballad, "A Bird in a Gilded Cage," she switched to the more upbeat "Bill Bailey, Won't You Please Come Home?"

Hidden in the shadows as the wagon bounced along,

Hope didn't feel compelled to mouth the words. No one would notice whether her lips moved or not. Listening to the music felt both comforting and sad as she was part of—yet apart from—the group.

As they sang about wanting Bill Bailey to come home, Hope pleaded in her heart with Ben to come home—to her, to their friendship, or whatever they could have together. She longed for what they'd shared before she'd messed up, again. The laughter, the teasing, the mutual interest in art. She had no one else to talk to who understood what creating something pleasing to the eye or inspiring meant to her.

Did he miss her? Was he having a good time tonight? It was impossible to tell in the dark with him at the other end of the wagon. A young woman who was sitting with several of her friends moved closer to Ben and leaned in, as though whispering in his ear. His head bobbed silently. Was he laughing at some witty thing she'd said?

How could one feel so alone in the midst of song and laughter? The blanket of hay no longer warmed her, and she shuddered. She should have never come. It was a mistake to pretend that Ben's distance didn't pierce her heart.

Annie and Jake were so focused on each other, they seemed to have forgotten Hope. She forgave them. How could she not, when she preferred it that way? They'd come on the hayride for fun, not a night of taking care of her and trying to mend her wounds. Hope lay back in the hay, not caring that her hair would be filled with it later, and watched the moon follow them wherever the wagon turned.

An owl hooted nearby, the sound barely noticeable in the mix of storytelling and jokes. But the bird's sad and eerie call echoed what Hope felt in her heart. *Who* would love her for who she was? Despite her faults? A stubborn, independent, creative woman, who out of good intentions, sometimes leapt ahead and did things without thinking. What was it in Hope that made her want to fix things, even rescue people? Was she willing to be used by God and in his own timing? Or had she too often raced ahead, believing she knew better than him?

"We're almost there." Annie tapped Hope's shoulder as the wagons emerged from the woods, and her view no longer held dark branches clawing the air, but an open sky filled with glittering stars. Annie pointed. "Ole's farm is up ahead."

Hope sat up and brushed hay from her sleeves. The wagon bounced as it moved onto an open field that had already been harvested, and she grabbed the side of the wagon to steady herself. Her gaze moved to the back of the wagon where Ben leaned against the wooden side, his face hidden in dark shadows. Was he staring at Hope, or giving a listening ear to the young woman who clearly wanted his attention?

The wagon train pulled into the farmyard lit with lanterns. Any other night, Hope might have thought the scene enchanting, but not tonight. She just wanted to go home and hide in her room, in her bed, under the covers, in the dark.

Be strong and of a good courage; be not afraid, neither be thou dismayed: for the Lord thy God is with thee whithersoever thou goest. Joshua 1:9 was a verse her mother quoted whenever Hope became fearful of going to new places, trying new things, or even making new friends. They had become words to cling to whenever she feared failing at anything, but it had been some time since she'd called upon them.

Benjamin Greene had undone her. Hope loved him, and she didn't know what to do about it. She should trust God in all matters, and she was trying to depend on him for answers pertaining to her design work, but when it came to love . . . Why would God let her feelings grow so strong for Ben, only to have them rejected? Why didn't God protect her from getting hurt—again? The people in Riverton had embraced her—and she them. But Ben was also a part of the community, and if she remained, every day could potentially bring fresh emotional injuries.

People riding on their wagon began climbing off. Hope followed Annie, and they trudged through the hay to the back of the wagon so they could follow suit, Hope's eyes focusing on where to step next. They reached the end, but Annie blocked the view straight ahead. Jake, already on the ground, whisked Annie into his arms and moved aside.

There Ben stood, ready to help Hope down from the wagon.

Her heart racing, she accepted his extended hand. "Thank you."

Annie's questioning eyes searched Hope's, but Jake grasped her arm and led her away. Brother looking out for brother.

Hope, the last person off the wagon, stepped with care down the wooden steps. All the other passengers had gone on ahead, eager to join the festivities. As soon as she reached the bottom and got her balance, Ben released his hold and hitched his thumbs in his front pockets. He nodded toward the crowd circling several tables set up in the front yard. "Martha and some of the other ladies from church have enough hot cider and cookies to feed the county."

Hope tucked a strand of loose hair behind her ear. "Sounds nice." She couldn't look at him. Why was he doing this? Was he just being polite because of the audience present?

"No one beats Martha's sugar cookies." He shuffled his feet. "It'd be rude not to try them."

"Cookies." Ben wanted to talk about food?

"And cider. I thought you might be hungry. Or thirsty."

"I see." Did he think this was funny? Hope crossed her arms and tilted her head to look up at him. Didn't he realize joking around with her like they were strangers was more painful than him ignoring her? "That's all you've got to say, Mr. Greene?"

"No," he said firmly. "But I hoped it might be a place to start." He took a deep breath. "Thought we'd get a cup of cider and find a place to talk. Maybe continue the conversation on the ride back."

The moon suddenly seemed to glow with more intensity, the stars twinkled more vividly, and laughter sounded more joyous. Ben must dislike the tension between them just as much as she did. Now they'd get a chance to repair things between them. Warmth flowed through her, melting the icy chill that had earlier claimed her body.

She smiled up at him. "I'd like that, Ben. I'd like that a lot."

To stroll beside him toward the tables felt natural. He poured her a cup of warm cider. The sweet apple nectar laced with cinnamon complemented the spices in the molasses cookie she nibbled on. A bonfire nearby helped light the area, and its heat gave comfort from cool evening breezes.

Ben grabbed a blanket lying over a chair. "Would you mind . . ."

He gestured to an area away from the group, and she followed him to a grassy spot not as well lit. The farther they moved from the fire, the cooler the night air. Hope shuddered.

"Will you be warm enough?" Ben sounded concerned, even a bit protective. "I can find another blanket."

"No, thank you. I'll be fine." With many thoughts and questions flying through her head, she sat on the blanket he spread out on the grass.

He dropped next to her, took a long drink of his own cider, then fiddled with the empty cup. "I don't like how things have gone between us."

"I don't either." Where was this conversation leading? She clutched her drink to steady her shaking hands. "I thought we'd become good friends, maybe even more. Was I wrong?"

"No." He put his cup to the side and lightly caressed her arm, but only for a brief moment.

That gesture—that simple touch—made her breath hitch and her heart start pounding all over again. Could she dare hope his feelings were strong enough for her that they could overcome mistakes made in the past? If he'd opened his arms to her, she would have dissolved into them, right there, in front of the entire congregation of Peace Lutheran Church.

"I've missed you, Hope. It's been almost four weeks since we've talked, or at least said anything meaningful to each other." He gazed up at the night sky, as though gathering courage from the stars, then turned back to her. "It's been difficult to stay away from you. I don't know why I thought I could—or even should."

"I've missed you too." There was so much she wanted to say, but something within told her to listen. "But we're here now, and I want to hear what's on your mind—and in your heart." She gave him a smile for encouragement.

"I've done a lot of thinking, and I need to apologize. I was too hard on you for not telling me about Henry earlier." His forehead furrowed, and he sounded earnest. "That was something not only personal, but painful, and I didn't have any right to get upset about you keeping it to yourself. I believe you'd have told me in time, when you were ready."

A weight lifted now that he'd accepted that truth. "I promise. I would have explained everything. I would never have kept my relationship with Henry a secret from you."

"When he laid his hands on you, all I felt was rage toward him. After the promise I'd made to myself, it scared me that I wanted to hurt him." He paused for a lengthy moment. "I realized how much I care about you." Ben's voice was thick with emotion. "That was pretty terrifying too."

He did have strong feelings for her, maybe even love her. She wanted to nestle in close to him and tell him she loved him, but he took a deep breath and hesitated. Ben wasn't finished. She forced herself to not move.

"I spent some time talking to Reverend Caswell, and I told him everything. About my painting. About Percy and what happened in that schoolyard. How losing my temper and fighting with him caused his blindness. Everything." Ben got quiet, as though lost in his own thoughts.

"What did he say?" she whispered.

Ben rubbed his eyes. "He said God had forgiven me a long

time ago, and that I needed to forgive myself."

"He's right."

"I know. I've spent a lot of time thinking and praying since then, and I've finally been able to do it. With my parents' help, I also did some digging and found out where Percy lives. You know, he's married and has two children. Knowing that gave me the courage to write him and ask for his forgiveness. I haven't heard from him yet, but I hope to. Anyway, it sure made me feel better."

"I'm glad." Maybe now Ben could move on. He wouldn't carry that burden or hide his art anymore.

"Me too. It feels good. Like one of those tall New York City buildings has been lifted from my shoulders." He chuckled.

She smiled at hearing the relief in his voice. "That's wonderful." Dare she suggest what she was thinking? They were just starting to find a tender new common ground. But if they valued honesty, she needed to tell him. She took a slow breath. "Now that you've let go of that burden, there's no reason for you not share your talent."

He twitched. "What?" Ben shook his head. "That's not what forgiving myself is about."

Ben still couldn't see. She shifted on the blanket. She had to convince him. Otherwise, if they were married one day, how could she carry on with her creativity while his languished away in a shed? "But you haven't shown anyone your work because you thought you had to do penance for hurting Percy." Her voice rose in volume, but she couldn't help herself. This was too important. "Now that you've realized there's no need, what reason would you possibly use to hide your artistic gifts?"

"Why are you being so stubborn about this?"

"I have too much faith in you to let you make weak excuses."

"Then you're believing in the wrong person. I don't have what it takes. If I had any talent, you would've heard from the man who's kept my painting for, what has it been now? Six weeks? Still no word. It's probably been tossed in the corner of the gallery's basement and is buried beneath a pile of rubbish."

"That's not true. You *will* hear from him." She clenched a fist. "Why do artists have to be so temperamental?"

"Don't forget, you're speaking about yourself."

"Maybe I am." She loosened her fingers and tried to calm her heart. "Ben, I don't want to fight."

"I don't either." He locked his fingers through hers. "It means a lot that you see me as a worthy artist, and I appreciate how much you care about me and my work. It was a crazy childhood wish to have my paintings on display, but they'll never hang in a gallery like Arthur Woodlin's. That's not ever going to happen. So, I'm going to continue painting for myself, and only myself, and I hope you'll be able to respect that." He squeezed her hand, and in the dim golden light cast by the bonfire, his gaze locked on hers. "I love you, Hope, and I want you in my life. So, I *need* you to accept that."

Hope's emotions mirrored a rainbow-colored kite being lifted by the wind. He wanted her as much as she wanted him. "I love you too."

Ben didn't understand why it was so important to her that he share his work, and there were times when she didn't understand her need to push him either. All she could do now was love him and pray for answers. Hope did know that Ben was a talented artist, and if his work inspired her to experience God and his love for his creation through paint brushed on canvas, it could move others too.

Twenty-seven

Almost in a mindless fog, Hope folded the women's handkerchiefs in front of her on the store counter. She'd gone through the morning, and now most of the afternoon, struggling to focus on customers' needs. Psalm 27:14 continued to run through her mind. *Wait on the Lord.*

"I know it's only been a few days since the hayride, Lord," Hope whispered as she fingered a white handkerchief's lace edging, "and I need to trust that an answer will come, but I sincerely pray that you don't keep me waiting too long."

She hadn't mentioned it again to Ben, but she'd been praying that God would reveal to both of them what he wanted for Ben in the art world.

"Miss Andrews?"

Her head jerked up, and her gaze flew from the cloth to her boss, who now stood before her. "Mr. Carter, sir."

Although she tried to appear relaxed, obviously Hope was startled by her employer's intrusion on her prayer. She didn't need a mirror to know that her face had turned a fiery red. She wouldn't have been surprised to see Mr. Carter calling for a bucket of water to douse out the flame.

Hope cleared her throat. "Is there something I can do for you?"

"Not me, but this gentleman is looking for you." Mr. Carter smiled, then stepped to the side and gestured toward the man next to him.

Hope suddenly felt a little lightheaded. She grabbed the edge of the counter as her knees threatened to buckle, but she gained her composure before toppling over. She'd asked for a quick answer to prayer, but none had ever come on the heels of saying *amen* before.

"I happened to be up front when he walked in and inquired about where to find you." He held out his hand. "Nice meeting you, Mr. Woodlin. I'm sure Miss Andrews will be able to assist you, but if you need anything else while you're in town, please don't hesitate to call upon me."

"Thank you, Mr. Carter. You've been very helpful." He shook the store owner's hand, then turned to Hope. "Hello again, Miss Andrews."

"Mr. Woodlin, I don't understand." She'd written letters, requesting that he return Ben's painting—her painting—but no response had come.

"I'm sure you don't, and for that, I owe you an apology." He placed his fedora on the counter. "I have a lot of explaining to do, but my reasons for not contacting you earlier will have to wait. You have a job, and I assured Mr. Carter that I wouldn't take much of your time."

She didn't care if he stayed all day. She only wished Ben were visiting the store at the moment. "How did you find me?"

He took a small stack of letters from his coat pocket. "I stopped at the post office to inquire where you lived and showed the stamped envelopes from the letters you sent me so the post master could be confident I wasn't a complete stranger. He told me I'd find you here." Mr. Woodlin returned the envelopes to their hiding place. "I sat down to write a week ago. But knowing I'd be taking the train through Martindale on my way to Chicago this week, I decided to take a short detour here so I could talk to you and Mr. Greene personally. I owe it to you both."

"Ben—Mr. Greene—lives on a farm with his brother just outside of town. I could take you there." Hope fought to keep her racing heart under control. *Wait. Wait on the Lord.*

"I need to leave in the morning. Would it be possible to see him this evening?"

"The store is closing in an hour." Her heart galloped. This would only be good news, she was certain. Why else would Mr. Woodlin have come so far? "I have a buggy and could take you out to the farm after supper."

"I would like that." Mr. Woodlin picked up his hat from the counter. "I'm staying at the Sherlock Hotel."

"Wonderful. You should be very comfortable there. The restaurant in the hotel isn't like those you're probably accustomed to in Minneapolis, but Mrs. Sherlock is a wonderful cook, and I think you'll be pleased." Excitement bubbled like champagne inside Hope. "Could I come by around six?"

"I'll be ready." Mr. Woodlin smiled. "I think this could prove to be an interesting evening for all of us, Miss Andrews."

ᏌᎦ

Hope led Mr. Woodlin up the porch steps to Ben and Jake's farmhouse, and knocked on the door. After hearing the gallery owner's explanation of why he wanted to meet Ben, Hope was anxious to arrive at the farm and had struggled to not command the horse pulling the buggy into a full run.

This could be an answer to her prayers, depending on how Ben reacted to what Mr. Woodlin had come to relay.

The door opened and light poured onto the dark porch, illuminating the area enough to see each other. Jake held the edge of the door in one hand while a book dangled from the other. "Hope, this is a surprise. Ben didn't say anything about you coming out tonight."

"Jake, I'd like you to meet Mr. Woodlin, of the Woodlin Gallery in Minneapolis." Hope grinned and fought to keep composed, when internally she wanted to squeal.

Jake's mouth gaped until he accepted Mr. Woodlin's hand. "Nice to meet you, sir!" Jake pumped the man's hand as though he expected liquid gold to flow from the man's fingertips. "Please, come in!"

It took strength for Hope not to jump up and down at seeing Jake's expression. He was just as excited as she at what the man's visit could mean. "Mr. Woodlin is here to see Ben. Is he inside?"

"No, he's where he usually is—in the shed with his paintings. Let me grab a lantern. I know the holes in the ground. Don't want you to trip."

It took only a moment for Jake to join them outside with a lantern to light their way, and by then, Mr. Woodlin had pulled Ben's painting from the buggy. The three of them made their way to the shed where a golden glow from the windows welcomed them.

How would Ben respond to her and the gallery owner showing up at the door of his private haven? Hope shivered either from the chilled air or from anticipation—maybe both. Maybe she should warn him before introducing them. "Let me go in first and prepare him."

Jake nodded.

"Whatever you think is best." Mr. Woodlin stepped to the side.

The door creaked as Hope swung it open. The hinges needed another oiling. "Hi, Ben."

Lanterns set in strategic spots filled the room with enough light. Ben set his palette and brush on the bench and wiped his hands on a rag. "Hope, what are you doing here?" He sounded pleased. That was a good start.

"I've brought a visitor. Someone who is quite anxious to meet you." Trying to keep her excitement controlled, Hope clasped her hands in front of her. "Mr. Woodlin from the gallery is here to deliver your painting in person."

"He's here?" Ben's shoulders rose, and he looked dumb-founded. "The painting belongs to you. Why would he want to see me?"

"He's come a long way. Please hear him out." *Please, God, help Ben listen with an open heart to whatever Mr. Woodlin has to say.*

"Of course, bring him in."

◌⳩

"It's a pleasure to meet a fine artist like you, Mr. Greene." Mr. Woodlin stepped forward and extended his hand.

Ben, skeptical, glanced at Jake, then at Hope before accepting the handshake. "I'd be lying if I didn't admit to being surprised, Mr. Woodlin. You referring to me that way." Ben had done a little research, and from what he'd discovered, Mr. Woodlin not only owned a reputable gallery, but he was highly regarded by people who traveled in the art world as well.

"You shouldn't be. But it's refreshing to come across a talent who is also humble. That rarely happens in my business. I assure you, it's usually quite the opposite." Mr. Woodlin began to unwrap the package he'd been holding in his left hand. "Miss Andrews has explained that although this artwork belongs to her, you're the one who has been adamant it be returned." He held up the painting of Jake as a boy, running in the field with his dog, Shep.

"Thank you for bringing it, sir." Ben accepted the painting and placed it on an easel. "You're right, it belongs to Hope— Miss Andrews. But there are personal reasons why I insisted that it not be displayed outside of her home."

"That's a shame." Mr. Woodlin took several steps to the right and eyed a wooded scene on canvas. "This is nice, but it lacks the same kind of soul as your work with the boy and the collie. That's where your deeper talent lies—showing life playing out—its joys, its spirit."

Ben glanced at Jake and Hope. By their blank expressions, they didn't know where this conversation was leading either.

Mr. Woodlin pointed to a stool. "May I sit?"

"We can go back up to the house, if you'd like," Jake said. "It'd be more comfortable there."

"No, no. I'd prefer to stay. I'm hoping that once I explain why I'm here, your brother will allow me to view more of his paintings."

The man seemed nice enough, but he talked in circles. "What's there to explain?" Ben leaned against a bench.

"Why it took me so long to return the painting, even though I received several letters from Miss Andrews requesting an immediate response." Mr. Woodlin pulled a handkerchief from his coat pocket and swiped his nose. "My wife and I are raising our eight-year-old grandson, Teddy, and he spends a great deal of time at the gallery with me. I've tried to teach him about art, but he's young and has never shown much interest. Not until he saw this painting. Your artwork captured his imagination, and he took such a liking to the picture, I allowed him take the piece home and hang it in his bedroom."

Ben caught Hope glancing his way, her eyes sparkling like sunshine on a rippling lake.

"We've talked about the painting every day since. Together we've made up stories about the boy and the collie. You know, adventures that all little boys want to have at his age. I think it helped when he missed his parents. They died a year ago."

"Thank you for telling me, sir." Ben's throat felt so thick, he could barely talk. "I'm humbled and honored."

"Thank you for making a little boy's life easier." Mr. Woodlin wiped his nose a second time and cleared his throat. "I certainly would have offered to purchase the piece, but Miss Andrews insisted on the painting's return."

Hope stepped forward and laid her hand on the gentleman's arm. "I'm sorry, Mr. Woodlin, but that's still true."

"I understand. However, aside from delivering the painting in person with an explanation as to its delayed arrival, I'd very much like to see more of your work, Mr. Greene. And if what I'm seeing around this room is any indication of what you have to offer, I'd like to discuss a possible showing at the gallery. That would be one opportunity to sell some of your paintings. Also, several people who have seen your artwork are interested in commissioning you to paint their children in informal settings. They're tired of typical portraits and would pay you well."

People were willing to pay for his work unseen? And Mr. Woodlin was talking about a possible showing at the gallery. Ben felt overwhelmed by the unexpected affirmations.

"Ben, listen to what this man is offering you!" Jake looked like he was going to jump out of his skin.

"What do you think, Hope?" She'd been quiet during the entire discussion, which was so unlike her. But Ben wanted—needed—to know what she felt.

She looked him in the eyes, her gaze unwavering. "I think it's more important what God thinks and wants, and I believe after hearing Mr. Woodlin's story, you know."

"Yes—I do." Ben wrapped his arms around her waist and swung her around several times before planting her back on her feet, the two of them both laughing. "Forgive me for my unprofessional exuberance, Mr. Woodlin, but I can't tell you what this means to me—to *us*." Ben smiled at Hope. "You've literally changed my life and provided answers to questions that—well, would take a long time to explain."

Ben had been praying for direction, and God had revealed a clear path. "Mr. Woodlin, we have a lot to discuss. Are you ready for that cup of coffee now?"

Twenty-eight

Hope's fingertips moved across the top of the envelope with Butterick Company's return address. Next to it sat a letter from Eva Lancaster. Both had arrived that morning—a miracle? Instead of opening any mail at the post office, she'd brought everything home where she could read her correspondence in private.

Only a week ago, Ben had not only accepted an invitation to show his paintings at the Woodlin Gallery, but he'd also received requests for commissioned work. The praise from a professional and also hearing how his painting had touched a little boy had brought out another side of Ben. He seemed happy and more at peace than Hope had ever seen him. Would these letters indicate similar success for Hope?

Staring at the mail wouldn't accomplish anything. Which one to reveal first? Hope grabbed the envelope from Butterick and slashed through the top with a letter opener. *Please, Lord, let there be good news.*

She pulled out the sheet of paper, unfolded it, and scanned the contents. The back of her eyes prickled and the writing before her began to blur. Another rejection. She should have known better than to get her hopes up. After fumbling in her pocket, she withdrew a handkerchief. Alone, she needn't be ladylike. Hope gave a good blow into the white embroidered cloth.

Eva Lancaster's letter sat to the side, taunting Hope. If she didn't open it, the unknown would torture her. Hope took a deep breath and slid the letter opener along the edge of the envelope. Miss Lancaster had filled three pages with her now-familiar script. Her truthful critiques included detailed suggestions, but overall she felt that Hope's designs still needed improvement in style and originality. As much as she respected Miss Lancaster, her words stung. How much more original could Hope make her designs without them appearing outrageous?

However, Miss Lancaster added that she felt confident Hope could be successful if she continued to work diligently. She'd even suggested that studying in Paris would be beneficial and could provide a turning point for Hope. Would she ever consider traveling to Europe? Encouraging—and challenging—words, but the thought of living alone in another country felt intimidating and impossible.

Three o'clock. Only a few hours before Annie would walk through the door, cheerful and eager for them to get ready for the evening's Harvest Dance. Hope propped her elbows on the table and cradled her head in her hands. Why did the dance have to be that night, when all she wanted to do was hide in her room and wallow in her misery?

Hope wiped a tear and sighed. Jake and Ben would arrive at seven to escort them, so she needed to stop feeling sorry for herself and put on a smile. Annie had been looking forward to the dance for weeks, and Hope didn't want to ruin the evening for her or anyone else.

However, she could do one thing for herself first. Hope pulled a warm coat from the hall closet. If she left now for Clara's, she'd have time to get back before Annie returned home from the store.

❧

The moon didn't offer much light that cold evening, and Annie's house appeared dark and unwelcoming as Ben, Hope, Jake, and Annie returned from the Harvest Dance. Quite a contrast to the cheery setting earlier where lively music had played. While townspeople danced in high spirits because of an abundant harvest and the satisfaction of knowing provisions were stocked for the fast-approaching winter, he and Hope had celebrated his arrangement with Mr. Woodlin. Ben had savored every moment he'd held Hope in his arms—felt her delicate hand in his, her touch on his shoulder.

He pulled the buggy up to the hitching post, climbed down, and tethered the horse before assisting Hope. Jake followed suit and helped Annie to the ground.

"I know you sampled most of the baked goods at the dance, but I insist you come in and try my apple cake." Annie practically skipped up the porch steps, and there was a lilt to her voice that Hope had never heard before.

"Can't turn that down." Jake bounded after her. "I worked up quite an appetite on the dance floor tonight."

Hope turned to Ben with a grin. "I guess you're staying."

"I don't mind at all," he whispered in her ear, and taking her arm, he walked with her to the door.

By the time they stepped inside, Annie had lit several lamps. "Jake, Ben, please make yourselves comfortable at the dining room table. Hope and I will get the cake. Would you like tea? Or should I brew some coffee?"

Jake's grin would have reached past his ears if it were any

larger. "Could I have a glass of milk instead of tea, please?"

"Of course. Milk, it is." Annie's cheeks were rosy in color.

The two women headed for the kitchen, and on the way Annie stopped at her mother's china cabinet for dessert plates.

Once in the kitchen, Annie chose several pieces of wood from the nearby box and threw them into the woodstove. "Water will heat up fast. We'll have hot tea in no time."

Enough suspense. What was her cousin up to? "What's going on? You're acting very mysterious."

"Am I?" Annie smiled, then proceeded to cut four pieces of apple cake and place them on her mother's china, used only for special occasions.

"It's fine that you have a secret. Just know that you won't get any sleep tonight until you share it." Hope pumped water into the tea kettle and placed it on top of the stove.

Annie and Hope delivered four servings of cake to the dining room table, then Annie pulled three china cups from the oak cabinet and one crystal goblet. She went back into the kitchen and returned with a pitcher of milk.

Jake couldn't seem to take his eyes off of Annie as she busied herself with setting the table.

Hope perched her hands on her hips and eyed each one of them. "I'm not waiting for the kettle to whistle to find out why you're all acting strange. Someone better fess up."

"I can't wait any longer either!" Annie squealed as she clapped her hands together.

"I should have brought champagne," Jake said as he stood and moved next to Annie.

"Champagne? Oh . . ." Hope didn't need to ask. The sparkle in Annie's and Jake's eyes relayed another reason besides the harvest to celebrate.

"We're engaged!" Annie withdrew a ring from her pocket and slipped it onto her finger. "Jake asked me tonight. Under the moonlight where we could hear the music." She beamed at her fiancé. "We didn't announce it at the dance because we wanted to tell you first before anyone else."

"I'm so happy for you." Hope hugged Annie, elated for her sweet cousin, yet feeling an ugly pang of jealousy. "Congratulations! Both of you." She turned to Ben. "Did you know?"

He grinned and nodded toward his brother. "We've talked."

"You haven't shown me the ring." Hope's love for Annie brought a true smile to her face.

With eyes shining, Annie held out her hand. "Isn't it the most beautiful thing you've ever seen?" The ring consisting of four rose-cut diamonds and an emerald set in a gold band was exquisite.

"It's lovely, Annie." Hope looked into Jake's proud eyes. "It's perfect."

"Whew!" He wiped his brow. "I could use that glass of milk now."

The tea kettle whistled, and Hope laughed. "I'll get that. You all sit down."

She returned and joined them at the table. Ben leaned back in his chair with a satisfied expression on his face, observing his little brother. From that smug look on his face you'd think Ben had guided the whole process. Maybe he had.

Annie kept holding her hand out to view the ring, as though she could barely believe it was still on her finger.

"Jake, what do you think about a spring wedding?"

He brought her hand to his lips and kissed it. "Whatever you want."

She glowed brighter than a jar filled with fireflies on a dark night. But then, why shouldn't she? Annie had just received everything she'd ever wanted. She enjoyed being a clerk at the store, she had the library, and the man she loved and would marry, adored her.

Hope glanced around the table. Jake was happy being a farmer. He never wanted anything more. Ben, appearing more relaxed than she'd ever seen him, seemed excited about the opportunities Mr. Woodlin had offered. But Hope might never see and taste fruit from her labor. After all the hard work, sacrifice, and prayers, how could she ever live with that?

"We could have the wedding in May." Annie stood and poured Jake another glass of milk, then kissed the top of his head before setting the pitcher down and returning to her chair. "My mother plans to come back to Riverton before then, and of course I'd love to have her home to help with all the details. She's always thrived on planning parties."

Ben swiped his mouth with a napkin. "Is your mother coming back to stay?" He'd already downed most of his cake, while Hope hadn't even touched hers.

"She loves being with her grandchildren, but she also misses her home and friends—and of course, me," Annie said with a wink. "And my sister's husband recently got a promotion, so they'll be able to hire someone to help with the children when my mother returns here."

Jake moved his chair closer to Annie and wrapped his arm around her shoulder. "Ben and I have agreed that Annie and I will live in our house on the farm."

Of course a young married couple would want privacy, but it didn't seem fair to throw Ben out. Hope caught his eye. "Where will you stay?"

Ben swallowed his last bite of cake and put his fork on the table. "I don't know where my art will lead me, so right now the future is unclear. But Jake and I have talked about some possibilities, and I'm thinking about building a cottage with a studio on one end of the farm."

Annie leaned forward and squeezed Hope's hand lying next to her tea cup, the contents now cold. "Of course you can stay here as long as you like. Mother would love to have your company."

How things had switched since Hope had first moved to Riverton. She'd thought when she first arrived it might be a temporary arrangement until her parents' return from Panama. She hadn't told Annie that her plans had altered as of that very afternoon, and she'd made a decision that would keep her in Riverton in a position that could prove both challenging and satisfying. There would be time for that later. This was Annie's night to share a life-changing moment, and Hope didn't want anything to distract from her cousin basking in it.

After an hour of talking about the engaged couple's future plans, Jake and Ben decided to leave.

"Would you join me outside while these two lovebirds say good night?" Ben gestured toward Jake and Annie, their heads together as they talked in voices too low for Ben and Hope to decipher what they were saying, and they shared an understanding smile.

She slipped her coat on and stepped out onto the porch.

Hope was staying in Riverton, and Ben was making plans to build his own place, so it sounded like he had no intention of leaving either. Dare she hope they might have a future together?

Ben closed the door behind them. "We haven't had much time to talk, Hope."

"We haven't had *any* time, but I understand. It's been less than a week since you met Mr. Woodlin and heard his offer. Your mind has probably been spinning with possibilities and details."

"There's been a lot to sort out. Mr. Woodlin's visit. Jake's proposal." He leaned against a post standing between the porch railing and roof. "But, I want you to know without a doubt—even though I fought you on it—that I appreciate your introducing my work to Mr. Woodlin. I wouldn't be in this position without you believing in me. I owe you."

"So, you finally admit that you've been given your artistic ability for a reason?"

"The story about Mr. Woodlin's grandson got to me. I'll never forget it."

"I won't either," she said quietly.

"The reason I was willing to talk to Woodlin at all that night was because I've been having some long conversations with God. The two of you finally got through to me." He shifted his weight and tipped his head back for a brief moment, as though thinking through what he wanted to say next. "Hope, I've been praying for God to change me."

"You have?" What did he mean by change? That he'd become more willing to share his work without reservation? That he'd forgive himself for hurting Percy? Or was there something else?

"I want to be the kind of man you need me to be."

"Ben . . ."

"Please. Hear me out." He reached for her hands and held them close to his chest, drawing her nearer to him.

His heart pulsed beneath her fingertips, and the heat from his body stole the night's chill from her own. Hope longed to rest her head on his chest and feel his arms envelop her like a cocoon where she could find love, comfort—and home. Instead, she gazed into his serious eyes.

"Hope, I know it hasn't been your plan to live in Riverton forever. But I'm asking you to stay and give us some time—see where God takes this relationship. I know there are things you want to do with your life, and I promise I'll do whatever I can to encourage and help you."

"You don't have to make any promises, Ben. I've accepted that I need to be realistic."

"Realistic?"

"No more big ambitions." A sob caught in her throat. She swallowed her unexpected grief, then took a deep breath and recovered. "No more fantasies about seeing my fashion designs in *The Delineator* or any other magazine. I talked to Clara earlier today. I'm not going back to New York. As a matter of fact, I'm not going anywhere at all. We're going to have our own dress shop right here in Riverton."

Twenty-nine

Large, delicate flakes danced outside like snow fairies at a winter ball. One landed on the Home Store window, and Hope marveled at its perfect, intricate design before it slowly dissolved. Two weeks before Thanksgiving and the ground was already blanketed.

This would be her place for now, but she and Clara hoped they'd soon have their own establishment. First, Mr. Edgewood would have to agree to sell them his mother's millinery shop. The elderly woman had stopped making hats some months ago because her sight had failed to the point where she could no longer continue the work, and she'd found no one interested in learning the trade while she was still able to see well enough to take on an apprentice. But if Hope and Clara were unable to purchase the building, where would they set up their dress-making business?

No time for daydreaming. As the holidays drew closer, the Home Store grew even busier. The place would open in ten minutes, and there was sure to be a flurry of people in and out. Although the *Sears, Roebuck and Co.* catalog was helpful for ordering almost anything people could need or want, there was something more intimate about shopping for gifts in person, and last-minute shoppers couldn't always count on items being delivered in time for Christmas.

Hope would miss seeing all the decorations in New York,

especially the elaborate window displays. Maybe Mr. Carter would let her help decorate the store to make it more festive. Ideas were already stirring in her head. They couldn't duplicate what the larger city stores achieved, but they could still accomplish plenty on a smaller scale.

Annie had explained a large wreath and garlands were traditionally hung outside, but she hadn't mentioned decorations inside, a Christmas tree, or if any treats were provided for customers. Serving hot apple cider and cookies, as well as giving out peppermint sticks to the children, wouldn't be difficult. Hope would present a list of suggestions to Mr. Carter in a day or two, so there would be time to prepare and get things in place—if he approved.

Annie and the other clerks moved into their positions as Mr. Carter unlocked the front door, and Hope stepped behind the sewing counter. Next year at this time, would she and Clara be decorating their own shop for Christmas?

℞

The day passed in a flurry. Hope had gulped down her lunch, not wanting to leave other clerks without needed help. A darkening sky signaled the workday's end. After a ride home chilling them to the bone, Hope and Annie would need to get a fire started in the woodstove first thing.

"Hope, I'm glad you're still here." Clara, sounding out of breath, frowned as several snowflakes fell from her hat. "I brushed myself off before coming in, but it looks like I missed a few."

"It's still snowing?"

"You haven't noticed?"

"I've barely had time to glance out the window since this morning. Thanksgiving is still two weeks away, but we were so busy you'd have thought it was the last shopping day before Christmas."

"The snow probably drove people in. They're sayin' we could be in for an early blizzard. If that happens we'll be stuck inside for a while, and I'm going to be prepared." Clara opened her handbag and took out a piece of paper. "I have a list of things I need. A snowstorm can be fun when you're safe at home and have enough supplies to last several days, but it can be dangerous when you don't."

"Then I'm even more thankful that Ben and Jake made sure we have ample wood for the winter."

"Those two have blessed me the same." Clara laid her hand clutching the paper on the counter. "When my Frank was alive, he could chop and stack wood faster than any man in the county. But he's not here to take care of us anymore, so we do the best we can with what we've got, and I try to let go of my pride and ask for help when needed. Rose is a mature fourteen-year-old, but she and I don't have the strength to chop that much wood, and the boys are too young to handle an ax."

"We're all here to help each other." Hope covered Clara's hand with her own and gently squeezed. "That's how God intends it." She smiled. "Now, what I can do for you?"

"Oh, oh my!" Clara's eyes lit up as she chuckled. "We have the best news! Mr. Edgewood stopped by this afternoon and said he'd like to meet with us tomorrow morning, if possible. He and his mother have decided to sell us the shop!"

Air whooshed from Hope's lungs, and her body felt twenty pounds lighter. *Thank you, Lord.* "Clara, how could you possibly talk about snow before mentioning something that will completely change our lives?"

"Forgive me." She shook her head and laughed. "I think I'm still in shock. I can't believe my wish is comin' true." Clara sighed. "Hope, you don't know how long I've wanted to have my own dress shop. A real business."

The joy in Clara's eyes warmed Hope's inside. What had she done to deserve this lovely friend and partner? "Did Mr. Eldridge and his mother agree to sign the papers and turning over the building the beginning of January?"

"Yes, he said they weren't in any great hurry because of the holidays. Waiting until January gives them plenty of time to clear her things from the shop." Clara sobered. "You're sure you want to do this? It doesn't seem right when I don't have any money to contribute to the purchase."

"Put your worries to rest. It's a fair collaboration. I can't do this without you." Hope understood Clara's concerns, but she was telling the truth. Without her friend's knowledge and skills, the shop would be doomed to fail before it even opened. "I have the funds to invest, because my parents trusted me enough to make sure I had access to money should anything happen to them. It's there to ensure that I have a future—and this is what I've chosen to do with it. I'll write our family's lawyer and get things set in motion."

"I still don't know about being a partner. Maybe you should just have your name on the deed. I could work for you."

"That's not what we agreed to, my friend. You're going to be an equal in every way. I'm providing the initial financial investment, but you're offering skills I don't possess. Once we establish ourselves, we'll create a plan for you to put some funds back into the business."

"My own financial contribution."

"Exactly." Hope glanced around the room. She wasn't neglecting any customers—the place had pretty much cleared out. "So, you see? It will all work out. Come spring, I might even fix up the apartment above the shop and move in. A place to live without paying rent could be an advantage to our deal."

"You don't want to live with Annie?" Clara's hand covered her open mouth. "Oh, that's right, she's getting married in the spring."

"And her mother is planning to return. I'm sure my aunt wouldn't mind me staying with her. She might even desire it, but I think it would be good for me to have my own place."

It was one thing to live with Annie and feel like they were two young women ready for adventure. It was another to be left behind like a maid doomed to be a spinster, and though she and Ben had been spending more time together, he hadn't even hinted he might be interested in marriage someday.

◌঵

"Brrrr . . . it's cold out there!" Hope hugged her chest to stop the shivering. The temperature wasn't much warmer inside. With both she and Annie gone for the day, they hadn't stoked the fire that morning. "Dear cousin, please get a fire going." She shuffled around the house, lighting several lamps.

"Good thing we brought in a stack of wood last night before the snow covered it up. It always burns better when it's warm and dry." Annie opened the door to the woodstove in the kitchen and placed kindling inside. "It won't take long to heat up the place once we get this thing going."

Hope pulled back a curtain and stared out the window at the white flurry outside. "We got home just in time. It's coming down harder." She dropped the curtain back into place. "I'm glad it wasn't like this all day. Your poor horse would have struggled pulling us through a foot of snow." Hope unbuttoned her coat, then re-buttoned. Better to wait until she could no longer see her breath. "I'm glad she's safe and sound in the barn."

Annie blew gently on the kindling, and the flame grew. "Abby will be fine. There's plenty of water and hay to keep her comfortable." She placed a small piece of wood on the flame, and then another, until it roared and she closed the door. "I could use something hot to drink. Tea?"

"Hot cocoa sounds better."

"It certainly does. There's a bit of cocoa left and plenty of milk." Annie opened the door to the icebox. "Ham and cheese sandwiches sound good?"

"I'm famished, and anything quick and easy will be perfect." Hope slipped out of her coat and draped it over a chair to dry.

"I can take care of simple sandwiches. You warm up."

"Thanks, Annie." Hope grabbed a shawl lying on the back of a sofa in the living room, returned to the kitchen, and drew a chair closer to the stove. Her eyelids grew heavy as her thoughts replayed the conversation with Clara.

The sound of a pot clanking on the stove jarred her.

"A feast of sandwiches and shortbread cookies." Annie bowed and placed several plates of food on the kitchen table.

Hope moved her chair back to the table with an apologetic smile. "I'm sorry. I should have been more help. You've been on your feet all day too."

"No apology needed. It's not like I spent hours in a hot kitchen preparing a lavish meal. You can cook tomorrow night." Annie stirred the pot of milk and cocoa with a large wooden spoon. "I think it's ready. Don't want it so hot it burns your mouth." She wrapped a towel around the handle and poured steaming liquid into two cups, then sat across from Hope.

"Thanks, Annie." Hope said a prayer of thanks, then took a bite of her sandwich and savored the meat's smoky flavor paired with the cheese's creamy texture. She sipped the warm, velvety, sweet drink. "I mean it. You're a jewel. All shiny, beautiful, and priceless."

Annie, giggling, almost choked on her food. "If all it takes to have you swoon is a little bit of ham and cheese, then I need to make one of my pumpkin pies. I'll really have you in my power."

Hope grinned, then took another bite.

"Oh, my goodness." Annie jumped up. "We were so busy at the store, I forgot. Something came for you today. It's in my bag." She left the room, then returned with an envelope and a letter opener.

The cream-colored envelope was smudged with dirt. Hope fingered the corner where Eva Lancaster's return address had been torn halfway through, but she didn't move to see what the parcel held.

Annie stared at Hope with raised eyebrows. "Aren't you going to open it?"

"I'm sure it's much of the same. She'll just say I show

some promise, and someday I'll be a true designer if I just keep working hard."

Here in her hand was yet another reminder of her failures, and that while those she cared for were seeing their desires become reality, she'd never experience the same. After deciding to help Clara open the dress shop, Hope had convinced herself she'd smothered that small flame of envy that fought to flare into a roaring blaze. Hope sighed, then laid the letter opener on the tray between them and tossed the envelope on top.

"If you're not going to read it, would you mind if I do?"

"Be my guest."

Annie moved to the edge of her seat and reached for the envelope and opener. She slid the sharp tool under the flap of the envelope, then pulled out delicate paper from within and sat back to read. Less than a minute passed in silence before Annie gasped and dropped the thin papers into her lap. She picked them up again and stared at the contents.

Something was terribly wrong. A sick feeling grew in Hope's stomach, and her heart picked up pace. "Annie, what's going on? Is Miss Lancaster ill?"

"No—nothing of the sort." Annie turned to Hope, her eyes sparkling like precious emeralds in brilliant sunlight. She pushed the pages into Hope's hands. "I think you need to read this for yourself."

"Don't you think you're being a little dramatic, Annie?"

A grin spread across Annie's face. "Just read!"

Hope held the letter and perused the message. Lightheadedness made her feel strangely weak. She needed to breathe, but if she took in air she might also release a sob. The words before her blurred as she fought moisture gathering in her eyes. The lovely, delicate lines of Miss Lancaster's penned strokes were being distorted as liquid pain hit the page.

"I hope those are tears of joy," Annie said, concern etched in her voice.

Hope couldn't speak. She could only shake her head. *An invitation. Paris.* So, when Miss Lancaster had asked in a previous letter if Hope would consider traveling there, she hadn't meant alone. Had she been purposely vague in earlier correspondence? Or had Hope been blind to what her mentor had tried to convey?

"I don't understand." Annie knelt at Hope's feet and grasped her hands. "This a wonderful opportunity."

It was difficult to swallow, let alone speak. Anyone would love to have three months in Paris with Miss Lancaster, learning from her and the other designers.

Hope took a deep breath. She'd try to explain her reaction to the charitable offer. Maybe it would make more sense even to her if she said the words out loud. "I'm so honored." Miss Lancaster must truly believe in her to extend such an offer. "Think of it, Annie. Spring in Paris. We'd leave for Europe in April and return the end of June. It's too wonderful to comprehend. She even suggests that with all that I could learn, Butterick would be eager to use my work."

"It sounds like a trip beyond imagination."

"In so many ways." Hope blinked back a rush of emotion. "Miss Lancaster and I share a common passion for fashion, and she's become my teacher. But I think our friendship has also continued to grow because I miss talking to my mother. Writing to Miss Lancaster helps fill that void, and I think my letters have helped her deal with her own loneliness since her mother died. I don't write just about my designs. I talk to her about Ben's paintings, what I've read in Scripture that day, and anything else that might brighten her day."

"So, this trip would be a wonderful time for the two of you to enjoy and share a great number of things."

As a tear escaped her lower lash and slid slowly down her cheek, Hope could only nod.

"Then, why aren't you dancing around the room like a person who's just won a valuable prize?"

"Because, dear cousin, I can't go." Hope could barely speak the words without falling apart.

"Why not?" Annie almost screamed the words. "Because of your plans with Clara?"

"How could I possible leave Riverton for three months when I've just committed to buying a dress shop with one of my dearest friends? I can't let Clara down. There's so much work to be done, and with the plan to open in February, we'll barely have the business up and running by April. To abandon her would be unfair, not to mention unwise after investing my money. Clara is a wonderful seamstress, but she needs me to oversee the business area of our partnership."

Annie opened her mouth, but Hope held up her hand to quiet her before she said a word.

"And there's Ben. I don't want to go away and risk losing what we've built between us. I love him, Annie, and now that he's embracing his talent, I can't risk him throwing it away again. Mr. Woodlin wants to schedule a showing at the gallery in April. Ben is excited about the opportunity, but we artists tend to live with a lot of self-doubt. Not only is he going to need a lot of encouragement until the showing, but I can't imagine not being there to share that with him."

Annie's shoulders sagged. "But, Hope . . ."

"I have to write Miss Lancaster and tell her I can't go. There's nothing else I can do."

Thirty

Ben reached for another gingersnap cookie from the plate Annie had sent home with Jake the night before. Then he gulped half a glass of cold milk.

Jake nudged him as he walked by. "You really going to do it?" He slid onto a chair opposite Ben and grabbed two cookies for himself.

"Tomorrow." One more night and he could share his plans. That reality sent a surge of adrenaline through his body.

"Going to be a big change."

"My life has already taken a big turn since Hope introduced me to Arthur Woodin. A new world has opened up for me, and I not only owe her for that, but I love her."

Jake chomped on a cookie. "Your feelings for Hope involve more than just gratitude, don't they?"

"Of course they do." He couldn't imagine living without Hope—her trust, her encouragement, her love. Ben prayed she'd see his plan as a new and exciting adventure for them both.

A sly grin spread across Jake's face. "Just teasing. What else are little brothers for? I know how you feel about Hope, and I'm happy for you."

"I owe you, Jake." Ben caught his brother's eyes. "I couldn't make this move without—"

"Ben, don't get all sentimental on me. This has been a long time coming. No need to worry about the farm. You've been good to stick around this long. This was never your dream—it was mine. Now that we've got things up and running, I'll be fine."

Jake and Ben both reached for the last cookie at the same time, but Jake was just a bit faster. He gave Ben a smug grin as he stood, reward in hand. "Better get some sleep. Big day tomorrow. I can taste that Thanksgiving turkey and pumpkin pie already."

Sleep? He'd be lucky to get a wink before morning.

ᴄ℈

Bible lying open across her lap, Hope trailed her fingers down the well-worn page as though caressing the words. She studied the photograph of her mother and aunt at a young age sitting on the mantel above the fireplace. More than ever, Hope missed her mother and her wisdom. "I wish you were here now, but it's all right. You're where God wants you, and I know what you would say if I asked."

A letter from her parents had arrived only two days before, and Hope kept it close at all times. She'd read the pages numerous times since, savoring each word. She ached with missing them, especially because of tomorrow's holiday, but they were both well despite others developing malaria, and for that, Hope was thankful.

She prayed for their continued health every day and would not stop until they returned. Her mother had received the boxes of supplies and special gifts the Ladies Aid Society had sent for the workers' families, and she expressed her gratitude for the generosity. The supplies were much needed and would be put to good use.

Hope leaned her head on the back of the rocking chair and closed her eyes, letting the warmth from the fire bathe her face as she prayed silently in the parlor, quiet except for the fire's crackling.

In the Bible, Jesus told a parable about a man who needed to go on a journey, so he entrusted his property to his servants and gave each a sum of money. Hope's father had often used the story to remind her that God had given her talent, and she'd be held accountable for what she did with it.

If she were to only follow that guidance, the simple answer would be to travel with Miss Lancaster to Paris. On the other hand, Hope yearned to be like her mother—unselfish, placing love above all else. She never seemed to think about how she'd be rewarded. She didn't serve to receive accolades.

As she prayed, completely opening her mind and heart to hear God's voice, she heard truth whispered. When she first arrived in Riverton, she was out to prove something, not only to herself but to the world. So, at times, Hope had been envious of other people's achievements because her desire for success carried some selfishness. Her pursuits weren't entirely for the right reasons, as much as she'd tried to convince herself they were. *Lord, please forgive me.*

For so long she'd tried to get Ben to accept responsibility concerning his abilities. But she needed to learn the very things she'd tried to teach him. *Take the log out of your own eye, Hope.*

She rocked back and forth, interchanging prayer with inner silence as she strived to hear God's voice.

Lord, I just want your approval. You've given me desires and gifts, but I need to trust you to use them for your glory and in your time. Only then will I be truly happy and ful-filled.

Invisible shackles fell away, and Hope, filled with a free-ing peace, silently praised God for his goodness and pa-tience.

"What are you still doing up?" Annie's hushed voice broke the sacred connection. "It's late, and we have a busy day tomorrow."

"We do." Hope closed her Bible. "So, what has *you* up at this hour?"

"Clever. Turning the question back on me." A yawn es-caped. "I've been tossing and turning, worrying about our Thanksgiving dinner. Whatever possessed me to invite guests when I've never cooked a turkey without my mother's help? What if I burn it? Or it's as dry and tasteless as stored hay from the barn?"

Hope stifled a laugh. "You've tasted Abby's hay?"

"No!" Annie scowled at her. "But Thanksgiving is an im-portant holiday, and I don't want to disappoint anyone with my cooking."

"Everything will be fine, Annie. If the turkey turns out dry, we'll just pour a little extra gravy over the servings."

"I'm still going to pray over the turkey and ask that God have mercy." Annie clutched her shawl and pulled it tighter around her shoulders. "So, what's on your mind? And why the parlor?"

"I've never understood using a room only on Sundays or special occasions. It seems like such a waste. Besides, it's cozy sitting by a fire, and staring into the flames helps me think." Hope rocked for a moment. How much was Annie ready to hear, especially when her eyelids looked like they could close at any minute? "I've also been having some serious conversations with God."

Annie dropped onto the settee. "You've been pretty quiet since Miss Lancaster asked you to go to Paris." She gave another big yawn, then rubbed her right eye. "It's been two weeks since you got her letter. Are you having second thoughts about refusing her invitation?"

"No, I'm not reconsidering my decision." Hope gave her a genuine smile—she was finally at peace about sacrificing the designer's generous offer. "I may have seemed a little aloof lately because I've been thinking and praying about that situation."

"Come to any conclusions?" Leave it to Annie to be direct. Her eyelids were no longer drooping. Hope had her full attention.

"If God wants me to remain in Riverton and run a dress shop with Clara, I need to believe that I'll be content doing that." Hope hugged her Bible to her chest. "I'm at peace, Annie, for the first time in a very long time. I'm truly delighted that you have the library and that you and Jake will have the farm together. I'm ecstatic that Ben will gain notice for his artistic talent. He deserves it."

"But, don't you deserve some big triumph for all your hard work? You love designing clothes."

"True, I'm passionate about my work, and I'll continue. But I think for different reasons than before. I'm happy here in Riverton. I have you, Jake, Ben, and so many other friends. People really care about each other here. I think I started to take that for granted. Maybe someday I'll get another chance to train under Miss Lancaster, but for now, Ben and Clara need me here."

The usually-playful Annie squirmed, and her eyebrows knit together. "But, what happens if opportunity comes knocking on your door?"

Thirty-one

The scent of roasting turkey mingled with the aroma of hot spiced cider, making the house feel warm and cozy on a cold Thanksgiving Day, as did the heat from the woodstove in the kitchen and the burning logs in the parlor fireplace. Later, Hope would start up the phonograph. Music always added a bit of festive ambience to an occasion, and Annie loved it.

Earlier that fall, Hope and Annie had pressed colored leaves to maintain their color. They'd added them to arrangements of twigs, apples, small gourds, and candles placed down the center of the dining room table large enough to seat ten people—four on each side and one on each end.

Hope had laid out eight place settings of her aunt's finest china for Ben, Jake, Clara and her three oldest children, Annie, and herself. Clara's youngest, Lucy, was only two years old, so Annie had cleaned her old high chair for the little one.

Since it was a holiday, the adults would make good use of the parlor and piano. Checkers, as well as other board games, were available for anyone who wanted to take on those challenges. Enough snow had fallen for the children to make snow angels, and thoughtful Annie had propped her sled against the house in case the children wanted to slide on the hill next to the barn.

Annie danced into the dining area with flushed cheeks and a grin on her face. "I think I've done it. The turkey is golden brown, and there are plenty of drippings for gravy."

"It smells heavenly, Annie."

"Thank you." She placed her hands on her hips as she gave a sigh that was filled with contentment. "The work we put into the garden paid off. Just think—the potatoes, corn, green beans, and squash all resulted from our toil. It kind of makes me feel like one of the pilgrims."

"I wouldn't go that far." Hope laughed.

Annie's eyes held a mischievous glint. Loud footsteps sounded on the porch, as well as children's giggles. "We have company." She reached the door at the same time someone knocked. Annie threw open the door. "Happy Thanksgiving!"

Somehow, they'd all arrived at once. The three younger children rushed in ahead of Clara and Rose, who were each carrying several pies. Little Lucy tried to keep up with ten-year-old Daniel and eight-year-old James, but they beat the toddler to the checkers. Jake and Ben followed with fresh milk and cream. Their main contribution was the wild turkey Jake had shot and cleaned for their dinner.

Hope caught Ben's eye, and he returned her smile, but there was something different in the way he looked at her. His expression felt—confusing and a little unsettling. Maybe her excitement over celebrating Thanksgiving with people she loved had set her imagination in motion.

The boys challenged Ben and Jake to a game of Tiddly-winks while the women finished preparing dinner. Rose entertained Lucy with the dolls and blocks they'd brought with them. With Ben occupied, Hope joined Annie and Clara in the kitchen.

Forty-five minutes later, Hope strolled out of the kitchen. "Dinner is ready. Would everyone find their places at the table?"

"Hope, the food is being kept warm, so eating can wait a few more minutes. But, something else can't." Annie's eyes gleamed with mischief. "The children are occupied in the living room for now. The rest of you follow me into the parlor so we can all explain something important to Hope." Annie gestured toward the room, then led the way.

"I'll bring coffee," Clara said as she scurried back to the kitchen.

What was going on that couldn't be put off until later? Hope settled into the rocking chair next to the fire, her heart thumping. "Annie, has something happened to one of my parents?" Hope could barely breathe, and her question came out sounding raspy. "Is my father or mother ill?"

"Oh, dear, no. Nothing is wrong. Quite the contrary." Annie sat on the settee.

Jake stood behind Annie, while Ben paced to the right. Clara returned with cups of steaming coffee. She moved around the room with the tray, delivering the hot liquid to any who were inclined to drink. Hope accepted a cup just because she wanted something to hold on to. Why didn't Annie just get on with it—whatever *it* was—the reason they were sitting in the parlor instead of dining on turkey and mashed potatoes?

"Hope, you know that Jake, Ben, Clara, and I all care for you." Annie moistened her lips and shifted in her seat, as though preparing to relay something important. "So, before you say anything, please hear us out."

Hope folded her hands in her lap and took a deep breath. "All right."

"I—*we*—understand that the reason you turned down Miss Lancaster's invitation to go with her to Paris was because you were concerned for people in this room."

Hope's cheeks heated. "Annie, you told them?" How could her cousin have betrayed her confidence? Not wanting anyone to feel responsible for her refusing the designer's generous offer, Hope had decided to not reveal that information. Now that they knew, did they see her as ungrateful to Miss Lancaster? Or fearful of traveling to Paris and failing?

"I had to, Hope. For your own good. It wasn't fair for them not to know."

Clara set down the tray. "And feeling mighty guilty and selfish because of your reasons. Don't you know we want the best for you too?"

Hope's gaze moved around the room. Annie, Jake, Clara, Ben—their expressions were filled with expectation. What did they all know that she didn't? What scheme were they all in on?

"We want you to go to Paris." Annie's eyes locked on Hope. "This is your chance." She glanced to the right, where Ben stood with his hands behind his back. "It was Ben's idea for the four of us to write Miss Lancaster and tell her how you've used your talent to create beautiful clothing for the women in Riverton. We explained you'd initially declined only because you were looking out for your friends. We told her you deserved to go, and she should expect to receive your acceptance letter soon."

Clara flashed a smile. "No procrastinating."

Of all the people in the room, save Ben, Clara must understand Hope's reasons for declining. *She* had the most to lose if Hope left and things fell apart. "But, Clara, it wouldn't be right to leave you alone with the shop for three months."

"Rose will help, and so will Annie if I need it." Clara gave a dismissive wave. "With their assistance, I can hold down the fort while you're gone. It's an investment in the shop's future. Who wouldn't want to have a dress designed by someone who's been to Paris? We'll have ladies coming from all parts of the county."

Seemed they'd addressed her every objection in regards to their new shop. Hope peered over at Ben. "I don't want to miss your showing at the gallery." She'd never forgive herself if she wasn't there to celebrate his success with him. She loved him too much.

Annie smiled at Ben, as though they shared a secret. "Ben, would you like to tell her?"

He stopped pacing and took a deep breath. "There's not going to be a showing in April like originally planned."

"What? No! Ben?" What could have possibly happened that Mr. Woodlin would cancel?

"It's not going to be in April because Mr. Woodlin has agreed that it should be postponed until later in the fall."

"But, why?" This was all so confusing.

Annie raised her eyebrows. "What better place than Paris for an artist to paint?"

Had she heard correctly? Ben was going to Paris? "I don't understand."

"God has provided a way for you both to go." Annie slid to the edge of her seat, grinning.

"Eva Lancaster has been a long-time patron of the arts, and she's acquainted with Mr. Woodlin and the gallery. They think it would be beneficial for me as an artist to also spend some time in France." His expression held restrained excitement, as though he felt unsure of setting it free. "I told her I would cover my expenses to join the two of you in Paris, but she's insisted on providing my voyage."

Hope's fingers touched her throat. "Ben, you're willing to leave for three months?" He'd delay his first showing for her—even abandon his brother during planting season? "What about Annie and Jake's wedding? They're planning it for May. You can't miss your own brother's wedding."

"We've already settled that." Annie reached her hand up toward Jake, and standing behind her, he grasped it and grinned. "We'll just move up the wedding to April and get married before the two of you need to sail into the sunset."

"This is all so unbelievable." Hope turned her gaze to Ben.

The love in his eyes almost took her breath away. "Hope, I need to take this trip to Paris—for you and for me. You always thought I was burying any desire to share my paintings with those who would find meaning in my work. It's true I've wanted that ever since I was a young boy. But more than anything, I've wanted to forgive myself for pain I caused. I've wanted to find a way to put the past behind. Going to Paris is part of moving forward with my life, and I couldn't have done that without you."

Hope's throat thickened and moisture gathered in the corners of her eyes. Ben had finally found his way, and God had provided answers to her prayers in ways she hadn't imagined. She wouldn't miss Annie's wedding or Ben's gallery showing. But spending time with him in one of the most romantic cities in the world was beyond her comprehension.

Ben slipped into a nearby chair, and with his elbows resting on his thighs, leaned forward. "Mr. Woodlin assures me he has a buyer for one of my paintings. With the money I'll make from that sale and several other commissioned pieces, I should have enough to take care of my needs while there. If not, I'll sell more paintings. And Jake is practically pushing me off the farm."

Jake nodded in agreement.

"Miss Lancaster's aunt married a Frenchman, and Miss Lancaster stays in their home whenever she's in Paris," Annie said. "The aunt has a guesthouse in the back where you can stay. She suggested Ben find an inexpensive flat in the city. On days that you and Miss Lancaster are exploring the new fall fashions and fabrics, Ben can paint. And when your time is free, the two of you can explore the country like two people in a romance novel."

Annie knelt in front of Hope. "Dear cousin, I asked you last night what you would do if opportunity knocked. In this case, I don't think it's knocking at all—it's downright pounding."

◌৪

This had to be a fantasy—one that would disappear in a puff of smoke any minute. Everyone she held most dear, except for her parents, were in that room. Their bodies were nourished and full from the earlier Thanksgiving feast, which was accompanied by lively conversation. Clara relaxed while Jake and Annie sat at the piano, teaching the children catchy tunes. Lucy had curled up in front of the fireplace with her blanket and fallen asleep. Ben, trying to avoid stepping on the toddler, added another log to the dwindling fire. Jake left after dinner to milk the cows, but he'd convinced Ben to stay. Jake needed to get used to doing things on his own once in a while. He'd return once milking was done.

Hope couldn't remember ever feeling as thankful as she did at that moment. Not only did she have her friends and family, but she had the dress shop to help keep her grounded as well. And then there was Paris. Not only with Miss Lancaster, but Ben would be there too. They could share that wonderful city together. She closed her eyes. *Heavenly father, you have shown me favor and blessed me. Thank you.*

A hand grasped hers, and she opened her eyes to see Ben smiling at her.

"Would you come outside with me?" he whispered. "Just for a minute?"

Hope nodded. "Let me get my coat."

They slipped out of the room without being noticed, or at least no one asked where they were going. Dressed in a wool coat, Hope felt no chill as they stepped onto the porch. Instead, the fresh air invigorated her.

The full moon in the cloudless sky shone on the snow, making it glow—magical.

Ben leaned against a post and drew Hope close to him until her back rested against his chest. He wrapped his arms around her like a blanket. They stood that way for a moment, and she quietly appreciated the beauty at the end of a surprising and delightful day.

Hope, soaking in the peace, could have remained in his arms for hours, but Ben withdrew and gently turned her around. His warms hands embraced her cool face, and he slowly lowered his mouth to hers. Heat ignited in her belly as he lightly caressed her lips with his. She'd never been kissed with such tenderness.

Hope wanted more—she needed more—so she pressed in close to his chest, giving permission. His kiss grew more ardent, and she returned it with enthusiasm.

Breathless, Ben carefully pulled away. He leaned his forehead against hers and caressed her arms. Even through the thick coat, his touch thrilled her senses.

"Hope, I love you," he whispered, then kissed her forehead. "But I don't want us to go to Paris as two people courting."

Her heart squeezed in alarm. "Then, what do you want?"

"I want you to be my wife." He kissed her fingertips. "We can make Paris a honeymoon to remember for the rest of our lives. I know a simple flat won't be as elegant as Miss Lancaster's accommodations, but I think we can make it work. So will you? Will you marry me?"

Hope threw her arms around his neck and on tiptoes, kissed him. "Yes—yes—I say, yes!"

Hugging her, he twirled her around, lifting her feet from the ground. Ben slowed, then lowered her feet until they touched the ground.

"I love you, Benjamin Greene," she said, out of breath from twirling, laughing, and the pure exhilaration of it all. "I'll marry you, and we'll have a wonderful three months in Paris. You'll paint and be brilliant, and I'll learn everything I can."

Ben removed something from his pocket. Then, taking her hand, he slipped a ring onto her finger. From the light emanating from inside the house and what the moon offered, Hope could see the exquisite piece—an opal surrounded by six diamonds.

"It's stunning." She tilted her head and met his lips with her own.

Hope's designs weren't published in magazines yet, but she still had opportunities to create beautiful garments for God's children, and he was fulfilling dreams she never knew she had. With more time and work, she believed those that had been planted in her heart years ago would also come to pass. He did know best. She could trust that without reservation.

Hope gazed into Ben's loving eyes and grinned. From now on, she was going to enjoy every challenging curve, stroke of adventure, and splash of color God added to his design for her life.

Questions for Discussion and Reflection

1. At the beginning of the story, Hope makes it clear that she will never marry a man who doesn't have the courage to pursue his own dream. What do you think about that?

2. While looking for a relationship (marriage or dating), what preconceived ideas have you had about the kind of person you want to be with?

3. Have you ever found yourself attracted to someone who was very different from the person you thought you would date or marry? What has been your experience?

4. Hope longs to find someone who will support her dreams. Would you marry someone who wasn't enthusiastic about your aspirations? If you're already married, how is your spouse supporting your dreams? If your spouse is not supportive, how are you handling it/getting what you need?

5. Do you think Henry really loved Hope? Why or why not?

6. How did Hope's willingness to talk about Henry's treatment of her affect her ability to be a thriving survivor and not an ongoing victim?

7. When Hope's designs are rejected, she tries to trust God to show her the path he's designed for her. How can having faith in God's divine plan help us through disappointment?

8. It's difficult to be patient and wait for breakthroughs while working hard to make our dreams come to fruition. How does being thankful for what we already have help us during discouraging times?

9. In the story, Hope comes to a point where she asks Clara for help with putting her designs into physical form. What situations in your own life might have gone better if you'd been willing to ask for help?

10. Sometimes in our humanness, pride gets in the way of accomplishing our dreams. We may become stubborn or embarrassed about confessing that we can't do it all on our own. Is there anything that you're trying to accomplish right now, or that you might want to accomplish in the future, but are afraid to ask for help?

11. Why does Annie let Rebecca help with getting the library established, even though she hasn't trusted Rebecca for a long time? Can you think of a situation where you've seen someone be held back from using their gifts and contributing because of their past?

12. If you've experienced situations where you or others weren't given opportunities to use personal gifts/talents because of not being as popular as someone else or others felt threatened by those gifts, how was it handled? How did you feel about the outcome?

13. After Ben donates his painting to the library auction, he regrets his decision. Have you ever held back on sharing your gifts/talents because you've been afraid you weren't good enough, or that others would criticize your work? What did that feel like? How might you handle the opportunity next time?

14. Hope has a desire to help people, but sometimes in her eagerness she leaps in before taking time to think things through. Why do you think she's so quick to jump in to try to fix things for people? Is this a positive or negative trait?

15. Hope recognizes that she too often moves on impulse without taking the time to pray and ask for direction. Has there been a time when you've moved too fast and wished you would have taken more time to think, research, explore, and pray before making a decision? What did you learn from that experience?

16. Later in the story, Ben becomes angry and hurt because he feels betrayed by Hope. He decides that he needs a little time to think and pray about what happened before offering forgiveness. What do you think about that? Are you quick to forgive, or do you take a long time?

17. Ben comes to a crossroads where he realizes that his life might be changed forever, which is both exhilarating and frightening. Have you ever been—or are you now at a crossroads in your own life? What fears are you experiencing? What possibilities excite you?

18. After Henry shows up in Riverton and Hope is forced to share the full story about her relationship with Henry, Ben wonders if she's holding more secrets, and he says he can't be with anyone who he can't trust. How do you feel about Ben's response?

19. There are several situations in the story where people do wrong things for the right reasons. What are they? How do you feel about that?

20. There comes a point in the story when Reverend Caswell states that, as Christians, there are times when we must fight both physical and spiritual battles in order to serve the kingdom of God. How do you feel about that statement?

21. There comes a point in the story where Hope wonders if she has been trying so hard to create opportunities to use her talent that she's risked those created by God. How might it apply to your own life?

22. The story talks about being accountable for the gifts/talents we're given. How are you being accountable—or not accountable—for the abilities God has given you?

Acknowledgements

How do you say "thank you" to people who have believed in you and walked with you through a long writing and publishing journey? Words seem inadequate, but that's all I have to give.

So, I'll say thank you to:

Ocieanna Fleiss . . . You've walked beside me for many years. What you've taught me about writing has helped bring me to this destination.

Annette M. Irby . . . You're more than my editor, you're my friend. I'm so grateful for the insight you provided on this story.

Sandra Byrd . . . Your friendship, prayers, and wisdom are all precious to me. Your feedback on *Hope's Design* was invaluable.

Tina Boyd and Leann St. Germain . . . You're always there to support and encourage me wherever I venture.

Debby Hartsock and Janene Durman . . . Your prayers have meant so much—they've sustained me while facing the challenges that come with this gig.

My Family . . . Sonny, I'm so glad I married a man who isn't afraid to dream. Brooke, Ana, and Katrina, you inspire me every day to go after my own heart's desires and not give up.

God, my Father . . . You gave me the dream, and then you provided the way.

Meet the Author

Dawn Kinzer, a mom and grandmother, lives with her husband in the beautiful Pacific Northwest. Favorite things include dark chocolate, cinnamon, popcorn, strong coffee, good wine, the mountains, family time, and *Masterpiece Theatre*.

You can find out more about Dawn and her books by visiting www.dawnkinzer.com.

She loves to hear from her readers. You may contact her at dawn@dawnkinzer.com.

Other places to connect: Facebook, Goodreads, Pinterest, Google+, and Instagram

FREEBIE! Download *Maggie's Miracle*—a short story—as a gift when you visit www.dawnkinzer.com and sign up to receive Dawn's author newsletter sharing interesting tidbits about her books, photos, and other fun stuff about her writing world.

Made in the USA
Charleston, SC
10 November 2016